Pushing Brilliance

Tim Tigner

ISBN: 9781652796121

For more information on this novel or Tim Tigner's other thrillers, please visit timtigner.com

This one's for mom. She's been pushing me to be brilliant for nearly five decades. Most people would have given up by now, but not Gwen Tigner. Love you, mom.

ACKNOWLEDGEMENTS

Writing novels full of twists and turns is relatively easy. Doing so logically and coherently while maintaining a rapid pace is much tougher. Surprising readers without confusing them is the real art.

And then there are the characters....

I'm grateful to the Editors and Beta Readers of *Pushing Brilliance* for their guidance with the finer points of plot and character, and for their assistance in fighting my natural inclination toward typos.

Brent Bird, Doug Branscombe, Anna Bruns, John Cabler, John Chaplin, Geof Ferrell, Lawrence Fulkerson, Andrew Gelsey, Emily Hagman, Robert Lawrence, Margaret Lovett, Tony McCafferty, Joe McKinley, Bill Overton, Bryon Quartermous, Stan Resnicoff, Chris Seelbach, Todd Simpson, Gwen Tigner, Rob Tigner, Steve Tigner, Slaven Tomasi, Judy Troyer, Igor Vocanec, and Jill Weinstein.

PART 1: AUDACITY

Chapter 1

The Kremlin

HOW DO YOU PITCH an audacious plan to the most powerful man in the world? Grigori Barsukov was about to find out.

Technically, the President of Russia was an old friend—although the last time they'd met, his old friend had punched him in the face. That was thirty years ago, but the memory remained fresh, and Grigori's nose still skewed to the right.

Back then, he and President Vladimir Korovin wore KGB lieutenant stars. Now both were clothed in the finest Italian suits. But his former roommate also sported the confidence of one who wielded unrivaled power, and the temper of a man ruthless enough to obtain it.

The world had spun on a different axis when they'd worked together, an east-west axis, running from Moscow to Washington. Now everything revolved around the West. America was the sole superpower.

Grigori could change that.

He could lever Russia back into a pole position.

But only if his old rival would risk joining him—way out on a limb.

As Grigori's footfalls fell into cadence with the boots of his escorts, he coughed twice, attempting to relax the lump in his throat. It didn't work. When the hardwood turned to red carpet, he willed his palms to stop sweating. They didn't listen. Then the big double doors rose before him and it was too late to do anything but take a deep breath, and hope for the best.

The presidential guards each took a single step to the side, then opened their doors with crisp efficiency and a click of their heels.

Across the office, a gilded double-headed eagle peered down from atop the dark wood paneling, but the lone living occupant of the Kremlin's inner sanctum did not look up.

President Vladimir Korovin was studying photographs.

Grigori stopped three steps in as the doors were closed behind him, unsure of the proper next move. He wondered if everyone felt this way the first time. Should he stand at attention until acknowledged? Take a seat by the wall?

He strolled to the nearest window, leaned his left shoulder up against the frame, and looked out at the Moscow River. Thirty seconds ticked by with nothing but the sound of shifting photos behind him. *Was it possible that Korovin still held a grudge?*

Desperate to break the ice without looking like a complete fool, he said, "This is much nicer than the view from our academy dorm room."

Korovin said nothing.

Grigori felt his forehead tickle. Drops of sweat were forming, getting ready to roll. As the first broke free, he heard the stack of photos being squared, and then at long last, the familiar voice. It posed a very unfamiliar question: "Ever see a crocodile catch a rabbit?"

Grigori whirled about to meet the Russian President's gaze. "What?"

Korovin waved the stack of photos. His eyes were the same cornflower blue Grigori remembered, but their youthful verve had yielded to something darker. "I recently returned from Venezuela. Nicolas took me crocodile hunting. Of course, we didn't have all day to spend on sport, so our guides cheated. They put rabbits on the riverbank, on the wide strip of dried mud between the water and the tall grass. Kind of like teeing up golf balls. Spaced them out so the critters couldn't see each other and gave each its own pile of alfalfa while we watched in silence from an electric boat." Korovin was clearly enjoying the telling of his intriguing tale. He gestured with broad sweeps as he spoke, but kept his eyes locked on Grigori.

"Nicolas told me these rabbits were brought in special from the hill country, where they'd survived a thousand generations amidst foxes and coyotes. When you put them on the riverbank, however, they're completely clueless. It's not their turf, so they stay where they're dropped, noses quivering, ears scanning, eating alfalfa and watching the wall of vegetation in front of them while crocodiles swim up silently from behind.

"The crocodiles were being fooled like the rabbits, of course. Eyes front, focused on food. Oblivious." Korovin shook his head as though bewildered. "Evolution somehow turned a cold-blooded reptile into a warm white furball, but kept both of the creature's brains the same. Hard to fathom. Anyway, the capture was quite a sight.

"Thing about a crocodile is, it's a log one moment and a set of snapping jaws the next, with nothing but a furious blur in between. One second the rabbit is chewing alfalfa, the next second the rabbit *is* alfalfa. Not because it's too slow or too stupid ... but because it's out of its element."

Grigori resisted the urge to swallow.

"When it comes to eating," Korovin continued, "crocs are like storybook monsters. They swallow their food whole. Unlike their legless cousins, however, they want it dead first. So once they've trapped dinner in their maw, they drag it underwater to drown it. This means the rabbit is usually alive and uninjured in the croc's mouth for a while—unsure what the hell just happened, but pretty damn certain it's not good."

The president leaned back in his chair, placing his feet on the desk and his hands behind his head. He was having fun.

Grigori felt like the rabbit.

"That's when Nicolas had us shoot the crocs. After they clamped down around the rabbits, but before they dragged 'em under. That became the goal, to get the rabbit back alive."

Grigori nodded appreciatively. "Gives a new meaning to the phrase, *catch and release.*"

Korovin continued as if Grigori hadn't spoken. "The trick was putting a bullet directly into the croc's tiny brain, preferably the medulla oblongata, right there where the spine meets the skull. Otherwise the croc would thrash around or go under before you could get off the kill shot, and the rabbit was toast.

"It was good sport, and an experience worth replicating. But we don't have crocodiles anywhere near Moscow, so I've been trying to come up with an equally engaging distraction for my honored guests. Any ideas?"

Grigori felt like he'd been brought in from the hills. The story hadn't helped the lump in his throat either. He managed to say, "Let me give it some thought."

Korovin just looked at him expectantly.

Comprehension struck after an uncomfortable silence. "What happened to the rabbits?"

Korovin returned his feet to the floor, and leaned forward in his chair. "Good question. I was curious to see that myself. I put my first survivor back on the riverbank beside a fresh pile of alfalfa. It ran for the tall grass as if I'd lit its tail on fire. That rabbit had learned life's most important lesson."

Grigori bit. "What's that?"

"Doesn't matter where you are. Doesn't matter if you're a crocodile or a rabbit. You best look around, because you're never safe.

"Now, what have you brought me, Grigori?"

Grigori breathed deeply, forcing the reptiles from his mind. He pictured his future atop a corporate tower, an oligarch on a golden throne. Then he spoke with all the gravitas of a wedding vow. "I brought you a plan, Mister President."

Chapter 2

Brillyanc

PRESIDENT KOROVIN REPEATED Grigori's assertion aloud. "You brought me a plan." He paused for a long second, as though tasting the words.

Grigori felt like he was looking up from the Colosseum floor after a gladiator fight. Would the emperor's thumb point up, or down?

Korovin was savoring the power. Finally, the president gestured toward the chess table abutting his desk, and Grigori's heart resumed beating.

The magnificent antique before which Grigori took a seat was handcrafted of the same highly polished hardwood as Korovin's desk, probably by a French craftsman now centuries dead. Korovin took the opposing chair and pulled a chess clock from his drawer. Setting it on the table, he pressed the button that activated Grigori's timer. "Give me the three-minute version."

Grigori wasn't a competitive chess player, but like any Russian who had risen through government ranks, he was familiar with the sport.

Chess clocks have two timers controlled by seesawing buttons. When one's up, the other's down, and vice versa. After each move, a player slaps his button, stopping his timer and setting his opponent's in motion. If a timer runs out, a little red plastic flag drops, and that player loses. Game over. There's the door. Thank you for playing.

Grigori planted his elbows on the table, leaned forward, and made his opening move. "While my business is oil and gas, my hobby is investing in startups. The heads of Russia's major research centers all know I'm a so-called *angel investor*, so they send me their best early-stage projects. I get everything from social media software, to solar power projects, to electric cars.

"A few years ago, I met a couple of brilliant biomedical researchers out of Kazan State Medical University. They had applied modern analytical tools to the data collected during tens of thousands of medical experiments performed on political prisoners during Stalin's reign. They were looking for factors that accelerated the human metabolism—and they found them. Long story short, a hundred million rubles later I've got a drug compound whose strategic potential I think you'll appreciate."

Grigori slapped his button, pausing his timer and setting the president's clock in motion. It was a risky move. If Korovin wasn't intrigued, Grigori wouldn't get to finish his pitch. But Grigori was confident that his old roommate was hooked. Now he would have to admit as much if he wanted to hear the rest.

The right side of the president's mouth contracted back a couple millimeters. A crocodile smile. He slapped the clock. "Go on."

"The human metabolism converts food and drink into the fuel and building blocks our bodies require. It's an exceptionally complex process that varies greatly from individual to individual, and within individuals over time. Metabolic differences mean some people naturally burn more fat, build more muscle, enjoy more energy, and think more clearly than others. This is obvious from the locker room to the boardroom to the battlefield. The doctors in Kazan focused on the mental aspects of metabolism, on factors that improved clarity of thought—"

Korovin interrupted, "Are you implying that my metabolism impacts my IQ?"

"Sounds a little funny at first, I know, but think about your own experience. Don't you think better after coffee than after vodka? After salad than fries? After a jog and a hot shower than an afternoon at a desk? All those actions impact the mental horsepower you enjoy at any given moment. What my doctors did was figure out what the body needs to optimize cognitive function."

"Something other than healthy food and sufficient rest?"

Perceptive question, Grigori thought. "Picture your metabolism like a funnel, with raw materials such as food and rest going in the top, cognitive power coming out the bottom, and dozens of complex metabolic processes in between."

"Okay," Korovin said, eager to engage in a battle of wits.

"Rather than following in the footsteps of others by attempting to modify one of the many metabolic processes, the doctors in Kazan took an entirely different approach, a brilliant approach. They figured out how to widen the narrow end of the funnel."

"So, bottom line, the brain gets more fuel?"

"Generally speaking, yes."

"With what result? Will every day be like my best day?"

"No," Grigori said, relishing the moment. "Every day will be better than your best day."

Korovin cocked his head. "How much better?"

Who's the rabbit now? "Twenty IQ points."

"Twenty points?"

"Tests show that's the average gain, and that it applies across the scale, regardless of base IQ. But it's most interesting at the high end."

Another few millimeters of smile. "Why is the high end the most interesting?"

"Take a person with an IQ of 140. Give him Brillyanc—that's the drug's name—and he'll score 160. May not sound like a big deal, but roughly speaking, those 20 points take his IQ from 1 in 200, to 1 in 20,000. Suddenly, instead of being the smartest guy in the room, he's the smartest guy in his discipline."

Korovin leaned forward and locked on Grigori's eyes. "Every

ambitious scientist, executive, lawyer ... and politician would give his left nut for that competitive advantage. Hell, his left and right."

Grigori nodded.

"And it really works?"

"It really works."

Korovin reached out and leveled the buttons, stopping both timers and pausing to think, his left hand still resting on the clock. "So your plan is to give Russians an intelligence edge over foreign competition? Kind of analogous to what you and I used to do, all those years ago."

Grigori shook his head. "No, that's not my plan."

The edges of the cornflower eyes contracted ever so slightly. "Why not?"

"Let's just say, widening the funnel does more than raise IQ."

Korovin frowned and leaned back, taking a moment to digest this twist. "Why have you brought this to me, Grigori?"

"As I said, Mister President, I have a plan I think you're going to like."

Chapter 3

2 Years Later

WHILE THE MELODIC CLINK of a silver spoon on Waterford crystal quieted the banquet's fifty guests and halted the jazz trio playing in the corner, Achilles leaned toward his brother and whispered, "Who's the speaker?"

Colin swallowed his last bite of steak. "Sometimes I forget you're from a different world. That's Vaughn Vondreesen. He's the venture capitalist who recruited dad to Vitalis."

Achilles really was from a different world, Colin mused. Whereas Colin and his father were entrepreneurial physicians, Achilles was a spy. Well, he used to be a spy. Currently, he was unemployed. Funny thought, that. An unemployed spy. *How did spies get jobs?*

"He looks like George Clooney," Achilles said.

"And he's just as charming. Even has a British accent from his Oxford days." Colin gave his younger brother one of those some-guys-have-all-the-luck nods. "They say Vondreesen is as powerful in Silicon Valley as Clooney is in Hollywood."

The brothers were at a four-top table in the back of a stylish Santa Barbara restaurant named Bouchon. Colin was seated beside his girlfriend, Katya. Achilles sat next to an empty chair. As the honoree's immediate family, custom would have seated them at the head table, but they'd ceded the seats to their father's favored colleagues. The businessmen had all driven down from Silicon Valley for the night, whereas the family would be dining together for another week.

As if on cue, Vondreesen began, his regal intonation instantly silencing the crowd. "We're here tonight in Santa Barbara's finest restaurant, with Silicon Valley's finest executives, to celebrate the sixtieth birthday of the finest man I've ever known, and alas, his retirement."

Applause erupted, and everyone stood. After a minute of heartfelt clapping, the guests returned to their seats and Vondreesen continued. "Let me tell you a few things you might not know about John ..."

Achilles again leaned toward his brother. "What's going on?"

"What do you mean?" Colin asked, knowing full well what he meant.

"You're nervous about something."

The brothers had no secrets. Achilles was just eighteen months younger, but their boyhood rivalry had long ago given way to brotherly love. As they'd grown, their careers and personalities had evolved as differently as the flower from the leaf. But with common roots and seed, they generally shared one mind. "No worries. I'll tell you later."

"And they say I'm the mysterious one," Achilles replied.

"What's mysterious?" Katya asked, more interested in their discussion than Vondreesen's speech.

Colin flashed Achilles a warning with his eyes, possibly confirming a suspicion but figuring that was better than the alternative.

"From my perspective," Katya continued, "The only mystery tonight is why Achilles hasn't been flirting with Sophie."

"Who's Sophie?" Colin asked.

"Our waitress," Katya said. "She's been eying Achilles all night."

"It's the clothes," Achilles said. "She thinks I'm a rebel."

"It's not the James Dean wardrobe," Katya said. "Trust me." While she spoke, Katya beckoned for Sophie to come over.

Katya was the love of Colin's life. He had fallen for her at first sight, and a year later she still electrified him every time she walked into a room. She was beautiful and brilliant, bold and brave, compassionate and kind. He was utterly, completely, and blissfully bewitched. In other words, he loved her dearly.

When the waitress arrived, Katya caught her eye. "Achilles here was just wondering where you're studying."

Sophie's face turned a cute combination of coy and confused. "Did she call you by your last name?"

"She did. I've always gone by Achilles."

"What's your first name?"

"It's a secret."

Sophie's expression indicated that she wasn't sure if Achilles was joking or not, but she moved on. "Okay. Now that we've kinda cleared that up, what makes you think I'm a student?"

"That was actually Katya's question."

"Oh," Sophie said, sounding wounded.

"I already know you study marine biology at UCSB," Achilles said.

Sophie and Katya both did double takes at that. Colin smiled.

"How do you know that?" Sophie asked.

"Is he right?" Katya asked.

"He's right," Colin said. "I don't know how he knows, but trust me, he knows." Colin beckoned Sophie closer. It was his turn to whisper. "Achilles used to work for the CIA." He met her widening eyes with a reassuring nod.

A round of applause broke the moment. Vondreesen had completed his toast. As a lawyerly-looking guest launched into his kind remarks, Sophie grabbed the empty seat next to Achilles and asked, "How did you know that about me? Do you have some facial recognition phone app? Were you *practicing tradecraft* on me?"

"Practicing tradecraft?" Achilles raised his eyebrows.

"I read Ludlum and Flynn," she replied, mock challenge in her voice.

"Well, Sophie, since you read Ludlum and Flynn, you can appreciate that I was conducting a basic threat assessment."

Sophie brought her hands to her proud chest, fingers splayed. "Surely I don't look threatening?"

"You were obviously concealing something over there on the side table, among the menus. Given the way you went back to it whenever you had a spare minute, I figured it was a book rather than a bomb. Either some fantastic fiction like Ludlum or Flynn, or perhaps a textbook, but I've learned not to assume. So I checked it out."

Colin was pleased to see Sophie's flirtatious reaction. He was happy to be out of the dating game, but still enjoyed it as a spectator sport. And his brother could use a good time.

"I have a chemistry test Monday," Sophie said. "That's a chemistry textbook. How'd you know I'm a marine biology student?"

Achilles held up both hands. They were big as a quarterback's, and calloused from thousands of hours climbing rocks. Very manly. He held his fingers wide and then brought them together like the overlapping circles of a Venn diagram. "Graduate level chemistry classes and scuba diving have a pretty limited overlap."

"Scuba diving? What makes you think I'm a scuba diver?"

"The tan lines on your face and wrists indicate you frequently wear a wetsuit with a hoodie."

"Maybe I surf, or dive as a hobby." Sophie was obviously enjoying the mental joust. "This is Santa Barbara, after all."

"It's scuba. Surfers don't typically wear wetsuit hoodies. Hobby doesn't fit either. You're working your way through graduate school as a waitress, and you're busy and diligent enough to risk sneaking a textbook to work on a Saturday night, so you don't have the kind of free time those tan lines would imply if coming from a hobby."

Rather than respond, Sophie studied Achilles for a moment. "Are you sailing later tonight, or in the morning?"

"Late morning. After brunch."

Colin looked Sophie's way and cleared his throat. She checked her watch and stood. "Time for dessert."

Katya threw a *you're welcome* look in Achilles' direction, followed by a toothy grin. She had a big beautiful mouth that used to remind Colin of the actress Anne Hathaway. Now Anne's smile reminded him of Katya. Apparently Katya was quite pleased with her good deed. Or maybe she wanted Achilles off the yacht for the night. Perhaps she sensed what was coming.

Chapter 4

A Cold Reception

TIME LIES. It masquerades in symmetrical guise, using clocks and calendars as accomplices. They cloak it in perfect uniformity, regular as hatch marks on a ruler, stretching forward and backward without variance of size or scale or import. As anyone who has lived even a little knows, this is a grand deception.

I was about to be served with the most pivotal of days, and the longest of my thirty-one years. The day that would forever split my life into *before* and *after*. But of course, I didn't know. We never do. Time only lets us look in one direction. So I had no clue what was to follow that knock at my hotel room door.

"Who is it, Achilles?" Sophie asked.

Turning my head from the peephole, I called back, "Are you in some kind of trouble?"

"I don't think so," she said, sitting up without covering up and sending my waking body in an altogether different direction from my brain. "Why? Who's at the door, the police?" She was joking, but she'd nailed it.

"Yeah."

That brought the sheet right up, but it didn't elicit panic. The deduction became pretty basic at that point. They were here for me.

I addressed the door. "Give me twenty seconds to get some clothes on, officers."

I pulled on my jeans and t-shirt, tied my shoes, and donned my leather jacket. Sixteen seconds. I gave Sophie a reassuring smile, and mouthed, "Sorry." Then I cracked the door in twenty flat.

"Kyle Achilles?"

"That's right."

"We need you to come with us, please."

I checked the authenticity of the officers' footwear and then their proffered credentials. "Okay."

I turned back to Sophie. "Looks like I'll have to give you a rain check on breakfast."

Her mouth said, "I understand. It was nice meeting you." Her face said she was unsure what to make of this and didn't necessarily want to find out.

That made two of us.

I knew she'd be okay a few seconds later when I heard her shout through the door, "So it's *Kyle*."

From outside, the Santa Barbara Police Department looked more like a Spanish mansion than a government office, right down to the lush manicured garden. White stucco walls and red-tiled roofs, with lots of arches and gables and a shady colonnade. Clearly the locals were proud of their heritage and their wealth.

Officer Williams swiped open the door to Interview Room One. Once he'd ushered me inside, he turned to leave. "Detective Frost will be with you shortly."

"Can I get some coffee? Big and black."

Williams replied, "Sure thing," but his tone was ambiguous and I couldn't see his face. As the lock clicked, leaving me in isolation, the implication of Officer Williams' words struck me. I was expecting some kind of CIA inquiry or debriefing, having just resurfaced back in the US for the first time since resigning a year earlier. But Langley wouldn't involve a police detective. They'd videoconference or send a local agent.

My empty stomach twitched a warning.

I looked at my watch: 10:49 a.m. My family would be polishing off their mimosas right about now at whatever local gem had earned the best Sunday brunch reviews. I had until 1:00 p.m. to get back to the *Emerging Sea* if we were going to stick to the schedule.

Dad was big on schedules, as was Colin. Martha and Katya seemed considerably more relaxed, although I was still getting to know them.

I started to pull out my phone to call my dad, but remembered that my cell's battery had died without the usual overnight recharge. I was debating pounding on the door and asking for a phone when it opened and a mid-fifties bureaucrat walked in. He had more hair sprouting from his ears than above them, like a continuation of his mustache, and his paunch was bigger than a bag of bagels. To be working here looking like that, this guy had to be either very good or well-connected.

"I'm Detective Frost." He took a seat across from me without offering either his hand or coffee. Well-connected it was.

"You don't appear to have brought coffee."

"What?"

"Williams said he'd send some coffee."

"Maybe later." Frost pulled a reporter's notebook from his back pocket, flipped past several penned pages to a blank one, and readied a cheap plastic pen.

Chapter 5

Revelations

MY STOMACH DROPPED with Detective Frost's first question. This was definitely not a CIA debriefing. "What brings you to Santa Barbara?"

I knew it would be pointless to press Frost for information before he was ready to give it. Interrogations didn't work that way —and that's exactly what this was beginning to feel like. About what, I hadn't the faintest idea. "I'm just passing through. I'm in the midst of a two-week cruise from San Francisco to San Diego with my family."

"How many are sailing with you?"

"Five, including me. My father, his wife, my brother, and his fiancée." Hoping to speed things along, I added, "We're celebrating my father's sixtieth birthday and retirement. Yesterday was his actual birthday, so last night we had the formal party right here in your fine city."

"Private cruise?"

"That's right. We're breaking in my father's new yacht." I would normally have said *boat* even though the *Emerging Sea* was clearly a yacht, because using *my* and *yacht* in the same sentence isn't in my nature, but here at the SBPD they were clearly used to bowing to *haves* while dealing with *have-nots*. I was hungry and budding a caffeine-withdrawal headache, so I was ready for a little less dealing and a little more bowing.

"When did you arrive?" Frost asked, flipping the page and continuing to write.

"We docked around 4:00 yesterday afternoon, and plan to set sail two hours from now." I tapped the face of my Timex.

"And what did you do after docking?"

"Once the ladies were ready, we went straight to Bouchon for the party."

"Bouchon," he repeated back. "That's very nice. How long did the ladies take to get ready?"

"An hour or so."

"Meanwhile the guys were doing what?"

"We put the yacht in order, and then got dressed ourselves."

"Did you go to the party, at Bouchon, dressed like that?"

"I did."

My answer seemed to disappoint Frost. Truth was, I'd been living out of a backpack for the last year, wandering Europe from rock-face to rock-face, climbing hard and contemplating life. Thirty-one might be a bit old for that, but I had my reasons.

The necessity of packing light had led to an appreciation for a simple wardrobe. By sticking with white t-shirts over cargo shorts or jeans, along with climber's approach shoes and a black leather jacket when required by circumstance or weather, I freed my backpack and my mind for more important things. Of course, this had made me the only person at Dad's retirement bash not in formal attire, but nobody, least of all my father, had seemed to mind. It was a California crowd, after all.

"And how late were you there?" Frost asked.

"Until about 1:00 this morning."

"And where did you go then?"

"Right next door to the hotel where your colleagues found me."

"Why not back to the yacht?"

"I met someone at the party, and opted for a little privacy."

"Do you do that kind of thing often?"

"Not often enough."

"You're being evasive."

You're being rude. "I only recall one other such occasion. That was about four months ago in Greece. Coincidentally, her name was Sophie too."

Frost jotted something, then closed his notebook and leaned forward. "Tell me about your brother's fiancée."

I didn't lean in to match Frost's posture, but rather stayed right where I was with my right leg crossed over my left knee. I was intrigued by his pivot but didn't want to show it. "Katya's Russian, like our mother. She's a doctoral candidate in mathematics at Moscow State University. They just got engaged last night over dessert, in fact. Made the night a triple celebration."

Frost wet his lips. "She's beautiful."

Katya had a classic Slavic face, as in the kind Czars paid Dutch Masters to paint. Perfectly proportioned features perched between high cheekbones. Thick honey-blonde hair framing a broad jaw, lithe neck, and lean shoulders. Beautiful was an understatement. Katya was spectacular. "She is. Smart too. I'm happy for Colin. They're good together."

"What's your relationship with her?"

"My relationship? I don't have one. Is this about Katya?"

Frost stood up and then leaned forward, placing both his fists on the table. I wasn't sure if he was going for hemorrhoid relief or the alpha-gorilla look. "If you don't have a relationship with her, then why did she spend last night in your stateroom?"

I kept my face passive, but inside was shocked, as much by Frost's apparent knowledge as by the fact itself. Every other night she'd been in Colin's bed. What had changed? "I wouldn't know, since I wasn't there. I was in a hotel. As we've already established."

"Doesn't Katya's behavior strike you as odd, spending her engagement night apart from her fiancé?"

"I've never been engaged, so I can't speak to that. But I have heard my brother snore after he's been drinking, so I can appreciate her wanting to seek a quieter refuge—afterwards."

"When did you first meet Katya?"

I wondered if it was always so frustrating on this side of the table, or if Frost just had a knack for irritation. "Your use of *first* implies a pattern. There is no pattern. Before leaving on the cruise last Sunday we'd only met one other time."

"Would you mind telling me where and when?"

I was starting to mind a lot of things, but I didn't want Frost to know it. "In Moscow. A little over a year ago. I was there on business. My brother was working there and dating Katya. He was crazy about her and brought her along when we hooked up for dinner."

"Are you telling me you had no contact with Katya between those meetings?"

"That's right."

"You sure?"

"Yes, I'm sure."

"That's not what she says. But we'll come back to that later."

"Wait a minute. Katya's here?"

Frost gave me a smug smile. "In the next room, speaking to my colleague."

I stood up. Put my own fists on the table. "It's time you told me what this is all about, detective."

"Sit down."

"I'll sit down when I'm ready."

"It's for your own good." Frost's timbre changed as he spoke. "There's something I need to tell you."

Chapter 6

Icebergs

FOR THE FIRST HALF of the movie *Titanic*, everyone is cruising along enjoying life, certain that tomorrow holds as much promise as today. Then they hit the iceberg, and their world turns upside down. Frost's voice sounded like ice ripping through the hull of my life. He sat down and I followed suit as a shiver ran up my spine.

Frost cleared his throat before he spoke. "I'm sorry to tell you that your brother, father, and stepmother all passed away this morning. Carbon monoxide poisoning appears to have been the cause."

I stared at Frost's mustached mouth with its coarse salt and pepper hair and crooked teeth.

Tears started streaming.

My jaw lost its grounding.

I couldn't speak. Couldn't process the news. Just hours ago we'd all been having the time of our lives. My father had worked his tail off for forty years and finally received the big payoff. Now he and Martha were set to spend the next forty years living the dream. And Colin ... that was ... unfathomable. He was the conservative Achilles. The responsible bookish older brother. A single grade ahead in school but six steps ahead in life, with a prestigious MD, a great girl, and a boundless horizon. A black body bag didn't fit in the frame.

"Katya called 911 at 6:00 a.m. after finding your brother, and then your parents," Frost continued. "A patrolman was there by 6:06, the paramedics by 6:08, and my partner and I by 6:45. The paramedics pronounced them dead on the scene. Are you familiar with carbon monoxide poisoning?"

I nodded once, my mind stuck on Colin. My self-identity was always evolving, but *brother* had been a constant from day one. Though half a world apart and as different as water and wine, Colin and I had been riding the river of life as a two-man team. Now I was completely alone, and reeling.

Frost continued speaking, but I wasn't really listening. "It's easy to diagnose as a cause of death because a fatal dose turns the cheeks cherry red. We see it a few times a year between suicides and accidents. Such a—"

The professional part of my brain suddenly kicked in like a safety light during a power outage. I interrupted Frost. "Why wasn't Katya killed as well?"

"We've been looking into that along with the source of the gas. Well, the source was the yacht's engine, obviously, so rather we're investigating how the gas circumvented the exhaust system and safeguards. Technicians are still on the scene. As for Katya's survival, we're working on that too. She's younger, slept in a different room, and got up early to work at the dining table. Apparently she has an important presentation coming up. Do you know anything about that?"

"She's scheduled to defend her doctoral dissertation in a few weeks, after five years of work. She's very nervous about it. It's in mathematics. Apparently people frequently fail the first time. Some never pass."

"Doctoral dissertation. In mathematics, no less. So she's practical? Clever?"

"She's brilliant." As the words came out of my mouth, Frost's line of reasoning came together in my head like a clap of thunder. I knew what he was up to. I felt my sea of grief becoming a swell of anger, but before my numbed mind computed my next move, someone knocked on the door.

Frost got up and stepped out into the corridor. When the heavy lock clicked behind him, I found myself facing the worst day of my life.

I took one deep breath, then another, counting down from six as I exhaled. My mind was racing, my pulse was pounding, my heart was broken. I knew how to rein in the physiological reactions. Controlling those had been a professional requirement. The grief, however, threatened to topple the cart.

I couldn't let that happen.

Not now.

Not until Frost believed in my innocence.

Chapter 7

Four Bags

TO RETURN REASON to the driver's seat, I had to relegate emotion to the back. To accomplish this, I did as I was trained. I painted my grief as a big gray blanket on the canvas of my mind, heavy and coarse and damp with tears. I folded it in half and half again until it was a manageable size. Then, reverently and temporarily, I set it aside.

Sometime later I heard the lock click. The door opened, and a very different detective walked in. She was ship-shape and petite and a good ten years younger than Frost. A huge and pleasant contrast.

The first thought to cross my refocused mind was that she too had to be either pretty darn good or well connected to get a plum detective job with her demographic profile. My second thought was that she hadn't brought me coffee either. Rather she was carrying a black backpack by the top handle as though it were a briefcase. She set it down on the floor and came around the table to introduce herself with an extended hand and a courteous smile. "I'm detective Flurry."

Her greeting surprised me. Not her words, but her actions. When I rose to shake her hand, I was a full foot taller and twice her size. Her hand disappeared into mine like a baseball into a glove. I could have tossed her like a ball too, literally pulling her in with my right while hoisting her over my head with my left, and sending her sailing with no more effort than a Sunday morning yawn. The contrast put me in a psychologically dominant position at a time when traditional police tactics called for the opposite. I watched her eyes closely as we shook, but she gave absolutely no sign of discomfort.

I liked her immediately. Decided to test my instincts.

"Why start with a lie?" I asked. "Aren't you supposed to be establishing trust?"

"Pardon?"

"Santa Barbara's population is only what, a hundred thousand? I'd be surprised if there were more than two detectives in the crimes-against-persons unit. You're telling me the two happen to be named Frost and Flurry?"

"You should find that reassuring."

"How so?" I asked.

"The names are real."

I chewed on that for half a second. "So you have a daily reminder that coincidences do happen."

She smiled.

One point for Flurry.

"I'd like you to take a look at something for me. Four things, actually." She unzipped her backpack and extracted a bunch of clear plastic bags. Evidence bags. She pulled them onto her lap where I couldn't see them. Setting the first on the table, she said, "Look, but don't touch."

The bag appeared empty.

Flurry studied me while I studied it.

I looked back up at her with a blank expression. She didn't comment either. She just dealt the second bag as if it were a poker card, watching me all the time for a reaction. It appeared empty at first too, but this one was less crumpled and the room's fluorescent light hit it at a different angle. I saw that it contained a piece of clear packing tape. I tilted my head to reexamine the first and then saw that it contained tape too.

I allowed my face to show my confusion.

The third bag was a bit more interesting, but still not very. It held an empty tube of superglue rolled up like a toothpaste tube to extract every last drop.

I said, "Three strikes."

She said nothing.

The fourth and final bag presented something very different. Something I definitely had seen before. That was when the worst day of my life became the worst day imaginable.

Flurry picked up on my reaction immediately. She finally asked a question that I could answer. "Recognize this?"

I said, "I'd like to speak to an attorney now."

Chapter 8

Emerging Sea

WHEN I INVOKED my right to counsel, Flurry didn't sigh and shake her head and slowly get up to leave the interrogation room. She didn't pull out her radio and inform Frost. Instead she said, "I believe your attorney just arrived."

That solved one mystery, but created another. Now I knew why she'd rushed to get my reaction to the evidence. She wanted to be sure she got it before I lawyered up. Another sound tactical move by an impressive detective. But I had no idea how my lawyer could have arrived. I didn't have a lawyer. I didn't know a single lawyer in the state of California. My best guess was that Katya was ahead of me, but that seemed a stretch for a foreigner just in from Moscow.

The door opened as if on cue and two men in dark suits and bright ties walked in. I recognized both from Bouchon. The first was Vaughn Vondreesen, the uber-charismatic guest and master of ceremonies. The second had also given a toast. He was handsome as well, but a mere mortal, and I didn't know his name. He spoke first. "Detective, I'm Casey McCallum, Mr. Achilles' attorney. Kindly give us the room and complete privacy." He motioned toward the camera on the ceiling.

As soon as the door clicked behind Flurry and the blinking red diode went out, Vondreesen closed the gap between us. "Casey's the best criminal defense attorney in the Bay Area. The minute I heard what happened to your family I took the liberty of asking him to stick around. Just in case." He put a hand on each of my shoulders. "I'm so sorry for your loss. Your father was the best man I knew."

Vondreesen radiated energy from his hands and eyes in a way that I found both comforting and disconcerting. Casey had a similar energetic vibe about him. Perhaps it came with being a captain of Silicon Valley. Perhaps it was a prerequisite. In any case, I was encouraged to know that it would be working for me against the aggressive detectives in the Santa Barbara Police Department.

Vondreesen lowered his arms with a final reassuring shoulder squeeze and I stepped forward to offer Casey my hand. "Thank you for coming. Your presence and Vaughn's prescience are most welcome."

Casey shook my hand reassuringly and then got right to it, a quality I was glad to find in a man who was undoubtedly charging my father's estate an astronomical hourly rate. "What have they told you?"

"They haven't told me anything, directly. But given the fact that they've been questioning rather than consoling me, they're clearly leaning toward a homicide ruling. Just before you walked in, Detective Flurry confronted me with four evidence bags. The first two contained pieces of clear packing tape. The third held an empty tube of superglue. They meant nothing to me. The fourth, however, contained a piece of PVC pipe with collars at both ends. I'd seen it last Sunday. As soon as she showed it to me I stopped talking and asked for counsel."

"Always a smart move. Where did you see it last Sunday?"

"When I first boarded the *Emerging Sea* I found it on my bunk along with a full tube of superglue and a roll of packing tape. Right there in the crease where the bedspread meets the pillow. I gave it a once-over, then put all three items in a drawer. Didn't think about them again until Flurry pulled out the piece of PVC. The moment I saw it, the darkest day of my life became midnight black, because I understood two things." I held up my fingers to count them off. "One, my family didn't die in an accident. They were murdered. And two, I'm being set up to take the fall."

Chapter 9

Deep Freeze

CASEY'S FACE reflected serious concern. He clearly shared my conclusion. But figuring out who was setting me up, and why, would have to wait. First, we had to deal with the evidence against me.

Casey wasted no time with sugarcoating or sentimentality. "So the police have your fingerprints on what we assume will be the piece of exhaust pipe that was loosened to release the carbon monoxide into the yacht's bedrooms. And if that proves to be true, then no doubt the tape and superglue will also be linked to the crime and covered with your prints. Have they fingerprinted you?"

I held up my hands in a reflexive but pointless display. "No need. My prints are already in the system."

Vondreesen chimed in for the first time. "Tell Casey about your professional background. He was a Marine, way back. I'm sure he'll appreciate it."

I looked at Casey who nodded. "Please."

"I used to work in the CIA's Special Operations Group."

"Used to?"

"I left a year ago, after five years of service."

"And what do you do now?"

Casey's question was simple, my answer anything but. "I've been traveling in Europe. Climbing rocks and contemplating life while trying to figure out what I want to do with the rest of mine."

"You're not currently employed?"

"No."

"And you don't have a family of your own?"

"No."

"But you've got family money. A recent development, from what I understand?"

I acknowledged what we both knew was coming. This was not going to look good. "My father was a physician in the Air Force. Not a highly paid position, but he enjoyed it and put in his twenty. Then he spent the last fifteen years working in biotech, kind of a continuation of his military specialty. Ten of those years were with a company that got acquired last year for half a billion. His net from stock options as their chief medical officer was around ten million dollars. He was going to retire then, but as I gather you know, Vaughn talked him into joining another start-up, Vitalis Pharmaceuticals."

Casey didn't comment.

"My stepmother wasn't wild about him giving up retirement, so as a compromise he bought the *Emerging Sea* and agreed to take her on a month-long cruise in conjunction with his sixtieth birthday. Then, as is so often the case in Silicon Valley, Vitalis folded and the birthday bash became a retirement party as well."

"And now you'll be inheriting an estate worth at least ten million?"

I knew the smart move was to come clean right away. While Casey watched, I double-checked that the camera was still off before replying. "I haven't seen the wills, but would expect to be the primary surviving beneficiary. Martha had no children. As for the money, I helped my father move it overseas, so I know your estimation is accurate."

"You helped him move it? Overseas?"

"A certain amount of know-how came with my CIA job."

"That won't look good if they find out, but at least it puts the money out of the court's reach for the moment. Can you access it?"

"I can."

Casey ran a hand through his thick gray hair, front to back, then massaged his neck for a second. "What exactly does the CIA's Special Operations Group do?"

"We're essentially the military arm of the State Department. We quietly attend to America's overseas interests."

"Military arm," Casey repeated. "Would I then be right to assume that in addition to banking, you have a lot of practical knowledge when it comes to mechanical things like engines and weapons of all kinds, including explosives and toxins?"

"That also went with the territory."

"How about investigations? Did your work involve those?"

"It did."

"Therefore you understand the challenge we're up against?"

"Ten million worth of motive, plus means, opportunity, and presumably compelling physical evidence. They're also exploring my relationship with my brother's fiancée Katya, in case there's a jealousy or a collusion angle."

Casey's face looked nearly as grim as I felt. He was exceptionally good at projecting empathy. He had to be. His income rose with the misfortune of others, but he could never let that calculation show. His acting skills would serve me well with a jury, if it ever came to that.

There was a sharp double rap on the door and then Frost walked in, followed by Flurry. Two more uniformed officers remained in the hall. Frost spoke clearly and officially, without preamble. "Kyle Achilles, you're under arrest for the murders of John Achilles, Martha Achilles, and Colin Achilles."

Chapter 10

Batter Up

ASSISTANT DISTRICT ATTORNEY Patrick Kilpatrick studied the two detectives seated across the table from him. They were far from a matched set. Frost was old-school. A middle-aged white male who knew how to work the system and benefited from being married to the mayor's cousin. He had the same rumpled appearance as television's Lt. Colombo, but from what Kilpatrick had seen during the years they'd worked together, little of Colombo's deductive power and none of his charm.

Flurry, on the other hand, looked nothing like a classic television detective. She was petite, vivacious, and Latina. This would be the first case he worked with her, and he was curious to see what she brought to the table. From what he'd heard, she was quick-witted and diligent, but garnered the resentment of many of her peers for a rapid rise they attributed more to her minority status than to her competence.

"I'm familiar with the evidence gathered and facts of the case," Kilpatrick began, "but I need to know more about the players. I understand we have a potential PR complication there? Our prime suspect won an Olympic medal?"

Frost's head whipped up from his notes. "A bronze medal. In a minor sport. No big deal."

Kilpatrick shifted his gaze to the junior officer. "Detective Flurry, why don't you tell me who we're dealing with."

Flurry began speaking from memory. This immediately differentiated her from Frost, who couldn't think without staring at his notes. "Kyle Achilles is the son of an Air Force physician and a

Russian Olympic gymnast. His only sibling was the brother who died with his father during the incident in question. Achilles went—"

"Wait a minute," Kilpatrick interrupted. "Didn't his mother die on the yacht as well?"

"That was his stepmother. I'm not sure what happened to his real mother."

"Huh. Go on."

"Achilles went to the University of Colorado, where he was a star skier. Apparently he was also an excellent marksman, as he made the Olympic biathlon team and eventually won bronze in Vancouver. Somehow he caught the attention of the CIA, and he ended up in their Special Operations Group, where he worked for five years before resigning suddenly, a year ago."

"Forget the past," Frost said, his tone dismissive. "Look at the present. At the time his multimillionaire father was murdered—along with the only other people who stood to inherit his fortune—Achilles was an exceptionally capable and highly trained but unemployed killer."

"That's one way to look at it," Flurry said.

"You have a better way?" Frost asked.

"Let's keep focused," Kilpatrick said. "What else do we know about him? What's he been doing since he left the CIA?"

"He hasn't earned a dime," Frost said.

"He's been traveling around Europe, competing in rock-climbing competitions," Flurry said.

"He's a bum," Frost said.

"He's an American hero who decided to take his college graduation trip a decade late," Flurry said.

"Climbing rocks?" Kilpatrick asked.

"It's his hobby," Flurry said. "According to a magazine profile, he poured his frustrations into rock climbing after a lower-back injury ended his biathlon career. They do a lot of climbing in Colorado, along with skiing and shooting. Apparently he's gotten pretty good at free-soloing. He set a couple of speed records in Greece."

"Free soloing?" Kilpatrick asked.

"That's the technical term for what you or I might call monkey-style. No ropes, tools, or safety equipment. Just special shoes and chalk for your hands."

"How do you know so much about it?" Frost asked.

"My college boyfriend was really into free-soloing—until it killed him."

Kilpatrick exhaled, pushed back from the table, and stood to pace. "What about the woman we found him with?"

"I checked her out," Frost said. "Sophie Gramercy is a UCSB graduate student who waitresses evenings at Bouchon. She's clean. They only just met at the party."

"And the Russian girl, the brother's fiancée?"

"Katya Kozara was our only other suspect," Flurry said. "But whereas Kyle Achilles stands to inherit over ten million dollars from the death of his family, Katya loses. She'd just gotten engaged to Colin Achilles at that party, just set herself up to be an American doctor's wife. She would have been in line to eventually share in that ten-million-dollar inheritance, but now she's getting nothing."

"No chance Kyle and Katya were working together?"

"It doesn't look that way. In any case, we appear to have a very solid case against him—clear motive, clear means, clear opportunity—so we'd rather not complicate it."

Kilpatrick stopped pacing to survey Frost. "Do you agree with that?"

"Not entirely. I think you should put the Russian before the grand jury as well. They probably won't indict her, but that will give us the chance to learn everything she knows. As soon as we kick her loose, she'll fly back to Russia and we'll never see her again."

Kilpatrick picked up a bat that Barry Bonds had autographed for him, and began swinging at the air. "Okay. Sounds like we've got our man and our plan. I happen to know Achilles' attorney. He's from the Bay Area, and he's top-notch. The best around. So I need you to keep on it until you've got all the facts buttoned down tight. I don't want any surprises." Kilpatrick brought the bat down on the desk like a judge's gavel.

"The DA is watching this one closely. A triple homicide at the yacht club makes for a very high-profile case with tourists and taxpayers alike, so she's ordered me to get a conviction. Whatever it takes."

Chapter 11

6 Months Later

804, 805, 806–

"Man, why you keep doing that? Looks painful."

I didn't pause, but redirected my focus across the hall long enough to appraise the new guy. He was pacing his cell like a caged panther. 812, 813, 814. He could have been straight from an NFL defensive line. Mid-twenties. A fit 300 pounds on a 6'6" frame. No visible gang tattoos. Conservative haircut. Healthy complexion. Reasonably intelligent, lucid eyes. 821, 822, 823. I'd worked with many a man who looked like him, and called more than one my friend. "A guy's got to do something, right?"

"You're not just passing time," NFL said, his voice thick and slow. "Nobody does a thousand sit-ups hanging by his toes jus' to pass the time. You're training for something."

"Domestic violence?"

"What?"

"You kill your girlfriend?"

"No, man. She's fine. It was an accident, but her old man's a cop. When a guy's my size, people make assumptions, you know?"

I understood, but I didn't reply immediately. This was fast approaching the longest conversation I'd had with a fellow inmate during the six months I'd been awaiting trial at Santa Barbara County Jail. On the hunter-gatherer spectrum, I was much more spear than basket. So rather than wasting time getting to know my fellow inmates, I was treating my time awaiting trial as though the SBCJ was a training camp.

While Casey's investigators were out looking for an alternative man and motive to wave before my jury, I was keeping to myself and getting into the best climbing shape of my life. 860, 861, 862.

I was also exercising my brain in a way I'd never done before. In *Moonwalking with Einstein*, I'd read that a person could win the US Memory Championship by practicing an hour a day for a year. Sounded pretty cool to me—not to mention therapeutic. I'd found that I could force myself to block out virtually any amount of physical or emotional pain if focused on a compelling goal.

While I wasn't planning on being in jail for a whole year, I could easily dedicate an hour a day to *each* of the competition's categories. After six months, I was up to 49 random words and 147 random digits. I was also getting competitive with memorizing decks of cards, my favorite.

At the moment however, I was focused on my physical routine —and my new neighbor. NFL was about as close to Miss Manners as they came in this place. 888, 889, 890. Since the endorphins were flowing and the inverted sit-ups were just the beginning of my routine, I answered his question. "I'm a climber. As in rock. Lots of core strength required. Can't be wimping out when you're a hundred meters up a cliff face and the wind starts—"

The distinctive double snick of an extending steel baton cut me off like a guillotine. I cursed my lack of vigilance even as I released my toes and twisted to absorb the fall to the concrete floor with my left deltoid rather than my skull.

The baton whistled and then cracked across my feet, creating a wave of pain powerful enough to loosen my dental work. "Hands and feet are to remain inside the cell at all times." Officer Grissel sneered down at me, exposing brown teeth.

My feet were screaming, but I clenched my jaw against the surging pain and building rage. Without responding, I rolled into a handstand and started doing pushups with my back to him. 1, 2, 3. I kept doing them until Grissel moved on. Then I piked down and into a cross-legged position to inspect the damage.

"Anything broken?" NFL asked.

"I got my toes clear of the bar in time. Might have been ugly otherwise. Could have ended my vacation plans then and there."

"Vacation plans? What you in here for?"

"Triple homicide. But I got a good lawyer."

NFL grunted at that. "They all like that here?" he asked, doing a head tilt in the direction of Grissel's departure.

"Grissel's the worst, and he doesn't like me very much. He confuses rank with superiority, and I've never done too well with that type. Plus I think he's suffering from a constant toothache." I rolled back into the handstand and continued my workout routine. "You smell that breath?" 18, 19, 20.

"Like he gargles with sewage."

NFL went back to pacing. Every once in a while he'd stop and watch me, shaking his head with his massive arms crossed. I figured we both targeted a thousand in our workouts, but whereas mine were reps, his were pounds.

I was in my fifth set of pushups when I heard approaching footsteps. They weren't Grissel's. Grissel was my height, and these belonged to someone considerably shorter in stature. I flipped back onto my feet and received an emphatic reminder of the foul guard's handiwork. I'd be leaving the burpees and jumping jacks out of my routine for a day or three.

Officer Hicks' mop of dirty blonde hair came into view. "You've got a visitor, Achilles. Your attorney."

I slipped into my shoes and stepped to the door without wincing audibly. Hicks unlocked it and escorted me toward the south holding cell block gate.

NFL called after me. "Give your attorney my name! Marcus Fry! Tell him I can pay!"

Chapter 12

Cui Bono

WITH MARCUS'S PLEAS echoing behind us, Officer Hicks prompted me down a long windowless corridor, through another gate, and finally into the visitation area. I'd learned that jails differ from prisons in a few key ways. They're designed for relatively short stays while inmates await trial. So, even though this one had room for 640 occupants, it didn't have all the amenities of a prison. There was no library, or gymnasium, or even a contact visitation room. I had to use a handset to speak to my visitors through the thick plexiglass window that separated us.

Not that I had many visitors.

Other than Casey, my only visitor had been Sergeant Dix, a Special Forces master sergeant. My CIA recruiter had enlisted Dix as part of the training program he'd designed to bring me up to par with the SOG's other recruits, most of whom hailed from elite military units. Dix and I had grown close over the course of a very intense year, and had kept in touch the way guys tend to do, which is to say very occasionally, or whenever it was important.

I didn't know Casey nearly as well as I knew Dix. My first battle beside him was still a couple of weeks away. But even without that familiarity, I could tell from the look in his bright eyes that the news wasn't going to be good.

Casey picked up his handset, and I picked up my handset, and he launched right into it. "The investigators still haven't come up with anything solid to support our *other man* defense."

As my heart sank ever deeper, he began counting off fingers.

"No witnesses who saw suspicious activity around the yacht.

"No witnesses who saw other people on the yacht.

"No credible reason to believe such a person exists.

"No unexplained fingerprints."

"They did, however, independently confirm that the section of PVC with your fingerprints on it exactly matches the rest of the PVC pipe connected to the motor. Your prints are on the original."

I wanted to pound my head against the plexiglass. This had been going on for months now. Lots of activity, no progress. Casey's investigators were like hamsters spinning wheels. Now we were virtually out of time. "Any good news? Anything at all?" I asked.

"There are traces of talcum powder on the packing tape used to cover the carbon monoxide detectors. That supports our assertion that the real killer used gloves while applying it, latex gloves in this case. But frankly, that's a lot more circumstantial than what the prosecution has, which is your actual fingerprints."

"Anything else?"

"I'm afraid so. As you know *Cui Bono* is the starting point of every murder investigation. *Who benefits* is also the question to which every juror will demand a satisfactory answer. Your inheritance gives the prosecution a ten-million-dollar motive, whereas the defense is broke. You're the only person who profits financially from your parents' death. Your brother's too, for that matter." Casey's expression was grim.

"As for other potential motives, we couldn't find anyone with a major grievance against any of the victims. None of the three appear to have been involved in anything that would make someone want to silence them. I trust you haven't thought of anything in either of those regards since the last time we spoke?"

"No, I haven't."

"Without some variant of those motives in play, we're left with homicidal mania and jealousy. Katya is beautiful enough that I could easily spin the jealousy motive, and her being from Russia would do a lot to open up the jury's imagination. But for that to work, you need to identify the individual. She swears there is nobody out there in a jealous fervor. My investigators kept her under tight surveillance in Russia and confirmed that she is not seeing or being stalked by anyone. She's back from Moscow, by the way. Arrived last weekend to start her post-doc at Stanford."

Katya had written me a couple of times. Long, despondent, tear-soaked letters written late at night. They were full of sorrow over shattered dreams and wistful memories of Colin. They'd also brought me up to date on her career progression. "Couldn't we say it's the police's job to find the stalker, not ours? Muddy the waters of reasonable doubt?"

"We could, but that would likely backfire. Assistant District Attorney Kilpatrick is pretty sharp. He'd position you at the top of that suspect list. They have you on tape lying to the police about having contact with her."

"It wasn't really contact. All I did was reply to an email she sent with a question about Colin. It slipped my mind in the interrogation room."

"But you see how they could spin the headline? Lying to the police about your history with her. Plus they could say the engagement was what threw you over the edge. It dashed your hopes. They'll say you were upset, infatuated, and intoxicated. Better we don't go there."

"What you're telling me is that with less than three weeks left until my trial you have nothing for me, other than a half million dollars in legal fees?"

"Actually I have Plan B all teed up and ready to go."

"Maybe you should have started with that."

The rebuke slid off Casey like water off a duck. "Kilpatrick owes me a few favors. I called them in, applied some leverage, played up your medaled Olympian status, and got him to agree to a sweetheart deal based on an alternative scenario."

"What alternative scenario?"

"Something got stuck in the exhaust pipe. Say a rat crawled in and died. You removed the dead rodent, but then didn't sufficiently reattach the piping."

"That's quite a scenario."

"As I said, he owes me."

"What about the tape over the carbon monoxide detectors, the portholes superglued shut, and all the other adjustments that had to be made to override the yacht's safety systems?"

"Those will be considered circumstantial and disregarded."

Casey was beginning to look like a miracle worker after all. "So what's the deal?"

"He'll drop the charges from the top end of the scale all the way to the bottom. From three counts of murder in the first degree, to three counts of involuntary manslaughter."

"And the number?"

"Involuntary manslaughter carries a sentence of one to four. I got you two."

"Two years?"

"Two years each, with consecutive sentences. Six years total."

Six years. I shuddered at the thought of what six years in captivity would do to me. "And I'd be a felon, convicted of killing his family."

Casey said nothing.

I'd run a million deal scenarios through my mind, fighting pride and weighing time. Figuring out where to draw the scrimmage line wasn't the hardest thing I'd ever done. But it was close. "Tell Kilpatrick I'll take my chances with the jury."

Chapter 13

The Fourth Man

FORTY-FOUR HOURS elapsed between the time Casey delivered his bad news and the moment I received my next message. It wasn't what most people would consider to be good news either. In fact, it would probably top the nightmare list for many. But my circumstances were special, in more ways than one, so I was happy to be the recipient.

It was Saturday morning, two weeks and two days from the start of my trial. I'd come to learn that like on the outside, jailhouse moods were best on weekend mornings. The inmates had visitation to look forward to, and the guards had a slightly more relaxed attitude without the warden around.

My message arrived in a shower bay. Three mountains of muscle cornered me the moment I was alone.

"Hello, pretty boy," the middle one said, identifying himself as their leader. "I heard you was lookin' for comp'ny."

These guys weren't going to be winning any genius awards, but they weren't complete fools either. They were going for the misdirect, trying to make me think rape rather than murder. It was a sound battlefield tactic. All war is based on deception, after all. But then I wasn't deceived. And despite outward appearances, I had the advantage.

I hadn't been granted bail while awaiting trial due to the nature of the crime, and the surfeit of compelling evidence. It also didn't help that I'd been trained to disappear. But I hadn't been convicted either. No one here had. This was jail, not prison. The three message boys had hope of seeing freedom someday soon.

They had a lot to lose.

Therefore, they would be highly motivated to make my death look accidental.

That gave me an advantage, because I didn't care about appearances.

Three on one would seem to most to be a lopsided fight, especially if all involved were of similar size and stature. I stand 6' 2" and weigh 220 pounds, which puts me an inch and 5 pounds below the average NFL quarterback, but still north of 19 out of 20 American males. The heights of the three facing me were also in that 1 of 20 range, but they'd register closer to 280 on the meat scale. More like defensive ends than quarterbacks. Advantage attackers. However, unlike football, where the rules of the game amplify the laws of physics, combat puts myriad additional factors into play. Among those applicable at the moment were tactics, technique, and attitude. I knew I had them on tactics and technique. The laws of probability made that a lock. Their need for *accidental* also tipped the scale. Advantage Achilles.

"You heard right." I sauntered toward the leader, acting all peaches and cream. "I've got six months of lonely all pent up inside."

As attacker one digested this unexpected twist in the conversation, I dropped to my right knee and drove my right fist up and into his exposed testicles like a battering ram on a castle door. I packed the blow with six months of pent-up rage, powering it with my shoulders and back, and punching it through as if I was reaching for the stars.

It was devastating.

As my fist lifted him up and back, I could hear his ancestors cursing the termination of their bloodline. My objective was to disable one of them before any knew the battle had even begun, and in that I succeeded with style points to spare.

But I was still two-thirds of the way from home.

As the eunuch heaved forward and vomited, I spun up and around to my right, where I delivered a rapid triple combination to the second slab of beef. First plowing my right elbow into his solar plexus and robbing him of his ability to breathe, then delivering a stunning backhand to the bridge of his nose. Finally, I whipped back around to yank his head downward into my lifting knee. *Oomph! Crack! Crunch!*

The crunch was gruesome. A ten-pound head colliding at speed with a ten-pound knee spelled all kinds of jeopardy for the two-ounce nose caught between. The sound alone sent a shudder down my spine.

I'd expected the third attacker to pause and assess the situation that was so rapidly veering from plan. But he didn't. The starting whistle had blown and so he jumped into play. He dove at me like people who weigh 280 pounds are inclined to do.

I couldn't get out of the way in time.

As my knee finished off number two, number three took me to the tiled floor. Hard.

Getting me on the ground worked in three's favor. My remaining opponent's only advantage was his weight, and a floor fight played to it. The bad news for him was that I'm not a football. There was no ref, and no whistle. He didn't know what to do next. He didn't know whether to try to hold me until one of his buddies recovered enough to help out, or to try to get on top and pummel me to death.

His moment of hesitation gave me all I needed, because I did know what to do.

For five long, hard, happy years, my government had sent me into kill-or-be-killed situations with enemies who did not hesitate. They didn't flinch or pause or think twice. They gave homicide no more forethought than insecticide. I hadn't become numb, but I had learned to postpone the self-recrimination until after the fact, after I'd done what needed doing to survive.

I reached down and grabbed the back of my third assailant's shaved head with my left and then I drove my right thumb into his left eye socket as if I was trying to ram a cork into a bottle. No hesitation. No half-measure. Full-on engagement powered by fury and frustration.

He spasmed and went limp. He'd likely lose the eye, but that was preferable to what he'd planned for me.

Attacker two remained motionless where he dropped, but the eunuch was struggling to regain his footing. Extricating myself from the muddle, I leapt up, grabbed him with both hands, and whacked his head into the wall with enough force to knock him out for hours. He hit with a nasty crack and collapsed like a fat sack of flour.

I moved beneath one of the running showerheads to rinse the vomit and gore from my bare flesh while giving the scene a quick survey. One thing wasn't quite right. I repositioned number two a bit, smearing his right thumb with the bloody goo oozing from number three's left eye socket.

Satisfied that there was no physical evidence to contradict the story that a trio had gone at it and beat each other senseless, I went for the fourth guy.

There had to be a fourth guy. He'd be just around the corner of our shower bay, leaning one shoulder against the wall, trying to look casual to any passing guard while he kept everyone else out. He'd surely have heard the scuffle behind him despite the running showers, but he wouldn't have been able to look without defeating the purpose of his mission. I'd probably find him snickering as he pictured the scene.

I moved quickly but quietly across the tile to the corner. Crept to within inches of where I was sure he'd be leaning. My plan was to step out, reach around, grab him by the throat and wrist, and pull him back around the corner where I could reason with him privately. Make him see the mutual advantage of not having seen or heard anything to contradict the three-way tussle story, lest it become a four-way.

I slipped around the corner, arms poised to pounce, and froze in place. The man before me wore a guard's uniform. It was Grissel.

Chapter 14

The Visitor

I DUCKED BACK into the shower bay and pulled my clothes on without pausing to towel off. For six months I'd held in a torrent of grief and a swarm of frustrations, but my cork had popped along with number three's eye. I wanted to grab Grissel by his big ears and head-butt him full on the nose. I wanted to feel his cartilage crushing and hear his nose cracking and see his blood spurting. Grissel's sworn duty was to protect me, but he had tried to kill me instead.

I closed my eyes and counted to three before stepping out directly behind him. "There are two ways to deal with this."

Grissel whipped around, his face showing surprise before flashing anger and then fear.

I kept my inner beast caged, but gave him a glimpse of the animal within. As he swallowed dry, I said, "Either both of us were here, or neither of us were here."

I walked past him without another word. I could almost hear his mind whirring behind me. Pride fighting fear, curiosity battling with self-preservation. I did hear his decision. I heard him walk away.

With Grissel off guard duty, an inmate would discover the bodies momentarily. I didn't want to be in the area when that happened. I hustled back to my cell and began flipping through my thick stack of playing cards.

"Why you spend so much time jus' looking at those?" Marcus asked, leaning against his bars.

"Really want to know?"

"Yeah, man. Ain't like I got no pressin' engagement."

"Pull out your deck. I'll show you."

Marcus did.

"Hold up the cards one at a time and show them to me, fast as you can. Just put them back down in the same order."

"Fast as I can?"

"The faster the better."

The toilet-sink combo unit was near the bars, so Marcus used it as a makeshift table. Holding the deck in his hand, he began flipping up cards one at a time, and discarding them in a pile on the sink's rim.

"Faster."

Marcus shook his head, but began flashing them at a rate of about one a second. Within a minute, he was done. " 'kay. Now what?"

"Four of clubs, six of spades, five of spades, nine of diamonds, jack of hearts … I was on the thirty-forth card, and Marcus's eyes were big as boiled eggs, when my ears triggered a warning. A guard was walking my way with a purposeful stride. It didn't sound like Grissel.

Hicks came into view. "You've got a visitor."

"My attorney?"

"She doesn't look like an attorney to me." The guard spoke with the inflection men use among themselves when referencing attractive women. I didn't know him well enough to tell if it was a ruse. Hicks was a new hire. He might be leading me to a closet where Grissel would be waiting with another crew.

I had no choice but to follow.

Hicks did usher me to the visitation room, where I spotted my visitor the moment he opened the door. About two-thirds of the way down the row of twenty stations, glowing like a lighthouse beacon on a stormy shore, was Katya.

She was wearing the same slim-cut toffee-colored suit she'd worn to the party and her preliminary hearing. In the courtroom I'd figured it was the only suit in her travel bag. Now I suspected it was the only one she owned. There was no need for it here, however. Most jailhouse visitors wore clothes anyone could buy at a truck stop or ball game. She must have associated jail with court and dressed accordingly. I guessed she was regretting the decision, given that she was also using three white tissues to shield her hand, chin, and ear from whatever might be growing on the handset's speaker.

I picked up my handset without taking protective measures. Between growing up with a military physician, and countless missions in hazardous places, I'd developed an immune system tougher than a buzzard's stomach. And I was eager to talk. Katya and I hadn't spoken since the day of our preliminary hearings, when I was indicted and she was released. She'd flown straight back to Moscow and her doctoral defense. I'd moved into cell 412.

"Hello, Achilles."

She wore a smile, but I could see worry in her amber eyes. "I heard you were back from Moscow. Congratulations. Do I call you Doctor now?"

"Maybe Professor someday. I see you're still waiting for your trial. It's been so long."

"My attorney delayed it as long as possible to give us more time to investigate. But we're only a couple of weeks out now."

She paused there, not sure what to say. I thought I understood her predicament. Talking about my case could easily suck up the entire 45 minutes visitors were allotted, but I suspected she hadn't driven five hours from Stanford for that. "What can I do for you?"

"It's so incongruous, you and this place. Colin loved to talk about you as *the guy who could do anything*. But here, they let you do nothing. I feel like a fool now for coming. I had a very different image in my mind." She shook her head, and looked down.

My mind stuck on her comment. I didn't know my brother had talked like that about me. I didn't know he'd talked about me at all.

Katya flicked something off the countertop with a long, elegant finger. "Clearly I didn't think things through. Forget about me. What can I do for you? I guess I should have brought you some cookies. Or, I don't know, a TV."

"Tell me what's worrying you. The best thing you could do for me is give me someone else's problems to worry about."

She looked back up and her eyes melted a bit. "I think someone's trying to kill me."

Chapter 15

Terminate Her

SOMEONE WAS TRYING to kill me too, but I wasn't about to tell Katya. I had a couple of competing theories playing out in my head. Her arrival fit both of them.

I met her eye, then made a point of glancing to the left and right. "Tell me about it, *po Russkie.*" In Russian.

Katya nodded her understanding. "Two days ago I was coming out of the math department when a big guy sitting in the courtyard made me nervous. It wasn't how he was dressed that first drew my eye—Stanford attracts all types—but rather his disposition. Even sitting there drinking coffee he radiated a predatory, soldierly vibe. Seemed to be directing it at me, although with his wraparound sunglasses I couldn't be sure."

"What did he look like?"

"He was even bigger than you. Chiseled face with a military-style haircut. Dressed in a black suit. He'd have looked like a Secret Service agent except that he was wearing a black t-shirt rather than a white shirt and tie."

Looking at Katya through the thick plexiglass, I couldn't help but admire the way her mind worked, her mathematical precision. She'd thought about this. Reduced it down.

Katya was one of those people who surprised everyone she met, because she confounded expectations. When someone's that beautiful, you expect her to play to it. Lots of mirror time, and selfie shots, and coquettish behavior. I was beginning to understand why she didn't behave that way, why her behavior didn't even acknowledge her physical status. Colin had pointed it out, but I hadn't latched on. Her mind was her best feature. "Then what happened?"

"I crossed the courtyard, heading for the parking garage. He got up and followed me. Not right behind, but close enough that a three-second sprint would put him on top of me. I've been followed before, in Moscow. Stalked even. But those instances were always a lone guy half acting out some sexual fantasy. Sometimes not so subtly. Nothing serious ever happened, but those experiences prompted me to take some self-defense courses. I learned how to avoid and escape those situations, and how to make use of my fists, elbows, knees, and teeth." She mimicked a few moves.

"I was preparing myself to jump into my car and lock the door and hit the horn when I saw a second guy. Same huge size. Same serious outfit. Same soldierly vibe." She rattled off the facts like premises in a proof.

"He was sitting in a black Escalade, which he'd parked facing my car from across the aisle. The moment I saw him, I changed direction and walked over toward a group of guys who had piled out of a Honda. There were five of them, Ultimate Frisbee players in their late teens. I told them my concern and one of them launched a Frisbee right at the head of the suit who was following me. It was a great throw, fast and straight. The suit saw it, stopped and leaned his head just far enough to the right for it to sail past within an inch of his ear. He was almost robotic. Then the Escalade started up and pulled around and he got in and they drove off."

Scary as that sounded, I was certain there was more to come. She'd used the word *kill*, and we weren't there yet. "Did you get a license plate?"

"Only subconsciously. Enough to recognize it later when I saw a black Escalade parked near the entrance to my cul-de-sac. When the familiar letter pattern registered I felt my heart turn to ice. I kept driving, right past my apartment complex. I wanted to get lost in a crowd, so I drove to the mall, got a hot tea, and sat in the food court, thinking about my options."

"What did you conclude?"

"I concluded that I wasn't a random target, a young body picked from the crowd at Stanford to be raped, or sold into prostitution, or whatever. And they weren't spying on me. These guys were definitely more *Terminator* than *Bond*. From there, I reduced my predicament down to two root conditions: either they were trying to harm me, or they weren't. If they weren't, then there were no mistakes to be made. If they were, and I made a mistake, then I'd either be hurting or dead. So the only logical move was to assume the worst, that a couple of professionals were trying to kill me, and act accordingly. Make sense?"

I couldn't speak to her psychological health, but her logic was bulletproof. "You've got a remarkably cool head. What'd you do next?"

"The first thing I did was make sure I'd stay alive in the short-term. The second thing I did was try to figure out how to stay alive in the long-term." She paused there to look me in the eye.

"And that plan involves me. Even though I'm locked up in jail 300 miles from Palo Alto."

Katya shrugged and smiled meekly. "I've only been in the US for a week. The only other people I know are mathematicians. Hardly a rough-and-ready crowd. And I don't know any of them well. You, on the other hand, are almost family. I also happen to know that you are very well-trained to deal with situations like these. I suspect that you can do more from behind bars than 99% of people could do on the outside."

"What's your backup plan?" My question was analytical— reflecting her preferred style—but I immediately regretted it.

Katya deflated. "No choice really. I can't afford to hire bodyguards, and that's not my style anyway. I'll have to leave

Stanford. Give up on my dream and go back to Russia."

"Well, then you're in luck." I locked my eyes on hers, leaned in, and mouthed the next sentence. "I'm about to break out of jail."

Chapter 16

Windbreakers

THEY CAME FOR ME at midnight. Grissel and a squirrelly guard with hairy ears named Willis.

Stopping before my cell, Grissel flicked open his baton and swished it through the air like a pirate testing a sword. "On your feet!"

The smell of his breath hit me with physical force. I'd almost have preferred the baton. I tried not to inhale while I slid on my sneakers and stood.

Willis dangled a set of handcuffs from his index finger like balls on a string, so I backed up to the door with my hands behind me as per prison protocol. He snapped them on with vigor and then unlocked my cell door while Grissel stood tapping the business end of his baton against the flat of his left palm. One way or the other, I knew I'd never see cell 412 again.

"Good luck, man," Marcus called, from across the corridor.

Grissel stayed about five feet behind me while we walked, far enough to remain out of kicking range, yet close enough to keep my skull within the baton's strike zone. I'd never traversed the jailhouse at night before. The darkness seemed to amplify the sounds and smells of bodily emissions, bringing the walls in even closer.

At the far end of my cellblock, we passed through a gate I'd never used to a hallway I'd never tread. The rhythmic smack of the guards' boots became the dominant sound until a lock buzzed and a steel door swung—and I found myself in a room occupied by two navy blue windbreakers adorned with bright yellow lettering. FBI.

The shortest but broadest of the two special agents turned to study my face, comparing it to a photo he had clipped to a fresh brown folder. "Kyle Achilles?" His bright white teeth flashed in sharp contrast with his shiny ebony skin as he spoke, drawing my gaze.

"Yes."

He pivoted left to face the window that partitioned our room from the control booth. This was one no-nonsense pro. High-speed, low-drag, and squared away, as my peers used to say. He signed a document that was waiting on the partition ledge, then pushed it through the receiving slot.

I stole a glimpse. It was a transfer of custody order, signed by a federal judge named Bartholomew Cooley.

"We've got him from here," the lead special agent said. "You can take the cuffs off. We brought our own."

Willis uncuffed me.

The guard behind the glass had me sign for my belongings.

The taller FBI agent then cuffed me again, hands in front this time so I could carry the paper grocery bag that held my watch, wallet, and clothes.

There was no more fanfare. A few buzzes and clicks later, we were outside in the crisp California air, walking towards a black Suburban with government plates.

They put me in the back.

The lead agent slid in beside me.

The taller one sat behind the wheel. He keyed the ignition, snicked the selector into drive, and pressed the gas, making it real.

I was out.

We turned north on Calle Real and the driver pressed the accelerator with enthusiasm. In less than a minute, the perimeter lights of the Santa Barbara Community Jail were out of sight.

I held up my arms. "I think it's safe to uncuff me now."

Sergeant Dix turned and gave me a big grin. "I kinda like it this way."

He unlocked me anyway.

"You do a pretty good special agent impersonation."

"Not my first time wearing blue. Just my first time without sanction." Dix's bonhomie morphed to a more serious tone. "Your girl came through. She called not more than a minute after I hung up with you. Don't know if that means you can trust her, but it's a good sign."

I agreed. "Did you come up with a passport for her?"

Special Forces units routinely generated false identities for their operatives. This was tightly controlled, of course, but Dix was a clever senior NCO, so he knew how to work the system and he had the connections to do it. Still, whereas he'd had months to prepare the other aspects of my backup plan, Katya was a late addition.

"Yep. Here you go." He handed me a hefty manila envelope. "In case you do travel together, we made her Kate Yates to match your Kyle alias. Couples attract less attention, as you know. You've got matching Indiana driver's licenses and credit cards too."

"How about the Russian travel visas?"

"Yep. Belorussian too, so you'll have a bolt hole."

"I like your thinking."

"Not my first rodeo. Is Russia your contingency plan?"

"More like a working theory. Why's the envelope so heavy?"

"Used a little of your money to pick up a couple of clean

iPhones."

"Outstanding, sergeant. What did you tell Katya about tonight?"

"Operationally, she's in the dark. She just knows to expect you around now."

"Perfect. Where is she?"

"She's in a hotel over between the airport and the university. About 10 minutes from here. Key's in the envelope. Room 229. I'll drop you off, but then we've got to run. Ortega needs to return the SUV to his brother, and then we're wheels-up out of Vandenberg at 02:00. Best we get back to Bragg before we're missed."

I opened the paper bag and began changing into my civilian clothes. "I see you switched to the new Sig."

"You noticed that, huh?"

"Yeah. Been meaning to try it out myself."

"I suppose you'd like to field-test mine?" Dix's teeth flashed in the dark.

"Thanks. You can keep the belt and holster. I'm sure it will fit in my pocket."

"I can keep my belt and holster? That's mighty kind of you."

The P320 did indeed slide easily into my jacket pocket, but then, like all my clothes, it was extra large. "How's life back at Bragg?" I asked.

"Same as always. Lots more practicing than doing. I was glad you finally green-lighted this op. For more reasons than one. It's good to see you. Why'd you wait so long? I was expecting to pull you out months ago."

"I wanted to exhaust my traditional options before going unconventional."

"You mean you thought your lawyer might work some magic? From what you told me, he didn't have a chance. Course, if I were him, I might have taken my time to tell you that as well. What's he charging you? Five hundred an hour? A thousand?"

"Enough to bring tears to your eyes, my friend."

Dix and I spent the rest of the short drive catching up in the quasi-awkward way old friends who rarely see each other do. Then Ortega pulled into a parking space near a side door to the UCSB Summer Inn, and our reunion ended. We all shook hands and I thanked them again.

"Consider yourself freed," Dix replied, referencing the Special Forces motto.

I had one foot out the door when I turned back to my old friend. "Who's Judge Cooley?"

"Just somebody Winks invented for the occasion," Dix replied, referring to Herald Winkle, the computer genius we'd worked with at the CIA. "He sends his best, by the way. As for old Bartholomew, he'll disappear from the DOJ database later tonight. I suggest you do the same."

I whipped off a salute. "Thanks. But I've got other plans."

Chapter 17

Telltale Tea

I KNOCKED on Katya's door and announced myself, knowing she'd be nervous. With anyone else, I'd have used the key to slip quietly inside, but with Katya that would have felt like a violation.

Ours was an unusual relationship, simultaneously intimate and awkward. The total number of hours we'd spent conversing could be counted on fingers and toes, but circumstances had rendered us closer to each other than to anyone else on the planet.

Katya opened the door and I stepped into a room that smelled of honeysuckle in bloom. Quite a treat for a nose that had just endured six months in lockup. The picture of a steaming tub with tiny bubbles and bare shoulders popped into my mind. I forced it right back out. She'd nearly been my brother's wife.

Katya threw the bolt and slid the chain, then turned to look at me with warm, wide eyes. "Did you really break out of jail?"

I paused for a second, reflecting on the fact that my résumé had a new bullet point, and aware of how atypical a career had to be for *successful jailbreak* to be a selling point. "I had a lot of help."

"Were those guys from the Special Operations Group?"

"For their sake, it's better if we don't get specific."

"Did you ... have to hurt anybody? To get out, I mean?"

Katya was clearly wound up tight and starved for information, which was easy enough to understand. I didn't mind talking. My tongue was due for some exercise. "There are two ways to break out of prison. You can either outsmart the engineers and guards, or you can outsmart the bureaucrats. We outsmarted the bureaucrats. We used uniforms, forged papers, and a very talented hacker who had access to the Department of Justice network. So no bullets were required."

"You tricked the guards?"

"We played to their weakness."

"Sounds risky."

"Fortune favors the bold. And the deck was rigged in our favor. A prison guard's entire world revolves around the chain of command. Blindly following orders is programmed into their autonomic nervous systems, like breathing. Once the hackers and forgers did their thing, all my guys had to do was look the part and exude authority."

Katya gave me a look that said she grasped the theory, if not much more. "I'm sorry if I offended you. I certainly appreciate it."

"No worries. I understand. People hear 'Special Operations' and they think snipers and explosives. We use those too, but only when that's the smartest way to complete a mission."

Katya double-checked the door lock.

"How are you feeling?"

"I'm a bit overwhelmed by recent developments, but I'm feeling a lot better, now that you're here."

If Katya had been anyone but my brother's fiancée, I'd have given her a big hug at that moment. As it was, I kept a healthy distance. "Glad to be of service. Now, we should get going."

"Going? It's one o'clock in the morning. Where are we going? Oh, are the police looking for you?"

"No. At this point, as far as my jailers know, I've become the FBI's problem. But there's a different clock counting down my fate, and it's very short on time."

She didn't press me to clarify, and three minutes later I was driving her Ford north on the 101.

"Where are we going?" Katya asked.

"Back to Palo Alto."

"Are your friends meeting us there?"

"No. They need to be back home before anyone notices they were gone. And we won't need them anyway."

As I activated the cruise control, she asked the question I'd been anticipating. "If you could have broken out of jail at any time, why did you wait? Don't get me wrong, I'm profoundly grateful, but as we mathematicians like to say, the equation doesn't appear to balance."

The truth was, I'd have broken out just to save Katya. I owed that to Colin. But she didn't need to know that. "I broke out the moment the benefits of doing so outweighed the benefits of staying in. Helping you added weight to the escape side, but I'd already green-lighted the plan. Good thing I did too."

"How so?"

"Three inmates tried to crack my skull in the shower this morning, with the help of a bent guard. It was a contracted kill, a coordinated assassination attempt."

"Assassination? Why? What could anyone gain by killing you?"

I liked how her mind jumped right to the unsolved part of the problem. "I need coffee. Please grab an iPhone out of the manila envelope in the glovebox and find us a diner that's open 24 hours."

She did. Denny's was just one exit and two right turns away.

As the waitress filled my cup with coffee, I said, "Please keep it coming."

Wendy said, "Sure thing, sugar."

Mid-fifties and working the graveyard shift at Denny's and our waitress still had a good attitude. I admired people like her. Wondered momentarily about her source of joy—a hobby or a granddaughter that offset the grind.

Katya tried her tea, and then looked at me expectantly.

I dove right in, answering the question she'd asked in the car. "There is exactly one person with something to gain by killing me. It's the same person who killed my family and framed me for it."

Katya processed that faster than most people over thirty can recall their age. "That doesn't make sense. If he'd wanted you dead, he'd have killed you at the same time. The frame was clearly part of the killer's calculation."

"You're thinking like a mathematician. I admire that, but this isn't like solving a mathematical proof."

Katya wrinkled her nose. "You don't think the rules of logic apply to investigations? Sherlock Holmes would disagree."

"That's not what I said. Logic is exactly what I'm using. But not a mathematician's logic."

"Mathematics is the purest form of logic."

"Purest, perhaps. But this isn't a pure situation." I paused, but didn't take my eyes off hers while I stole a sip of coffee. "It's evolving."

Her face flushed a bit as comprehension dawned. "Of course. It's game theory, not algebra. Do you have any suspects?"

"I have two. One for each motive."

"And what are those motives?"

"The first motive is money."

"What money?"

"My father's money."

"But you got it all."

"I did, for now. Whether or not I get to keep it is a different question. Someone could be playing a long game. Someone with the ability to predict the result of a complicated series of events ... the solution to a long equation."

I studied Katya's face as I spoke. I liked coffee as much as the next guy and more than most, but we were in Denny's rather than her car for one reason: so that I could study her face at this moment. Katya didn't go through the usual feigned surprise or delayed reaction that the rules of etiquette call for when polite discussion turns accusatory. Perhaps that was because it was 2:00 a.m. at Denny's and not 4:00 p.m. at Harrod's, but I took it as a sign of her character.

"How could I benefit financially? Colin and I weren't married. We were barely engaged."

"In Russia, that would be the end of it. But as everyone knows, the US has a very special legal environment. People sue for things here. It's practically a national sport. First, you get the murders pinned on me. Then you sue the estate for damages. You were almost killed. Certainly traumatized. A jury would likely be very sympathetic, especially with the money coming from a convicted murderer."

Chapter 18

Motives

KATYA DIGESTED my accusation in silence, intermittently sipping her tea and flicking her fingernails off the pad of her left thumb. One, two, three, four. One, two, three, four. She probably ran a thousand iterations through that big brain of hers before she looked up. "What's the second potential motive? The one that isn't money."

I'd seen what I wanted to see. "Let's hit the road. I'll tell you in the car."

I paid at the counter while Katya visited the restroom. Using Kyle Yates's new credit card, I tipped Wendy more than the cost of our beverages. It felt good to be back in society. Signing the check, it occurred to me that coffee at Denny's had been my first purchase as a rich man, legal fees aside. Alas, the money would likely all be gone before the credit card bill came due.

Katya took the driver's seat this time. As she moved it forward I racked the passenger seat all the way back. I still couldn't fully stretch out my legs, but wasn't complaining. This was the most comfortable I'd been for months. Not that there wasn't tension. In fact, I thought I detected a bit of anger in the way Katya handled the steering and pressed the gas as we navigated back onto the highway, but I had no comparison. She'd never driven me before.

Once Katya had engaged the cruise control, she turned my way. "Why did you tell me that? If you suspect me, wouldn't the smart tactical move be feigning ignorance?"

"You just answered your own question, but on top of that, it was a tactical decision. The odds of my making a mistake go up considerably if I have to split my attention between two investigations. And I can't afford any mistakes. Plus, I don't have time to play it subtle, which isn't really my style anyway."

"What do you mean, you don't have time?"

"You'll see."

"Anyone ever tell you that you're cryptic?"

"Cryptic used to be my job description."

Katya kept quiet for a few miles.

I felt her relaxing.

"Why did you quit? You never really told me. The first time we met, when you were on that case in Moscow, you seemed so happy."

I didn't want to add that emotional maelstrom to the mix I was already feeling. "That's a long story for another time."

"There you are being cryptic again."

I said nothing.

A minute later, she asked her next question. "What's the second motive?"

"It's a bit more nebulous than the first. Let me tell you what I'm thinking. You can tell me if my deduction passes muster."

That pepped her right up. "Okay."

"Watch your speed."

"Sorry."

"Let's begin with the reason for framing me. In this scenario, that would be misdirecting the police investigation."

Katya was all over that theory. Clearly, she'd given it some thought while I was in jail. "Wouldn't it be better if they weren't investigating anybody at all? They could accomplish that by making the murders appear to be an accident. Surely that would be simpler. We should be looking for the simplest explanation. Occam's razor."

"You're right. And you've just hit on the key. The best way to avoid a serious investigation would have been to make the murders look like an accident. So that's what they would have done—if they could have."

"You're implying they couldn't?"

"Exactly. They couldn't. But *why* couldn't they? More specifically, what would make it difficult to credibly stage the murder as an accident?"

Katya turned from the road to look at me. "You've obviously run the permutations. What did you conclude?"

"I figure they needed to kill more than one person. They needed to kill at least two of the three, one of which had to be my brother."

"Why did one have to be Colin?"

"Because it would have been easy to stage an accident killing my father and mother. They're always together. A hit and run car crash would have been quick, and clean, and credible."

"There could be a hit and run with Colin in the car too."

"Sure, if Colin was with them on any kind of a regular, predictable basis. But he was in Moscow. The sixtieth birthday cruise, however, was tightly scheduled well in advance. There were plane tickets on both ends, and a detailed itinerary in the middle. Two weeks' worth. It also provided a controlled and isolated environment. Perfect for a planned murder."

I gave her a second to think that through.

"I've never heard of a fatal yacht crash."

"Exactly. So what kind of accidents can you have on a yacht? Not a lot of pirates off the coast of California. You're left with poison and explosions."

She mulled that over as a black Lamborghini screamed past at twice our speed like the shadow of an airplane. "Suppose that's true. Suppose they implemented a scenario that framed you, with inheritance as the obvious motive. Why? What was their motive? How did they benefit?"

"That's the rub, and it's driving me crazy."

Chapter 19

Invisible Enemies

DURING MY DISCUSSION with Katya, I began to feel something unexpected: a great sense of relief. The district attorney, the detectives, and the actual perpetrators were all still out to get me, but talking to Katya made me feel better. As they say, a problem shared is a problem halved.

I was no longer waging this war alone.

Sure, back in jail, I had Casey. But when the meter's running at an obscene rate, you don't really feel like a team. And while Dix had been beyond great, he was also remote, and our contact infrequent. Interaction feels different live, and when people are truly in it together, as Katya and I were now.

I looked over at my unlikely comrade in arms, seated behind the wheel of her little red Ford, and continued presenting my analysis under this new light. "I can't come up with a direct financial motive for the killings. Therefore I've concluded that there must be some *indirect* benefit."

"Indirect benefit. What could that be?"

"My best and only guess is that it's a *business* benefit. Colin and my father both worked at the same startup."

Katya shook her head. "But it wasn't making any money. The product was still in clinical trials when it folded."

"True, but startup valuations are based on expectations of future earnings. With pharmaceutical companies, I'm sure nine-figure valuations aren't uncommon."

"Do you know what Vitalis was valued at?"

"I have no idea, but with a big name like Vondreesen involved in the financing, it had to be significant."

Katya's expression told me she wasn't impressed with my deduction. "It really doesn't matter. The company folded a couple of months before the ... incident. Vitalis's valuation dropped to zero. Your father retired and Colin got a new job."

"I know. That's why I'm stuck."

"If there's a business benefit behind this, it could just as easily be Colin's new job. He talked about it with your father, doctor to doctor, businessman to businessman."

"I know. You're right. I've got a lot of investigating to do. That's another reason I needed to be out of jail."

Katya chewed on that for a while.

I started to doze.

"There's a third option, a third motive."

That woke me up. "I'm all ears."

"You started this conversation by saying that the reason for framing you was to misdirect the police investigation, but what if that's wrong? What if everything was done for revenge against you? I suspect you made some cunning enemies during your government career?"

"You're right. I left that one off the list. It had been at the top for months. In my cell I cranked out hundreds of thousands of sit-ups and pull-ups and leg-lifts and crunches while working up my list of suspects and how to get at them. But that motive faded the moment someone ordered a hit on me. It vanished when they also went after you."

"Why?"

"Because they were winning. My case was looking hopeless. And because killing you doesn't fit that scenario at all."

She was quick processing that one too. "You're right. I agree."

"Somebody has a business interest they're trying to protect, Katya. A business interest that my father and brother somehow threatened. A business interest that's still vulnerable."

"And you plan to expose them?"

"I plan to destroy them. These people killed my family. When I get done with them, they will–" I stopped myself there, remembering that I wasn't talking to Dix or one of the guys. "They'll regret it, for a second or two."

Katya didn't seem put off by this glimpse of my inner animal, reminding me of where she'd come from and what she'd been through growing up in Moscow during perestroika.

"Where are we going to start?" she asked.

Her use of the plural pronoun rang sweet in my ears. "We're going to start with one of the things that changed. We're going to start with the guys who are trying to kill you."

Chapter 20

Cul-de-sac

I FELT LIKE I'd spotted the Loch Ness Monster. It was two hours after sunset, but the East Palo Alto rooftop was still warming us from below when a black Escalade entered the cul-de-sac, running dark. A shiny black hole in the calm California night. Katya inhaled sharply beside me as we watched it glide to a stop beside a red curb.

The driver kept the motor running.

"What are they doing?" she whispered.

"They're counting the windows to be sure your light is on. They'll get excited in a second when the oscillating fan shifts the curtains. After two days of reporting failure, you can be sure they're eager for good news and redemption."

The Escalade rolled forward, lights still off. It drove quietly past the entrance to Katya's apartment building before backing into a visitor's spot. This time, the driver cut the engine. The passenger pushed a button on the ceiling before they opened the doors, killing the cabin light. Katya had told me they were disciplined. Apparently they were also meticulous.

I smiled. If I was right, their professionalism would soon be working in my favor.

Both the goons' heads crested the Escalade when they stood. I put them at 6'4" or 6'5"—Katya had been right, they were taller than me. Her mind hadn't exaggerated despite the fear and stress. I tucked that observation away for future reference.

They weren't wearing wraparound sunglasses, but otherwise the pair matched her description. Black suits and buzz cuts, or as she'd put it, Secret Service agents with t-shirts rather than ties. I saw no evidence of firearms, and knew their mission wouldn't require them. Against Katya's relatively fragile frame, 500 pounds of beef would more than suffice. I watched them turn and walk toward Katya's building, without locking their car.

"Will you be okay up here alone for a few minutes?" I asked Katya.

"I'll be fine. Will you? I'm worried about you." She inclined her head toward the giant receding figures. "Maybe we should call the police?"

"No worries. These guys won't know what hit them until it's too late."

Rolling to my left, I pulled out my iPhone and tapped the only stored contact. As Katya's phone began to vibrate, I dropped over the side of the two-story building and lowered myself to the ground using nothing but handholds, a technique climbers called *campusing* because of the campus boards widely used to practice climbing with only hands.

I was halfway across the parking lot when Katya's whispered words came across my wireless earpiece. "You didn't tell me your plan."

"The general plan is to disable one of them and question the other. I was planning to strike when they exited your apartment. Whack one and push the other back inside. But now I think I'll wait to jump them in their car. More private, and the confinement will work to my advantage." As we spoke, I slipped in the rear driver's side door and ducked behind the second-row passenger seat. "Let me know when you see them coming."

I pulled on a black balaclava. I'd swapped my habitual white tee for a long-sleeved black one, and with the headgear was now sufficiently shadow-like. "When they find your place empty, they might wait inside to ambush you, but my guess is that they'll come back to the car to wait for your return."

"Why is that your guess?"

"It gives them more control and options if you don't come home alone."

We lapsed into silence.

The most recent twelve months aside, my entire adult life had been one competitive mission after another. First with the Olympic biathlon team, then with the CIA's Special Operations Group. Observation and assault. Measures and countermeasures. Winners and losers. This was what I knew. My comfort zone.

Katya, on the other hand, had spent her adult life immersed in probability theory. Distribution functions and stochastic processes and the theorems of Kolmogorov and Cardano. No doubt she found my tools and techniques as foreign and intimidating as I'd find the equations in her notebooks.

"How did you end up at the CIA?" she asked, burning off nervous energy.

I played with the release lever on the bucket seat before me as I formulated my response. It flipped the seat forward, first pancaking it and then rolling the whole assembly against the front passenger seat. It was quick and quiet, yielding sufficient room to operate.

I decided to answer Katya's question with a question. "Suppose you tripped and hit your head, and lost your ability to solve equations. What would you do?"

"I don't know." Her voice was wrought with emotion. "I'd be devastated. Mathematics is my life. Oh, I see. That's essentially what happened to you with the Olympics. But I don't see the connection, except that biathletes and spies both need to be sharpshooters."

Boy was she quick. Her mind hummed like a Gatling gun. "The connection was indirect. Not wanting to become bitter after my injury, I funneled all my energy and frustrations into rock climbing. I went straight for free-soloing, tackling cliffs like they were battlefields, and I was my ancient namesake. I was reckless. But with my Olympic conditioning, I quickly set a couple of speed records. Nothing newsworthy anywhere outside Colorado or climbing circles, but enough to make the local papers. The top guy at the Special Operations Group, Granger, was visiting the Air Force Academy when he saw an article and got curious. He ended up recruiting me. Kinda made me his pet project and brought in top guns like Dix for my training, since I didn't have a Special Forces background. I was very fortunate."

"So why did you leave? Wait! Here they come!"

"Both of them?"

"Both."

"Okay. Please mute your microphone. If bad becomes worse, call 911 and give them the Escalade's license plate number."

Chapter 21

Bad Connection

EARLIER IN THE DAY, I'd hit a military surplus store to stock up for our little operation. My purchases included the black tee and balaclava I now wore, plus a sap—a heavy little flexible club designed for knockout blows to the head.

As the assassins approached, I readied Dix's new Sig in my left hand, palmed the sap in my right, and rehearsed the combat sequence in my head.

The driver was the first to reach his door. He slid in and started the car. His partner hopped in a second later, rocking the whole car.

"*Zdec budem zhdat?* We going to wait here?" the driver asked in Russian.

"*Ona machinu znayet.* She knows the car. *Luche sprachemsya.* Better to hide."

The driver flipped the selector and pulled out slowly. I hoped Katya had heard them so she wouldn't panic. The seatbelt reminder began to chime. *Listen to it, guys*, I willed them. *Buckle up. Strap yourselves in.* The passenger complied but the driver ignored the chime's warning. He circled the cul-de-sac, looking for an inconspicuous parking place with the right vantage point. I didn't dare raise my head to look, but the map in my mind had them driving a route similar to the one Katya and I had used that morning when searching for their Escalade.

The passenger pointed. "Look, her car's in its spot. She must be at a neighbor's. Or maybe the gym. This dump have a gym?"

"I don't know."

I decided not to wait to find out what would happen next. I wanted the driver busy driving and the passenger strapped in. I brought my right hand across my body, preparing it for a backhanded knockout sap strike to the side of the passenger's skull. Still holding the Sig in my left, I readied my middle finger on the seat lever. I pictured the two giant enforcers attacking Katya, pummeling her tiny frame with their massive arms. Rabid dogs with a rag doll, begging to be put down. I felt my muscles twitch and my adrenaline rise and then I flipped the seat lever.

I rocketed forward, swinging the sap as I flew. Whether the move took a quarter of a second or a half, it proved to be all the time they needed to react. These were no ordinary men. They weren't rent-a-cops or mob enforcers or strip mall martial artists. They had combat-hardened reflexes as quick and true as those of any elite soldier I'd known. And their eyes, their piercing, intelligent eyes were so unexpected that their gaze nearly stopped me in my tracks.

But it didn't.

I adapted instead.

Ratcheted it up.

The passenger spun fast enough that the sap struck him between the eyes. The driver was faster still. He had his Glock out and sweeping in my direction before the sap's sickening crack had fully registered on my ears.

From there on it was a race.

I was bringing my Sig up from below.

He was bringing his Glock around from the front.

I still had a three-foot arc to traverse.

He only had two.

It didn't matter how much faster his gun would be lined up with my head than my gun with his. Ten seconds or a tenth of a second, the end result would be the same.

He was leaning forward, giving his shoulder room to move.

I was leaning left, forcing his arc to extend.

I was straining and groaning and willing my muscles to move faster than they'd ever moved before. But I couldn't move my whole body faster than he could move his arm.

He was going to win.

My whole reason for being collapsed down to completing a single task. My brain didn't need to think. My heart didn't need to beat. My lungs didn't need to breathe. For that one split second of time, the only thing I had to do was prevent that arm from traversing those three feet.

The Escalade is a luxury vehicle. It's high on polish and full on feature, kind on the eye and cruel on the wallet. The driver's seat is designed to make its occupant feel like a million bucks. It's wrapped in rich leather, coddling the captain, while a tough plastic shell defends his backside from kicking kids and clumsy cargo. Inside, the driver's seat is packed with framing tubes and motion systems, heating elements and cooling fans. Wires and rods and cushions and sensors. It's a miracle of modern engineering.

A nine millimeter parabellum, while an engineering marvel in its own right, is a far less sophisticated artifact. A quarter ounce of lead wearing a full metal jacket, it escapes the barrel of a Sig P320 at 1,300 feet per second. Minimal weight, but tremendous velocity, and spec'd to punch through 14 inches of hog muscle. I didn't know how 14 inches of pork compared to an Escalade seat, but I was about to find out.

I didn't wait for the headshot. I didn't even wait to clear the seat. I started squeezing the trigger as soon as there was flesh in the flight path. Bang. Bang. Bang. Buttocks. Kidney. Heart. The driver's arm dropped, head slumped, and body rolled—lifeless, onto the door.

Glancing beyond the windshield, I saw that while I'd stopped the driver, I'd failed to halt the car. We were now seconds from colliding with a parked pickup and attracting attention.

I dove for the selector switch and slammed it into park with my right while I swung the Sig back at the passenger with my left. My eyes met his, but they weren't looking back. He wasn't dazed, he was dead.

I'd killed them both.

That was a problem. Dead men tell no tales.

Chapter 22

Travel Plans

I PUT AN ARM around Katya's shoulders as she averted her eyes from the fresh corpses of her would-be killers. She was shivering, but her mind wasn't shaken.

"What are we going to do now?" Her query was analytical, not accusatory, and it nailed the big question on the head. We'd just lost our only leads.

I was amazed by her resilience. She was a 28-year-old academic, not a homicide detective. "Are you all right? I know this isn't your comfort zone."

"I may not have been in jail, but I've been out of my comfort zone since I found Colin's body. Then these killers came for me. Twice. You saved my life. So while I may not be all right, I am a lot better with them gone. But, now that we don't have anyone to question, I am quite anxious to learn what's next?"

I was happy to keep the analytical side of her mind occupied. "We've got a tactical decision, and a strategic decision."

She gave me a lay-it-on-me wag of her chin.

"Tactically, we have to decide what to do with the bodies. Leave them or hide them."

"Why would you hide them?"

"To confuse the enemy. Always a good move." I paused there to help the point stick, like Granger always did. "Put yourself in your assailants' shoes for a minute. They've been reporting failure for nearly a week now. Odds are their boss is pretty upset. Odds are he's not the warm-and-fuzzy type. Life and death situation like this, I'm guessing he threatened them. Applied a bit of stick. So if they disappear now, he won't be certain if they were killed—or they ran."

Katya took a second to process our unusual problem. "Where would you hide them?"

"We could dumpster the bodies and leave the Escalade to be stolen. Or we could cover the bodies with a blanket in the back of the Escalade and leave it in long-term parking at the airport."

While Katya wrapped her big brain around our body-disposal options—a first for her, I'm guessing—a car entered the cul-de-sac, headlights blazing.

We were in her Ford, parked in her assigned spot like a couple at the end of a date. But the corpses were exposed. They were bleeding out where they'd died, in the front seats of a car badly parked in a fire lane. If anybody bothered to look, they'd be on 911 before their screaming stopped. Whatever we decided to do, we had to do it quickly.

"You also referenced a strategic decision?"

My brain had bridged that gap while Katya was contemplating. "I think I just figured that out. We should head for the airport. And since we're going there anyway—"

"We have our plan for the bodies." Katya's voice was upbeat, given the circumstances.

"Right. Let's run inside so you can change into jeans and throw your travel essentials into your backpack. If you'll give me your two worst blankets, some window cleaner, and a roll of paper towels, I'll get to work down here."

"Slow down, Achilles. You're being cryptic again."

"I don't mean to be. I'm just excited. I found the common thread connecting your assailants with the death of my family. It's just a thread, but it's enough for us to start unraveling this thing."

"But we didn't learn anything from the hit men. You killed them before question one."

"That was my first reaction too. But then I realized that I was overlooking the obvious." I wanted to let her figure it out. She'd feel better if she did.

The dim light from a streetlamp filtered through the windshield onto Katya's contemplative face. I watched her mind working it. She seemed to appreciate the mental exercise and momentary distraction. After a few blank seconds, I threw her a prompt. "Remember our discussion last night about motive?"

She nodded. "You concluded that your father and Colin were killed to gain some unknown business benefit. You convinced me that no other motive explained the incident."

"Right. Now think about the hit men. What do they have in common with a business interest my brother and father shared?"

"We didn't learn anything from the hit men. At least I didn't. Did you see something?"

"It wasn't what I saw. It was what we heard."

Katya was clearly frustrated that she couldn't grasp it, but I knew that she would. She began thinking out loud. "They were talking about what to do. Where to wait for me. They saw my car and figured I was at a neighbor's house or the gym. Nothing about themselves or their boss ..." Her voice trailed off, then I saw her get it. "Russian. They were speaking Russian. Your father and brother had business in Russia."

"Can't be a coincidence. Do you happen to know who Colin worked with?"

"The company folded."

"The company may no longer exist, but hopefully some of the former employees still do. Did you know any of them?"

She thought about that for a moment, her face delightfully animated. "I didn't move in with him until after Vitalis closed, so I don't know much about it at all. I do know that he was the only company employee in Russia. As a startup they outsourced everything. His focus as chief medical officer was the clinical trial, and for that he worked with a contract research organization based out of the Sechenov Medical School. The *Clinical Connection* or something like that. It's over near Moscow State University. The only person Colin ever mentioned was the clinical coordinator, Dr. Tarasova. Tanya Tarasova. She called him more than once. I can look up the office number and ask for her."

"Excellent. When we get to the airport, give her a call and make an appointment."

"We're going to Moscow? That's the flight we have to catch?"

"You got it."

Chapter 23

Bad Call

NINETY MINUTES LATER the assassins' Escalade was in a distant corner of SFO's long-term lot, Dix's disassembled Sig was on its way home compliments of an express mail drop box, and Kyle and Kate Yates were ticketed for Moscow via Frankfurt. They were already calling our flight when we cleared security.

I pointed Katya toward our gate. "Why don't you see if you can get through to Dr. Tarasova before boarding. I have another call to make, but I want to use a payphone."

"Moscow as well?"

"No, local."

"At eleven o'clock on a Sunday night? This part of the strategic plan?"

"Just the first move. The second call will be the big one. I'll make that from Frankfurt during our layover. Go ahead and board as soon as you're done with Tarasova. No sense making it easy for anyone watching the video surveillance of my call to figure out we're together."

"I should have guessed," Katya said, with the hint of a smile.

One tough girl.

I ran to the other international wing and began stuffing quarters into a pay phone that wasn't under direct surveillance from a security camera.

My call was answered on the second ring. "Santa Barbara Police Department."

"ADA Kilpatrick, please."

"I'm sorry, the District Attorney's office is closed right now."

"I'm sure it is. I need to get ADA Kilpatrick an urgent message. Can you do that for me?"

"I can try."

I dictated the message, then added, "Please be sure to tell him the number from which I called."

Ten hours and nine time zones later, I picked up a different pay phone. I fed this one with euros while Katya stood by my side. I didn't dial the SBPD directly, but rather a CIA relay. With that trick, the caller ID would show up as *Unknown* even if I dialed the White House or the Hoover Building.

"Santa Barbara District Attorney's Office."

"ADA Kilpatrick, please. He's expecting my call."

"Hold on."

Katya leaned up and in to hear.

"Mister Achilles?"

"Morning Mister Kilpatrick. Do you have Casey McCallum and Detective Flurry with you?"

"We're all here, as is Detective Frost," Casey said. "And anxious for your, ah, update."

"Thank you for getting together on short notice. I appreciate your time, and will get right to the point. I'm calling to arrange for bail."

As we listened to silence, I pictured the faces of the three senior officers of the court, first looking at each other and then staring into space. The brooding eyes and furrowed brows of professionals who just moments ago had thought they'd already heard it all.

Kilpatrick broke the silence. "Your request for bail was denied some six months ago, Mister Achilles. I'm about to have a bench warrant issued for your arrest. I would have done so already if your attorney hadn't convinced me that you could be made to see reason."

"I thought it might be in everyone's best interests if you reconsidered my bail request."

"I don't see how granting you bail would be in anyone's interest but yours."

Patrick Kilpatrick was a boy-faced redhead, with freckles and sad eyes that seemed to reflect all the misery he'd witnessed in the course of prosecuting cases of domestic violence, child abuse, murder, and rape. I could picture those eyes now, dark tranquil pools concealing the shark within. "Well, first of all, if I'm not out on bail, then the nightly news will carry a story that makes your boss look bad, Mister Kilpatrick. Secondly, compared to the alternative, it's a win-win situation. If I show up for my trial, then no one looks incompetent. If I don't show up, then I'm just another bail-skip, and the city gets a fat payout. No news story there."

"Are you planning to show up for your trial?"

"Absolutely—if I get bail. There's no other reason to ask for it, given the circumstances."

"Then why did you break out? You'd already been in jail for six months. What's the big deal about two weeks more?"

"It wasn't a question of time. It was a question of necessity. It became clear that I was going to have to conduct my own investigation in order to prove my innocence."

"That's what you're currently doing, investigating?"

"Exactly. And that's why I wanted Detective Flurry on the phone. I may need some help."

"Detective Frost and I have already concluded our investigation," Flurry said.

"Yes, but I got the feeling your gut was at odds with the evidence against me. I thought you'd want the chance to help get it right."

Before Flurry could answer, Kilpatrick said, "I don't think we can go for this. There's no precedent for it. Without precedent, the DA would be out on a limb."

My stomach dropped.

I needed bail.

Without bail, my odds of walking away free and clear plummeted from low to near zero. Precedent or not, granting bail in these conditions seemed like a no-brainer to me. I suppose I should have known better after working for the CIA. Risk aversion was a way of life for people counting on government paychecks and pensions. But I'd felt certain that with elected officials like the DA involved, the desire to CYA would trump all. "Check with your boss, Kilpatrick," I said, trying to sound more upbeat than I felt. "I'll call you back tomorrow."

Chapter 24

Tricky Situation

FROST SLAPPED HIS NOTEBOOK against his palm the moment Casey left the conference room. "I really want to nail this bastard. First he manipulates the system to make us look incompetent, then he tries to use that very fact to blackmail us. Fuck him and his special request."

Kilpatrick rose from the table, but the detectives remained seated. By now, they both knew that the ADA literally liked to think on his feet. Anyone visiting his office figured that out pretty quickly. Kilpatrick had stacked old Martindale-Hubbell law directories under the legs of his desk, raising it an additional eighteen inches so that he could stand while working. If anyone commented, he'd note that each volume included the name of at least one attorney he'd trampled in court.

Kilpatrick began pacing with his bat. "I think we're all agreed on the goal, as you so eloquently put it, detective. Let's make sure we don't underestimate Achilles again. As I see it, we have two options for putting him back in jail. We can either find him, or we can trick him."

Flurry scooted forward in her chair. "What do you mean by trick him?"

"The use of deceptive tactics in situations like these is sanctioned. Let's think about what we could tell him the next time he calls to lead him into a trap. Detective Flurry, why don't you focus on that."

"Okay."

Frost looked up from his notebook. "Shall I focus on finding him?"

Kilpatrick shook his head without turning his gaze from the garden outside the window. "I don't want any attention drawn to this situation. It's too politically sensitive. That means no BOLO's or other forms of outside involvement. Given that, and the fact that Achilles has almost certainly fled the jurisdiction, and most likely the country, there's nothing you can do. Our hands are tied, for now."

"What about the jailbreak? Shall I look into that?" Frost asked.

"Not yet. Same reason. For now, besides the perpetrator and his attorney, we're the only people who know that there's been a jailbreak. I'd like to keep it that way until he's back behind bars, or ..." Kilpatrick drifted off into thought.

Frost and Flurry sat in silence, watching and waiting until the ADA spun back around. When he did, there was excitement plastered across his ruddy cheeks.

"Achilles inherited about ten million dollars, right?"

Flurry was faster off the mark. "He did. I moved to seize it, but his father kept it overseas, and Achilles was smart enough to have it moved again before we could get to it. It's gone."

"So let's get him to bring it back."

Frost chuffed. "You mean as bail? All of it? No way he's going to do that. The guy's in the wind with ten million in the bank. He'd be a fool to take that deal."

Kilpatrick swung his bat in slow motion at an imaginary target. "Let me worry about the negotiation. Meanwhile, let's figure out how to catch him quietly, on our own. If we apprehend him now, we've got a lock on an escape conviction. With that, the triple homicide conviction will be virtually guaranteed. He'll go away for life."

PART 2: CONNECTIONS

Chapter 25

Déjà Vu

WE REGISTERED our fresh passports at a big old hotel near Katya's former dormitory. Perched in the woody Sparrow Hills, the Korston Hotel overlooks a big bend in the Moscow river and many of the city's most notable landmarks. It also transports visitors through time and space.

Walking through the Korston's lobby doors, tourists exchange views of Moscow State University's iconic stone spires and the legendary gardens of Gorky Park, for those of old Las Vegas. Red carpets, colored lights, and cocktail lounges abound—all designed to put people in a playful mood. A round-the-clock buffet keeps clientele inside and fueled while noisy slot machines and chatty prostitutes drain their pockets. Hardly my definition of paradise, but to each his own.

Katya and I skipped the glamour and glitz and headed straight for our room, aiming for power naps amidst piles of pseudo-silk pillows.

I woke after forty minutes, and hit the shower. It was my first since the prison attack and I welcomed it like vindication. I listened to half of Adele's latest album under the hot torrent of a large showerhead, part of it performing maintenance, all of it enjoying a simple pleasure six-months denied.

Exiting the bathroom wrapped in a towel and surrounded by a refreshing cloud of steam, I walked into a trap I thought I'd avoided. I found myself flanked by two enormous black suits, both wearing wraparound shades.

To the left, a gorilla with a shaved head held Katya's throat in his fist. He looked ready to crush it like an empty beer can. Straight ahead, a brute with a wicked scar covering half his left cheek held a Glock pointed at my heart. Rock steady. *The G43 slimline subcompact*, I noted reflexively. Ideal for concealed carry. A considered purchase. A professional shooter. And the same model used by the boys in Palo Alto.

Scar pointed to the pile of clothes outside the bathroom door. "*Odevaicya*. Get dressed."

I played out the next ten minutes like a fast-forward movie, scrambling to find a place to splice an escape into the film. The pressure points were the hand on Katya's throat, and the finger on the Glock's trigger. I needed a situation that would enable me to neutralize both long enough to work some magic.

Our hotel room was no good. They'd established advantageous positions and had space to maneuver.

The doorway was better. A pinch point that split their attention.

The hallway was bad. They'd be behind us with straight shots, unless we were lucky enough to run into a crowd. I wasn't feeling lucky.

The descent was the first situation that held promise. Ten flights of elevator or stairs. Holding someone by the throat on an elevator was risky, since they didn't know how often the doors would open, or who'd be there when it did. For that reason, I figured they'd go for the stairs. Nobody used those. Plus, they were more isolated and controlled.

They'd exit us into a waiting vehicle, probably through an exit that avoided the lobby. That would take us through back hallways, and potentially past fire extinguishers, cleaning carts, and maintenance supplies. All were potentially useful, but none were predictable.

I needed something I could rely on. Something in my control. Once we were in the car, or truck, or van, then rope, or handcuffs, or duct tape would come into play, and our odds of escape would plummet.

I had to act before we got that far.

I had to come up with a plan before we left the room.

In my mind, I backed up to the stairwell and pictured it as a battlefield. A jungle of concrete walls and metal rails slathered in gray paint. Twenty flights of tripping points and sharp turns, of rigid corners and precipitous drops.

I made my decision.

Raising my hands slowly, I put quiver in my voice. "Don't shoot. Don't shoot me. I'll give you whatever you want."

"*Odevaicya*," Scar repeated, the right side of his mouth drawing back in a sneer.

I pulled my t-shirt on first, followed by my jeans and leather jacket. I was consciously fumbling in fear on the outside while my mind raced, surreptitiously searching for weapons or tools. The floor was bare, and there were no tabletop trinkets within range. I settled my mind on the Bic pen I'd used to complete our customs forms. A simple yellow cylinder in my back jeans pocket, next to the paperclips I always carried as makeshift tools. I tied my shoes and stood slowly, shoulders slumped, palming the pen out of sight while dangling my arms like broken wings.

Scar gestured toward the door with his gun. "Let's go."

Chapter 26

Making a Point

WHEN CONFRONTED with superior numbers, the first rule is split the opposing force. Divide and conquer.

I beckoned to Katya with my head, urging her to go first and allowing my eyes to flash lucidity as they met hers. I wanted her to know I was on my game. I wanted her prepared.

She started walking as though there wasn't a fist wrapped around her throat. The gorilla slid his grip to her shoulder, covering it like a baseball mitt as she led us out of the room.

"To the right," Gorilla said, steering her toward the stairs. The hallway was empty. Not so much as a maid's cart to be seen. Two steps in front of me, Gorilla had his paw on Katya's shoulder. Two steps behind me, Scar had his Glock leveled on my center of mass. He'd literally be shooting from the hip, firing through his suit coat pocket, but at that range, a drunk blind man couldn't miss.

At the stairwell entry, Gorilla swapped his left hand to Katya's shoulder so he could use his right to open the fire door, which was no doubt held closed from the inside by a heavy pneumatic spring. We accordianned back together as a foursome and I followed the leading couple through.

I reached up with my left hand to prop the door for Scar, glancing over my left shoulder as people in polite company do. Of course, people in polite company don't have guns pointed at each other's backs, so Scar was left with a dilemma. Should he pull his gun hand out to prop the door, or should he let me hold it while he walked through, or should he reach awkwardly across with his left?

I was ready for all three.

He went with option one, pulling the gun from his pocket and using the butt to prop the door. He had four inches and fifty pounds on me, and three minutes prior had heard me quiver with fright. Hardly high-tension for him. Just another day on the brute-squad job.

My left hand followed my gaze, rocketing up from my waist to grab his right wrist from below, pushing it up while my fingers clamped down like emergency brakes. The moment they locked on, I sprang up and back with my legs, pulling Scar off balance and on top of me.

He began squeezing the trigger as he toppled forward, his sunglasses flying from his face. Once, twice. Crack! Crack!

We went airborne, nose to nose, with concrete chips flying and the echoes of gunshots reverberating.

I brought my rigid right arm around, pen now clenched like an icepick in my fist, eager to extinguish the confident gleam in his eyes. Ignoring the threat of the rising concrete floor, I put my back and shoulder into the swing, driving the exposed inch straight into his left ear canal. This stunned him, but it didn't put him down. His grip on the gun remained firm as we smacked down on my left side.

If Gorilla also had a gun, this was the moment where I'd meet my maker. I hadn't seen a telltale bulge on his breast or ankle or in the hollow of his back, but that was far from definitive with slimline semiautomatics against that much bulk. In any case, it was out of my hands, so I put it out of my mind.

I used Scar's moment of shock to wrap my legs around one of his, taking knees out of play and gaining some control. Our arms began a desperate two-front tug-of-war. My right hand kept pressure on the pen puncturing his ear, as Scar struggled with savage fury to pull it out the way it had gone in. Meanwhile my left hand battled his right for control of the gun. I couldn't pull the trigger, but he couldn't aim.

I looked up and back, over my head, and along my arm.

I saw Gorilla making the decision to abandon Katya and go for Scar's gun.

Then I witnessed the bravest act I'd ever seen.

The strongest muscle in the human body isn't the arm's biceps brachii or the thigh's rectus femoris. Pound for pound, the jaw's masseter muscle takes the prize. Delivering up to 270 pounds of force through dense mandibular bone and teeth designed to cut and grind, it powers nature's original weapon, and it functions with equal ferocity whether the object encountered is dead or alive.

Katya twisted her long slender neck down to the left and clamped the full breadth of her jaw around Gorilla's left hand. The move was amazing, both for its accuracy and its speed, like a chameleon catching a fly. She must have been rehearsing it in her head. Must have spent the walk screwing her courage tight and preparing for that strike.

And that wasn't all.

While maintaining the grip with her teeth, Katya swung her fist down and back between her tormentor's legs, making audible contact and eliciting a tortured groan. The combination blow momentarily knocked Gorilla out of commission, and saved both our lives.

Or at least it postponed our deaths by a few auspicious seconds.

I pushed my left arm up while vising my thighs in and down, leaving Scar's shoulder with minimal leverage so I could direct the gun. I didn't need it pointed anywhere in particular. I just needed it clear of Katya. With her safe for a second, I focused on the pen. Scar was desperate to pull it out. I was determined to drive it in. But I didn't have the room. The pen was only five and a half inches long, and my fist was covering four. We were at a stalemate, but one that wouldn't last. Katya's bite had bought us the ability to keep fighting, but Gorilla would knock her aside and get to Scar's gun in a heartbeat or two.

I rolled, torquing to the right with everything I had, as if swinging for survival on the face of a cliff. I pulled Scar on top of me and then over, all the way from my left side to my right. A hundred-eighty-degree roll of five hundred furious pounds. The instant my right side hit the bottom I released my left hand from around Scar's wrist, and prepared it to deliver a powerful palm strike to his upturned ear.

His gun hand now freed, Scar began swinging the Glock toward my head.

I was in a race all over again. The second in as many days. Two lives in the balance, milliseconds on the clock.

As Scar's Glock neared the completion of the arc that would end my life, my left palm pummeled his exposed ear with a powerful thud, driving his head down on the pen like a hammer on an inverted nail.

His head hit the floor.

The Bic disappeared.

The lights went out.

Once again, I'd beaten my rival to the punch by the breadth of a hair.

Scar fired wide as he spasmed in death. Somewhere in the back of my brain I registered that there would be three rounds left if he'd started with a full load, four if he kept one in the chamber. I reached and rolled and took it down to two. Gorilla took my round in the heart and collapsed like a duck blown out of the air. His body hit the stairs and slid to the next landing, lifeless and limp, his head thunking surrender on each bloody step.

Chapter 27

Wheels Turning

I LEAPT to my feet and wrapped my arms around Katya, pulling her to my chest. "You were amazing," I whispered. "You saved us both."

She was trembling like a baby in an ice bath.

I guided her across our landing to the upward staircase and sat her down on the second step. "Just close your eyes and breathe deep for a couple of seconds."

She nodded weakly, maintaining a thousand-yard stare rather than closing her eyes.

I picked up the Glock and zipped down the adjacent stairs, sticking to the right to avoid leaving footprints in the smeared and spattered blood. Rummaging through Gorilla's pockets, I found nothing but a wad of rubles and a slim ceramic lock-blade knife. No papers. No identification. No phone. I pocketed the plunder along with the Glock and bounded back up to search Scar. A Mercedes key, more rubles, and a folded sheet of paper. I was curious, but it could wait.

I extended my hand to Katya. "Okay. Let's go."

We didn't have a key to our room, but a couple of warm smiles and a hundred-ruble note convinced a gray-haired janitor to let us in. I didn't like leaving impressions, but figured our secret was safe with his generation. Stalin had taught them to keep their heads down and tongues tight.

I spoke the moment our door closed. "Let's gather our things and go. An investigation is going to erupt the moment someone uses those stairs, and we need to be gone by then."

I retrieved our passports, wallets, and phones from under the mattress while Katya stuffed her clothes and our toiletries into her backpack. We left the Korston without checking out, as people often do. The morning maid would find that the bed had been slept in and the shower used, so there would be nothing to draw suspicion to Mr. and Mrs. Yates.

"Metro?" Katya asked, as we traded the dim hotel lobby for afternoon sunlight.

I held up a finger. "Maybe. Wait here. I'll be back in thirty seconds."

I headed toward the hotel's back parking lot.

Katya began to follow. "Talk to me, Achilles. Tell me what's going on."

I stopped and turned. "They had a car, and I've got the key. We may as well use it. Plus, it may yield clues. These guys didn't have cell phones or wallets on them."

She stared at me. "What if they have a driver waiting in the car? He'll shoot you on sight."

"That's why I asked you to wait. You have to trust me, Katya. I promise to explain everything once we're clear. I just don't want to stop to do that now. We're too exposed here."

Her mouth started to tremble, and I knew I'd screwed up. I had to get better at working with an amateur partner. "I don't think anyone will be in the car. It's much more common to work in twos than threes. And if there were a getaway driver, then why would Scar have a key? Besides, I have a gun now too. By asking you to wait, I'm just being cautious. Make sense?"

She nodded.

"I'll be right back. Okay?"

"Okay."

I made a mental note to work some decompression into our schedule. As soon as possible. Next stop.

Rounding the back corner of the building, I saw an old beer

truck parked before the delivery door, and beyond it a likely candidate. A shiny new Mercedes van sat backed up to the employee entrance. The beer truck rumbled to life as I approached, and pulled out after its loud transmission clanked into gear. The bearded driver paid me no attention in his side mirror.

The Mercedes was a white panel van emblazoned with the blue logo of the GasEx corporation. I walked around it as though it were my own, visually confirming that it was empty while listening intently. Satisfied, I returned to the driver's door, yanked it open, and hopped in with my Glock covering the cargo area. Nothing there but a large stainless-steel storage box and an ominous packet of heavy duty cable ties.

I located the cover for the fuse box under the steering column, popped it open, and extracted the fuse for the entertainment console. Starting the engine, I confirmed that there was no power to the GPS system, and drove to pick up Katya.

"Won't they be able to track us?" Katya asked, as we rolled over the Metro Bridge into central Moscow.

"If they use LoJack, then yes. But they're more likely to use GPS, if anything at all, and I've disabled that."

"And if it is LoJacked?"

"They won't get around to tracking it for hours. How about dinner? We'll eat and see if anyone shows up looking for it."

I followed Katya's guidance to a neighborhood a couple of kilometers south of the Kremlin, stopping along the way to purchase a couple of movie posters and a roll of packing tape. We parked strategically in a courtyard near the Frunzenskaya Embankment, and covered the GasEx logos with the posters. Ours was now just another of the thousands of panel vans in the city that twenty-million Russians called home.

"Do you think the van really belongs to the GasEx Corporation?" Katya asked, as we walked the Moscow River embankment. "Or is that camouflage?"

"Camouflage seems more likely to me. I can't imagine how an oil and gas behemoth could be connected to Vitalis Pharmaceuticals, but it might be genuine. A big part of our problem is that we have no idea what we're up against. I'm beginning to get the feeling that this is big. Very big."

"What do you mean by that?"

"The murder of my family was the biggest event of my life, with framing me for it a close second. So I naturally assumed that it was a big event for the perpetrator too, and I've been looking at this like a murder investigation. But what if it wasn't? What if I got the scale wrong? What if Colin, and Martha, and my father were just three victims in a war?"

Chapter 28

A Thousand Words

WE STROLLED in contemplative silence toward the shadow of the Crimean Bridge, as the dark waters of the Moscow River rippled past. Ahead on our left, the sign for a Georgian restaurant Katya favored glowed like the light at the end of a long tunnel.

Opening Guria's arched pinewood door for her, I saw heavy pinewood tables with matching chairs, forest-green curtains, and a bit of Georgian bric-a-brac. The decor was nothing special, but the smells were divine. Roasting meats and melting cheeses and spices I knew I'd love but couldn't identify. The dining room was packed with jovial patrons sucking down juicy dumplings and dark red wine, toasting to health, and looking for love. We got lucky with a table, and a motherly waitress in a green apron and headscarf was soon with us.

"I'm thinking we should get it all," I said to Katya so the waitress could hear. "Pork and lamb shashlik, khinkali, and khachapuri, with beans and greens. Does that sound good to you?"

"Sounds great." Katya's voice was noticeably less tense than the last time she'd spoken.

"Wine?" the waitress asked.

"Borjomi," I said, referencing the famous Georgian sparkling water.

The waitress gave me a spirited look that said I'd earned a B-plus.

I pulled up an iPhone app and found a couple of private apartments in the area advertising as B&B's. Got the thumbs up from Katya and made note of the addresses as the Borjomi and khachapuri arrived. I stuck my nose out over the steam, closed my eyes, and inhaled deeply. Freshly baked bread browned just so, rimming a buttery puddle of melted cheese. Hard to beat that.

I put a slice on each of our plates and raised my effervescent glass. Katya raised hers back at me in the Georgian tradition. "Survival of the fittest. It's nature's primary rule. Adapt and flourish, or freeze and perish. In my line of work, I've seen a lot of it, but I've never seen anyone adapt like you, Katya. Colin was right, you are amazing."

She blushed and clinked my glass.

"I'll never forget the image of you biting that guy. It was so perfect, but so out of character. How did you ... what made ... where did that ferocity come from?"

"Remember that self-defense course I told you about the day I visited you in jail?"

"Sure."

"The instructor primed us to change our character when threatened with physical violence. He showed us some pretty scary surveillance videos of attempted rapes so that we wouldn't have any illusions about what attackers would be willing to do to us. Then he conditioned us to react to *rape* as a trigger word, a word that would instantly recall those horrible images and evoke that fighting mentality. He made us shout it as we practiced his defensive techniques, both as a means of attracting help, and to act as a psychological trigger. So I screamed *RAPE* in my head, and bore my teeth."

"Wow. I'll remember that one. And if I ever meet your teacher, I'll be buying him a couple of drinks."

"I must say, I never thought I'd need to use it."

I raised my glass. "Let's hope you never do again."

As the dumplings and shashlik arrived, I asked, "Have you heard back from Dr. Tarasova?"

"Nope. But I left a message saying that I'd stop by first thing in the morning. They open at nine. What is it you expect her to tell us?"

That was the big question. We were only at the beginning of a complex international investigation, an investigation I had less than two weeks to solve. If we failed, I'd likely spend the rest of my life in jail. It was going to be tight, intense, and apparently very dangerous.

"We have a general motive we need to make specific. To do that we need to learn about Vitalis's business. We don't know what its product was supposed to do, or why it failed. As their clinical coordinator, Dr. Tarasova should have a pretty good understanding of the basics, but I doubt they told her more than that."

Katya cocked her head. "Why would they hide things from her?"

I used a finger to wipe a thin string of cheese from Katya's chin. "Pharmaceutical companies are very secretive before patents issue and products launch. There's so much competition, with billions potentially on the line. But at a minimum, she'll know what Vitalis's product was supposed to do, for whom, and how. She'd have to know that to recruit patients."

Katya pushed her plate back and leaned in. "And she'd have to know why they cancelled the trial."

"Not necessarily. The lab results would likely have gone straight to Colin as the chief medical officer. All part of the secrecy thing. How much Tarasova knows really depends on whether Colin regarded her as a partner or a contractor."

"I got the impression he thought of her as a partner. He was very collegial with her on the phone. I could tell that he liked and respected her."

"Great. The more she knows, the easier it will be for us to figure out what was worth killing for."

My poor choice of words put a shadow on our conversation, and we turned our focus back to the food. As we finished off the last of the dumplings, Katya asked, "How did they find us at the hotel?"

I set the paper I'd snatched from Scar onto the table, still folded closed into quarters. "How do you think? Work it like an equation. You have the result. What are the predicates?"

She gave me an appraising smile, her eyes aglow. "Thank you."

"For what?"

"For understanding me." She blushed a bit. "The most basic predicate is that they were looking for us, which is disturbing news."

"It's a good sign actually, given our race against the clock. It will be easier to find them if they're also looking for us."

"Do you think they followed us from California, or picked us up here?"

"There wasn't time for anyone to follow us. We went straight from your place to SFO and onto a plane, so they picked us up here."

"But no one knew we were going to that hotel."

"Right ..."

Katya chewed on that for a second. "So they spotted us at the airport?"

"That's my hypothesis. If I'm right, the paper I took off our assailants will back it up." I slid the folded white sheet across the table to Katya. She opened it up, exposing a printout of four pictures. It was a format I was familiar with, the kind generated by facial recognition programs and used during stakeouts. It displayed a full frontal shot and a profile shot for two people, complete with calibration marks. The background was familiar too. It was the Santa Barbara County Superior Court. We were looking at our own faces.

Chapter 29

Knock Knock

I SET ASIDE my breakfast plate and stood to go. "I think you should wait here while I talk to Tarasova. This is going to be dangerous."

Katya shot me a glance that reflected a feisty combination of anger and fear. "The last time you left me alone in a hotel room I ended up with a gorilla at my throat. And that was just for a trip to the shower."

"This is different."

"How is it different? You promised me you weren't going to be cryptic."

She was right. "Do you want the long answer?"

"I would love the long answer."

To signal my commitment to acting partner-like, I moved from the breakfast table to the couch that had served as my bed. Plunking down onto the coarse green fabric, I signaled her to join me. "My work at the CIA revolved around the neutralization of very bad guys. As my employers put it when talking to their congressional overseers, these were 'individuals actively engaged in actions sufficiently hostile to the American people or government to warrant targeted covert action.' Do you follow?"

"Are you saying you hunted down the CIA's equivalent of the FBI's most wanted list?"

"Pretty much, although my list was unpublished. Too sensitive. For that reason, my work was not officially sanctioned either, so if I got caught doing something unsavory on foreign soil, there was always the chance I'd be on my own."

"You volunteered for that?"

"I jumped at the chance. It was exciting, meaningful work. And special operatives don't think about the downside any more than policemen or firemen or soldiers do. I suppose that's a testosterone thing."

"Uh-huh. I trust that *neutralize* is a euphemism?"

"For lead therapy?"

Katya elbowed me.

"Actually, the more beneficial and interesting operations involved turning the perpetrator into an asset. That was my specialty. Of course we had to locate them first. Given that these were people working very hard to stay hidden, I had to get creative. The secret to my success was becoming adept at arranging circumstances that would bring our targets to a predictable place within a predictable window. Rather than hunting them, I'd figure out a way to draw them to me. The corollary to this, as you would say, is that I've become well-attuned to not acting predictably."

I paused there to let Katya digest.

She didn't take long. "And going to the clinical trial site is predictable."

"Very. Assuming we're right, and all this is somehow related to Vitalis."

"Well then *we'll* just have to be extra careful."

I wasn't about to challenge her informed decision. For all I knew, she'd be the one saving the day again.

We arrived at the medical school campus promptly at nine o'clock and ostensibly undetected. We'd camouflaged ourselves within a group walking from the metro, so I was pretty sure we hadn't been spotted. Yet.

Tarasova's building bordered a construction site on one side and the Palace of Youth's park on the other. Number 28 was a long, eight-story structure clad with white tile and adorned with wraparound balconies on the higher floors. Lots of places to put a spotter, but I didn't see any. Speaking loud enough to be heard over the rattle and hum of earth-moving equipment, I said, "Nice building."

Katya had apparently been thinking the same thing. "The medical school's lucky to have it. I'm sure that renting it out to commercial enterprises helps to keep their lights on."

Speaking of keeping the lights on, a sign on the elevator door recommended using the stairs on account of frequent electrical outages. A result of the neighboring construction. A couple of students approached and bravely pressed the up button while we read. "Which floor?" I asked Katya.

"Top one, of course. The eighth."

"Feel like some exercise?"

I felt my stomach squirming as we began to climb. If this visit wasn't successful, I wasn't sure what we'd do next, but I did know that losing momentum could be deadly. Speaking of which, I slid my hand into my jacket pocket and around the butt of Scar's Glock.

My focus shifted to Katya, who was breezing up the stairs as though she did a thousand a day. It occurred to me that I had no idea what she did to keep so fit. I'd have to ask. After 126 stairs, the Clinical Connection's office door opened to reveal a typical medical practice.

Except that nobody was there.

Chapter 30

Sirens

I SLIPPED THE GLOCK back into my pocket as we entered the Clinical Connection. The small reception area was outfitted with soft chairs, a rack of well-thumbed magazines about pop stars and fast cars, and a reception counter beside the door that led to all the action. There were no patients, and no receptionist. It was quiet as midnight.

"Hello," I called. Once. Twice.

Footsteps broke the silence, high heels double-clicking across hard floors. A moment later, a matronly woman appeared wearing gray wool slacks and a white lab coat. Her nameplate read Perova. "Yeah?" she asked, as though picking up a call from a telemarketer.

"We're here to see Dr. Tarasova."

"She's not here. If she was, you'd be talking to her, and I'd still be working."

"We had an appointment," Katya pressed.

Perova frowned. "Really? She wrapped everything up last week."

"Last week?"

"The Vitalis trial. That's why you're here to see Dr. Tarasova, right? I don't see you on the calendar. What are your names?"

I leaned forward on an elbow and spoke softly. "When do you expect her?"

Perova gave me an appraising glance. "I don't know. She was here earlier. She's supposed to be here now. We have a lot of cleanup to do."

"Would you please double-check?" Katya asked. "Maybe she's on the phone."

Perova practically rolled her eyes, but whirled and clattered off.

Katya and I exchanged surprised glances the moment Perova turned. "Last week? The company folded eight months ago."

I thought about it. "Maybe there's some Ministry of Health regulation requiring follow-up visits, regardless."

Katya shrugged.

The office was quiet enough that we could hear Perova's progression as she moved from room to room. I leaned over the counter and looked around. Nothing notable. In fact, not much at all. Looked like a bare-bones operation. "They're not very busy. I wonder how many trials the Clinical Connection has going?"

"Don't know, but the elevator situation can't help."

The footsteps signaled Perova's return a few seconds before her head appeared. "I told you. She's not here. What time was your appointment?"

"I left her a message requesting one first thing this morning, but didn't hear back," Katya said.

"Well, that's hardly the same thing as having an appointment, is it? I need to get back to my work now. Apparently I'm the only one working today."

Katya smiled sympathetically. "We'll check back in a bit. I saw a Coffee Mania back by the metro. Can we bring you something? Cappuccino and a pastry, perhaps?"

Perova seemed shocked by the offer. "This is a clinic. No food or beverage allowed."

I liked Katya's idea. I was feeling the jet lag. Ready for that second cup. I gestured toward the elevator. "What's the deal? Is it safe?"

"We've had patients get stuck. Don't get me started."

"That can't be good for business."

Perova snorted. "Especially if you're running an incontinence trial. We're moving. That's why it's so quiet around here. All the action is at the new office."

"Is Vitalis there now too?" Katya asked.

"Didn't I just tell you that they wrapped up last week?" Perova wheeled about without waiting for an answer.

"You did."

We took Perova's advice and used the stairs, which wrapped around the elevator shaft. "How did Colin explain Vitalis folding?" I asked.

"He didn't want to talk about it. I remember him staring at some paperwork and shaking his head while repeating 'game over' as though he couldn't believe it."

"Yeah, I also got that impression and didn't want to press, especially on the phone. Now I wish I had. Would you say Colin was surprised, or just disappointed?"

"He was more than surprised. He was shocked and devastated. One day he was on top of the world, certain he had the best thing since penicillin, the next he was unemployed."

Noise echoed up the stairwell from below, disrupting our discussion and growing louder as we descended. The clamor of a crowd was being augmented by the two-tone wail of an approaching ambulance.

Emerging into the front lobby, we found it packed with people facing the street. I took Katya's hand and guided us toward the exit and the epicenter of the excitement, brushing shoulders and making holes. A few steps revealed a couple of police cars parked in V-formation, their lights flashing red and blue. I went up on my toes, using my height to beat the crowd.

"What do you see?" Katya asked.

"Three uniformed officers, circled up and looking at the ground. A fourth studying the sky, shielding his eyes against the reflection of the rising sun." I nudged us closer, glancing skyward like the fourth cop, then back at the ground.

"What?" Katya persisted.

I tightened my grip on her hand and started plowing us through the crowd toward the approaching siren and the main road, cataloguing cars and faces as we walked, my senses on high alert. "Someone fell from the roof. Brunette in her mid-thirties. Landed on her back. She was wearing a white lab coat. I couldn't see her whole name tag, but it started with *Tar*."

Chapter 31

The Rocket

CLEAR OF THE GAWKING CROWD, we continued walking briskly, digesting the latest turn of events in silence, not sure where to go. As we neared Komsomolskiy Prospect, Katya spoke, her voice showing strain. "Are you certain the dead woman was Tarasova?"

"You can do the math. What are the odds of having a last name starting with Tar?"

"Any chance it was a suicide? Maybe from guilt over complaisance in whatever killed Colin. Perhaps my call triggered it?"

I wanted to ease Katya's mind, but noise from the approaching ambulance made conversation awkward. As the siren passed us racing toward the scene, and the Doppler effect changed the *ah ah* to *oh oh*, a white panel van rolled past in the other direction, a blue GasEx logo on its side.

Our matching van was still a kilometer away, so I released Katya's hand and spun around to face the oncoming traffic. I stuck my arm out to flag any driver willing to work as a cab and began waving. To my great relief, a maroon Lada 5 pulled right over.

"Change of plans?" Katya asked as I ushered her inside. "Tired of walking?"

Speaking rapid Russian to the Lada's young driver, I said, "We're following the white van that just turned right on Komsomolskiy. I've got a hundred dollars US for you if you can stick behind it."

"You got it!" he said, accelerating after his target. "Where's it going?"

"That's what I want to find out." I extracted a Benjamin from my wallet so he could see that I meant business. "But I don't want the van's driver to know he's being followed. Think you can manage that?"

"Depends where he goes." The driver repositioned his rearview mirror to study Katya and me. "This car is about as anonymous as they come. We should be fine as long as it stays on busy streets. And they're all busy at this hour."

As we crossed the Moscow River on the same long bridge we'd driven the evening before, I turned to face Katya and spoke in English. "No chance at all."

She took a second to pair the answer with her suicide question.

"How can you be sure?"

"First of all, a GasEx van just left the scene. Secondly, I saw the passenger and driver."

Her expression ran a gamut of emotions before stopping on fear. "Black suits?"

"With black t-shirts and sunglasses."

"It looks like GasEx is where we're heading," the driver said in English, pointing to the distinctive skyscraper now visible on the horizon. GasEx's Moscow headquarters looked like the Washington Monument, but made of blue glass and with auxiliary towers running up each of the four corners, giving it an X-shaped footprint. The glass pyramid at the top reminded me of the entrance to the Louvre Museum.

"They call it Barsukov's Rocket," the driver said.

"I get the rocket part. But who's Barsukov?"

"The new chairman of GasEx," Katya and the driver replied in unison.

"Why don't I know that? The name's not familiar."

"He stays behind the scenes," Katya said. "The CEO, Antipin, is the public face. He's much more presentable. I'm sure you've heard of him."

"Arkady Antipin, sure. Looks like a cross between a sweet grandfather and an elder statesman. Trustworthy and competent. What makes Barsukov unpresentable?"

The driver hopped on my question. "He's got dark, deep-set eyes and a face they say is allergic to smiling."

Katya nodded. "I can confirm that. He spoke at MSU last year. Part of his victory lap after landing the chairmanship. He hosted a recruiting dinner afterwards for PhD candidates in STEM disciplines, and I was seated at his table. He's incredibly smart and very smooth, but inherently creepy. When you look into his eyes you see a crocodile's soul."

I found my curiosity growing the closer we came to his monumental headquarters. "Seems an odd choice for a chairmanship appointment."

"They say he's an old KGB friend of President Korovin's," the driver said. "Do you want me to try to follow the van onto the GasEx complex if it turns in?"

A friend of the president's. "Oh yes."

Chapter 32

Evil Eye

KATYA TURNED to me as we neared the GasEx gate. "Isn't it risky, going in unprepared?"

"The way things are going, standing still is risky too. We won't do anything rash, but at the very least, we'll see which building they enter."

She put on a brave smile.

I wondered if I should try to hide her away in some suburban hotel until this was over. I doubted she'd go for that, but resolved to ask her later.

The fence that surrounded the GasEx complex rolled by to our right, black iron spears, tightly spaced, with a deep lawn beyond. Modern high-security of the sort used by Bel-Air estates, and G7 embassies. Closer now, we could see a circle of smaller buildings and flagpoles surrounding The Rocket, again reminding me of the Washington Monument atop the National Mall.

A couple of cars ahead, the white van's turn signal began to blink right. I watched it roll to a stop before a card reader in the employee lane. A black sleeve extended a blue card, and the iron gate swung open in response.

While we waited behind a black Mercedes S550 in the visitor's lane, I rolled down my window. "I'll do the talking."

I felt Katya tense beside me as our turn came and we stopped before a beefy guard in a black suit. His appearance and demeanor were similar to that of our friends, but rather than sunglasses and a black t-shirt, he wore a black collar shirt with a blue tie the same hue as the GasEx logo.

My eyes moved to his left hand as he greeted us. It held something similar to a laser pointer. A metallic cylinder with an eye. He directed it at each of us for a second. I didn't recognize it until the damage was done.

In English, I said, "Good morning. We're tourists and stockholders and were just curious and attracted by your beautiful building. Do you have a museum or anything like that?"

"I'm sorry, sir," he replied in perfect English. "You're welcome to visit in June during the annual stockholders' meeting, but otherwise the grounds are closed to visitors. However, I'm sure that if you reached out to investor relations, a tour could be arranged." He produced a business card from his breast pocket. "Here's their contact information." He turned to the driver and gestured while saying, "You can exit to the left."

"Where to?" the driver asked once we were facing the street again.

"The nearest metro. As fast as you can get us there."

"Sixty seconds fast enough?"

"Why'd you give up so easily?" Katya asked, disappointment evident. "I thought you'd planned to finesse our way in."

"That was before we were fucked."

The driver turned to look at me as Katya said, "What are you talking about?"

"I was stupid. Should have anticipated."

"What?"

"First thing the guard did was take our pictures. No doubt they went directly into a facial recognition program, probably the same one that processed the courtroom photos. They've got a bead on us now. And worse, they know we've got a bead on them. We need to disappear, fast."

I turned to the driver. "You'll be fine if you keep a low profile and stick to a slim version of the truth. If asked, tell them we flagged you down on Komsomolskiy Prospect and paid you a hundred rubles to drive us to GasEx. Then you dropped us at the metro when we couldn't get in. That's it. We didn't say anything during the drive, and for God's sake don't mention following a van. Keep it boring and they'll get bored with you. Sorry for the hassle. Here's an extra hundred bucks."

The driver sighed somber resignation and a couple of seconds later pulled to the curb near the entrance to Kaluzhskaya metro station.

We made for the escalator without another word.

Once we were underground, Katya asked, "What now?"

I grabbed her hand and increased our pace. "It's time to deploy a secret weapon."

Chapter 33

Dim

GRIGORI BARSUKOV had his feet on his office desk and a cigar in his mouth when he got the news. He was celebrating. It was thirty months to the hour since he'd walked the lonely Kremlin corridor and made his initial pitch to President Korovin.

He'd been a bundle of nerves walking into the meeting. He could admit that to himself now. The president's hunting allegory had nearly pushed him over the edge. But he'd hung in there, steeled his will, and kept his eye on the prize.

They'd met three more times. The first had just been an update on the Brillyanc rollout, but the second and third had been much more. At the second meeting, Grigori revealed an unexpected twist. A tantalizing, delicious, unbelievable twist. At the third, they'd agreed on an audacious plan to exploit it.

Now Grigori was sitting on a chair made from the hide of the very crocodile Vladimir had referenced in their initial meeting. A gift from the big man himself. A daily reminder of who had given him his position, and who could pluck him from it. But Grigori chose to regard the chair as a symbol of his own strength and guile. Evidence of the type of tactics that prevailed in a predatory world.

The modern chime of his private elevator struck a chord dissonant with the Beethoven symphony playing in the background. Then the brushed-aluminum doors opened to reveal his head of security.

From the outside, Grigori's office/apartment looked like the entrance to the Louvre Museum, except that it was perched thirty-stories up, atop GasEx's Moscow headquarters, rather than in a

Parisian palace courtyard. The pyramid forming the walls of Grigori's office consisted of 576 panes of a special blue glass, the clarity or opacity of which Grigori could control electronically from a tablet. His power to block out the sun with the flick of a wrist was a little godlike, as of course was the Olympus-like view from atop his 'rocket.'

Grigori had one of his technical people write a program that kept the window pattern arranged so that the sun spotlighted anyone exiting the elevator. This gave Grigori a physical and psychological advantage in the crucial first seconds of every meeting. This time, the spotlight told him Pyotr was about to ruin his day.

"Achilles just showed up at the front gate," Pyotr said, removing his wraparound shades now that he was clear of the sun. "He's with Katya and a guy we have yet to identify. Probably a cabbie, but my guys are checking as we speak."

"Excellent. Do you need my help disposing of the bodies?"

Pyotr's big bald head reddened. "We don't have them. They turned around at the gate, after their images were captured, but before the facial recognition program alerted us to the match."

Grigori drummed his fingers audibly on the back of the tablet. "Not so excellent. In fact, that's pretty much the opposite of excellent, wouldn't you say? Now we need to worry about what brought them here. Coming to Moscow was one thing. That was a logical move given the data available to them. Any competent investigator would have done the same. But coming here, to my property specifically? Well, that presents an entirely different deck of cards. That indicates significant progress. Which indicates the existence of a trail. Which indicates a breach in security. Which indicates incompetence. Wouldn't you say?"

Pyotr's whole head flushed red again. "Yes, sir. We're trying to identify the trail, even as we search for them. It's not the Clinical Connection. We retrieved all the records and eliminated the doctor before they arrived."

"That's too bad."

"Sir?"

"There aren't a lot of trails to cover. Not here in Moscow anyway. If it's not the clinical people, that leaves your guys. Doesn't it?"

Pyotr just blinked.

"We assume they got your guys in California. We know they got your guys in the hotel. Maybe your guys talked?"

"They wouldn't talk."

"Then how do you explain Achilles showing up on my doorstep?"

"I can't."

"If you're this stupid after Brillyanc, I don't know how you survived before it."

"Yes, sir."

"Put guys at the airports and train stations. Good guys. Brillyanc guys. Sooner or later, they're bound to flee. I'm going to call in some outside help to try and make it sooner."

"Yes, sir. We only have eight Brillyanc guys left, but there are three airports and nine train stations."

"Prioritize. Improvise. Get your own butt out in the field. I don't want to call in help. It increases my exposure and makes me look weak."

"Yes, sir."

"And Pyotr?"

"Sir?"

"You're only understaffed because you're down four to Achilles. If he makes it five, I'm going to make it six. Are we clear?"

A few more blinks. "Yes, sir."

His celebratory mood ruined by the incompetence of others, Grigori grabbed a special cell phone and headed for the terrace door. He had an important call to make.

Chapter 34

Pets

GRIGORI'S OFFICE SUITE had three points of egress. All
biometrically controlled. All locking down at night—leaving him
safe as an eaglet in a nest. The first was the private elevator that had
just swooshed closed behind Pyotr. The second was the entrance to
his residence—a sliding slab of granite resembling a square of
sandy beach still wet from a wave. The third exit led to the roof, or
more accurately, a circumferential terrace.

Surrounding the pyramid to a depth of three meters, the
limestone terrace provided a hundred-meter circuit for walking off
frustrations, as well as access to his helipad, which topped the south
tower. It was Grigori's refuge, retreat, and secret weapon.

Grigori pressed his palm against a plate embedded in one of the
big glass triangles. A powerful electric motor engaged with a whir
and a whoosh and lifted the heavy window up and out along its
hinge, creating a doorway that measured two meters on each of its
three sides. Cool April air blasted in and blew ash from Grigori's
cigar back onto the granite tile behind his feet, where it disappeared
into a mélange of earth tones. Ignoring it, he stepped through,
bringing the phone to his ear. "Call Kazan."

With his left hand, he side-pitched his spent cigar out and over
the edge like he was skipping a stone. He followed it, all the way to
the edge so he could watch the cigar's thirty-story plummet.

There was no rail, no ridge, no barrier of any kind between him
and five seconds of free fall. A single solid gust would send him to
Splatsville. But life on a tightrope had made Grigori immune to
heights. The metaphorical had translated into the physical via

nervous system fatigue. He'd run out of fear. A discovery he routinely used to his advantage during negotiations and power plays. Nothing like a casual walk inches from the edge to establish an alpha position.

Grigori had come to enjoy life on the edge. Aided by toys and girls, of course. Fantastic toys, like the new Ansat helicopter parked a few steps to his left. And breathtaking girls, like those downtown at Angels on Fire.

His call connected before the cigar landed. "This is Doctor Galkin."

"Mikhail, it's Grigori. I'm looking for good news."

"Afternoon, Grigori. I've got good news. Very good news. Two vectors have proven viable. They'll be available with time to spare."

The cigar crashed onto a mature bloom, scattering red tulip petals across green grass like drops of blood. "Redundancy and time to spare. That's impressive. I've got a role for you running my security if biotechnology ever begins to bore you."

"Pardon me?"

"Never mind. Long story. I greatly appreciate your competence. A ten-million-ruble bonus will be headed your way."

"Thank you. Thank you very much, Grigori."

"You're welcome. Now, when can I expect my new pets?"

Chapter 35

Behind the Curtain

WE TOOK THE METRO back to central Moscow, and then walked to our stolen van. As I keyed the ignition, Katya pointed to the storage container bolted to the floor behind us. "Aren't we going to see what's in the big metal box first?"

I hit the gas. "I wish we could. It's basically a safe. I know the brand, and unfortunately we're not going to be able to get in without either the combination or special equipment."

"Couldn't you shoot it open?"

"No. The steel is much too thick for that, and the lock incorporates multiple deadbolts."

"Power tools?"

"I like your attitude, but it would take a lot of time, make a lot of noise, and require some serious equipment."

"What do you think's in there?"

"The guys that attacked us didn't have wallets with them, and only one was armed, so at a minimum I figure we'll find ID and key cards and another weapon."

She percolated on that for a second. "Where are we going?"

I didn't want to worry her, but she had a right to know. "If the car is LoJacked, they'll pounce once we start moving. I want to go just far enough to either draw them out, or be sure they're never coming. We'll stash the van someplace similar, a couple of kilometers from here. I'll show you something interesting while we watch for them from safety."

"Why not forget the van? We can take taxis."

"Investigations are about stirring things up. Plus the van is a ticket into the complex, if we ever get our hands on those IDs."

As we pulled off the embankment road onto side streets, Katya returned to the discussion of motives. "Did you figure out what an energy company has to do with a pharmaceutical company? I can't think of a single connection."

"Yes and no. Both are high-risk, high-reward. Pharmaceutical development is often compared to energy exploration. Both require massive upfront investment with no guarantee of any return at all. Both also rely heavily on lobbyists to maintain favorable tax and legislative environments. But I don't see how any of those similarities could play into our situation."

"What are you thinking then?"

"I'm thinking that it's an indirect connection, as per last night's big-picture discussion. And I'm thinking that if the connection isn't at the industry level, it's at the individual level."

I could almost hear Katya's brain working that idea as we drove the next few blocks. Police cars were all over the place, but no other GasEx vans were in sight. We crossed Komsomolskiy and drove toward the famous New Maiden Convent and Cemetery. After a quick lap to check for tails, I parked within sight of both the convent and the hotel Randevu. An interesting choice of name, given its pious neighbor.

I paid cash for a room that overlooked the van while Katya talked the manager into letting us rent his laser printer for an hour. Then I went to work on my iPhone while Katya maintained lookout.

By this point, I was ready to trust Katya with my life. But my next move involved a different kind of trust. The CIA had given me access to some very sensitive tools. I needed to make use of those tools now, and there was no way to do so without making Katya aware of their existence. She was too smart to attempt to fool, and there was no mundane explanation for the magic I was about to work.

I whirled the desk chair around to face the bed. Katya had kicked off her shoes and shed her sweater and was lying chest down in skinny jeans and a caramel-colored cotton shirt. She'd propped her chest up on a pillow and had her bare feet crossed in the air. All she was doing was watching the van through the open balcony blinds, but she looked as sexy as anything I'd ever seen in my life. She glanced over, studied my face, and then grew an inquisitive half-smile. "What?"

I dove right into the deep end of business. "When I worked for that other government agency, they didn't give us special computers. Those would have marked and encumbered us. Instead, they gave us protocols for accessing hidden websites from any connected device."

Katya pulled herself up into a cross-legged position that made it easy for her to rotate her head back and forth between me and the street. "What kind of websites?" she asked, her intonation reminding me of the excitement I'd felt when Granger pulled back the curtain for me.

"Some are portals to access databases we can query. Others are operation-specific repositories. The operation-specific ones are deleted as soon as the mission wraps up, but the portals are permanent. I'm logged into one of them now."

I wasn't going to tell her that this particular portal queried both Interpol and the equivalent of the FBI for most of the industrialized world, including Russia's FSB. I'd never actually been told that was what it did, but I figured that was the only way it could work its magic. "And here she is: Tatiana Tarasova, MD, born in Moscow on October 10, 1980, residing at ... married to ... graduating from ... home phone ... work phone ... cell phone. There we go! Now, I'll take Tarasova's phone numbers to another portal, identify the one she used to call my brother's cell, and then get us a printout of the other numbers she called from that phone."

Two minutes later, I'd identified Tarasova's cell phone as the one she'd used to call Colin, and we were in business. Five minutes after that, the printer was spitting out records of Dr. Tarasova's cell phone calls for the past twelve months.

"What are you going to do with that information?"

"We'll use it to identify other Vitalis patients. Then we'll pick a few to interview."

I set to work turning numbers into names, and names into profiles. Katya went to work analyzing the results, looking for patterns and attempting to identify individuals whose backgrounds indicated that they'd be knowledgeable about pharmacology. A few dozen candidates into it, she yelled, "Bingo!"

Chapter 36

Clinical Connection

"BINGO?" I repeated back to Katya, wondering what could have elicited so much excitement.

"Saba Mamaladze is on the list. We're classmates. He's still in the doctoral program at MSU. Brilliant mathematician, and a good guy."

"You sure it's the same Saba Mamaladze?" I couldn't keep a straight face while repeating the melodic name. "What kind of a name is that?"

"It's Georgian. And yes, Achilles, I'm sure."

"You know him socially?"

"Sure do. I've been to his dorm room many times. He lived in the same building, the next entrance over. Should I give him a call, tell him we'll be stopping by?"

"No. That would be poor operational security."

"You told me you were going to work on the cryptic thing."

"It's best that we don't let anyone know that we're coming. We don't know who may be listening. We called Tarasova in advance, and she ended up dead before we could speak to her. There may or may not be causality there, but let's not take that chance with your friend." Not wanting her to dwell on that topic, I hastened to add, "I want to go back to the Clinical Connection on the way. We might as well come clean with Perova and see what we can get out of her."

"You think she'll be receptive?"

"I'm not sure about receptive, but I think we can get her talking if we give her a bit of information."

"What are you planning to tell her?"

"The truth."

No one had paid any attention to the van while we were at the Hotel Randevu, so I was comfortable that it wasn't being tracked. Still, we parked a few blocks from the medical school to be safe, and approached cautiously on foot.

I rang the bell in the empty reception room. "We're back."

We got the sound of high heels in response. They were moving slower than before. Perova's face, already visibly shaken by the morning's events, turned even paler at the sight of us.

"We know what happened," I said, saving her the pain of breaking the news. "And I have a confession to make. We're not patients, we're investigators. My brother was Dr. Tarasova's contact at Vitalis Pharmaceuticals, Dr. Colin Achilles."

Perova pursed her freshly painted lips, not sure what to make of all that. Finally, she composed herself. "I don't know your brother. I wasn't involved with the trial. Vitalis was all Dr. Tarasova."

"We were coming to talk to Dr. Tarasova this morning because my brother was murdered. We think it was related to his work. Katya was his fiancée," I added, inclining my head in Katya's direction. "Now Tarasova is dead too."

Perova's red eyes grew wide. "Oh my God! Am I in danger?"

"We're not certain what to think at this point."

"But the police said there was no evidence of foul play." Perova's tempo was quick and her voice high. "I told them I didn't think Dr. Tarasova was suicidal, but they said it was often completely unexpected. Do you think she was killed by the same person who killed your brother?"

"That's our theory. What can you tell us about the Vitalis trial? We thought Vitalis had ceased operations months ago around the time of my brother's death, so we were surprised this morning when you said the clinical trial had concluded last week."

"It did wrap up last week." Perova took a seat behind the

counter. "The last patients were in Friday."

Katya and I exchanged glances.

"What can you tell us about the product?" Katya asked.

"The only thing I know is that the codename was *Brilliance*—spelled with y-a-n-c to be cute or something." She rolled her eyes.

"All our clients are secretive, but Vitalis was over the top. Dr. Tarasova was the only person who knew anything. She had to do everything herself, from briefing the patients, to running their labs, to hooking up their IVs."

"IVs?" Katya asked.

"Yes, Brillyanc is a parenteral delivered once every three months during a six-hour infusion. We've never had anything else like it. Dr. Tarasova had a good setup for it though, with comfortable chairs and snacks and personal televisions. And the patients were all upscale, well dressed, and educated. Usually we get the opposite here. That's why I immediately associated you with the Vitalis trial this morning."

"What about records?" I asked.

"Everything was managed electronically. Dr. Tarasova had a laptop for her own use and a tablet for patient input. The police were looking for both of them this morning, but neither is here."

"Isn't that strange?" Katya asked. "Surely she'd have brought her laptop to work today."

"Ordinarily, yes. But she didn't have a project to work on, so maybe she didn't bother. The metro is so crowded these days, the less baggage you have the better. Today she was supposed to be helping me out, preparing for the move."

"Who else has been asking questions today?" I asked.

"The police were here most of the morning, followed by a couple of investigators. They left just before you got here."

"Did they ask the same questions?" Katya asked.

"More or less. They wanted to know who Tanya discussed her work with, and what I knew about it. Like I told you, the answers were *nobody* and *not much*."

"Did you see identification?" I asked. "For the investigators."

"No, but it was obvious who they were. Very police-like."

"Big guys?"

"Yes, with square jaws, bright eyes, short haircuts, and black suits."

Chapter 37

Connecting the Dots

SABA MAMALADZE had thick, curly black hair, lively eyes, and a nose that belonged on an eagle. He wore faded jeans, a yellow polo shirt, and a smile that wouldn't quit—at least around Katya. He hugged her for a good five seconds while saying, "It's so good to see you, so good." Releasing her, he stepped back like a tailor admiring a suit. "Once you left for Palo Alto, I figured I wouldn't see you again unless I managed to score a post-doc at Stanford for myself. Speaking of which, I'm still counting on your help with that, you know."

"Stanford would be lucky to get you, Saba. When the time comes, let me know and I'll be sure the right people pay attention to your application."

Saba put his hands on his hips. "Well, aren't you a peach. So what does bring you back? Get a craving for Max's dumplings?"

Katya turned to me. "Max is Saba's roommate. He's also Georgian, and his family owns the best restaurant in Tbilisi. Every once in a while, when he's overly stressed out, he'll spend a day making dumplings. Hundreds of them. The best you ever tasted. So Saba and I do our best to keep him stressed."

"The secret is the meat." A convivial voice spoke from the hallway. "I use three kinds, but I'm not going to tell you which."

We all turned to see another beaming Georgian face. "How are you, Katya?"

Max had a slim, academic build similar to Saba's. He also wore faded jeans and a big grin shaded beneath a prominent nose, but his polo was royal blue, to match his intelligent eyes.

"I'm okay. You're looking great, Max. So are you, Saba. Have you guys adopted a new exercise routine or something? I want your secret."

The Georgians exchanged knowing glances.

"Who's your friend?" Max asked Katya.

"Guys, this is Achilles. He's Colin's younger brother."

The jovial Georgian faces turned solemn at the mention of Colin's name. Obviously they'd heard the news. We took turns shaking hands.

"To what do we owe the pleasure of your company?" Max asked. "Assuming it's not my dumplings."

"We had a few questions for Saba. And we brought a little something to loosen his tongue." Katya turned toward me.

I held up the bottle of Georgian wine we'd picked up on the way over. After Perova's mention of black suits, I figured a good bottle would satisfy both etiquette and Katya's nerves.

"Khvanchkara!" Saba accepted the precious bottle of semisweet red with smiling eyes. "Ooh la la. I'll get four glasses."

While Saba Mamaladze was obviously naturally exuberant—how could he not be with a name like that—he was clearly very fond of Katya. Watching the trio's interaction I had the feeling Max was even more fond of her. Max rolled two desk chairs over by their old Ikea couch and then grabbed a stool from the kitchenette for us to use as a drink table.

Feeling Katya relax beside me, I realized that I'd never seen her with friends before. I kicked myself for not thinking to suggest something like this earlier, given all she'd been through in the past couple of days. Katya was holding up as well as most professionals, so I had to work to keep in mind that she was a civilian swept up in circumstance.

"What questions did you have for me?" Saba asked, pouring the rich red.

"I just learned that you were participating in Colin's clinical trial.

I want to learn more about it."

Saba exchanged a glance with Max again like they were an old married couple. "I didn't know Brillyanc was Colin's. I'm sorry, this is a bit awkward given the circumstances and all. What are you trying to find out?"

"We're investigating Colin's death, and as part of that we want to learn everything we can about Brillyanc. We didn't even know the drug's name until an hour ago."

"I thought he died in a boating accident," Saba said, his voice suddenly slow, deliberate, and tense. "Carbon monoxide poisoning."

"That's right. We don't think Brillyanc killed him. No need for you to worry about that. But the carbon monoxide poisoning wasn't accidental, so we're looking for motives."

Max said, "I heard they'd arrested Colin's brother for that." He turned to me, connecting the dots.

"It wasn't me. But to prove that I need to find out who it really was. Right now, our only evidence points to the company where my brother and father worked. We know next to nothing about it. So when we learned that you were part of the Vitalis trial, we came right over. Will you please tell us what you know about Vitalis and Brillyanc?"

"Of course. We both will. Max was in the trial too."

Chapter 38

Priceless

OUR FIRST BREAK, I thought, as Max confirmed that he'd also been in the clinical trial. If I was remembering correctly, Katya had said Max was getting his PhD in biochemistry.

Katya brought her hand to her chest. "I saw your name, but there must be ten thousand Max Ivanov's in Moscow, so I read right over it. When I hit Mamaladze however…"

"Please start with the basics," I said, eager to dive in. "Other than the intriguing name, we don't know anything about the drug."

Saba set down his wine glass, and began. "They told us it was a 'metabolic enhancement product.' Those were the words they used. When we pressed them for details, they told us we'd notice improvements in the way we felt. They refused to get more specific because of the placebo effect, and because individual metabolisms vary greatly."

Katya and I nodded along, not wanting to disrupt the flow.

"Of course, our primary concern was side effects. But they told us there weren't any related to the product itself, just those related to the delivery, to being hooked up to an IV for six hours."

"And that was all little stuff," Max added. "Like redness and swelling around the puncture site, headache, and nausea. The typical panoply of minor maladies you find on most medications if you read the fine print."

"But Max, being Max, ran his own tests. He did blood work on both of us before and during the trial."

"What did you test?" I asked Max.

"I tested the typical annual-physical parameters: a complete blood count and chemistry panel, fibrinogen, hemoglobin, hormones, and PSA. None of them changed significantly for either of us. If anything, they trended slightly better."

"What did change was our mental clarity," Saba continued, lifting his refilled wine glass as if in a toast to the medical gods. "It's been every student's dream. I started breezing through my research, digesting everything I read on the first pass. I actually began stopping by Dr. Abramov's office to discuss *Annals of Mathematics* articles with him. Just for fun. Can you imagine that, Katya? Well actually I'm sure *you* can, you were always his darling. But can you imagine *me* doing that?"

"You were always your own harshest critic, Saba. Are you sure it isn't the placebo effect? Perhaps brought on by the name?"

"If it is, it's the best placebo effect ever. My dissertation is done. I wrapped it up last week, a full half-year ahead of schedule." In reaction to Katya's surprised expression, he added, "I know I didn't mention it the last time I saw you. Things were going so unbelievably well, I was afraid to jinx it."

Max set his wine glass down. "My results were similar. I'll be finishing my dissertation months ahead of schedule as well, and my adviser has been a lot more complimentary than he was before I started."

"How long have you been taking it?" I asked.

"Eighteen months. It's been fantastic. Frankly, I'm worried about what's going to happen now that we're off it. One more dose and I'd have been set, dissertation done and defended."

Katya gave Max a discerning glance. "Given your expertise and the lab equipment at your disposal, why don't you whip yourself up a batch, now that the free supply has ended? Is it tough to make?"

"I have no idea. They were very secretive about the formulation. The ingredients weren't written on the IV bags. Believe me, I checked. I also stole a look in their refrigerator one day when nobody was watching, but there were no spare bags. In retrospect, I wish I'd siphoned off some of my IV to analyze. But I didn't know the trial was going to be ending when it did, and I didn't want to risk jeopardizing my continued participation."

"What tests did they run on you?" I asked.

"During each session they gave us an IQ test. They also took blood and urine samples. Last week when we went in, we did the test and gave the samples, but we didn't get the infusion. They told us that was it."

"Did they ever share the results?"

"No."

"And do you feel it wearing off?"

"Definitely. Frankly, I'm nervous about it."

"Would you pay to keep taking it, if that were an option?"

"Sure."

"How much?"

Max grew a wistful smile. "I'd pay anything."

Chapter 39

BOLO

THE BUOYANCY brought about by an hour's reprieve with old friends and a bottle of wine evaporated as we exited Saba's building.

A police car was waiting.

Two militia officers sat smoking inside, their attention on the next entrance over. I put my arm around Katya's shoulder and casually guided her in the opposite direction while slouching to take a couple of inches off my height.

She leaned in and whispered. "That's the entryway to my old apartment they're watching."

"I assumed as much."

"Do you think they were looking for me?"

"Have you ever seen the police hanging around like that before?"

"No."

"Then yes, I think they were looking for you."

"But why? I haven't done anything."

Me either, I thought. *But look at me now.* "Apparently we've upset powerful people just by surviving, and I'm not inclined to placate them."

"Why are the police suddenly involved?"

"I'm guessing that when we tripped the facial recognition system at GasEx, we spooked them, whoever they are. Apparently they decided to go beyond their own goon squad."

Katya gave me a dubious look. "What would they tell the police? How could they get them looking for us?"

"If it's a powerful person making the request through someone high up in the force, they could feed us into the system as *persons of interest*. That could generate a priority BOLO, a Be-On-Look-Out dispatch, without requiring specifics as to why. The beat cops would just be ordered to bring us in for questioning. Then they'd have us."

"So what do we do?"

"We keep out of sight and hope we figure this thing out quickly, because Moscow's no longer safe." Katya's lower lip quivered, so I hastened to add, "On the good news front, we know the investigation is heading in the right direction, and we know they're not tracking our van."

We drove into the setting sun without speaking, lost in our own thoughts, trying to cope with a situation that had started badly and was spiraling downward. I noted that Katya was now mimicking my vigilance, constantly but subtly scanning the windows and mirrors for black suits, white vans, and police cars.

It took us thirty minutes to reach Dr. Tarasova's address. Her five-story apartment was an old, undesirable style of apartment building built back in the 1960's throughout the Soviet Union under Nikita Khrushchev's reign. I drove past it and parked in a shadow a couple of hundred meters further up the side road. "We have to assume they'll be watching the place. I'd have a man posted either within sight of Tarasova's door, or within the apartment itself. So we should assume both."

"Okay, what's our next move?"

"I'm going to ask you to stay here in the van and keep an eye on Tarasova's entrance while I scope out the twin neighboring building and figure out which apartment is number 32." I put in my earbuds and called Katya's iPhone. She donned her own set and answered by saying, "Don't bother. Hers is the second window from the right end on the top floor." She pointed. "The kitchen ventilation window's open and the lights in the main room are on."

"How do you know that one's hers?"

"The five-story Khrushchyovkas are all the same. I had a friend who lived in 32. I'm sure it's freezing in the winter and the roof leaks into the kitchen."

"What's the floorplan?"

"It's an efficiency. There's a kitchen, bath, entry hall, main room, closet, and balcony."

"Not a lot of places to hide."

"That's for sure."

"Won't 32 be on the third floor?"

"No, they're numbered sequentially. What's all this about? What's your plan?"

"I'm going in through the window."

Katya's face wouldn't have looked more skeptical if I'd told her I could fly. "How? It's on the fifth floor."

"Climbing to the window will be a snap. It's getting through it undetected that has me concerned. I'll have to play that part by ear. Same plan as before. You keep an eye on things from down here."

"But someone will see you."

"Not if I'm fast and time it right."

"What will you do if someone starts yelling?"

"I'll go over the roof and be down the back side before anyone can react. Don't worry about it. As long as you're keeping a watch out from below, I'll be able to focus on a quick ascent and quiet entry. Agreed?"

"Okay. You really think you can climb the building? Without falling?"

"Most residential buildings are as easy to climb as ladders. They have all kinds of pinch points, edges, and ledges. All reasonably spaced and regularly repeated. These walls are concrete panel rather than brick, which would make it a challenge if there weren't windows and balconies everywhere, but there are. And this one even has a drainpipe, which may as well be an elevator."

Katya didn't look convinced. "We're talking about five stories. That's probably sixty feet. One heck of a tree."

"See my shoes?" I crossed my left leg over my right to put my approach shoe on display. "They're designed for climbing. The tread is gummy, the support excellent, and they fit like a glove. With them, I'll stick to that wall like a spider." This wasn't quite true, of course. But to comfort her I was going for attitude rather than accuracy. "To answer your other question, the best way to avoid attention while doing something surreptitious in public is to act like you're someone in charge."

"And how do you plan to do that?"

"It will be a combination of what I do and don't do. I'll avoid cautious movements and furtive glances since they arouse suspicion —triggering alarms built into our DNA. My goal will be to avoid detection altogether, so as not to generate any reaction at all, but even if I get stuck walking past an audience that can't miss me, all I'll have to do is keep my head up and shoulders back like an authority figure. That posturing triggers the submissive sectors in most people's minds, and usually lets one slip under the radar without a second glance." I nodded, subliminally reinforcing the veracity of what I'd said. "Time to go."

Chapter 40

Monkey Business

I GOT OUT of the van, but waited to cross the road until a couple of people walking dogs had rounded the corner. With the sun down, the air had taken on a chill, but it was dry. Good climbing weather.

I made my way to Tarasova's building with my head down and hands in my pockets, like a local resident on his way home. I didn't have chalk for my palms, but they wouldn't be sweating, and with a drainpipe to climb, it really didn't matter. "Am I clear?" I asked, speaking into the mike.

Katya came right back like a pro. "There's a couple on a bench about twenty meters ahead of you, but they're looking at each other. And across the street there are numerous open curtains, but I don't see anyone actually standing at their window looking out."

"Good enough. Here goes." The concrete panels were about nine feet tall, so there wasn't much to grip. The surface itself, while ostensibly smooth, was plenty rough for smearing, the raw face-to-face friction move that would give my feet purchase. As for the ten-centimeter drainpipe, it was built fifty years ago by the Soviet war machine. Designed to withstand the never-ending strains of a brutal climate and communal living, it wasn't going anywhere. I put a hooked hand around each side at head level, and pulled back until my arms were straight and my back was engaged. Then I brought my feet up onto the wall one at a time, and began to ascend like a hungry monkey scaling a coconut palm.

It felt great.

I never feel better than when I'm climbing. There's something about the combination of mortal risk, physical exertion, and discernible progress that stimulates my brainstem like nothing else. And the greater the risk, the tougher the climb, and higher the ascent, the better I feel.

I wear approach shoes wherever I go because I'm always eager for a fix. I don't go around climbing telephone poles, but I feel better knowing the option is there. And sometimes kittens get stuck.

It took me about fifteen seconds to get my head level with the bottom of Tarasova's kitchen window, which was about two meters off to my left. As a climber I knew that my 'ape index' was 1.05, meaning that my arm-span was five percent greater than my height, or about six-foot-six. If my two-meter estimate was accurate, my reach would come up short.

"Anybody notice me?"

"Not that I can tell. You climb like a chimpanzee."

"Nicest thing you ever said to me."

I leaned as far as I could to my left, but was still a couple of inches shy of the windowsill. Rather than leaping for it, I repositioned my feet so that my right foot was pressing against the pipe from the left side, and then extended both my left arm and leg. To Katya, it would look as if I splatted against the wall in the midst of a jumping jack, but it did the trick. My left fingers found two knuckles' worth of purchase amidst the city grime and pigeon crap.

I released my right.

A shuffle and chin-up later I was looking into Tarasova's kitchen window. Fortunately, no one was looking back. "Katya, I want you to hang up on me and call Tarasova's home number. If someone answers, find some reason to keep him talking and distracted. Otherwise, let it ring for a few minutes."

"Okay. Be careful."

I positioned myself so that I was peeking through a corner of the window that was partially concealed by a potted plant. From there I could see through the kitchen and into the better-lit hallway beyond, without risk of detection by the casual glance of a resident. Of course, this only applied to people inside the apartment. From the outside, I was totally exposed.

The apartment's phone began to ring.

It kept ringing.

On the fifth ring I made my move. I pulled myself up and onto the exterior windowsill, which was only about an inch wide. From there, I reached through the small ventilation window in the top right corner, and then used the curtain to snag the latch handle and unlock the larger window.

With Scar's Glock in my hand, I pushed the window open on the eighth ring. Apparently the Tarasovs opened it on a regular basis, because the mechanism was smooth and the windowsill was clear of clutter. Either that, or karma was on my side.

Climbers learn to become a part of the rock they're climbing. It's a feeling, a mindset, a flow. They shut off all other senses and feel the rock, living from its perspective, moving in harmony with its surroundings. Serene, secure, and silent. I slipped into that mindset as I eased through the window, onto the sink, and down to the floor. Quiet as a summer breeze. Then I reengaged with the rest of the world.

The phone was still ringing.

I used a ring to cross the kitchen floor and tiny hall. On the next, I peered into the main room, the living room/bedroom combo. It contained a convertible couch, television, wardrobe, and display cabinet, but no pulse.

I exhaled. That left me the balcony, closet, and bath to clear. I could see the entire top half of the enclosed balcony from where I stood. It looked empty, but would be a good place to hide. I glided across the floor and peered through the glass. Nothing but boxes and cross-country skis.

The closet's contents also proved to be inanimate.

On my way to the bathroom, I stopped by the front door and looked out the peephole. No one appeared to be on the landing, but that didn't mean a black suit wasn't waiting behind a door or in the stairwell—locked, loaded, and listening.

Two silent steps took me to the bathroom door. Light shown through the crack at the bottom. I listened for a full minute before opening it from a crouched position, the Glock raised and ready.

Mr. Tarasov stared back at me. He was in the shower, hanging by his neck.

Chapter 41

Health Food

I WAS DETECTING A PATTERN.

I was also tiring of being one step behind.

I needed to figure out how to get one step ahead.

That was the problem with following clues: you were following. Behind by definition. Getting ahead required ideas.

I had a couple to try.

But first things first. There was no need to check Tarasov for a pulse. A swollen tongue protruded from his mouth, and stains on his jeans indicated that he'd voided his bowels. I glanced around the bathroom for a fake suicide note, something referencing his not wanting to go on without his beloved wife, but the black suits hadn't bothered with those finer details. No need. The setup itself looked good. Perfect motive. No signs of struggle.

My guess was that they'd tranquilized him before stringing him up on a belt in the shower. No other way to do it, really, since his feet were touching the bathtub floor. There would be traces of the tranquilizer in his bloodstream, but the police wouldn't find it if they weren't looking.

Getting them looking was one of my ideas.

I pulled the bathroom door shut behind me and dialed Katya. "I'm okay, but Tarasov's not. They killed him. How are you? I'm going to need about twenty minutes."

Katya took a few silent seconds to absorb that blow before coming back with, "I'm fine. The group of teenagers has grown into the double digits, but no sign of unfriendliness. Are you in danger? What are you going to be doing?"

"I'm working on getting us leads. I'll be fine." I hung up and began searching the apartment for computers, notebooks, or papers —anything that Dr. Tarasova might have brought home from work. I was sure the black suits had beat me to it, but I couldn't not look.

The size of the apartment made it a quick job, and I came up empty on all accounts. But I'd saved the best for last. That was where my second idea came into play.

Tarasova wouldn't have bothered to hide her notes or computer, because taking those home was part of her job. Not just permitted, but required. One thing, however, probably wasn't allowed. It wouldn't be left laying around in plain sight, not that there was a great deal of choice in where to lay it.

I rubbed my palms together like I was getting ready to roll dice or pick a card, and opened the refrigerator door. Milk, juice, sausage, cheese, condiments, various plastic storage containers, and a six-pack of probiotic yogurt drinks in a cardboard box.

The plastic containers were the obvious first choice, so I removed the yogurt box instead. It felt full—and it clanked. I looked inside. A dozen glass vials winked back at me. "Now we're talking."

Setting the yogurt box off to the side, I grabbed an insulated lunch box off the kitchen counter, and checked the freezer for cooling agents. No ice, corn, or peas. Although it did yield bags of frozen strawberries, blueberries, and blackberries—the constituents of a smoothie I was guessing, noting the bananas, blender, and thermos on the counter.

Seeing them gave me another idea.

I loaded the blender with fruit and milk, then secured the lid. I put the yogurt box in the lunch box, set a quart-sized ziplock bag on each side, and packed in as many frozen blueberries as would fit. Satisfied that the Brillyanc would keep cool for hours, I slung the lunch box's shoulder strap around my neck, and went out the way I'd come in.

Chapter 42
112

"WHAT'S THAT?" Katya asked, her face awash in relief and curiosity.

"That," I said, "is one step ahead."

"What?"

I was back in the driver's seat, with the lunch box on my lap. "Figuratively speaking. Literally, it's a couple of pints of frozen blueberries, and a dozen vials of Brillyanc."

"No way!"

I passed her the box. "See for yourself."

Katya unzipped the lid and pulled out the yogurt carton. She opened it up and extracted a glass vial. "Two fluid ounces. I was expecting IV bags."

"I assume the Brillyanc gets diluted with saline or some other buffering solution for the infusion. If it takes six hours to go in, there's probably some sophisticated biochemistry involved."

Katya brightened even more. "Fortunately we know a sophisticated biochemist."

"My thoughts exactly."

"What made you think to look? In a yogurt carton in the refrigerator, I mean."

"A sophisticated biochemist. Max made it clear that he'd do whatever it took to keep taking Brillyanc after the clinical trial ended. The only reason he didn't arrange it was that he didn't know the trial was ending."

"So?"

"So I figured Tarasova would feel the same. Only she did know the trial was ending. And she had access to the product. And since Brillyanc has to be kept refrigerated, I knew where to look."

Katya grew the face of a professor who'd heard the right answer. "What do we do now?"

"Call Saba, and see if he and or Max can meet us now at Leningrad train station. You can let him know we've got something for him, but don't hint as to what it is. Just in case."

"Okay. Are we going to St. Petersburg?"

"No, that's a red herring. Just in case."

"I'm picking up on a motif."

I couldn't help but smile at that. It felt good. "Leningrad station also provides tactical advantages. We do need to get out of Moscow ASAP though. Between the black suits and the police, there are too many forces working against us here. But we need more information first, and I'm not sure how best to get it. I'll give that some thought. Meanwhile, I'm going to work on getting us two steps ahead."

Katya had learned better than to ask, but her eyes flashed concern.

I put calm in my tone, and a grin on my face. "I'll be back in ten minutes."

"Be careful."

I retraced my steps from earlier that evening, and a few minutes later was back in Tarasova's kitchen. I reversed the lighting pattern in the apartment, turning on the kitchen light and turning off the main room light. After checking the blender's lid to be sure it was secure, I flipped the on switch. As the violent roar disrupted the silence, I ran back to the main room, stepped behind the curtains, raised the Glock, and waited for a black suit to come through the door.

I didn't have to wait long.

The front door opened, slowly—just a crack. The blender drowned out any noise as it screamed for attention. After a ponderous second, the door crashed all the way open, its thunk loud enough to hear over the high-pitched mechanical drone.

It was followed by nothing.

For six long seconds there was no other sign of movement from the hall. Then the chrome barrel of a large semiautomatic emerged. Probably a Desert Eagle. Next came a leather gloved hand followed by a black sleeve. A powerful shoulder panned it back and forth nearly six feet above the floor, like a tank turret. Hallway, kitchen, main room. Light to light to dark.

The Desert Eagle stopped on dark. Then quickly, suddenly, smoothly, the rest of the body followed in from the hall. As he kicked the door shut, I squeezed my Glock's trigger.

When a bullet rips through your heart, you don't bring a hand to your chest and wobble around moaning before sagging slowly to your knees, and then toppling forward to the floor. When a bullet rips through your heart, the blood stops pumping and the oxygen stops flowing and the central nervous system effectively shorts out. It's like someone yanking your power cord. You simply drop.

Suit collapsed.

Three hundred pounds of muscle turned to three hundred pounds of beef in three-hundredths of a second. His joints all gave way at once: ankles and knees, hips and shoulders. Because he'd been a pro ready to release a magnum round, his center of gravity had been a vertical dead center. When the quarter ounce of lead I'd thrown his way came calling at 1300 feet per second it was enough to tip the balance, so when he dropped, he dropped on his back.

Well, mostly.

His legs fell akimbo in an entirely unnatural pose, and his head came to rest propped up against the edge of the wall as if he was looking at his own misplaced legs and thinking *WTF*.

The bark of my gun followed by the thud of his body and crack of his skull would normally have alerted even the most dimwitted of neighbors. But the blender was still doing its thing. I was eager to silence it, but wanted to lock the door first.

Since suit had kicked the door closed behind him, I was relatively certain that he was alone, but I wasn't willing to risk being wrong. So far I'd only seen suits in pairs.

I crept toward the front door, remaining near the wall but keeping the soft soles of my shoes on the oriental carpet rather than the hardwood floor. Stepping over the corpse and resisting the urge to look through the peephole, I slid the lock into place from the protected position of the far side.

The blender stopped wailing. A failsafe to prevent overheating, I assumed. I stood still, listened for thirty seconds, then crept to the peephole. The landing was clear.

This suit had worked alone.

I didn't bother searching the body, certain that he'd be as sterile as the last guys and wanting to leave him untouched with my next move in mind.

I was pleased with the little bit of progress I'd made—another thug down and some Brillyanc in my bag—but I felt like a climber who, having conquered a foothill, was looking up at the mountain ahead. As crazy as it sounded, even in my own head, it was time to turn up the heat.

I dialed 112, the Russian equivalent of 911, and reported a shot fired at this address.

Chapter 43

Smoothie

I SLID INTO the driver's seat, started up the van, and hit the gas.

Katya looked up from the Brillyanc bottles, her face awash in curiosity. "What's up?"

"The police are on the way."

Katya looked around. Listened. "How do you know?"

"I called them."

"Why on Earth would you do that?"

"I left a suit upstairs. Wanted to make sure they'd find him. Put a little heat on our pursuers."

"You killed another one?" Katya's face morphed to an expression somewhere between marveled and horrified.

"They did a convincing job of making it look like Tarasov killed himself. I wanted to make sure the police didn't fall for it, so I added another body to the scene, reducing the forces against us at the same time. Kind of a two-for-one deal."

We were on the third ring road around Moscow, driving counterclockwise toward the Leningrad train station. With the fall of the Soviet Union, they'd changed the name of the city founded by Peter the Great from Leningrad back to St. Petersburg, but the train station retained its communist name.

Wanting to lighten the mood, I pulled the thermos from my pocket and handed it to Katya. "I made a smoothie."

"What!"

"Want some? It's triple berry with banana."

She didn't reply.

It was getting colder. I added a notch to the van's heater. After a couple of silent minutes, I said, "I trust you got through to Saba, and he's meeting us at the station?"

"I did. They'll both be there."

"Did he sound normal on the phone?"

"You mean, did it sound like someone had a gun to his head?"

"Yes, I suppose that's exactly what I mean."

"No, he sounded fine."

I could tell by the way she trailed off the last word that Katya had more to say, so I waited. It had been two days since we had laid on a warm rooftop in Palo Alto and watched death visit Katya's door. Since then, death had kept calling: at the hotel, at the clinic, and at the Tarasov's.

Sergeant Dix told me that at Fort Bragg they found that two to three days of constant tension was what it took to figure out if a soldier was going to break. Most who made it to the Special Forces Qualification Course could take anything the Army cared to throw at them for forty-eight hours. But by day three, with reserves depleted and nothing but misery on the horizon, a soldier's core became exposed. His baseline ability. His essence. Superficially, this was evidenced by the decision to quit or continue, a temptation the drill sergeants dangled every time they spoke.

The real game, of course, was mental. Beating the Q boiled down to a soldier's ability to disassociate his body from his mind, his being from his circumstance. This was relatively easy during the mindless procedures—the hikes, runs, and repetitive drills that form the backbone of military training. Disassociation became much tougher, however, when the physical activity was paired with judgment calls and problem solving. If a soldier could engage his higher-order thinking while simultaneously ignoring the pain and willing his body to continue beyond fatigue, then he had a chance at making it to the end. If he couldn't, then the strength of his back, heart, and lungs didn't matter.

Dix had concluded that the Q-Course was as much about self-discovery as a prestigious shoulder patch.

Katya was in that discovery phase now.

The big question was what we'd do if she decided to quit.

She broke the silence after a few miles. "Do you ever get used to it?"

"The killing?"

"Yes."

"We're all used to killing—just not people. We kill when we spray for bugs, or squash a spider, or buy a leather bag, or order a hamburger. I don't think of the individuals I've killed as people any more than you thought of the last steak you ate as Bessie."

"But they are people."

"When people are trying to kill me, I categorize them as a virus in need of eradication. I know that sounds cold, and I'm aware that the violent life I've led has skewed my perspective, but I don't want to lie to you and tell you that I cry a little every time I squeeze a trigger."

"How did you do it this time?"

"I set a trap and encouraged him to walk into it. I used the gun his colleague pressed against your temple last night in the stairwell."

I wanted to watch her process this, but we were nearing the train station so I had to keep my eyes on the road, and there was no time to stop for tea. Would she be able to rise above the individual acts and look at the big picture? Could her mathematical mind parse it into a simple kill-or-be-killed, them-or-us, details be damned? Or would the hurdle be too much for her moral framework to handle, now that her reserves were depleted, and her baseline exposed?

"You made a smoothie," she said, her voice tentative. It was a statement. A challenge. An opportunity.

"The blender was the trap. The smoothie's a reminder that we're just doing what it takes to stay alive. That we've got to play the cards we're dealt, with the big picture in mind. That despite all the crap that fate has thrown our way, life still has a lot to offer."

I looked over at Katya.

She looked back, meeting my eye. Then she unscrewed the thermos's lid and took a sip. Then another. "Pretty good."

I had my answer.

Once the smoothie was gone, Katya busied herself playing with the Brillyanc bottles. They clinked about like gold coins as I maneuvered the van through the city center's stop-and-go traffic.

When I finally hit the parking selector in an undersized spot in Leningrad station's long-term lot, I looked over to find Katya beaming her beautiful smile back at me, excitement in her eyes. "What?"

"Do you know who Rita is?"

"Rita? No, I can't say that I do."

"I don't know either. But Tarasova did. And she wrote her phone number on the inside of the yogurt carton." Katya opened the lid to reveal the note, handwritten in blue pen on the cardboard. "If I'm not mistaken, that area code is in Washington, DC."

Chapter 44

Blending

I STARED at the handwritten name paired with a 202 number and ran various scenarios through my mind.

"Who do you think Rita is?" Katya asked.

"Not a patient. Not with a DC phone number."

"Do you think she's connected to Brillyanc?"

That was my hope. "If Tarasova was just using the yogurt box as a notepad because it was handy, she'd have written it on the outside. Or torn the lid off. And this is written carefully, not a quick scribble. Given that, and the way it's hidden, I think it's clear that Rita's somehow connected to Brillyanc. What expiration date is stamped on the bottom?"

Katya closed the lid and carefully inverted the carton. "May 20."

"Still nearly a month to go. So the box is fresh, meaning the note is fresh."

"Should we call it?"

I shook my head. "Not yet. I like your attitude, but I'd like to do some research first. Meanwhile, I think your friends are probably here by now. Where are they waiting?"

"Beneath the clock in the main hallway."

I locked the van with an enthusiastic press of my thumb and hid the key under the fender. Now that we had a solid lead to follow, the smart move was to get out of Moscow before either the suits or the police got lucky. My intuition was that our investigation would eventually lead us back to Moscow, and I wanted the van ready and waiting when it did.

Katya came around to my side of the car. "What did you mean

earlier when you said this meeting location gives us tactical advantages? The police are bound to be looking for us at all the major transportation hubs."

"Major train stations have thousands of people mulling about, looking this way and that, walking here and there. Having been on the other end of an operation in a place like this, I can tell you that visual fatigue sets in quickly. By now, anyone posted will have been at it for hours. Meanwhile, it gives us an anonymous place to leave the van long-term, and the ability to quickly and inconspicuously conduct counter-surveillance."

I led Katya in the direction of the road rather than the station, and ducked into a kiosk I'd noted while driving in. It yielded winter jackets and watchman's caps, black for me and white for Katya. We studied our reflections in the saleswoman's smudged mirror before handing over our cash. Picking us out of the crowd dressed like this would be nearly impossible. We'd probably have to introduce ourselves to Max and Saba.

"How does it work?" Katya asked. "Counter-surveillance, I mean. What do we do?"

"Well, for starters, there are two types of people who may be looking for us: black suits, and police. The police will have seen our photos as part of a BOLO. But they'll have other duties on their plates as well. So as long as we don't do anything conspicuous, we're not likely to ping their radar. Our primary concern is the black suits. Make sense?"

"Sure."

"In essence, what we're doing is looking for people who are looking for us. Of course we need to do this in a way that allows us to see them, before they see us. Let's begin by thinking about *where* they'll be looking for us. Any guesses?"

Katya gave me a mysterious look that made my heart skip a beat. "Obviously they'll be looking at anyone approaching Saba and Max, if they know that's who we'll be meeting. If they don't, then I guess they'll be watching the entrances."

"Very good. What other focal points would be of interest? What will be the best vantage points?"

Katya tilted her head. "I suppose any perspective that also yields a view of the faces of people in line for tickets or getting onto trains would be doubly advantageous."

"Excellent. Now, *how* are they going to be doing that? Assuming they're good and they're resourceful, which they certainly appear to be."

"How are they going to be doing that?" she repeated back to herself. "Hum. In a manner that looks natural, I suppose."

"That's right. Or?"

"Or ... from someplace they either can't be seen at all, or wouldn't be noticed."

"For a theoretical mathematician, your analytical skills are pretty practical."

"Thank you."

"Given all that, *how* can we expect them to have set up surveillance?"

"How? You mean *hidden*?"

"Exactly. But hidden how? What are the two ways to hide?"

"Out of sight, or ... what's the word ... camo'd?"

"Camouflaged. How do you camouflage yourself in a train station? Keeping in mind the primary objective, which is studying faces in the locations you noted."

"You mean dressed like a ticket agent, or a janitor?"

"You're on the right track. Ticket agent would be good if it weren't for the limited perspective. Although if they were really thorough, they'd have our pictures taped in front of all the ticket agents. By contrast, janitors have freedom of movement, but they're not going to look natural studying faces, only floors."

"Okay. How about conductors or baggage handlers?"

"Now you're thinking. Limo drivers looking for their clients would be another example. Also people who would otherwise appear harmless, like a mother watching a child, or a businessman nervously checking his watch while looking around for a late colleague. And as for the hidden, that would be someone watching from above with binoculars, or studying the monitors in the security office. Whoever and wherever they are, our goal is to avoid catching their eye while we try to identify them."

"And how do we do that?"

"We begin by blending into the background. Come on, I'll show you."

Chapter 45

Reunion

I HELD OUT MY ELBOW for Katya. She looped her arm through and we began walking toward a *marshroutka*, a privately operated passenger van that served as a bus. "We'll start with the lingo," I said. "The direction we're heading is 12, as in the top of a watch face, and our rear is our 6. With our arms intertwined and our mouths conversing, you'll look natural with your head traversing 9 to 2, and I'll look natural with mine moving 10 to 3. Also, as long as your eyes follow sudden noises, or track something interesting, like a sexy skirt or a big dog or a running child, it will look natural to glance backwards. The key is to make any head movement look casual. That make sense?"

Katya swept her head to her 9. "Yes." And swept her head back to 12.

"Good," I said, performing a similar reverse move. "This applies while we're walking side by side. When we need a three-sixty search, we stop and face each other while I appear to check my phone, or you rummage through your purse."

Katya had developed a bounce in her step that I took as a good sign, although whether it meant she was enjoying the lesson or looking forward to seeing Saba, I couldn't tell. "That gives you the general idea of how to study your surroundings without appearing to do so. Offense, as it were. For defense, we modify not only our behavior, but also the context in which we'll be seen. Since they'll be looking for a couple, we want to appear as anything but. We can separate, so long as we keep a live call going, but more preferable is blending into a larger group. That could be as simple as walking beside a luggage porter with a full cart, or blending into a group of people whose outward appearance fits with our own. A warmly dressed Caucasian family would work, but not a hockey team."

I guided us so that we were next to another couple approaching the station, walking four abreast with the women in the middle. "As we enter the station, turn to the woman and compliment her on something. Get her talking to you. Try to keep it going until they stop moving."

While Katya engaged the woman to her right, I pulled out the paper I'd taken from Scar. It was folded in quarters with the photos inside. I held it in front of me like a ticket, and began glancing back and forth between it and the arc of surveillance points that afforded good views of the entrance. I saw nothing. No stationary figure in a group or alone watching the main entrance. Not near, not far. Not uniformed, not in plain clothes. There were shadows and blind spots I couldn't examine covertly, but I was confident we'd be all right if they hadn't sent their A-team.

The center of the station was bustling and clamorous. The overnight trains to St. Petersburg were the most popular, which was why I'd selected that particular station. There were tired businessmen and couples with quarreling children. There were groups of excited students and large families that appeared to be hauling everything they owned in big bags and brown boxes. All were being serviced by eager porters and weary vendors and sly hawkers and patient conductors. Controlled chaos, with a rhythm shared the world over in transportation hubs.

We stayed beside our cover couple as we walked right past an oblivious Saba and Max and onto the couple's train, but then went left as they turned right, with Katya and her new friend exchanging bon voyages.

"You did great," I said, stopping by a window that offered a good view of the way we'd come, the only way onto our train.

"Thanks. That was fun. Saba and Max didn't even notice us.

What now?"

"Now call Saba and ask them to join us for a minute on the first car of this train."

Katya complied while I continued watching the pier that led to our train. We were near the front car, nearly a hundred meters down the pier. It was filling up, with departure just ten minutes away.

When the familiar Georgian forms came into view, strolling side by side along the pier, I motioned for Katya to stay there in the hallway beside the private sleeper cabins, while I moved to a position near the doorway. I called Saba when the guys were about ten feet away. Once I caught his eye, I turned so they'd follow without fanfare, leading them back to Katya's side.

"We meet again." Max held out his hand to shake mine after hugging Katya.

"Thanks for coming. Anybody ask about us or follow you or anything like that since we left?"

The Georgians looked at one another, then shrugged. "No excitement at our end, other than the curious summons," Saba said. "Katya said you had something for us?"

I pivoted to unsling the lunch box and felt my cheek burn as the window shattered to my left, and Saba's head exploded to my right.

Chapter 46

Tight Squeeze

SCREAMS ERUPTED FROM other passengers in the hallway as I dove onto Katya and Max. Three more bullets followed the first in rapid succession as we flew to the floor, suppressed sniper shots from a single gun, shattering glass and splintering wood. I shouted, "Stay down, but follow me!" and scrambled through the doorway a meter ahead to our right.

The sleeping compartment I'd invaded had upper and lower berths on each side, and a table against the back beneath a big window. Katya and Max tumbled in after me, stunned and sobbing.

The thwack of impacting bullets gave way to the silence of expectation as my friends looked up at me with wide eyes. Was the sniper adjusting his angle, preparing to begin another barrage with the first sign of life, or had he packed up and fled?

I kicked the door closed as soon as they were clear, and threw the lock. Reaching down with both hands, I helped Katya to her feet. She was trembling, but not hysterical. Max appeared to be in shock. "Max. Open the window. All the way down. Can you do that for me? Can you handle that, Max?"

He nodded.

The window split horizontally, so when opened it created a gap about four feet across, and a foot high. Enough to squeeze through.

The clock in my head said it had been about twenty seconds since the sniper's first shot signaled his presence and position. That sliver of time would feel like an eternity to an exposed professional whose modus operandi was concealment and stealth. It also created what I'd consider an unacceptable risk. By now, a hardened pro would have relocated in anticipation of our next move, and most lesser shooters would have fled. Plenty of mad men and fools also played the killing game, bringing unpredictability and adding risk, but they didn't fit in with the black suits I'd seen. I ran the odds, and made a call. "Katya, stay down. I'll be right back."

I removed Katya's backpack and the lunch box from around my neck, then crouched, opened the door, and rolled back out into the corridor. It was empty for the moment, but would soon be swarming with police. I couldn't low-crawl to Saba through a pool of blood, given what we had to do next, so I duckwalked instead, keeping my head well below the window line.

Seeing my new friend's yellow polo drenched in crimson like a perverted New Mexico state flag made me want to forget retreat and go hunt the sniper. I was angry with myself for getting him killed, and I wanted to vent that anger by venting the shooter. But this was no time for self-indulgence. Two living souls were counting on me, and I had a mission to complete, so I did as I was trained.

I went over Saba's pockets and person, removing everything I found: watch, wallet, keys, passport, comb, a handkerchief, and a pack of gum. The longer Saba remained anonymous, the safer Max would be. I piled everything into my own pockets, and was about to return the way I'd come when I caught sight of a gold chain beneath his shirt, no doubt holding an Orthodox cross. Removing it would cost precious seconds and make a mess, but a thief would pilfer it if I didn't, so it went in my pocket as well.

Back in our commandeered cabin, Katya and Max were hugging and sobbing before the open window. "Time to go," I said. "Max, you mind going first?" Normally I'd go point, but I wanted to stay between Katya and the killer.

Max gave Katya an extra squeeze, then climbed onto the table. He worked his right arm and leg through the gap, then he pulled the rest of his body up and over the sill, dropping with a crunch to the gravel below. Katya followed with the grace of a springboarding gymnast, reminding me that she'd been one in her youth.

I passed the backpack and lunch box through to Max, then handed my new black coat and leather jacket through to Katya, concerned that my chest would be a tight squeeze. "Put my black coat on over your white one, and remove your hat. For camouflage." I was more concerned with Katya covering the bloody streaks screaming for attention than I was with altering her general profile, but avoided mention of them. I was learning.

On an exhale, I wriggled myself through the opening without drawing blood, and crunched down on the gravel beside them. We hopped the chain guardrail between the neighboring train's cars and stepped inside the proximal car with the swoosh of a pneumatic door and a short sigh of relief.

I grabbed Katya's hand and led them toward the back of the train and the front of the station, nodding politely to the other passengers we passed while hoping that the panicked looks on my colleagues' faces wouldn't cause concern. But I'd forgotten something. I felt the blood rolling down my nose just as the woman started to scream.

Chapter 47

Burner

THE SCREAMING WOMAN raised her tattooed arm and pointed. Right at me. Right at my bleeding face. Didn't she know it was rude to point?

I ignored her, but went to work wiping the blood with my left sleeve and hand as I guided Katya and Max toward the exit.

The woman didn't scream again.

We reached the last car about six minutes after the sniper's first bullet. Six minutes was long enough for the screams to have put the station authorities on alert, but too short for the city police to have sealed the station. I guessed we had another minute or two before that curtain came down.

It was going to be tight.

"We're going to run for the street where we'll grab the first taxi we can find. Forget trying to blend in, go for speed."

"What about the shooter?" Max asked with wavering voice. "Won't we be exposed?"

Only the world's best, battle-hardened professional snipers would have the nerve to stick around this long with the police closing in. Of course Russia was home to many of the best, but the odds were still in our favor. This wasn't a government operation, it was a private affair, and our choice of transportation hub had been random. "As long as we're quick, we'll be out the door before we're spotted."

And we were.

We ran right into a white Lada that had probably been working as a cab for twenty years. Once we'd disappeared onto the ring road, heading west, Katya turned my way. "I can't believe the station wasn't going crazy after the shooting."

She was seated between Max and me on the back seat, and speaking in English, lest the driver get involved. While plenty of Muscovites spoke English, the odds of an English-speaker driving a twenty-year-old cab in that economy were slim. "Judging by the lack of reaction, you'd think someone gets shot there every day."

"Maybe they do," Max replied without turning from the window.

He was right. It wouldn't be clear until ballistics were performed that a long gun had been used. Meanwhile, a Georgian with his face blown off wouldn't look that different from a Chechen, and Chechens had been terrorizing Moscow for decades. The police were probably numbed.

"Do you have someplace you can go for a few weeks?" I asked Max. "A friend or relative you can stay with until I get this sorted out?"

"You're going to sort this out?"

Max's despondent voice showed a trace of hope. I wanted to play to that, and keep him energized until he was free and clear. "Oh yeah. No doubt about that. No doubt at all. But meanwhile, it would be wise for you to keep out of sight."

He turned and leaned forward to study my face, looking for reassurance.

I saw that he was still on the dark side of despair.

"I lost a partner once. Also to a distant sniper. Also when I was standing beside him. I made that sniper wish he'd never heard my name. Made him wish he'd never been born. Took me ten days, but I did it, and I did it right. I'm going to break that record with this guy. Count on it." I lifted my chin and pointed to the spot on my cheek that burned. "If for no other reason than because the bullet was meant for me."

Max held my gaze for a few more seconds, then shifted his eyes to Katya for a few more before saying, "I've got friends with a couch."

"Good. Now, I've got something for you. Something you're going to like." I passed the lunch box to Katya.

She passed it on to Max. "Twelve vials of Brillyanc."

Max unzipped the box and looked inside. "Make that nine. Three are broken. What's with the bags of berries? An ice substitute, I assume."

"Correct. You'll need to keep it refrigerated. How long will it take you to analyze?"

"That depends on when I can get time on the mass spec. Probably a few days at least. Is there a rush?"

"Oh yeah. If I don't figure this out in the next ten days, it will be a long time before I get another chance."

"I'll see what I can do. Where are you guys headed? Or shouldn't I ask?"

"Back to the US. But we'll be in touch. Actually, you should probably keep your cell phone powered off with the battery out until things clear up. Just to be safe. Buy a burner phone to use in the meantime." I typed our cell numbers onto a note on my phone, and showed it to Max. "Memorize these and call from your burner once you learn something."

"Got it. Will do."

Chapter 48

Balancing Act

HALF AN HOUR LATER, Katya and I were on a different train departing a different station for a different country. This one was headed 720 kilometers west to Minsk. Katya curled up and fell asleep within minutes of my locking our first-class cabin's door.

I was bone-weary, but had a call to make. Assistant District Attorney Kilpatrick was expecting to hear from me, and I didn't want to disappoint. I weighed the pros against the cons and decided to remain in our cabin for the call. The train's clackety-clack provided good cover, added a bit of intrigue, and I was planning to speak softly enough that Katya would be able to sleep right through.

In the last 72, hours I'd survived multiple assassination attempts. I'd seen three people killed, and had killed five men myself. But it was dialing a phone number that put a lump in my throat. "Mister Kilpatrick. It's Kyle Achilles calling."

"Kyle Achilles. I'd say good afternoon, but that comment assumes I know what time zone you're in. Which I don't. Which I guess gets to the point of your call."

"Did you discuss my proposal with the DA?"

"I did. That was an interesting conversation, to say the least."

I waited for Kilpatrick to continue, but he was going to make me ask. Perhaps he wanted me to sweat a little. If he only knew. "What did you conclude?"

"We concluded that bail was a risky proposition. If you don't show up for trial, people will ask why you were granted bail in the first place, having been arrested for a triple homicide and all—with compelling physical evidence, the oldest motive in the book, and a colorful professional history. The discussion gets particularly awkward at that point, because of course we didn't grant bail. Not initially. That was reported in the local press. So if anyone asks, we'll be on the losing end of a news story involving a jailbreak and a cover-up. The DA asked me to tell you, 'Thanks, but no thanks.' "

Kilpatrick had some good points. Each felt like an ice pick in my ear. Or maybe a Bic.

I took a deep breath and reminded myself that assistant district attorneys spent their careers negotiating. He hadn't come close to *yes*, but he hadn't given me a flat-out *no* either.

He wanted something.

I had a pretty good idea what that was going to be. Before we went there, I wanted to balance the scorecard.

"That's not nearly as juicy or scandalous as the bumbling incompetence involved in letting me walk right out the front door."

"You had accomplices. Accomplices posing as federal agents. They'll be in nearly as much trouble as you are when we catch them."

"I don't know what you're talking about, Kilpatrick. Those were legitimate FBI agents, as far as I know. Either way, it makes the story national news if the story comes out. And it makes the FBI look bad. Of course, the master politicians in the Hoover Building aren't going to let that story spin against them. No way, no how. They'll be using your little department as a shield. Your boss will become a scapegoat, a bug deflector. Plus, you'll have the Fibbi's in your shorts for the foreseeable future. Certainly through the next election cycle."

Kilpatrick didn't respond immediately. Got me thinking he had the DA in the room with him, and they'd put me on mute. It was a good minute before he came back on the line. "I suppose you have a less controversial scenario in mind?"

"The morning of the day I was released from jail, there was an attempt made on my life. A serious, sponsored attempt involving three other inmates and a senior corrections officer. The inmates came at me in the shower while the guard stood watch. Given the nature of the attack and the imminent threat to my life, you had no alternative but to pull me out of SBCJ, at which point granting bail seemed the most sensible option."

"Is there any evidence of this alleged attempt on your life?"

"The three inmates all required medical treatment afterwards. The guard's name is Grissel. I'm sure he was paid off. I'm also confident it wasn't the first time. That's both justification for my relocation and four hashmarks in the DA's win column."

Again there was a pause. "Even in that scenario, it would be difficult for bail to make sense."

"But you'll discuss it with the DA?"

"Yes. I'll discuss it with the DA."

"I'll call you back tomorrow."

Chapter 49

Pattern Recognition

AS I CLICKED OFF the call with Kilpatrick, Katya rolled over to face me. "That didn't sound overly encouraging."

I turned so that I could study the lines of her face while I spoke. "I'm sorry I woke you. I had to get that call in today, but didn't want to risk the chance that you'd wake up here alone."

"Thank you. I got enough sleep for now. Kilpatrick's not cooperating?"

She did appear to have rebounded. Remarkable. "He is playing it out longer than I expected."

"Playing it out?"

"Negotiating."

"Negotiating for what?"

"Money."

"Doesn't he get to dictate the amount?"

"He does. But I can always walk away. I've already walked away. He has to get me to come back."

"Why do you care if you get bail? Since you're out, I mean."

"If I don't get bail, then I'm guilty of a prison escape. It was nonviolent, but they could still give me three years in jail for it. Furthermore, it makes me look guilty in the eyes of the jury. That alone would push most over the edge of reasonable doubt on the murder charges. Plus there will be a warrant out for my arrest. That could impede my investigation. Given the time pressure, I can't afford any impediments."

"And where is the investigation taking us next?"

I felt a twinge, a little warm wave scurry across my skin with her use of *us*. "Washington, if we're lucky."

I opened the iPhone's web browser and began navigating.

"You accessing one of those special CIA websites again? Tracing the yogurt box number?"

"Exactly."

"You access it through a weather website?"

I looked behind me, saw the phone's screen reflected on the window, and adjusted the angle of the screen. "You know I trust you completely, right? It's just not my call."

"I understand."

Once I reached the hidden portal, I drilled down to the page I needed, input the DC phone number, and queried the owner detail. "Unregistered. No big surprise there." I queried the call log next.

"When we get to Minsk, if there's time before our flight to Washington or wherever, can we get a room with a tub? Even if it's just for an hour?"

"Count on it."

The screen populated.

I scanned the results and then checked the header to be sure I hadn't limited the search parameters. "Rita's phone number has only been active for three weeks."

"Is that a good thing?"

"It means the trail is fresh, which is good news. But it limits the amount of data, which isn't so good."

Katya sat up and I moved next to her so she could see the screen. She scooted in closer. "All the calls are 202 area codes."

"And they're almost all outgoing. Just a few incoming calls—and those just started this week. And they're only from numbers she called during the first week." I copied the entire list and then pasted it into the phone's spreadsheet app. Then I sorted the list by number. "Most of the numbers were only dialed once, but there were a few twos, threes, and a four."

Katya pointed. "The repeated calls are all on consecutive

evenings, each roughly an hour later than the one before."

Leave it to a mathematician to pick up on a pattern faster than you could spell Pythagoras. "Conclusion?"

"She was trying to catch them at home. And she doesn't leave messages. The call durations are too short."

"I agree. Now look at the last one and tell me what you see."

"It was just ten minutes ago and only lasted two seconds. And it was the second time she called that number in as many days."

"That's accurate, but not quite what I see."

Katya turned to me and raised her eyebrows.

"I see an opportunity."

Chapter 50

No Dope

WE SPENT the next couple of hours researching the recipients of Rita's calls, beginning with the latest. Chris Pine was a 35-year-old manager at Kenzie Consulting, a top-tier firm. His specialty was the public sector, which as far as I could tell meant that he helped make government operations efficient. Talk about a growth industry.

Rita's earlier calls all went to people with similarly prestigious positions. Three more management consultants, five investment bankers, a dozen big-firm lawyers, and no less than four members of Congress. All were mid-career, with most in their thirties or early forties.

I set my phone on the bed and rubbed my eyes. That tiny screen wasn't the best way to view a spreadsheet—but I wasn't complaining, I was just hurting. And feeling sleep deprived. "Congressmen aside, I don't think there's a person on the list earning less than three hundred thousand a year. I'd guess many are closer to a million."

Katya pointed to the picture on her screen. "Chris Pine looks like the actor with the same name. Took me a second to be sure it wasn't. Same square jaw, mischievous smile, and smoldering blue eyes." She cocked her head in a gesture that was growing on me. "Now that I think about it, so do you. Except you've got that Spartacus chin dimple."

"That's good news. The resemblance, I mean."

"Why's that? You planning to go into acting?"

I was glad to hear that Katya's sense of humor had remained intact. Her resilience astounded me. "No, but I suspect that I may be impersonating Mr. Pine before this is over. In person, I mean. Of course first I'll be impersonating him on the phone, about twenty-two hours and thirty-seven minutes from now."

"You're planning to be in his home when Rita calls?"

"Of course."

"But what if he's there? What if his family is there?"

"He's not married. We already know that from his file. If he's there or a girlfriend or boyfriend is there, that will complicate things, although not insurmountably. But management consultants travel all the time. Their engagements typically last for months, and the consultants only fly home on the weekends, if at all."

"How do you know that?"

"The CIA used them on occasion. Paid them more for a month than they paid me for a year." I changed the subject. "Bet you'd like some tea."

"You'd win that bet. But I don't think the overnight trains have dining cars."

"I thought I'd check with the conductor."

"You don't think he'll be sleeping?"

"He works nights. Besides, we've got the Belorussian border coming up. He'll be getting the paperwork ready for that. Lock the door behind me."

I found our conductor in a good mood, for which I decided to take credit. I'd paid him a hefty premium in cash to sell us tickets on the spot. He was in his little nook at the end of the car, sipping tea with his feet up on the edge of his mini kitchenette, and reading a Russian detective story. For twenty dollars I got us a couple of piping hot teas, a small box of chocolates, and the explanation that they only stocked enough complimentary breakfast boxes to cover the number of tickets officially sold. "Free refills on the tea," he'd said as I was leaving.

Katya cleared the chocolate box like a hustler playing pool, and I ended up taking double advantage of the free refill offer. Once the last truffle had melted in her mouth, she smiled and asked, "Why do you think you'll be impersonating Chris Pine in person after the phone call?"

"What kind of calls do you think Rita's making?"

"What kind? How should I know?"

"Deduction. A process I know you're both fond of and proficient with."

Katya humphed, but her mind started spinning. She began paging through screens on her phone, examining the downloaded records. "The calls are all placed in the evenings, to home numbers. And no messages are left. That's an unusual combination, except for sales calls. So these are likely sales calls."

"That was my conclusion."

"You think she's trying to set up a clinical trial?"

"No. Consider the recipients. What do we know about them?"

Katya plucked crumbs from the box with a moist index finger while she thought that through. "They're all successful professionals in the second quartile of their careers."

"Right. What else?"

"They're all influential and affluent. All are well-educated. All are excelling in very competitive industries."

"What does that last point tell you about them? About their personalities?"

"They're hardworking and ambitious."

"Exactly. So we've got ambitious plus affluent. I think that's the common denominator."

"Common denominator for what?"

"Selection."

"Selection for what?"

"A sales pitch."

Katya's eyes went wide and her voice kicked up a notch. "Of course. Only instead of dope, she's pushing Brillyanc."

Chapter 51

Shared Secrets

KATYA AND I stared at each other, digesting our breakthrough. I repeated it, just because it felt good. "Rita's pushing Brillyanc. In the US."

Katya's eyes flashed the same excitement I was feeling. "Max said he'd pay anything."

"To gain a significant competitive advantage, most ambitious people would."

"But she doesn't want *most* people. She wants the *most-affluent* people."

"Exactly." I grabbed a seat at the foot of Katya's bunk.

"Why? Why not cast a broad net and let the customers figure out the money part? Why not act like a typical drug dealer?"

"Secrecy."

"Drug dealers work in secret. They have to, since it's illegal."

"They work to keep their identities secret. Rita's working to keep Brillyanc's existence secret."

Katya's head rocked back skeptically. "Is that a realistic expectation? In Russia we have a saying: *Three people can keep a secret, as long as two of them are dead.*"

"We have that saying too, and it's been bugging me. But the one thing we know for sure. The one thing we know with absolute certainty, is that these people will kill to keep a secret."

"You think they're threatening their clients? 'Buy our product, and oh, by the way, if you tell anyone about it we'll kill you?'"

"No. That wouldn't be sustainable. But back to secret-keeping. The history of the world is full of it. There are state secrets, trade secrets, secret societies, and of course, clandestine organizations like the KGB and CIA. All managed to keep secrets for generations by doing one thing."

"And what's that?"

"Making their members *want* to keep the secret."

Katya began flicking her fingernails off the pad of her thumb while her big brain tackled that twist. One, two, three, four. One, two, three, four. "Seems to me that when you discover something amazing, your first impulse is to share it. But maybe that's a female thing."

"No, it applies to us hunters as well." I leaned back against the wall. Felt the train rocking rhythmically on the rails. "I remember one time in college, the ski team was on a road trip and I snuck into the home team's gymnasium to do my stretching routine. It was closed off due to construction, but I found a way in. I heard some laughter and went exploring. I found a grate in the floor that looked down over a locker room, which at that moment was packed with dozens of sorority girls posing in their bathing suits for a fundraising calendar. Every college guy's dream, right? But my first impulse wasn't to pull up a chair and enjoy the frivolity, it was to go get my fellow Buffs and share the thrill."

"Did you?"

"I did. Brought three back and we spent the next half hour enjoying a private modeling show while the girls giggled and the photographer did his thing. We began clapping as they were wrapping up with a group photo. None of us stuck around to see what happened next, but I found out later that one of our clapping shots made the cover. There was something particularly sexy about their expressions at that instant of discovery."

I stood up and began pacing. I was exhausted, but needed to keep my head in the game. "But getting back to the secret keeping, I think your point is valid. And I don't have an answer. I don't know what you do to keep a Brillyanc user from telling his closest friends."

"Maybe that's why they're targeting these professions. They want cutthroats who'll be unwilling to share any advantage that gives them a leg up."

The simplicity of her solution hit me like a splash of cold water. "Yes! That works. Although my gut tells me there's more. Something more predictable. Something the makers of Brillyanc could count on with absolute certainty."

Neither of us could crack that nut. After a long silence, Katya said, "You still haven't told me why you think you'll be impersonating Chris Pine in person before this is over."

I stopped pacing and turned to face her. "Three reasons. First of all, look at the call pattern. For starters, the calls are all under ten minutes. That's too short to close a sale on something as complicated and nuanced as Brillyanc. Second, they're all in DC. Why limit yourself geographically, unless personal contact will be involved? Finally, we know what's being sold, and it requires you to be hooked up to an IV for six hours."

"Do you think the call is just to set up a meeting?"

"I do."

"What do you tell people as smart and sophisticated as these to get them to attend that meeting?"

"That's what we're going to find out—about twenty-two hours from now."

Chapter 52

Touchdown

GRIGORI WAS NOT a big man in the physical sense. At 5'8" and weighing in at a hundred and fifty-two pounds he'd be described as *average* and *slight*. In the company of his security head, however, he looked downright diminutive. At least from afar. Up close, body language warped perceptions. Pyotr was a tiger, but Grigori had tamed him.

While Grigori adjusted his crimson tie in the big mirror that dominated his bedroom, Pyotr stood silently at attention a few steps behind. Satisfied with his appearance, Grigori turned to face his security chief. "You lost another one to Achilles. That makes it five now, if I'm not mistaken. Am I mistaken?"

"No, sir."

"I thought not." Grigori let that hang there for a second, then checked his watch. "Let's go. President Korovin is the one man I won't keep waiting."

Grigori opened the terrace door and stepped out into the inviting air of an April afternoon. He was excited. His first flight to the Kremlin's new helipad was just minutes away.

But he had one more bit of business first.

Grigori detoured from the direct route to his favorite toy, leading Pyotr right up to the rim in the corner where the south tower and the main building met at a ninety-degree angle. On clear spring days like this, a constant slipstream bellowed up from below, warm wind powered by the sunbaked southwest exposure and channeled by the cornering facades. He'd tried tossing a cigar into the gust once, to see what would happen. It had come right back up and marred his blue suit with gray ash.

Once Pyotr was beside him at the edge, Grigori pointed to the ground a hundred meters below. "Do you see that?"

Pyotr had not developed Grigori's immunity to acrophobia, but given his role he couldn't show it. Grigori punished him this way, and Pyotr had no choice but to grin and take it. Pyotr was the beast, but Grigori held the whip. "What am I looking for?" Pyotr asked.

"Not what. Who."

"All I see is tulips."

"Closer to the building. Right below where you're standing."

Pyotr scooched and leaned. "I see him now. Black suit. Who is he?"

"Your replacement."

Grigori was a hands-on guy who loved the feel of life's furry edge. That was what had driven him to the KGB all those years ago, and that was what drove him to discipline Pyotr personally today. There was a challenge inherent in Grigori's selected means, however, which boiled down to basic physics. His security chief had every physical advantage there was, working in his favor. A greater reach, younger reflexes, and a hundred pounds of muscle, to name a few. Grigori balanced the equation by adding electricity to his side. Six million volts of electricity.

Palming a mini stun gun like a magician would a card, he pointed down with his left hand, and zapped Pyotr's ass with his right.

The jolt shot Pyotr's hips forward as if they were propelled by rubber bands. As the stun gun took his central nervous system offline, Pyotr's center of gravity swung out over a hundred meters of open space, dooming him before his body had a clue what was happening. Just a tenth of a second from A-Okay to complete-systems-failure. Grigori may as well have put a bullet through his brain for all the chance Pyotr had of recovering—but this approach was much more satisfying.

Pyotr yelped, then Grigori got a couple of words in before Pyotr began wailing. "As promised."

Unlike the cigar, Pyotr wasn't blown back.

Grigori looked up before Pyotr touched down. Such a disappointment.

Back to business.

Chapter 53

Full Circle

THE HELICOPTER PILOT, a chisel-faced veteran of the Afghan war, met Grigori's eyes with a level gaze as he approached the big black bird. He showed no reaction to Pyotr's demise.

Grigori made the lasso sign.

Erik flicked a switch and the rotors started spinning with effortless grace. The twin Pratt & Whitney turbines, each capable of delivering the power of 630 horses, emitted more of a throaty growl than a thundering whine. Grigori loved the sound. Tremendous raw power. At his command.

He liked his pilot too. Ten years his senior, Erik was the only employee with whom Grigori felt a natural ease conversing man-to-man. He'd come with the helicopter, but was now Grigori's chauffeur as well.

Grigori would have preferred to sit in the front to better take in the memory of this flight, but it wouldn't do to be seen exiting from the cockpit. So he hopped in back, and donned his headset.

"We got the go-ahead from the presidential security service," Erik said by way of greeting, his voice calm and cool like a captain's should be. It was hard to faze an Afghan vet.

"Ever flown to the Kremlin before?" Grigori asked.

"Almost no one has flown to the Kremlin before. They only put the helipad in a few years ago, and it's typically reserved for the president himself and visiting heads of state. How'd you get the privilege, if you don't mind my asking?"

Truth was, there were at least a dozen Russian oligarchs who had been granted the perk by a president eager to maintain an iron-clad support base at home. But it was still the hottest ticket in aviation, and Grigori's pride swelled every time he thought of it. "A few years ago the president asked me a question. A sports question, of sorts. A year ago, I gave him an answer he liked."

"Must have been one hell of an answer."

"You should have heard the question."

As they hit the Moscow river from the south and turned northeast to follow it to the Kremlin, Erik risked a glance at Grigori. "If you were granted the privilege a year ago, why haven't you used it until today?"

"I was waiting to make a special delivery. Something worthy of the honor." He reached up to touch the vials in the left breast pocket of his suit coat. Then, remembering, he removed the mini stun gun from his right side pocket. "I'll leave your toy in the cup holder. Thanks. It was the perfect tool for the job."

~ ~ ~

This time Grigori's throat was relaxed and his palms were dry as the presidential guards escorted him to the big office. This time he knew exactly what to do upon entering. And this time he knew exactly how to answer the question: "What have you brought me, Grigori?"

As the guards clicked their heels and closed the gilded doors, Grigori walked straight to Vladimir's chess desk and took a seat. He removed two finger-sized vials from his breast pocket and positioned them upright on the squares reserved for the black king and queen. When the president looked over, he said, "Something for the hunter watching the crocodile watching the rabbit. Kind of completes the circle."

"You really did it?"

"We really did it."

"When I saw you fly in, I figured as much. What are they?"

"The king is a flea. The queen a tick."

"Okay to pick them up?"

"Sure. To you and me they're as harmless as any other flea or tick."

"And to our hunter?"

"He'll start having vision issues about a month after he's bitten. Within three months he'll be blind."

Korovin toppled the king vial and began to roll it back and forth with his index finger, watching the flea tumble while churning the scenario in his mind. "How's that possible?"

"The technology is the same that's used to create custom cancer therapies. Only instead of going after cancer cells, they're going after retinal cells. They used gene sequencers, mass spectrometers, and micro-array scanners to analyze his DNA and create a molecular profile of his cells, using the hair follicle your office supplied. Then they went to work with genetic databases and synthetic biology software to create a very specific synthetic DNA. They booted that DNA up in host cells, and then transferred those cells into pests indigenous to the Moscow region. The pests, in turn, will transmit the synthetic DNA to our hunter with their bites."

Korovin leaned forward, making no attempt to mask his enthusiasm.

Grigori was loving it.

"When I get bug bites, my doctor always inspects them. If he doesn't like what he sees, he loads me up with vitamins and antibiotics."

"The bite will look normal, as will his blood work. Even if they prophylactically treat him for everything from plague to Lyme disease it won't matter. This is a personalized bioweapon, based on his DNA. It's not anything that's ever been transmitted by a bug bite or anything else before. It won't be detected."

"Really?"

"Really. That said, I suggest we go with fleas. They're much less conspicuous, and quickly forgotten. They don't latch on and hang out the way ticks do. The docs weren't sure which host vectors would prove viable, so they tried three species. These two worked."

"How do we know they'll bite him?"

"It only takes one bite. Given the quantity of fleas that will be in the vial, and the condition they'll be in, my people tell me it's a mathematical certainty so long as you remove the cap within a meter of the target while you're both stationary. A hunting blind will be perfect."

"Will they be able to trace the condition back to the bite?"

"No. At best, it will be one of many hypotheses. But there won't be any evidence."

Korovin stood and began to pace. "But will it look natural? If they suspect foul play, they'll look for motive, and we all know where that investigation will start."

"*Cui bono.*"

"Exactly. We can't have that."

"It doesn't get any more natural than this."

"Be specific."

Grigori leaned back in his chair, tilting it up on two legs and then placing his hands behind his head. "My guys looked for a region where his DNA was already weak, something his doctors will likely be aware of. They found the predisposition we're exploiting, which is one reason we picked blindness rather than, say, cancer or a heart attack. Furthermore, since it's not an outright assassination, it doesn't fit the mold. Finally, there's the timeframe. It's quick in the big scheme of things, but there will be a full month between the flea bite and the first symptom."

Korovin sat back down. "So in summary, it's natural, untraceable, and inconspicuous?"

Grigori nodded.

After a moment of quiet appraisal, the President of Russia said the two magic words. "I'm pleased."

Chapter 54

Bubbles

THE BORDER CROSSING into Belorussia proved to be a non-event, and the flight from Minsk to DC uneventful. That was good, we were overdue for *uneventful*. The bad news was the timeline. Not only had the rush forced me to renege on my promise to get Katya a hot bath before the flight, but it also left us precious little time for reconnaissance after. By the time we got to Chris Pine's part of the city, the anticipated call was just three hours away.

Pine's apartment was a few blocks northeast of DuPont Circle on New Hampshire, which coincidentally put it within a stone's throw of the Belorussian embassy. We managed to find a hotel room directly across the street. A couple of major conventions left little selection when it came to rooms, so I sprang for a two-bedroom suite. That was fine with me—in part because it put us on the top floor with direct line of sight to Pine's apartment, and in part because I was in the mood to splurge on creature comforts. Gather ye rosebuds while ye may, and all that. Going with a suite also enabled me to keep Katya in the same room, but on the other side of a door. Something that was good for both her security and my waning willpower.

"The bath is perfect," Katya called out. "Worth the wait."

"So I'm forgiven?"

"Indeed."

It felt weird talking to Katya while she was in the tub, which itself was odd, given all that we'd been through. "Do you have your phone in there?"

"I do."

"I need you to make a call to Chris Pine's office."

"Okay. What's the goal?"

"We want to find out if he's in town, and if he is, how late he'll be in the office. If he's not in town, we want to find out when he's going to be back, and the name of his assistant."

"Okay. You know I'm the analytical type, right? Creativity isn't my thing."

I heard the Jacuzzi's jets kick in, so I spoke louder. "Would you like a little coaching?"

"Please. You can come in. I've got bubbles."

She's got bubbles. Great. Nothing sexy about that.

She did have bubbles. The Jacuzzi jets had blown them up to the rim of the tub. Besides her head, which was now plastered with wet hair, only the tops of her shoulders and her neck were visible. I moved the little vanity stool next to the tub and sat with my back to the wall so that all I saw was the bubbles covering her feet.

"If Chris answers, say, 'It's me. When are you going to be home?' If he asks you to clarify, use a silly-boy voice and say, 'It's Cathy, from across the hall. I've got a little something for you.' If he doesn't go along, tell him you must have a wrong number."

"And if he doesn't answer?"

"Ask for his assistant. Get her name—that's important—and tell her you're Chris's sister Cathy, and you want to surprise him with a visit. Say you know he travels a lot, so you wanted to know when you can expect him home."

"Wouldn't this be easier if you pretended to be his brother?"

"You think I'm being lazy?"

"I think you have a reason, and I'd like to know it. This spy stuff is new to me—and surprisingly fascinating."

Giving in to temptation, I turned to look at her. "People are generally less suspicious of women. Plus, we may be playing the distress card later on. That works best woman to woman."

"Distress card?"

"Don't muddle your mind with those details yet. Let's get this right first. Are you ready for the number?"

"What about my accent?"

"Good point." My jet lag was showing. Not a good sign.

"I could be his ex-girlfriend?"

"No. That will raise defenses. Can you fake a British accent?"

A second later, Katya replied with, "I suppose. Why would I want to talk this way, luv?"

"That's good. Say you're his sister and you've got a layover on your way back to England. If she says anything that throws you off, complain about your jet lag and ask her to repeat it." I handed her a dry washcloth to wipe her hands, and then her phone.

"What's the number?"

I gave it to her.

"It's ringing." "Yes, good afternoon. This is Catherine Pine calling for Christopher, please. Yes, Chris Pine. Is his secretary available? Yes, what's her name, please? Emma. Thank you. Yes, I'll hold." Katya looked over at me and smiled. She seemed to be enjoying herself. "Yes, good afternoon, Emma. This is Catherine calling, Christopher's sister. Yes, that's what the operator said. Are you expecting him later? Well, I guess not. That's a shame. I've got a layover I wasn't expecting and thought I'd surprise him. But I'm headed back to London in the morning, so I guess it wasn't meant to be."

I had a brainstorm and mouthed some words to Katya.

"Can you hold a second, luv?" Katya hit the mute button. A second later she unmuted. "Where was I? Oh yes. Don't tell him I called, luv. I'm going to leave a little something in his apartment and I want it to be a surprise. Thank you, you're a dear."

I clapped as Katya hung up. "You're hired."

"He won't be back until next weekend, ten days from now. He's in Hong Kong. What was that last bit about?"

I stood and stretched, my eyes averted. "Just priming the pump. I'm going to go recce Pine's place. You enjoy your soak."

"Recce?"

"Sorry. Reconnoiter. Conduct reconnaissance. I'm going to check out your brother's apartment. You be okay for half an hour or so?"

"Mmm hum."

I headed for the door, hoping I wasn't making the mistake of a lifetime by leaving her alone in the tub.

Chapter 55

To The Nines

IN THE HOTEL LOBBY, I paid eight bucks for a small roll of packing tape. It disappeared into my jacket pocket.

Chris Pine lived across the street in an Italianate eight-story. Constructed long ago from red brick and limestone, his building boasted bay windows, and looked more inviting than the smaller gray stone residences to its left and right.

I walked past the canvas-covered portico and through an alley to the back. I'd come for the view, but my nose couldn't help noticing the battle raging between the dumpster and the laundry room vent. For the moment, the fabric softener was winning.

I backed up all the way to the neighboring wall and surveyed Pine's building like I would a boulder I wanted to summit. Technically, I wouldn't be bouldering but *buildering*, although my current objective was the same. Route planning.

The easiest way to the top takes the whole ascent into account, not just the first dozen moves. There was no fire escape or drainpipe, but the middle third of the building was bumped out a couple of feet all the way to the top, to accommodate a different floor plan for the inside units, I assumed. The corner this created was a climber's dream. The ninety-degree angle gave enough opposing resistance to support a wide variety of hand and foot holds, and would speed both ascent and descent dramatically.

I moved in to inspect the bricks, and once again was delighted. Their height was a standard 76 mm, and the mortar set back a good 5 mm. That made them prime for pinching, as well as the crimping and edging I'd employ with larger masonry. Climbing Pine's place wouldn't be quite as quick as Tarasova's, but the difficulty was only about a 2 on a scale that ran all the way to 16, so I was a happy climber.

I turned around to check my exposure before heading to the lobby. Not bad. The building behind Pine's also had smaller, opaque windows on its backsides, primarily for bathrooms and stairwells, I assumed. People were more concerned about privacy than the view when it came to alleys.

Finished with the back, I headed around front. Pine's building didn't have a doorman, but it did have a concierge. This made sense to me. A traveling executive would want someone there to receive dry cleaning and packages and tend to the occasional personal request. This one was tall and lanky, with thinning hair and round, wire-rimmed glasses that made me think of colonial times. "Hi, I'm Adam," I said, holding out my hand.

"Charles. How may I help you?"

"A colleague of mine said this was a great building. Do you have any vacancies?"

"Not at the moment. We typically only see vacancies once or twice a year, and those are usually rented out in advance."

"Any coming up?"

"We've got a one bedroom becoming available in June."

"Does it have the same view as Chris's? He's in 8A."

"Mr. Pine's unit is a corner penthouse overlooking New Hampshire. The one becoming available is 8E, which isn't a corner unit, but it's also a one bedroom, and it also looks over New Hampshire."

"Could I see it?"

"I'm afraid it's occupied."

"Maybe just from the doorway?" I asked. Then I added the magic words, "I would be most grateful."

What's the difference between a bribe and a gratuity? Same two parties, same special service, same discreet transfer of cash. But the timing shifts, and timing is everything.

"I do have some dry cleaning to drop off in 8E."

Charles produced a back-in-five-minutes sign and then extracted three hangars' worth of bagged clothing from a closet behind the counter.

"I'll take the stairs," I said. "It's a thing."

No flicker of whimsy from Charles. Just a respectful, "See you up there."

I raced up eight flights of stairs and then a ninth to the roof. Cracking the door, I found the typical bare concrete architecture, with exhaust pipes and vents and a perimeter raised about eighteen inches. Someone had set up lawn chairs, the cheap folding kind you find in beachfront convenience stores. They'd also left a plastic bucket half filled with water that I presumed had once been ice. It was easy to see why. The view was fantastic. The fountain in DuPont circle was visible to the south, and beyond it, the Washington Monument, which would likely forever remind me of Barsukov's Rocket.

I tore a six-inch strip of packing tape off the roll using the built-in cutter, and plastered it over the door-latch holes. Then I tore off another to double its strength. Satisfied that it would hold, I eased the door shut, descended to eight, and joined Charles in the hallway before 8E.

Charles pulled out a Schlage master key.

I could pick most conventional locks with the paperclips I kept in my back pocket, but that could take time. With this information, breaking in would be cake. He worked the lock and said, "Kindly hold the door while I hang these. By the way, the kitchen is on the right, the bathroom's on the left, and the living room is straight ahead. The bedroom has the same southwest view."

And no alarm panel. I had everything I needed. "It's beautiful. Thank you so very much."

As he relocked 8E, Charles said, "Would you like to fill out an application?"

I pulled a hundred dollar bill from my wallet. "Let me think about it. I'm not sure about the eighth floor thing. How late will you be here?"

"Jason relieves me at eight o'clock."

I took my time going down the stairs so Charles would see me exit, which I did with a polite nod.

He reciprocated.

I took a right on New Hampshire, then a left on R. At the corner of Seventeenth, I entered what Google assured me was the nearest chain hardware store. After a quick survey of the hired help, I approached the youngest of the three employees. A skinny boy in his late teens. He was still losing the fight with acne, but no doubt winning plenty on his Xbox. "Hey Brad, I need a key," I said, reading his nameplate. "Can you hook me up?"

"You got it." Brad spun around and took me to the key machine.

Before he could ask, I said, "I need an L-style Schlage key, cut to nine on all five positions."

He took a minute to mentally process the order, which didn't follow the default input parameters. "You got the original?"

"No. I lost it. But it really doesn't matter since I know the pattern. Nine all the way across, so it will look like a little saw when it's done, with five tiny teeth. Can you do that? I can show you, if you'd like."

"I got it. Just kinda weird."

"Thanks. I got some other shopping to do. I'll be right back."

I heard the whir and metallic grind of the key-cutter going to work as I found a rubber O-ring with a quarter-inch hole. By the time I'd picked up a small screwdriver and returned to Brad, he was pulling the Schlage off his machine. He pushed it in and out of a deburring hole a couple of times, and presented it for my approval. "To the nines," he said with a touch of pride. Then chuckling to himself, he added, "Sounds like something my grandfather used to say, but I don't think he had this in mind."

It was exactly what I had in mind, however. So I thanked him, paid, and left to commit a felony.

Chapter 56

Backpacking

"I WANT TO GO WITH YOU," Katya said, her eyes twinkling and her hair aglow after the bath.

I was thrilled, but stunned. "Why? It's just a phone call. I can put Rita's call on speaker, and you can listen in on your cell phone. Same as being there, but risk free."

Katya put her hands on her hips. "Do you have any idea what this past week has been like for me?"

That wasn't the comeback I was expecting, and I had no idea where she was going with it. "I've got a pretty good idea."

"No, you don't. Not really. You're a professional, a trained spy with years in the field. You live in a world where breaking into a building or out of a jail holds as much weight as a trip to the supermarket. For you, putting a bullet through a brain or crossing a border with false papers is the equivalent of ordering brunch."

"So?"

"So I'm a twenty-eight-year-old with a PhD in mathematics from Moscow State University. My world is ethereal. I deal with probability theory and predictive computations and confused students. You and I live on the same planet, but our work lives have less in common than fish with fowl."

"I don't follow. I mean, I hear what you're saying, but I don't see what it has to do with your joining me for a felony B&E. Kinda seems you're making my point for me?"

Katya picked her mug of tea off the kitchenette counter and took a sip. Then another. "Everyone wants to visit Paris once in their lives," she said, tilting her head to the right and staring into her own mind. "Women, at least, all seem to have that common dream. But we differ on how. The vast majority opt for a tour bus trip. They want safe hotels, familiar food, and guides who speak their language. They want to hit all the must-see sights, without fail. They're willing to settle for a guaranteed B-minus experience, because it's predictable. The tourism industry has evolved to cater to them—the multitudes, the risk-averse." She met my eyes and I saw fire within.

"Then there are the backpackers. A paper map in their pocket and a few euros in their shoe. They figure things out on the fly, and enjoy an unscripted experience. They're the only people who have a shot at experiencing the real Paris, and that's only because they're willing to risk an F in order to earn an A. You follow?"

"Sure."

"I'm a backpacker, Achilles. I want to live. I want to suck up every second I can of this strange new world of yours, because I know that I'll never see it again. Soon, I'll be back in my ivory tower. And that's fine. I love it there. But while I'm here in your world, I want to live it. I'm not one to settle for a guaranteed B-minus in life."

Looking at her standing there making her case, I was overcome by the desire to walk over and crush her body to mine, kiss her like she was the last remaining source of oxygen in the universe. I wanted to run my hands up and down her slim back and through the tangles of her hair. I wanted to pick her up and take her to my bed and forget all about men in black suits and assistant district attorneys. But I was a grieving brother, and a gentleman, so I said, "As you wish."

Her mouth formed a funny smile, not unlike that famous must-see painting in Paris. "Thank you."

"But you're going to have to earn it. I'm climbing to the roof, and entering the building from there. You'll need to find another way to get past the concierge."

"What about a fire escape?"

"Building doesn't have one."

"Huh. Well, what was your Plan B? You had one, right? Back when you had me make the call to Chris's assistant?"

"That was in case there was an alarm. I was going to have you call her back from Chris's door and tell her you have a key, but forgot the alarm code, and now you'll be stuck dealing with the police if she doesn't give it to you in the next forty seconds."

Katya smiled like an eager backpacker as she pictured that scene. "But how were you going to get me to the door in the first place?"

"Charm, deceit, or subterfuge. I'd have thought of something on the fly."

Katya raised a fist. "So that's what I'll do. You ready to go?"

I took off my leather jacket, transferring my hardware store purchases to the back pocket of my jeans. "Now I'm ready. Don't you need time to plan?"

"Backpacker, remember? I'll think of something."

Chapter 57

Greasy Ladders

I EXITED Chris Pine's stairwell, winded and sweaty, ten minutes after Katya accepted my challenge. She was already there, waiting in the corridor, looking fresh as a daisy and somewhat pleased with herself.

"You have a key?" she asked.

"In a manner of speaking." I emptied my back pocket. "A *bump key* to be precise." I slipped the O-ring around Brad's handiwork and slid it back to the base. Then I inserted the key into the lock. "I'm going to put a tiny amount of torque on the key, barely enough to turn it. Now when I hit the back of the key like this..." I gave it a few straight-on whacks with the handle of the screwdriver. "The teeth bump the lower set of pins. If I get it right, the lower pins hit the upper pins like pool balls, creating a gap between the cylinder and the housing for a split-second, thereby allowing the cylinder to rotate if there's tension on it." The key turned after half a dozen bumps.

Katya grinned like a little girl on her birthday. "What's that rubber ring for?"

"It puts the teeth in the right place to bump the keys. Without it, I'd need to reposition the key every time. Still works, but it's much slower. Why don't you get your phone ready to call Emma? Just in case Chris had an alarm put in."

She did.

I opened the door.

The ringing started almost immediately.

It wasn't like any alarm countdown I'd ever heard. This was

more like a digital ring tone, one of the preset options on a modern home phone. Which, of course, was exactly what it was.

Katya stepped out of my way, noting, "Rita's early."

I ran toward the source of the noise, which emanated from a wireless home phone system on the counter between the kitchen and the living room. Katya locked the door behind us as I picked up the handset and hit the speaker button. "Hello."

"Is this Chris?" The voice was a late-twenties Caucasian female with a British accent. Katya and I exchanged fancy-that glances at the ironic coincidence.

"Yes, who's this?"

"My name's Rita. A colleague of yours referred me. I've got a proposition for you."

Intriguing start. Professional and self-assured. "What kind of proposition?"

"Not the type you'd expect, I assure you. I understand that you're doing well at Kenzie. You're working hard and it's paying off, but of course the future has yet to be written. As you're well aware, ninety percent of your class will slip off the greasy ladder before reaching the partnership rung, despite their Ivy League graduate degrees, herculean work-ethics, and killer instincts."

"That's probably right. It's a high-risk, high-reward business."

"What would you say if I told you that I can eliminate the high-risk component, that I can virtually guarantee that you'll make partner? That's my proposition. Are you interested?"

"Am I interested in making partner? Of course. But your proposal doesn't strike me as credible."

"Of course it doesn't. If it did, then it wouldn't be extraordinary. And it is extraordinary, Chris, I assure you. But no doubt my assurances aren't enough—so I'd like to prove it to you."

"Prove it? How can you prove what's going to happen years from now?"

"Meet me this Friday at the Hay Adams and I'll show you."

"How do I know this isn't some kind of a scam or swindle?"

"It's the Hay Adams, Chris, not a dark alley. And I'm not asking you to show up with a bag of gold bricks. But you can't mention this to anybody, and you do need to come alone. This is a *very* exclusive offer."

I paused for a sufficient interval. "What time?"

"Eight o'clock at the bar. It's appropriately named Off the Record."

"Okay."

"And Chris?"

"Yes."

"This is a one-time offer. If you're not there for any reason, you'll never hear from me again. Then someone else gets the offer, and you'll be left alone on the greasy ladder."

Chapter 58

Naked

I LOOKED ACROSS Chris's kitchen counter at Katya. "See if you can find a spare key. I'm going to program Chris's phone to forward to my cell, in case Rita calls back."

Katya didn't even have to move to find the key. She opened the drawer before her and there it was, in an organizer that also held an assortment of business cards and office supplies. "Why do we want a key? You need it to lock the door?"

"The bump key would suffice, but this will make it easier to return if required. Tell the concierge you're a guest with a key and there's not much he can do to contradict you, not with Chris in Hong Kong."

"You're big on contingency planning."

"I run into a lot of contingencies."

"Speaking of the concierge, how are you going to explain your presence when you leave, seeing as you came in through the roof? Or are you planning to go out that way too?"

"Charles got off at eight. Jason's working now. He won't know that I didn't come in earlier. You planning to tell me how you got past Charles?"

"A woman has her secrets."

Jason barely looked up from the monitor behind his counter as we passed. Perhaps the Washington Wizards were playing. I hadn't been following the playoffs. When we were out on the street, Katya asked, "What's next?"

"I've got to call Kilpatrick right away. While I'm on the phone, would you mind checking into flights to San Francisco? There's nothing for us to do here before Friday evening."

"San Francisco? Isn't that risky?"

"There's no sense in looking around anyplace that isn't risky. Would you rather hang back here?"

"Do I have to explain the whole tour bus and backpack thing again?"

"No ma'am."

"Good. I'll look into our flight options."

Back in our suite, I scrolled through my recent calls and redialed Kilpatrick's number.

"I'd almost given up on you," Kilpatrick said by way of greeting. "Then I saw the now familiar *Blocked* message on my caller ID screen. That's quite some service you're using."

"How'd it go with your boss?" I asked.

"It was an interesting conversation. A lesson in risk management from a master politician. She's keen to avoid the hit she'll take from a prison escape, and she has no desire to become the FBI's scapegoat. But she's been at this too long not to have learned that getting caught in the cover-up is usually worse than getting caught in the crime. So even after spreading the potential blame by consulting with Senator Collins—who apparently knows your reputation from your CIA days—she's still not going to go for it without assurances."

Here it comes. "What kind of assurances."

"Well, that's just it, isn't it? There's nothing you can say. There's only what you can do."

"And what can I do?"

"It's come to our attention that your father kept his money offshore."

"You noticed that, huh?"

"We did. You've got to bring it all back, and you've got to put it all on the line. The DA is setting your bail at ten million dollars, cash. Have it wired to the account posted on our website by close of business Friday, and you've got bail. Fail to do so, and the jailbreak story goes out first thing Saturday morning, along with a warrant for your arrest and a global BOLO."

"First thing Saturday morning," I repeated. "When nobody's watching the news."

"Like I said, she's a master politician. But that's going to be working in your favor, now."

"How so?"

"She's instructed Flurry and me to support you in any way we can. She recognizes that the stronger the case for your innocence, the more likely you are to show."

"And the more interaction we have, the easier it will be for you to track me down if I don't."

"Again, master politician. But that's not all there is to it. She rounded your bail back to ten million even, from the $10.2 million I'd proposed. I wanted everything you had left from your inheritance, less your attorney's retainer, but the DA didn't want your investigation to suffer from a lack of funding."

"That was considerate of her," I said. And I meant it. "You'll get the ten million Friday."

As I pushed the button that ended the call, I felt a big gorilla climb off my back, only to become aware that I still had a whole ark on my shoulders. I'd never been into money, but ten million dollars did provide a security blanket of sorts. Now I was practically naked and feeling an unexpected breeze. A very cool breeze. I was facing a formidable opposing force, a ticking clock, and life behind bars—but I had yet to figure out why.

Chapter 59

Bad Stats

WITH TEN MILLION DOLLARS now on the line, I closed my eyes and took a deep calming breath. When Dix was putting me through the worst of my training, when I was neck-deep in the slog and sucking wind with a world of hurt ahead, he would have me focus on momentum rather than position.

I tried that now.

Just a few days ago, I'd been locked up under Grissel's thumb and slugging it out in the shower. Now I had eleven days of freedom ahead of me, several solid leads behind me, and a remarkable woman by my side. I rolled my shoulders and threw a dozen rapid jabs into the air, like a boxer headed for the ring. With the blood flowing, I used my right palm to push my chin up to the left until my neck cracked. *Bastards didn't have a chance.*

"I see it went well," Katya said, reading my face as I returned to our suite's central room.

"I had to put the ten million I inherited up as bail."

Katya did a double-take. "I had no idea your family had so much money until the police detective brought it up while questioning me. I mean, I knew your father had done well, being a doctor and having a yacht and all, but I had no idea it was seventh-power money."

"Seventh power?"

"Ten million, ten to the seventh power."

"Yeah, well, that was a recent development. While we were growing up, my dad worked for the military, so the pay was very modest by physician standards. He really only became wealthy a couple of years ago when some stock options paid off."

"So you really are putting it all on the line? There aren't millions stashed elsewhere?"

"Yep, all on the line. Crazy, right? But then, I intend to show up, so it really doesn't matter."

Katya pursed her lips. "Have you transferred the money yet?"

"No. I was going to do that now. Why do you ask?"

"I think you should reconsider. Your attorney's investigators had six months to work the case, a hundred eighty-two days. That's sixteen and a half times the amount of days we have left to solve this thing. They came up with nothing. Even if we're ten times as good as they were, we're still going to fail, statistically speaking."

"Not necessarily. What did you find out about flights to SFO?"

"There's a flight at ten tonight that gets in at one a.m. And the flights start back up at six in the morning. Personally, I say we grab a nice dinner and get a good night's sleep, and head to San Francisco in the morning. I'm guessing there's not much we can do there at one in the morning anyway. And besides, isn't there some soldier's axiom about eating and sleeping when you can?"

"You an expert on soldiers now?"

"No, but I'm pretty good with axioms."

I laughed. Just a quick, spontaneous snort, but it felt good. I realized I hadn't laughed since the party, since Colin had recalled some of the more challenging moments presented by raising two boys while toasting my father.

Katya watched me enjoy the recollection before continuing. "When I said we'd have to be ten times as good as the other investigators to catch them in the time you have left, you said 'not necessarily.' What did you mean?"

"Your equation assumes the investigators were equally competent and motivated. I can't speak to their competence, but I'm beginning to think they weren't motivated at all. So first I'm going to take you to the Old Ebbitt Grill for some lobster. Then we're going to get a few hours of sleep. Then we're going to fly to San Francisco and confront an old friend."

PART 3: ENLIGHTENMENT

Chapter 60

Finding Fear

NEW YORK CITY has a street that serves as an address and an icon and a center for its financial activity. On the opposite coast, three thousand miles and a ditched-necktie away, Silicon Valley has a road that serves the same purpose. Vondreesen Ventures boasted its Sand Hill Road address on engraved linen stationery and crisp bone business cards. According to the shapely blonde at reception, however, the firm could no longer brag of the presence of the man for which it was named.

"Mr. Vondreesen retired at the end of last year," Megan said. "We're still here to administer existing funds, but there's no new business being conducted." She was cordial and intelligent and pleasant to watch, but Megan left no doubt that her words could be taken to the bank, like a weather girl who'd made news anchor.

"I hadn't heard. I'm an old friend. Vaughn worked with my father."

Her face brightened, then clouded. Recognition then realization before her diplomatic training kicked in. "You're John's son. That dimpled chin's pretty distinctive. I should have known right away."

I bowed my head as though doffing a hat. "I need to speak with Vaughn. Some old business related to my father. Is he still living in Atherton?"

Megan gave a perfect little shake of her head. "He moved. I'm afraid I have strict instructions not to pass his contact information along to anyone. Venture capital is a stressful business, and despite his success, he was happy to leave it behind."

"Why the office, then? The rent here can't be cheap, and surely the storefront is no longer necessary, if all that's left is administration?"

She gave me an appraising stare. "I'd heard you did, shall we say, government work. It shows. To answer your question, there was a lease and a legacy to consider. I can pass along the information that you called, if you'd like to leave a number."

I knew a cue when I heard one. "No need, I'll call him directly. I trust his old cell is still in service?"

"Some things never change."

Once we were back in the parking lot, where our Tesla waited in the shade of a redwood tree, Katya said, "You gave up pretty easily back there. That tells me you already have a Plan B."

"In the modern world, people who expect privacy are bound to be disappointed. Vondreesen is no exception." I looked up his cell phone number on one program, then pasted it into another. Twenty seconds later I got a set of GPS coordinates, which I punched into the Tesla's navigation system.

A voice remarkably similar to Megan's told me the route was being calculated.

I muted her without prejudice.

"He stayed in Northern California, or at least his cell phone did. It's near the far end of Napa Valley. Should be a lovely drive."

I'd rented the Tesla because its combination of speed, style, and silence were great for covert work in Silicon Valley, but I was still surprised by the quiet operation. Just touch and go. No rumble or revving, no jolting or shifting. Just velvety power on tap. Now I had the Golden Gate Bridge and the Marin County headlands and the windy roads of the Napa hills ahead. This was going to be fun.

As we left the 101, Katya said, "You still haven't explained what you expect to learn from Vondreesen? Or how he's related to the investigation? Or why Casey's investigators would be anything but motivated?"

I adjusted my seat with a whir and a purr, dropping my right arm onto the tan leather armrest and opening myself up in Katya's direction. "The morning of the incident, a couple of beat cops picked me up in a hotel room. By then the detectives had already spent hours scouring the yacht, but I was oblivious to what had happened. I'd enjoyed a very late night, and had slept in accordingly. When Frost finally broke the news to me, Flurry was already done with you. By the time I learned they were looking at me for the murders, I already had a lawyer."

"How'd you get a lawyer before you knew you needed one?"

"I'd wondered that too, at first. But I also knew I was a few hours behind the curve, so when Vondreesen appeared with his lawyer already working the system, I didn't question it. Lawyers go with venture capitalists like salt with pepper."

"And now?"

"Now I'm wondering if that wasn't a little too convenient."

"Convenient for whom?"

"That's what I want to learn from Vondreesen."

We were driving north through Napa Valley now on the St. Helena Highway. The sun was out, the fields were green, and the air was fresh with the scent of bloom. In a sense, I'd been told I only had a few days to live, and this wasn't a bad way to spend one of them.

"Vondreesen introduced you to Casey just moments before your arrest?"

"Yup."

"If you suspect Vondreesen, then by extension you suspect Casey too. Which is why you're not convinced the investigators were fully motivated. Since Casey hired them."

"It's a working theory. But it has a big fat hole, which is why I didn't start there."

"What big fat hole?"

"If you'll recall from the party, Vondreesen is about as far from the killer profile as you can get. Rich, handsome, extremely well-connected, and a longtime friend of my father."

"When did you start to suspect him?"

"He was always a suspect. But he didn't top the list until the Brillyanc connection emerged. As it is, I still don't have the most important piece of the puzzle." I tossed the question to Katya with my eyes.

She fielded it immediately. "Motive. What could he possibly gain by killing your family and framing you for it?"

"I think I've got the motive piece, but you're close. I'm missing the linking piece."

"What's his motive? You told me he has it all: fame, fortune, influence."

"Exactly. So his motive isn't *gain*, it's *avoiding loss*. Vondreesen's motivated by fear. But fear of what? That's the missing link."

"If something scares him enough to involve him in the murder of friends, then he's not likely to open up to us about it."

"I agree. I'm going to have to put the pressure on. And since I've got my trial coming up, and he's the kind of witness who could sway a jury, I've got to do it in a way that doesn't deeply offend him."

"How do you do that?"

"I'm not sure yet, but I think it will involve your being the *bad cop* to my *good*. Are you up for that?"

Katya waited for me to look over at her before saying, "Always," with a gleam in her eye.

Chapter 61

Time Travel

AS WE MULLED OVER the upcoming confrontation with Vondreesen, our electronic guide took us off the main road and up into the wooded hills. "I've never been anyplace more beautiful," Katya said. "Not that I've been that many places."

"What about Paris?"

"Apples and oranges. Paris is man-made. This beauty is natural. But now that you mention it, with its colorful homes and rolling vineyards, Napa Valley fits the image I have of the French countryside."

"Did you grow up in Moscow?"

"I did. Spent my whole life there. Russia's not like the US. Here, you've got New York, but you've also got Washington, and Chicago, and LA, and Dallas, and Miami, and, and, and. They might not all be considered quite equal, but to each her own. In Russia, on the other hand, there's just Moscow. Everywhere else is, I don't know, Des Moines. I suppose St. Petersburg is like, say, Buffalo, but you get the point. Once you make it there you never think about going anyplace else domestic. Other than to the Black Sea for vacation. Or Paris," she added with a wink.

"What did your parents do?"

"My father was a geologist. He had a PhD from the Moscow School of Mines. My mother was a technical translator for the patent office. They were relatively prosperous, but not well-connected. When I got into MSU it was a big deal for them."

"You used the past tense."

"They passed away a couple of years ago."

"Siblings?"

"None."

None. Did I check that box now too? Or did forms have a *deceased* box for siblings? I wasn't sure. It was going to take a long time to adapt to my new status.

At a quarter to twelve, we rounded a bend on a quiet winding road and approached the last turn on our route, a few hundred yards from our destination. I stopped the Tesla beneath the arching bows of ancient oaks to study the turnoff that I presumed was Vondreesen's drive. Large blocks of chiseled gray stone flanked the entrance to an unnamed road like silent sentries. No name. No number.

"This is the place." I lowered the windows to inhale the fresh air, then checked the display on my phone. "Vondreesen's still here. Or at least his cell phone is."

Twitters of the biological variety emanated from sunny treetops all around us, but otherwise the scene was silent and serene. That changed when the Tesla's tires met the fine gravel of Vondreesen's oak-lined drive with a crunch that sounded like money.

The drive arced and rose and the woods gave way, yielding to sun-drenched fields on both left and right. They were planted with acres of new vines in long contoured rows, each wrapped in a brown tube to protect it from foraging beasts and birds.

"Oh my God," Katya said, as we crested the rise. "We *are* in the French countryside."

I eased off the gas and we crunched to a halt with wonder in our eyes. Rising above us in the midst of a clearing backed by an oak and evergreen forest was a castle the likes of which I'd only seen in storybooks and European travel brochures. "Vondreesen didn't just leave Silicon Valley when he retired. He left the twenty-first century."

Katya couldn't stop gawking. "Looks like a remnant of the Hundred Years War. Like it was lifted from the Loire Valley by a magical crane and dropped here six hundred years later."

"Moat and all."

We studied the spectacle in stunned silence for a few seconds. Square towers with crenelations and merlons rose forty feet to the left and right, while the central entryway was located on the second floor. It was reached by crossing a heavy timber drawbridge that sloped up across a moat, and was protected on both sides by a barbican. Katya asked, "What do we do now?"

"It's a bit extravagant, but at the end of the day it's just a house. We park and knock." I earned an elbow to the kidney by adding, "Just keep an eye out for archers."

The driveway wrapped around to the back of the castle, but I parked to the left of the drawbridge in a bump-out big enough to handle a dozen Teslas, or two dozen horses.

Katya wasted no time getting out of the car. "This is really cool and really creepy at the same time. And what's with the second-story entrance?"

"No weak zones on the first floor. Standard defense against barbarians."

We passed beneath the spikes of a wooden portcullis dangling above, and stopped before the massive arched oak door. True to form, there was no doorbell, although I detected electronic eyes cleverly concealed in caricatures carved into either side of the framework. A dragon and a frog. The knocker was a heavy ring of wrought iron, which I clinked three times. I half expected to hear the clank of armored footsteps, but got no response for what felt like an eternity. Then the door swung open with the grace and ease of a big bird's wing, and the king of the castle spoke—with a British accent. "Hello, Achilles."

Chapter 62

Block by Block

VONDREESEN GAVE KATYA a warm smile. "Hello Katya. Welcome. Won't you come in?" He still looked every bit a George Clooney twin, but he seemed to have lost the energetic glow that had radiated from his eyes. Perhaps retirement, while good for the spirit, took its toll on the soul.

He stepped back with a graceful move to reveal an attractive architectural amalgam of fifteenth and twenty-first-century styles. Or so I guessed, not having much experience with the former. "Still feels like you're outdoors, doesn't it?" Vondreesen said, closing the door. "It's the lighting. It's all indirect, and it uses full-spectrum bulbs that automatically adjust in brightness depending on the time of day. The chandelier is for show." He gave me a proud grin.

"The floors are original, and come from the same mix of stones as the walls, but I had them sliced thin and installed over heating elements. Now I've got the first castle in history with floors that are warm to the touch. But forgive me for prattling on. My new toys and I are still in the honeymoon phase."

I spun around, admiring the architecture. "Not at all. We're naturally curious. This is the first castle we've been to today."

"You're too kind." Vondreesen put a hand on each of our shoulders.

"The painting," I said, gesturing to the large oil that filled the wall between stairways arcing up to the left and right. "Is that Raphael's *St. George and the Dragon*?" Since this was Vondreesen's place, I wondered if it could be the original.

"Something about it doesn't feel quite right, eh?"

Man, was he good at reading people. "Yes, although I'm no expert."

"But your mind is trained to detect incongruity and remember detail. It's neither a copy nor a Raphael, but it is from his workshop. That's an original Penni. It's sixty-four times the size of Raphael's original work, and it's painted on canvas rather than wood. A great find. This way, please." He motioned to his right.

"So what's the story?" I said, spreading my arms.

"Can't a man have a castle without a story?"

"Not a chance. Not a thousand years ago. Not today."

"It was relocated and reconstructed by a French Baron and wine enthusiast named Crespin who fancied himself an entrepreneur. There's not a lot of innovative entrepreneurship going on in the French wine industry, so Crespin came to the land of opportunity. He tried to bring old-world charm to the new land, figuring that he could one-up all his competition by adding a new dimension to the wine tasting experience. He thought he could create the hottest vineyard in Northern California—a tourist attraction in addition to a tasting room."

"Kind of a Walt Disney approach."

"Indeed, although Disney chose a German castle. This was originally built in the fifteenth century in what's now a nowhere village in south-central France. He bought it for a song, and reassembled it here, block by block."

"So what happened?" Katya asked.

"He died and the project stalled. By the time his heirs quit quarreling, an Italian had beat them to the punch with *Castello di Amorosa*, which is an even grander castle not ten miles from here. The Crespin heirs missed the window of opportunity and were stuck with a pink elephant. Napa Valley doesn't need two medieval castles. I was looking for a place when it came on the market, and I liked the extra dimension it added. It's hard to beat for dinner parties, or for getting the grandkids to visit."

"It certainly has cachet."

Vondreesen gestured toward the staircase. "Please join me in the library. It's also rather special."

Chapter 63

Duped

VONDREESEN LED US up the left semicircular staircase, past St. George and the mammoth wrought-iron chandelier and through oversized double-doors into the grand library beyond, where polished hardwood floors and rich oriental rugs treated our eyes. Classic floor-to ceiling bookshelves surrounded us, complete with rolling oak ladders, but our eyes flew to the opposite wall and grew wide.

A glass, semicircular wall bowed out into the room, running floor to ceiling and dancing with flames. The enormous ultra-modern fireplace reminded me of a commercial aquarium, but with flames rather than fish. It was a spectacular centerpiece, and made the library a memorable place to entertain Silicon Valley's most distinguished. No doubt that was Vaughn's intent. "There's a natural gas field on the property," he continued, in answer to an unstated question. "It's not large enough to justify a commercial effort, but it is sufficient to keep the home fire burning for decades."

"Why are we hardly feeling any heat?" Katya asked, as we

accepted seats around the central of the three coffee tables situated before it.

"The glass wall is double-paned, with a vacuum in between, and the glass itself is coated with infrared film. I wouldn't mind a bit more heat myself, but it wouldn't be good for the books." He plucked a smoldering stogie from the oddest looking ashtray I'd ever seen, and took a puff to keep it lit. Following my eye toward the softball sized hunk of pockmarked stone, he said, "It's a moon rock."

"Never heard of them. Do they do something to the smoke?"

Vondreesen smiled at my misunderstanding. "It's literally a rock from the moon. A gift from … well, I shouldn't say."

"And you use it as an ashtray?"

"At first I just had it on the table for display purposes. Then a guest mistook it for an ashtray, and, well …"

He picked up the mini-tablet that lay beside the moon rock and asked us, "Coffee? Espresso? Something stronger?" He swiped the screen as if planning to place our order electronically.

I caught a glimpse of the display before his first stroke. It showed live images of the barbican from the dragon's and frog's points of view. Perhaps that explained why a man who lived in a castle and could order up drinks on a tablet would answer his own door. "Black coffee would be great. And I'm guessing Katya would appreciate some chamomile tea, if it's no trouble."

She gave me a smile. "Please."

Vondreesen tapped his screen. "Melanie, two black coffees and some chamomile tea, please."

He set the tablet down with a reverent touch of pride. "Now, how can I help you?"

This was the big moment.

The moment for which I'd traveled halfway around the world and back.

The moment that could change the course of my life, sending it either into the freedom of the open seas, or crashing onto the rocks. At the very least, Vondreesen's reaction would be a barometer of my odds of avoiding jail. "As you may be aware, I've been granted bail in order to investigate my family's death. In that context, I wanted to learn more about Vitalis Pharmaceuticals. Specifically, why it folded."

Vondreesen picked up his cigar, found it lacking, and rekindled it with a torch lighter. Turning to Katya he said, "No worries," and motioned upward with his chin. "The ventilation system scrubs the air."

Turning back to me, he nodded solemnly, a grave expression on his charismatic face. Compassion and wisdom, with perhaps a hint of fear around the corners of his eyes. "You think Vitalis might somehow be connected to your tragedy?"

"It's a common denominator, shared by both my father and my brother. The police are looking at me due to economic motives, so naturally I'm looking into others."

"I see. Well, as you pointed out, Vitalis folded. It's bankrupt. Its shares are virtually worthless."

"In the US. But what about abroad? We've learned that the clinical trial only wrapped up last week."

"Is that what this is about?" He leaned back and blew smoke for a couple of beats. "Megan told me you stopped by, which means you know my office is still working, even though I retired at the end of last year. I believe she explained the logic behind that decision to you?"

"That's right."

"Well, the same goes for Vitalis. The clinical trial was prepaid, and the Russian Ministry of Health requires follow through, so we let it play out. No reason not to. Plenty of reason to let it run. It's my fiduciary responsibility to recover whatever I can for my investors, and that includes the sale of assets. Clinical trial results fall into that category."

I kept a friendly expression, but put some bite in my tone. "I can see that. But you still haven't answered my original question." I didn't repeat it. Vondreesen knew full well what it was, and of course he knew exactly why Vitalis folded.

Just then a woman walked into the room through a large oak door to the right of the fire, carrying a silver tray with a matching teapot, a French press full of coffee, three bone china cups on platinum-rimmed saucers, and a silver bowl of coco-dusted chocolate truffles. Melanie looked like she might be Megan's sister, and I wonder if Vaughn had collected the set. She unloaded the tray onto the coffee table, smiling at Katya while setting down the truffles. She poured the tea and coffee, then disappeared without a word.

Glancing up from the table, Vondreesen seemed surprised to see us looking back at him. His eyes went back and forth between us as though he was searching for something. For a good five seconds, I watched him struggle mentally while his face turned from confused to panicked. Then all at once his eyes lit up and his normal expression returned. It was as though his mind had suddenly tuned back in to its previous channel.

He leaned forward and put his elbows on his knees, cupping his right hand over his left so the cigar jutted out like a lance. Meeting my eye, he said, "Vitalis folded because I got duped."

Chapter 64

Synthetic

I LEFT MY COFFEE where it lay, and repeated Vondreesen's words. "You got duped. My family was murdered, and you tell me 'you got duped.' What the hell does that even mean?"

Two men appeared in the same doorway through which Melanie had disappeared, like guard dogs sensing a threatening change in tone. They weren't wearing suit coats or wraparound shades, but otherwise they appeared to have come from the same store as our earlier acquaintances. It could be a coincidence. Google *bodyguard* and *big, beefy, crewcut* was the image you got, more often than not with a black suit and sunglasses.

But I wasn't a believer in coincidences.

A part of me wanted them to intervene, giving me a chance to turn this discussion into an interrogation after working off some pent-up aggression. But Vondreesen held up a palm, and they backed off through the door. The scene reminded me of the way some guys will pull back their coat to reveal a concealed carry. Tactically, it was just as stupid a move.

Vondreesen seemed to sense this and dove right into the answer to my question. "Brillyanc wasn't my creation, you understand. It was brought to me. I'm a venture capitalist, not a biomedical researcher. An investor, not an inventor."

It was sad to see the great Vaughn Vondreesen making excuses. But I wasn't going to let the sympathy card distract me. It did get me wondering, however, if the castle was the late-life crisis equivalent of the mid-life crisis Ferrari, or something else entirely. "Surely you performed due diligence? In-depth analysis before pouring in millions of OPM?"

Katya recoiled at my words. "Hold on. I didn't know Colin was working with narcotics. That adds a whole new dimension to things."

"Not opium," Vondreesen said. "O.P.M. Other People's Money. And Achilles, actually VC's invest all the time without knowing if a compound is going to work. You can't definitively determine the efficacy of a new compound without performing clinical trials, and clinical trials are very expensive. That said, efficacy wasn't the problem."

"It wasn't?" Katya and I said in chorus.

"No. Brillyanc works. Beautifully, in fact. The problem was its formulation."

It was my turn to recoil. "The formulation? You mean the list of ingredients? Surely you didn't invest without knowing that?"

"No, of course not. But as I said, I was duped. The formula we were given for due diligence wasn't the same as the formulation used in the previous clinical trials—the preclinical studies, and the Phase I and II trials. It was almost the same, but a couple of amino acid side chains were different, and they make all the difference."

"You're saying they disclosed actual clinical results, but shared the wrong formulation?"

"Exactly. And furthermore, as part of the deal, we agreed to continue with their contract manufacturer—who used the original formulation without our knowledge. The result was that we didn't detect the discrepancy until we were a year into it, and then only because Colin was at the top of his game."

"What does it matter? Once you found out, couldn't you switch to the correct formulation?"

"If only! But no. Two reasons. One was the patents, all of which were filed around the wrong compound. That was critical, but not necessarily lethal. The other, however, was vital." Vondreesen, relaxing a little now that his story was flowing, took a few long puffs on his cigar before continuing. "Ask yourself why the inventors would do that? Why would they pull a switcheroo?"

I was willing to play along for now. But I wouldn't be leaving without the answers I'd come for. Barbicans and black suits didn't frighten me. Life in jail did. "You implied that it wasn't patents. So I'd guess that it was to get you to pay for the clinical trials, but not actually own anything of value in the end." I felt I'd found a thread, so I shifted my gaze to the flames and kept pulling it. "They'd keep two sets of books, so to speak, and leave you holding the bad ones while they run off to the bank with the good ones." I saw it now. I was getting excited. "My brother discovered this. He told my dad. The inventors found out and killed them to keep the se–" I cut myself off. My hopes dashed. "They killed them after Vitalis folded. There was no secret to keep at that point."

Vondreesen grew a 'nice try' smile.

Katya threw her idea into the ring. "They knew you wouldn't invest if you knew the real formulation."

"Correct."

"Because there's something that would prevent you from marketing the real formulation. Something other than efficacy or intellectual property."

"Correct again."

Katya and I each stared into the flames, racking our brains. This wasn't a twist I'd anticipated. After a minute we looked at each other. Neither of us had a clue. I started thinking aloud. "You said the product works, so we'll assume there's demand. Unless the actual formulation is too expensive?"

Vondreesen shook his head. "The pricing is inelastic. There are enough buyers to support a healthy business at virtually any price point."

"Okay. Well, we also know they can manufacture it, so we'll assume there's supply. If it's not supply or demand, what's left?"

"A regulatory issue," Katya said.

"It's all of the above," Vondreesen said. "The difference between the formulations was the difference between *organic* and *synthetic*. The formula they showed us was synthetic. The actual formula is organic, and it can't be synthesized. At least not with current technology."

"So what? You told me that price doesn't matter."

"That's right. It's not an issue of price. It's an issue of source. Unlike, say insulin, which came from pigs and cattle before it was synthesized, one of Brillyanc's key ingredients comes from an endangered species. The gallbladder of a sun bear, to be precise. Sun bears are the small ones that look like Winnie the Pooh, by the way." He spread his arms wide and rolled his eyes. "So out of the blue, we found ourselves with an insurmountable supply issue, a potential demand issue, and a killer regulatory issue."

"Three strikes and you're out," I muttered, as the implications began crashing down like the big stone blocks of castle walls.

Chapter 65

Vanishing Act

VONDREESEN SHOWED SIGNS of relaxing after dropping his bomb. His complexion improved and his facial wrinkles faded. I suspected that my appearance had gone in the opposite direction.

"Three strikes and you're out," Vondreesen repeated. "That's exactly right."

"Four, now that I think about it," I added. "In addition to a supply issue, a demand issue, and a regulatory issue, the public-opinion referees have you for ethics violations to boot."

"No choice but to fold," Katya said. "Now I understand why Colin was so confident one day, and so despondent the next. There was nothing he could do about it."

"Was this why you retired?" I asked Vondreesen.

Vondreesen blew out smoke and shook his head at the memory. "It was humiliating and it was discouraging. I let a lot of people down."

"That explains everything. Everything except the most important thing." I turned in my chair to face Vondreesen full-on. "Why would they kill my family, if there was nothing to protect?"

Vondreesen shrugged. "I asked myself that question six months ago, when it happened, and I asked myself that question six minutes ago, when you arrived. I got the same answer both times. *They* wouldn't. I can only conclude that your family's death was not related to Vitalis."

If that was true, I was screwed. I had no other leads.

But I knew it wasn't true.

The murders of Dr. Tarasova and her husband made the

connection clear. "Who are *they*?" I asked.

"I'm afraid I can't tell you that."

"Can't, or won't?"

Vondreesen collapsed back into his chair, spreading his arms and exposing his chest with his hands extended well over the sides. "Anonymity was a big deal to them. Frankly, I don't think they even needed the money. What they needed was an American face. They chose mine, and I agreed because the product was so spectacular."

"You mean you let greed override your better judgment?"

Vondreesen met my verbal jab with a remorseful smile so genuine that it might have saved Nixon. What a politician. "You have to understand, that's what VC's do. We spend our lives looking for investments with the potential for phenomenal return. That's our opium. Our bliss and our addiction. Brillyanc was the biggest deal I saw in thirty years."

"Who are they?" I repeated.

"They're Russian. That's all I know. They did everything through an offshore corporation that no longer exists. The officers who signed the forms were straw men. Caribbean islanders paid for their time."

"Isn't that suspicious?"

"If you look at it as venture capital, it's atypical. But if you look at it as a large financial transaction by a wealthy party, it's commonplace. I wasn't suspicious until Colin made his discovery. Then they disappeared, and we shut it down."

"What do you mean, they disappeared?"

"Their phone number and email server went out of service. All contact was severed. Recourse became impossible."

"And all that happened before my family was murdered?"

"Months before."

I had no idea where to take the discussion. This wasn't what I was expecting—and apparently my Brillyanc had worn off. Suddenly I wasn't so sure about my decision to post bail.

I looked over at Katya. She nodded back at me. We were done here. "Thank you for your time, Vaughn. Enjoy your castle."

Chapter 66

Forgetfulness

WE SAT QUIETLY as I backed away from the moat and headed down the winding drive, the gravel crunching beneath the Tesla's tires while Vondreesen's words reverberated in our ears. The moment we touched pavement, however, Katya hit me with, "What did you think of Vondreesen's story?"

I replied in a tone that showed my frustration. "It explains everything, and it leaves us nowhere. I feel like a reporter who interviewed a presidential candidate. I know I've been fed a salad of truth and lies, but I'm struggling to separate the mix. What did you think?"

Katya twisted in her seat so that she could face me, and drew her knees up toward her chest. "The use of endangered species in medicine rings true enough. I'm not familiar with sun bears, but in Russia we hear about endangered fish often enough, due to our love of caviar. Sun bear gallbladder sounds like an Asian thing to me—lots of traditional medicine there for sure. Anyway, it would certainly explain Colin's reaction and Vitalis's sudden demise."

I concurred and watched picturesque vineyards roll by on the left and right. I was trying to remember something I knew I was forgetting. It wouldn't come. The memory-palace technique I'd drilled in prison only applied to things I deliberately worked to memorize.

The helpless frustration I was feeling made me think of Max, cut off from Brillyanc just shy of completing his dissertation. His words rang truer than ever: *I would pay anything.*

God, what a nightmare Alzheimer's must be.

I was sorely tempted to stop at one of the beautiful wineries we were passing for a glass of pinot noir and a few minutes of reflection, but we didn't have time. I'd have to hope the drive jogged my memory, and settle for whatever red they served on the plane.

I decided to attempt tricking my mind into relaxing. "Sun bears are the smallest bears, but they have the longest tongues for eating honey."

"How in the world do you know that?" Katya asked. "Did you used to work at a zoo?"

"No. I was into Winnie the Pooh as a kid. What did you think of the rest of Vondreesen's story?"

"I can't really speak to the whole investment part of the equation, but I believe Switzerland has one of the highest per capita GDP's on the planet, and their economy is based largely on secretive banking. So I suppose I buy that too." She looked back at me with her big amber eyes. "What's making you skeptical?"

"I'm always skeptical. What's bothering me is that Vondreesen's explanation is flawless. I don't like flawless. It implies engineering. Natural phenomenon are rough around the edges. They have imperfections, holes, and grit."

"He got duped. That's a pretty big hole."

"I buy that part. I'm just not sure about the details. I also don't believe that he doesn't know the identity of the Russian owner. He's too savvy to go for that."

"But?"

"But those are just feelings. Feelings are useless. We need facts. And I feel like I'm overlooking some of those. Speaking of which, did you catch that senior moment of his?"

"Right after Melanie dropped off the coffee. He seemed spooked by it. You think that may have contributed to his retirement decision?"

"It may have. It's certainly a confounding factor, and our investigation doesn't need any more of those. It also surprised me. The other times I met him he seemed, I don't know, superhuman. But for a second there I thought he was going to have a breakdown. Anyway, time to focus on the next meeting."

"Rita?"

"Exactly. By tomorrow night I have to become Chris Pine. That's not a lot of time."

"You already look like him. What else do you need?"

"I resemble him from across a room. I need to pass muster face to face. Plus, I need to brush up on his biography, and study any online videos of him I can find so that my behavior and mannerisms match. We don't know what kind of research Rita did, but whatever it was, I need to fit what she found."

"There's something else." Katya reached over and put her hand on my arm. She'd never touched me like that before. Not pointedly. Purposefully. It was something we both seemed to understand was best avoided.

"What's that?"

"I want to go with you to the pitch. I want to meet Rita."

I thought about the hand on my arm, while I contemplated my answer. "She made it clear that I was to come alone. That I couldn't mention this to anybody. But you know that, and you still want to go, which means you think your presence won't blow the deal. Why's that?"

Her hand didn't move. "Because I'm going to be just as strong a candidate for Brillyanc as Chris Pine is. I'll find someone I can play.

Someone equally bright and ambitious and no less bent on climbing a greasy ladder. Perhaps Chris's coworker. Bottom line, Rita's a salesperson, right? She's not the boss. Her mandate is to sell. Sure, she might have second thoughts about working with someone who's less than perfectly obedient. But once I'm there her options become *two sales* or *zero*."

Katya had some good points, but I wasn't sure how far she'd thought this through. "When I ran covert meetings like Rita's doing, if I saw that my contact wasn't following instructions, I wouldn't show. If Rita's tactics are similar, she'll never know that you're a perfect second sale."

Katya tilted her head. "You're testing me, aren't you?"

I winked back. "I want to help you think things through. My mentor, Granger, was always guiding me that way."

"That's easy enough to manage. I'll keep out of sight until Rita shows. Also, she must have come to expect a little disobedience from her clients, given the egos she's working with. Furthermore, we know what she's going to pitch, so we know I'm a fit. We don't have to worry about it being a guy thing or something in very limited supply. She'll want me as a client. But still, it's your call. You're the one looking at life behind bars. I'm thinking that I can help you, if I'm there by your side." She gave my arm a squeeze, and then withdrew her hand. "No pressure."

No pressure. Right. And oh, by the way, does this dress make me look fat?

Our arrival at SFO's rental car garage saved me from an immediate answer. Pulling up next to the yellow-shirted attendant, I had a thousand things on my mind, not the least of which was the warm feel of Katya's hand.

As I looked up at the attendant's smiling face, I finally remembered what I'd forgotten: returning a rental car was predictable. Detective Frost spoke to me over the barrel of his gun. "Kyle Achilles, you're under arrest."

Chapter 67

Bad Note

"WHAT'S THE CHARGE?" I asked Frost as he locked the cuffs around my wrists with a bit too much verve.

"Prison escape."

"I'm out on bail."

"No, you're not."

Frost's smugness made me want to kick his teeth in. I held back, as I was reserving the first couple of kicks for myself.

I'd screwed up big time. Twice. I'd made a predictable move, and I'd failed to factor banking delays into my thinking. It was only Thursday. My bail payment probably still hadn't cleared. I was no expert, but this felt like a legal gray zone. I definitely didn't have time for one of those.

Frost barked across the Tesla's roof at Katya. "Stay where you are, Miss Kozara. If you interfere in any way, I'll arrest you for obstructing justice."

I looked over at Katya. Tears were streaming down her cheeks. "Stick with the plan you proposed," I said, trying to sound optimistic. I'll work this out and catch up with you as soon as possible."

"Should I call Casey?"

"Yes, but don't miss the plane. The big clock is still ticking, regardless of my current situation. Please focus on that, and let me worry about this. Now go."

Frost spun me around before Katya replied, and started marching me in what I assumed was the direction of his hidden police cruiser. I didn't resist. Once my cuffs were on, he'd swapped his Glock for a Taser, and I was sure he wouldn't hesitate to use it.

"I'll see you soon," Katya called after me, her voice squeaky, but resolute.

"So, you are sleeping with your brother's wife." Frost smirked. "The jury was still out on that, so to speak. I'll be sure to let them know."

"Why are you doing this? I have a deal with the DA. She even instructed Kilpatrick and Flurry to support my investigation. Surely, you know that."

"I know no such thing."

I wasn't inclined to believe him, but couldn't be certain. Frost was behind me in a control position, so I couldn't see his face. "We agreed on the terms for my bail yesterday. I initiated the payment as soon as we were off the phone. It's a done deal."

"Perhaps this changes things."

That was my fear, although I was screwed either way. If I went to Santa Barbara rather than DC, I'd miss the meeting with Rita.

I decided to go on the offensive. Test some hunches. Shake things up. What did I have to lose? "You're acting alone, aren't you? You've gone renegade, looking for a win."

"Caught you all by myself."

"Kilpatrick isn't going to be happy that you went behind his back. Maybe you should call him now, before this goes any further."

"Kilpatrick isn't my boss."

"That may be true, but you both work for the mayor, and I'm sure he wants harmony, not renegades."

"You seem to think you're above the law, Mister Achilles. I'm here to tell you that owning a yacht doesn't make the legal system optional."

"And apparently having the title of detective doesn't mean you have a clue," I replied. To be honest, I understood Frost's point of view. But that understanding didn't change my situation. If I wasn't at Off the Record at eight o'clock tomorrow night, I'd lose my best link to the real killers. Then the clock would run out, and I'd be living under the heel of men like Frost and Grissel for the rest of my life.

Where was Frost's car? I was scanning the rows of parked cars ahead looking for government vehicles, when it hit me. "Did you fly here?"

"Straight from Vandenberg."

That was bad news.

I had to act quickly.

As we were passing one of the garage's supporting pillars, I stopped walking and turned to face Frost. "Where's Detective Flurry? I'm sure she's in the loop. Call her if you won't call Kilpatrick."

"Keep walking."

I stuck out my chest. "Flurry's what, ten years younger than you? Fifteen? But she makes you look like the rookie."

I did my best to look smug and egg Frost on while he blasted me with his rambling retort, but my mind was elsewhere and the words didn't register.

A handcuff key has more in common with a standard screwdriver than it does with the device that unlocks your door. Like standard screwdrivers, handcuff keys are essentially identical. Like all screwdrivers, handcuff keys are merely tools designed to apply torque. Just as you can use a coin or letter opener to turn a slotted screw, you can use another improvised torquing device to release a handcuff ratchet. All you need is a tool that fits the slot, and the knowledge of how to twist it.

I pulled a paperclip from my back pocket and quickly kinked it in the proper place for Smith & Wesson cuffs. Frost had double-locked them, so working the locks was painfully slow—about four seconds for the counterclockwise move that released the locking pin, and three seconds more for the clockwise twist that retracted the ratchet. Fortunately, Frost had more than seven seconds of blathering in him.

Palming the freed left cuff in my right, I tuned Frost back in, and prepared myself for the inevitable prompt. I didn't have long to wait.

"... I'm done with you. Now get moving."

I gave Frost a defiant stare for good measure and began pivoting to my right in compliance, only to stop almost immediately. "One more thing..." Reversing my pivot to face him again, I threw my left hand at Frost's Taser arm while my right swung for the left side of his head. It was a move similar to the sap strike that had failed me in the Escalade, but Frost didn't have the black suit's lightning reflexes, so this time the blow was true to its target. The impact of the handcuff was solid enough to hurt my hand, but nothing his thick head couldn't handle. Frost wobbled for a second or two, then his eyes rolled up, his knees gave way, and he dropped into my arms.

I hoisted the unconscious detective into the bed of a nearby pickup, and laid him on his left side in what EMTs call the recovery position, with his mouth down, chin up, and arms and legs in stabilizing positions.

Pulling the reporter's notebook from the breast pocket of his blazer, I began flipping pages. The last scrawled entry was, "Silver Tesla," followed by our rental's plate number. I tucked that informational nugget away for later analysis, and penned Frost a note with my left hand on the next blank page. "Sorry about the headache. I'll make it up to you when this is over."

Chapter 68

Conflicting Interests

"YOU LEFT HIM A NOTE?" Katya said, still beaming and unable to believe my sudden reappearance on the plane.

"The guy might be a stick in the mud, but he didn't deserve a club to the head. I'll do something to make it up to him once I'm free and clear of this mess. Maybe season tickets to the Lakers."

"Not the opera, or the Polo & Racquet Club?" She replied with a wink.

I'd just made our flight to DC. When I'd plunked down next to Katya, she'd been curled up in her seat, knees to chest and phone to ear, trying to get through to Casey for the twenty-third time. Now we were cruising at 36,000 feet and giddily sipping airline wine.

"Where'd you learn to pick handcuffs? Why'd you learn to pick handcuffs?" Katya asked, giddily.

I responded in kind. "There's a lot of sit-around-and-wait time during covert operations. Usually we sparred or goofed off, but sometimes we got more inventive. That particular trick came up when we were brainstorming on all the things you could do with a paperclip. There's quite a list, actually. An impressive enough list that I've kept a couple in my back pocket ever since. You can find paperclips everywhere, and take them anywhere, and they've got dozens of practical uses. Picking handcuffs with them was the most interesting. It began as a typical male *challenge-issued, challenge-accepted* thing with a former MP, but we all ended up spending hours learning to do it blind."

"I'll never look at a paperclip the same." Katya's face clouded over as she spoke. "Wait a minute. Won't Frost have people waiting for you when we land in DC?"

"That's a distinct possibility. But I doubt it. I don't think he'll have either the time or the inclination."

"Really? It won't take him long, now that he knows the name you're using. From the rental car, I mean."

"There's still a lot of bureaucracy to press through, and it's only a five-hour flight. But I'm guessing he won't even try."

"Why ever not?"

"Couple of factors. First, he was acting alone, trying to be the hero, trying to upstage Flurry. I don't think anyone else knew what he was doing. Not Flurry or Kilpatrick anyway. So nobody is expecting an update. Why admit an embarrassing failure if you don't have to? 'Guess what? I caught him, but then he got away.' I don't think so. That goes against human nature. Second, once my wire transfer completes, I'll be out on bail. So they'd be doing my in-processing and out-processing simultaneously. That won't be good for Frost's reputation."

"In other words, you've got pride and practicality working for you."

"And spite working against me."

"So it all boils down to Frost's character."

"Exactly."

Katya finished off her Chardonnay before speaking again. "Assuming Frost's character goes your way, is it still okay with you if I come along to the meeting with Rita?"

"If you can find a solid fit, I'd love to have you by my side. But that's no small order. Remember, on top of everything else, the person you're impersonating will need to be unreachable, presumably traveling overseas. You better get started right away."

Katya did, right there on the plane using inflight Wi-Fi. By the time we arrived at Washington National, she'd found her woman.

Then we learned that Frost's pride and practicality had won out over his spitefulness. As our taxi pulled away from Washington National Airport beneath overcast skies, I thought I saw the clouds parting ahead. But maybe that was an illusion.

Chapter 69

Rules

BEFORE I KNEW IT, I was headed for the Hay Adams, free on bail, with Katya by my side. Or should I say Chris was headed there, with Alisa. I had a fresh haircut with a bit of premature gray on my temples and some makeup that altered the shape of my face and diminished my dimple. Katya was now a brunette with shoulder-length hair and black Versace glasses. We went early and entered separately, so that we'd be properly positioned when Rita arrived.

Off the Record was known as Washington's best place to be seen and not heard. It had dim lights and wood-paneled walls and plenty of plush alcoves upholstered in red. Katya went to the bar while I grabbed a corner booth. I scooted over so that it would be easy for Katya to slip in beside me once Rita took the opposite seat.

Ambient jazz music played in the background, just loud enough to keep quiet conversations private without being obtrusive. I didn't recognize the artist's sultry voice. I don't have a memory for that kind of thing, but I loved the way it melted into the piano and double bass like a dab of churned butter on a sizzling steak. I had the waitress bring me a club soda with lime, and studied the other patrons while waiting for Rita to arrive.

At the bar, lawyers and lobbyists were buzzing around Katya like yellow jackets smelling grilled meat. She was holding her own, fending them off without offending. No doubt the result of years of practice.

At precisely eight o'clock, a woman I pegged as Rita glided through the doorway like she was expecting to fuck the president. Confident. Poised. And sexy as hell.

I estimated that her outfit cost six-figures, including a low-cut couture suit of fine cream-colored wool, pumpkin-toned heels with a matching bag, and heavy gold jewelry splashed with diamonds. Rita herself had sparkling green eyes, suntanned skin, and dark hair coiffed up to reveal a long and slender neck. Marilyn Monroe and Jackie Kennedy rolled into one—here to meet me.

Here to make a sale.

She'd sold me and she had yet to say word one.

I stood as she spotted me and walked toward our booth. "I'm Rita, and I'm glad you came." It was the British voice from the phone. She held out her hand. A French manicure and a bracelet that likely cost as much as the average car. As soon as we were seated, Katya slid in beside me and extended her own hand. "I'm Alisa."

Alarm crossed Rita's face like the passing shadow of a predatory bird, but she took Katya's hand. "Pleased to meet you."

"Alisa is also an ambitious junior partner at Kenzie," I said. "She's a Princeton PhD with two great talents: predicting competitive reactions, and climbing greasy ladders."

"We're a team of sorts," Katya said, mimicking Rita's poise and confidence. "We serve as each other's sounding boards, and help each other out behind the scenes. Kind of a secret alliance."

I leaned closer to Rita. "So whatever your career-enhancing service may be, she'll be equally interested. I'm sure that with a little research you'll find that Alisa is every bit as attractive a candidate as I am. So I figured you'd be happy to include her—and double your commission check."

Rita processed this like Miss Manners finding an unexpected crunch in her food. A dab of distaste and a smidgeon of surprise, but she swallowed and smiled. "What's your last name, Alisa?"

"Abroskina. As you may have guessed from my accent, I'm originally from Russia."

"And yet you graduated Princeton, with a PhD no less. Most impressive. When were you born?"

Katya gave her Alisa's DOB.

"If you'll excuse me for a minute, I'll be right back." Rita got up and made for the door.

"Do we follow her?" Katya asked.

"We stay. She's not leaving."

"How can you be sure? I'm sorry. I shouldn't have pushed for this. That was selfish of me."

"I think you sold her. I was watching her body language. Once she got past the initial shock, she was leaning in and analyzing, not leaning out and thinking about escape. And I didn't detect deception when she said she'd be right back. There was an apologetic intonation. Slight, but detectable. She went outside to check you out. She's being cautious."

"I hope you're right."

Rita didn't return in a minute. She didn't return in two, or three, or ten. But after twelve minutes she walked back in, just like before, the belle of the ball. She slid back into her seat, proffering a stern smile. "There are rules."

Chapter 70

The Pitch

RITA MET EACH of our eyes in turn, her gaze suddenly as serious as a sphinx. "I'm making a special exception for you. A big exception. Fortunately for you and me, there is a precedent for allowing multiple members of the same organization to become clients. But as you will see, we are adamant about our rules. I need to advise you that no further exceptions will be made."

I didn't blink. "We understand."

"Very well. Rule One is Absolute Secrecy. The reasons for that will become clear shortly, but I need to get that on the table up-front. Think of it as joining the KGB. I'd say CIA, but American-style secrecy doesn't conjure up quite the same vision as the old Soviet-style. You have to accept that you will never be able to discuss what you are about to learn with anyone. Ever. And for what it's worth, you won't want to."

Rita paused to look us each in the eye. "Assuming I can deliver what I promised, are you okay with that? Please consider your answer as seriously as you would an oath of office."

"We deal with confidential client information all the time," Katya said, as we'd rehearsed. "Some of which is quite inflammatory. We're comfortable with this version of attorney-client privilege, assuming the business is legitimate."

Rita looked at me.

I nodded.

"Very good. Forgive the theatrics. You'll understand them in a moment. Now let me ask you," Rita said, leaning in. "If you had to name the one quality your firm's global managing partner possesses that got him to the position he holds today, what would it be?"

"Easy enough. He's affable and well-connected, but the driving distinction is the perception that he's always the smartest person in the room."

"Precisely. Thank you for doing my job for me. That's what I have to offer. I can make you the two smartest people in virtually any room." Rita leaned back, and gave what appeared to be a prearranged signal to our passing waitress.

"Literally, or figuratively?" I asked. "Are you selling covert information, or improved cognition?"

"You both hold advanced degrees from Ivy League universities and fast-track positions at the most prestigious consulting firm on the planet. That puts your IQ's somewhere in the range of 140, or 1 in 200. Sound about right?"

We nodded, our eyes locked on hers in rapt attention.

"I can take your IQs to 160. From 1 in 200 people, to 1 in 20,000. Add in your good looks, strong interpersonal skills, and killer work ethic, and you'll truly be one in a million."

"How's that possible?" Katya asked after a suitable period of stunned silence.

Rita was all too ready with the answer. "A new pharmaceutical. A very exclusive, very expensive new pharmaceutical. Which brings us to the next bridge you need to cross if we are to proceed."

"The cost," I said.

Rita smiled. "As junior partners at Kenzie, you're earning somewhere in the neighborhood of half a million, all in. Once you move up to partner, you'll begin earning twice that amount. And then five, ten, and even twenty times as much as you move into and through the director ranks. You know all this. It's why you're there. It's the dream. The dream, as you now see, that I can virtually guarantee." She grinned wryly.

"The cost of that dream is, of course, commensurate with the benefit. Something I'm sure you, as management consultants, can appreciate. It's ninety thousand dollars a quarter."

"That's a thousand dollars a day." I blurted my calculation a bit louder than intended. Perhaps not a bad thing. I'd fully expected a large number, but wasn't really prepared for that one. The $180,000 I'd need to cover Katya's and my first dose was virtually everything I had left after bail and this operation's other expenses.

Rita didn't miss a beat. "Roughly one-fourth the amount Kenzie charges clients for your services. Surely you wouldn't expect to pay less?"

Chapter 71

Meritocracy

THE WAITRESS ARRIVED carrying a shiny silver bucket pebbled with condensation. She set a crystal flute before each of us, and then set about unwrapping and popping the cork. Cristal Champagne, I noted. Probably costs north of $400 a bottle here. Nothing next to the $720,000 annuity Rita had just pitched, but noteworthy nonetheless.

Once the flutes were bubbling away before us and the server had moved on, I said, "You know we can afford it, but you also know that it will be a struggle at this point in our careers. You timed your pitch to ensure our complete dedication to maintaining the integrity of your system."

"I timed it to help you make the biggest leap of your careers. A single promotion at this point is worth as much as all your other advances combined." Rita picked up her flute. "Is that a financial commitment you'd be willing to take? We can either drink to your careers, or we can end the discussion here and just enjoy a nice bottle of bubbly. It's entirely up to you."

She was smooth. The perfect recruit for her job. Whoever had hired Rita knew his stuff. "You tell a good story," I said. "But how do we know there's more to it than that? Talk is cheap."

"You will, of course, have the opportunity to try before you buy. But we need to know you're committed before crossing that bridge. To put it in your parlance, we'd want a figurative LOI from you, a Letter of Intent. Your agreement to proceed at the terms discussed, assuming the product passes your scrutiny."

Katya and I looked at each other, then down at our glasses. We picked them up, and Katya said, "Here's to our careers."

The Cristal was delicious. Crisp and dry, yet smooth and buttery with a honeyed aroma that reminded me of a garden restaurant I'd visited on the Cote d'Azur. I wasn't sure if it was worth twenty bucks a swallow, but it sure beat prison fare. "How does this new pharmaceutical of yours work?"

Rita set her glass down. "An inquisitive mind. Why am I not surprised? There are two other hurdles I want to be sure you're comfortable with, before we come to that. There's a practical issue, and a philosophical one. First, the philosophical." Rita paused, meeting my gaze.

"The manufacturer has weighed the options and decided that Brillyanc—that's the name of the pharmaceutical—will be reserved for the elite. The true ruling class. They believe there's a line beyond which a democracy must yield to a meritocracy, and Brillyanc is on the other side of that line. Put another way, access to Brillyanc will be like one of Washington's exclusive clubs, where you need both an invitation to join, and the funds to do so."

Rita gave us a just-look-around-you gaze. "Now, while Brillyanc is not a club, it's also not like other pharmaceuticals. It's not medicine. It doesn't remedy a malady. There's no condition it's fixing or preventing. Everyone can live a normal, healthy life without it. Just like everyone can live without a Metropolitan Club membership." Rita paused to look at each of us. "Are you with me?"

"We understand," Katya and I replied in chorus.

"Good. Given that, the manufacturer believes there's no moral obligation to supply it to anyone. Or even to make it accessible to the majority of the population. They acknowledge, however, that the argument could be made that the greater good would be served if we were to put it in the water supply, so to speak. Like fluoride.

"With Brillyanc, we have the power to raise the IQ of the entire population, the whole human race. We could boost mankind a few rungs higher on the evolutionary ladder. But we're choosing to be selective instead. We're going surgical, rather than systemic." Again, she paused to aid our digestion.

We remained silent.

"If word of Brillyanc were to get out, the argument for widespread distribution would surely be made. Loudly and frequently. There would also be outrage regarding the pricing, since the vast majority of the population couldn't afford it even at one-tenth the price. Both of these would eventually lead to backlash against Brillyanc users. There would be witch hunts fueled by fear and jealousy."

"Like the X-Men comic books," I said.

Rita raised her sculpted eyebrows. "Exactly. So the manufacturer is not going to be marketing the product publicly, and therefore will not be seeking regulatory approval. You need to be going into this with eyes wide open. You need to be philosophically comfortable with the meritocracy approach. And you need to be one hundred percent committed to maintaining our secret, recognizing that there could be devastating personal consequences if it ever came to light."

"Why so harsh?" I asked, curious as to how much Rita would reveal.

"Not harsh. Balanced. You'd be betraying a network of the world's most powerful people, and putting billions of dollars at risk.

"So we're all in it together," Katya said. "KGB style."

"Are you okay with that?" Rita asked.

"We're used to taking risks to reap rewards," I said. "To dancing close to the line if that's what it takes to win. We know it's a dog-eat-dog world. And we're comfortable with our positions atop the food chain. What's the practical issue you referenced?"

"The practical issue," Rita repeated, her voice switching from belligerent to bemused. "That's the best part."

Chapter 72

Perks

RITA TOPPED OFF our champagne flutes, but set hers down without imbibing. "The practical issue involves the drug's administration. Once a quarter, you'll need to free up a weekend to get your Brillyanc infusion. Specifically, the second weekend of the second month of each quarter. Is that something to which you can commit?"

"We have pretty busy travel schedules," I said. "Is there any flexibility?"

Rita pursed her lips and twisted her neck to look down to the left. "Not much. The last weekend of the first month of the quarter is the only alternative, but that's on the West Coast. Over the next year we'll be adding options on other weekends, probably in Dallas and Chicago, but for now it's just DC and San Francisco on the schedule I mentioned."

She paused, and her face brightened. "Trust me, after you try it once, you'll be happy to do whatever it takes to make it thereafter. It's an unforgettable event.

"The magic begins with the pre-party. Imagine what we're talking about here." Rita flared her hands and fingers like a starburst as her voice took on the excitement of a game show host. "We're bringing together a group of the wealthiest, most powerful people in America, and we're doing it in a context where everyone wants to remain anonymous. So, we turn it into a party, the likes of which, trust me, you've never experienced. Even a Kenzie annual director's retreat wouldn't compare.

"First of all, everyone wears a costume we provide. It is a

medical procedure, after all. But rather than an extra-large back-split cotton smock, you're wearing tailored black silk pajamas and Zorro-style masks to conceal your identity." Addressing Alisa, she asked, "Can you get by without your glasses? The mask will work much better without."

"No problem."

"Good. Picture yourself walking into a cocktail party the likes of which is suitable for a gathering of captains of the universe. The Cristal will be flowing freely, along with every other exquisite indulgence known to man. Some simply treat it like an exclusive costume party. Most guests, however, take it further. Imagine how the emperors partied near the end of the Roman Empire and you'll have some idea. Combine that with the fact that everyone there is, shall we say, healthy and energetic and high on the good life, then throw in the anonymity, and most tend to lose the pesky inhibitions that constrain us in our daily lives."

Rita brought her hand down to the top button of her blouse while giving us a minute to let our imaginations run with that imagery.

Mine surely did.

"People arrive for the party between six and midnight, and then filter back to the infusion room as early as ten and as late as four in the morning to begin their overnight procedure. At that point, they're as carnally satisfied as they've ever been in their lives." She paused to take a slow sip of champagne before shifting gears.

"Now, let me tell you what's involved in the procedure itself. Brillyanc is a parenteral, so it's infused intravenously. The infusion process takes six hours, during which you'll be hooked up to an IV. Rather than a hospital bed, however, you'll enjoy a setup similar to a first-class transoceanic flight. Very chic and comfortable. After six relaxing hours, you'll be good to go for another three months. How's that sound?"

"That, uh ... sounds better than what I was expecting," I said.

"Trust me. Whatever you're imagining, it's better."

"You'll be there?"

"Best job perk in the world."

"Is it safe?" Katya asked. "Brillyanc, I mean. Not the sex."

"Totally. It naturally enhances your metabolism in a way that supplies the brain with a richer, cleaner supply of fuel. I know that sounds funny, but only until you think about it for a second, then you realize that your cognitive powers are always in flux based on how much sleep or exercise you're getting, or what you're eating or drinking." Rita raised her glass. "Right?"

"Sure. I get that," I said. "Tell me, our job requires occasional drug testing. Will anything show up there?"

"No. The only thing that will potentially test differently is your cholesterol level. If your LDL and triglycerides have increased over time, they'll drift back down as a result of your metabolic improvements. No extra charge for that."

"Is it addictive?" Katya asked.

Rita smiled—no doubt reflecting on her commission checks. "Not physically. But once you try it, you won't want to live without it."

Chapter 73

The Big Question

YOU WON'T WANT TO LIVE WITHOUT IT. I wondered if that was just an expression. I decided it was. Rita seemed genuinely excited about it, and Max and Saba had been disappointed at losing their supply, but not suicidal. "Who invented it?"

My question soured Rita's sweet expression, if only for a second. "I don't know. I'll be frank with you—this experience is like joining the Manhattan Project. The level of secrecy, I mean. We're working in a highly regulated field without an approved product, so we have to fly under the radar. On top of that, and again like the Manhattan Project, we're working with a secret weapon."

"A secret weapon?" Katya repeated.

"Brillyanc gives you the power to trounce your competition. So you'll be guarding that secret like a winning lottery ticket. That said, like using the atomic bomb, there are ethical issues. It could be considered cheating, or worse. So Brillyanc is not for the faint of heart. It's for people who are willing to do whatever it takes to succeed. True leaders, like Truman. The planet's elite."

Rita drained her glass and set it down. "That's my pitch. I know it's a lot to think about."

"Not really," I said. "When you're climbing a ladder as greasy as ours, that's all you think about. You work hard. You work smart. You make sacrifices. And you take every advantage you can get."

"Exactly," Katya said.

Rita looked back and forth between us both. "Well, all right then. The sample doesn't require a six-hour infusion. It's a shot. It will make you Brillyant for about four days, but I'll give you a week to decide if you want to go ahead. That way you'll also have a few days to begin missing your new superpower after it wears off. I'll call you exactly seven days from now, at which point you'll tell me *yes* or *no*. If *yes*, I'll give you a bank account number and you'll have 48 hours to deposit your first payment. If *no*, or if the funds don't arrive, you'll never hear from me again and the opportunity will be lost to you forever. Sound fair?"

"Sounds fair," we both said.

"Excellent. Well, I was taught to stop talking once I made a sale so I'll do that. I have a room upstairs if you'd like–" Rita had started to rise, but cut herself off and plopped back into her seat. "I only have one sample with me."

"Can we split it?" I asked. "Will that give us each a couple of days of Brillyanc?"

Rita brought forefinger to chin. "I believe the titration curve is more or less linear, so that should work. There's a bit of a ramp on either side, so you may only get the full effect for a day, but in my experience, that's really all it takes to seal the deal. Do you think a day will be enough to convince you?"

"We're pretty quick with the data processing," Katya said. "Which brings me to a question. Why not give weekly shots instead of a quarterly infusion?"

Rita was ready for that one. "The logistics don't work, given the amount of confidentiality and control required. Shall we go?" She stood, handed our waitress a stack of hundreds, and headed for the door. Not the first time she'd done this.

Walking through the lobby of the Hay Adams toward the elevators with two of the most beautiful women on the planet, I was struck by a feeling I knew I'd never forget. For those thirty seconds or so I was *that guy*. The man all others envied. Or so it appeared. As we passed a large wall mirror, I took mental photos for my album. Gathering the rosebuds while I may. If I was going to be spending the rest of my life behind bars, well, this was one record that was going to get a lot of plays.

The Hay Adams was, quite simply, the pinnacle of elegance. You can't trump a hotel that looks over the White House when it comes to glamour or prestige. Rita's room was neither glamorous nor prestigious, as its large third-floor windows looked out over a courtyard at other windows, but it was plenty elegant. Traditional decor in espresso hues, with a molded ceiling, and a queen-size bed covered in enough thick linens and puffy pillows to make you want to leap and bounce.

A sofa was positioned at the foot of the bed. Before it, the room's only light shone down on a glass coffee table. Rita led us right to it.

I took the middle seat, which wasn't optimal for talking. My relative size made me a wall of sorts between the women, as was my intent. Despite her charms, Rita was the enemy, and I wanted to shield Katya.

Rita set her small, pumpkin-toned purse on the table where it seemed to glow like a log on a fire. She flipped the gold clasp, and withdrew a couple of alcohol swabs and a Romeo & Julieta cigar tube. Noting my appraisal, she said, "Camouflage, always camouflage."

She unscrewed the little aluminum lid, tilting a filled syringe out onto her palm where it looked innocuous as baby vaccine. Then she asked the big question. "You ready to up your game? Ready to become one in a million?"

Chapter 74

Adroitly Ambitious

RITA'S INJECTION PROCEDURE was reminiscent of a phlebotomist drawing blood, except this was a deposit rather than a withdrawal. A small deposit. The syringe was just two cc's and I only got half. Katya was watching me wide-eyed the whole time, as though my transformation would be visual.

"That's all there is to it," Rita said. "You'll be a different person when you wake up in the morning."

As Katya and I switched positions on the couch, I asked, "Is there some test we should be doing to calibrate?"

Rita paused and looked up from the alcohol swab. "Good question. It's not a shades-of-gray difference. The change is dramatic enough that there's no need for a validated questionnaire like you'd be taking if this were, say, an Alzheimer's screening. You can test-drive your new neural performance any number of ways, and the neat part is that I don't need to tell you what they are. You'll know. Which, ironically, is a form of calibration in and of itself."

I was beginning to think this might be real. So far, I'd been intuitively assuming there was some trick involved. "How long have you been using it?" Katya asked, as the needle pierced her flesh.

"No personal questions. That's Rule Two: Complete Anonymity. You remember Rule One?"

"Absolute Secrecy," we said in chorus.

"Good. You'll get Rule Three when you show up for your first infusion. Or rather, on the way there."

"Speaking of which," I said. "I'd like to participate in the infusion event this weekend on the West Coast. I have a big presentation coming up in a week. Career making or breaking. So I'd love it to be Brillyant."

Rita mulled that over for a second. Looked like she hadn't received that question before. It would lock in a double commission check. I watched her struggle, but lose the fight. "I wish I could help you, but payment is required in advance. Since it's Friday night, your funds won't arrive before Monday. I learned the hard way that while many private banks work Saturdays, wire transfers don't post when the federal banks are closed."

"Suppose we were to make the transfer together, right now, using my phone?" I pulled my iPhone out of my breast pocket. I had prepared it ahead of time, as well as Katya's. Setting it on the table, I invited Rita to watch as I unlocked it with one-zero-one-zero.

"Ten-ten. Your birthdate."

"You really have done your homework."

While I logged into my numbered, offshore account, Katya extracted her own phone, pulled up a blank note, and offered it to Rita. "This will help. You can enter your account info here. That way, we'll have it for future transfers as well."

Rita's head moved back and forth between us. "You two really are on the same page." She took the phone, keying in routing and account numbers.

"You have it memorized," I said. "I'm impressed."

Rita didn't look up from her task while replying. "Wait till you see what you can do once you're Brillyant. Ten-ten will be way behind you." She finished typing and returned the phone to Katya, who set it carefully on my thigh where I could read it.

I keyed in the transfer order. "Since it's a numbered account, I put Alisa Abroskina and Chris Pine in the memo line." I presented it to Rita. "If that looks right, go ahead and hit the *send-funds* button."

She took the phone from me and studied it carefully. Not just the payee details but the website address as well. She looked up. "Looks good." She made a point of pressing send. Then she watched the transaction complete and returned the phone, which I slid gingerly back into my outer breast pocket.

"It's a good day for you," I said. "Two for one, with both signed, sealed, and delivered."

Rita returned a genuine smile. She was beautiful, and seemed sincere. "This brings us to our last point of business, a week ahead of schedule. Tomorrow evening at six o'clock a limo will meet you curbside outside Door One on the departures level of the domestic terminal at SFO. You got that?"

I repeated it back.

Katya asked, "How do we dress?"

"It doesn't matter. You'll be given a new wardrobe to change into in the car. You'll also be leaving everything with your driver. Jewelry. Cell phones. Everything. Anonymity is our first concern."

"That sounds kinda creepy," Katya said.

"Wait until you get there. You'll find it tremendously liberating. It's amazing what absolute anonymity will do for you. In fact, Alisa, for that very reason, I'd suggest that you go to the event here. Let Chris go to SF by himself. It's best if you don't know anybody, and nobody knows you."

"No worries there," I said. "We're not involved. Our relationship is strictly, shall we say, Machiavellian."

"As you wish. Just a suggestion, from experience."

"What if we have questions?" Katya asked.

"Ask them now. Once you go out the door, you'll never see or hear from me again. Rule Two."

"How did you find me?" I asked. "What made you pick me from the phonebook?"

"Rule One, Chris. But you should consider it an honor. It's not quite the Nobel Prize, but we're far more selective than either your employer or your alma mater. Anything else?"

"Yes. What do you do when people decline? Either after the initial pitch, or after the free sample?"

"It's never happened." Reading my incredulous expression, Rita added, "I'm very selective in whom I approach. I don't just look for people with sufficient income at the right point in their careers. I also look at character. I only approach people who are adroitly ambitious."

"How do you know if someone is *adroitly ambitious*?" Katya asked.

Rita looked down as the right side of her mouth drew back in a smile. Then she looked back up to meet each of our eyes in turn as hers glowed with intelligence. "It's a demonstrable quality. Picture a politician weathering a sex scandal. Or a CEO fighting corruption charges. Or a trial attorney defending a wealthy killer. In your case, Alisa, you hired a Russian hacker known as *Sciborg7* to identify and alter competing admissions applications at Princeton."

Katya was so into her role as Alisa that she blushed at Rita's revelation, while I let my eyes grow wide in wonderment. Rita had discovered that scandalous secret in just a few minutes. She had to be plugged into a resource that rivaled my CIA system. This added a new dimension to things, but I couldn't dwell on it now. "What would you do if someone declined? If they walked away?"

"And went to the authorities? To the police or FDA?" Rita clarified.

I nodded.

"Nothing."

"Nothing?"

"We'd do nothing because that's exactly what the authorities would do: nothing. What would they really have to investigate? No product. No company. No witnesses. Nothing but crazy talk." She canted her head and shrugged with open palms. "Anything else?"

She had a point. Anyone whose house had been robbed or car

stolen knew that if there wasn't blood on the ground, nobody really cared.

Rita stood and we followed suit. I wasn't sure if we'd been foolish or brilliant, but we were one step closer to the truth, the truth that was trying to kill us.

Chapter 75

White Powder

WE LEFT RITA in her room and caught a cab to a Thai restaurant near Chris's apartment. Tam yum soup and a red curry dish to go. I wanted to get some non-alcoholic calories in us, and Katya was in the mood for spicy.

The wait for our order gave me time to confirm that we hadn't been followed, five minutes of which I used to visit the corner drugstore and make a few purchases. Confident that we were clean, we returned to our neighboring hotel suite with Thai in tow. "Feeling Brillyant?" I asked, while snicking the deadbolt into place.

"Feeling hungry."

"You go ahead and start. I want to check the prints."

Katya pushed the food bag. "I gotta see this. The soup will wait."

I removed a bottle of talcum powder, a big blush brush, and a can of compressed air from the drugstore bag. Then I gingerly slid the iPhone from my breast pocket, holding it only by the edges as I had when giving it to and taking it from Rita.

Katya placed hers on the table beside mine with similar care.

"I'm a bit surprised we got these," I said, delicately pouring talcum powder onto the shined surface of the dark wooden desk. "When I saw her using the cigar tube, I concluded she'd been schooled in tradecraft, but apparently it wasn't an extensive course."

I dabbed the blush brush into the talc, just enough to dust it. I'd selected the brush with the longest bristles I could find, but their grouping was still a bit dense. Using pressure as light as hummingbirds' breath, I swirled the brush around the front surface of both iPhones. The white powder revealed multiple partial prints on the bottom half of my screen, including a decent index pad in the right corner. As Katya leaned over my shoulder, I said, "That's from when she hit send."

Katya's phone had fewer prints, but we knew they were all Rita's. The jewel there was an upside-down thumbprint on the top, from when she'd handed it back. Satisfied with the dustings I'd applied, I held the compressed air can about a foot above the phone and began dispensing micro bursts through the straw, a half-second puff at a time until most of the non-adhered powder was gone.

Katya watched with fascination. "Wow! Looks good."

"White powder on black glass is about as good as it gets. I don't think fingerprinting was what Steve Jobs had in mind when designing his phones, but he got it right."

I put the camera on Katya's phone in macro mode, snapped a few pictures of the index print on my phone, then reversed the procedure and captured the thumb off hers. I used AirDrop to get both photos on my phone, and then enhanced the contrast. "We got lucky. It's better than I'd hoped. This will definitely do it if her prints are in the system."

"You think they will be?"

"She's got a British accent. If she's living here and hasn't been an American citizen since birth, she should be. We print most foreigners entering the country these days, and everyone applying for a work or immigration visa. Most professional licensures require it as well, although I'm not sure about pharmaceutical reps."

"Surely you don't think Rita's licensed?"

"Not for her current job, of course. But I'd wager she used to be legit. The pharmaceutical industry is famous for using sharp, attractive young women for reps. The way she talked about titration curves and validated questionnaires makes me think she's experienced. If I were looking for someone to sell Brillyanc, that's where I'd go to recruit."

"How long will it take to check?"

"It's usually just minutes, given computer speeds these days. The FBI processes about a hundred million fingerprint checks a year, so it's got to be quick. Their algorithms have gotten really good too. With latent prints like these, their accuracy is up over ninety percent."

I was navigating my way back through my magic CIA portal, typing while I spoke. "Why don't you get our tickets back to San Francisco while I input this. Then we'll be done for the evening and can enjoy our dinner."

I finished before Katya, and laid our food out on the table.

"How's a noon flight sound?" she asked. "Gets us there at three. I figure we'll want some buffer in case there's a delay."

When I didn't respond, she looked over at me. "What?"

"We already got a match on Rita."

Chapter 76

Dangerous Territory

KATYA'S FACE REFLECTED her marvel at the power and speed of the technology I'd employed. "Who is she? Is Rita her real name?"

I read from the fingerprint analysis report. "Margaret Rosen. Birthdate is July 30, 1988. Born in London, England. Granted an F1 student visa in 2004 to attend Columbia University. Granted permanent residency in 2014. At that time, she had a New York City address. Her employer is listed as Bricks, the pharmaceutical multinational. No criminal record."

"Anything else?"

"That's all the good stuff the FBI has, other than her social security number. I'm sure Homeland Security has extensive biographical files as a result of her immigration applications, but I'm not going to bother with that now. We've got a back door into their organization if we need it."

"If we need it?"

"If tomorrow's assault doesn't work."

Katya started in on her soup. "What did you think of her pitch?"

"I thought it was masterful. She sold me, despite the exorbitant price. I'd bet she really does bat 1000."

"But?"

"Her pitch was seamless, like Vondreesen's, but it was also fundamentally different from Vondreesen's. No mention of sun bears. Makes me wonder."

"Wonder what?"

"We've heard two entirely different reasons why Brillyanc is kept secret. Vondreesen's endangered-species explanation, and Rita's backlash-avoidance explanation. Both fit perfectly. Both feel authentic."

Katya set her spoon down and brought her hand to her chin. "There's no reason they both can't be true. They're not mutually exclusive. Perhaps they keep it simple, and just mention the one most meaningful to the recipient. Endangered-species for investors, and backlash-avoidance for users."

"Could be. I just wonder if we have the whole truth between those two parts, or if there's more. I wonder if the Russians are playing Rita, the way they did Vondreesen."

"I think you're over-analyzing."

"We'll find out tomorrow night."

"Do you think the Russians will be there?"

"You heard Rita explain the event. She made it sound like the party of a lifetime. In my experience, a person only okays that kind of expense when he plans to enjoy it himself."

Our conversation yielded to the consumption of Thai food and thoughts of what was to come. A mysterious meeting. A debaucherous party. A treacherous investigation. And the ultimate confrontation.

I still found it hard to fathom how completely my life had changed from one minute to the next, just six months ago in Santa Barbara. It was like that interrogation room had been a cocoon, only I'd gone in a butterfly and come out a caterpillar. Tomorrow I'd once again be walking into an entirely different world, masked no less, in more ways than one. That would be another cocoon. I'd either become a butterfly again, or never emerge.

"What are you thinking about?" Katya asked, with a mellowed voice and empty bowl.

"It's all coming down to tomorrow night. Exoneration, or incarceration. If they send me back to jail, it's going to be maximum security. The dullest inmates. The cruelest guards. The worst conditions. And no end in sight."

Katya's expression assumed an intensity I'd never seen her exhibit before. "It won't come to that, Achilles. You underestimate yourself. They've been sending monsters at you from every direction, and you've been swatting them away like so many flies. You seem to think it's routine, but I'm in awe. After seeing what you've done this past week, I'd bet against the sun rising before I'd bet against you winning." Her eyes were misting up. Her voice, quivering.

There was nothing I wanted to do more than cross the two steps between us and crush her body to mine. I wanted to kiss her and caress her like there was no tomorrow. But if I took those two steps now, it would all be over. Her emotions were high, her reserves depleted. She'd either recoil or reciprocate. Either way I'd be going into the most important day of my life feeling like a rat. I'd be the guy who made a pass at his brother's girl.

No doubt Katya would be similarly impacted. She'd hung in there as well as any covert operative I'd ever worked with. She seemed to have a nervous system welded from stainless steel. Bulletproof. But guilt and revulsion were entirely different forms of strain. They could bend and twist and deform. "We better get some sleep." With a wink I added, "Even superheroes need shuteye."

I drifted off, having forgotten something that would soon become unforgettable. I'd forgotten about the Brillyanc coursing through my veins.

Chapter 77

Brillyant Minds

WHEN I AWOKE, I knew what to do.

My mind was experiencing a clarity I'd only enjoyed while sitting cross-legged on sunny mountaintops after long climbs. My thoughts didn't stutter, or get hung-up, or repeat. They flowed.

Testing my Brillyanc seemed superfluous, but I needed to be sure it wasn't a hallucination. I started by trying to multiply our ten-digit phone numbers in my head. I'd taken plenty of math in college, but since graduation I'd relied on a calculator like everyone else. The Brillyanc in my blood didn't cause the result to pop up like it did on a computer screen. I had to work it out. But I could work it out. I could keep track of the digits and decimals without paper. I did know instantly that it would be one-point-something times ten to the nineteenth power, since both had 317 area codes, and 317 squared gave me 100,489. The rest took about a minute. Brillyant.

For fun, I tried calculating the square root of the product. Instantly I knew that it would begin with 317—no great leap there. However, the next seven figures flowed as well, even though I couldn't remember ever mechanically calculating a square root before. That took about ninety seconds.

I went out to the central room, intent on retrieving the newspaper, only to find that Katya had beaten me to it. She too was dressed in a white hotel robe, but had also gone for the slippers. She lowered the paper into her lap to reveal tousled hair and a big grin. "I read the paper. The whole paper, straight through. My mind sucked up the words like a vacuum cleaner. Line after line without distraction or fuss." She folded the paper and held it out. "I remember it all. Ask me a question."

I took the paper and opened it to a random page. "What percentage of the US population–"

"One percent," Katya said, before I could finish, "is affected by schizophrenia."

"Okay. There's an article written by Bill Clinton's Drug Czar–"

"Barry McCaffrey."

Two for two. I decided to try a different kind of thinking. "Got a puzzle for you. You need to measure out exactly four liters of water, but all you've got is two jars and a water hose. One jar holds exactly three liters, the other exactly five. There are no markings on the jars. How do you do it?"

She didn't even hesitate. "Fill the five jar. Dump what you can into the three, leaving two liters. Empty the three jar, then pour the remaining two into it, leaving space for one. Refill the empty five, and pour what you can into the three. Exactly four liters will be left."

We continued to test-drive our new processors all morning, switching from trivia to the investigation as we boarded the plane and our stomachs started to tense with the knowledge of what lay ahead.

"Have you figured out how Brillyanc links to Colin's murder?" Katya asked.

I had been hoping that answer would just pop into my head. So far, no pop. "I haven't nailed down the exact motive, but there's no longer any doubt that it was some kind of cover-up related to Brillyanc. Given the way its got us thinking, this drug is clearly destined to change the world—and make many billions in the process."

"Maybe it was just money. Lots of money. Isn't that the oldest motive?" Katya looked hopeful.

I hated to dim her glow. "I don't think so. They could have just fired my father and brother. There would have been a payout involved, but nothing consequential. And it had to be something consequential against a backdrop of billions. Something that put everything at risk."

"But isn't that exactly what the sun bear sourcing does? If Colin refused to go along with the cover-up, he'd have put billions at risk."

I shook my head. "There had to be more to it than that. Sun bear sourcing doesn't explain murder. Confidentiality agreements would keep him quiet. Confidentiality agreements silence executives all the time—just look at the tobacco industry. Plus, they're marketing Brillyanc in secret, so regulatory approval and whistleblower protection doesn't apply. Meanwhile, the operation goes on. In fact, it appears to be picking up steam. Rita clearly feels like she's riding a gravy train that's got nothing but acceleration ahead. And given the way our minds are working at the moment, I can see why."

"So what then?"

I looked out the window, hoping to find the answer written in the clouds. It wasn't.

"Come on, put that Brillyant brain to work."

I tried, but just couldn't make the leap.

Speaking of leaps, the next thing I knew we were landing in San Francisco. Put another way, we were about to leap from the frying pan into the fire.

Chapter 78

Squawk

WE LANDED at SFO with time to burn, so we swung by long-term parking to check on the Escalade. It was still parked where we'd left it. That surprised me. The smell of decomposing corpses should have drawn attention by now. I noted that the bay breeze created constant air circulation. Maybe the stench didn't have the opportunity to accumulate. For precaution's sake, we decided not to get close enough to check.

I stashed our Yates passports along with our iPhones at the baggage storage desk. That left us with just 202 area code burner phones in our pockets. Our absence of identification would raise questions if discovered, but the alternative was worse.

This whole operation was half-baked. I didn't feel good about that, but I couldn't change it either. Risk increased as prep-time decreased, and I'd had little. I was running out of time and cash and options.

Katya was drawing many an appreciative eye. Sporting the same royal blue dress she'd worn to meet Rita, she looked like she'd come off a catwalk rather than a plane. Like she'd be met by a Maserati rather than a black sedan.

"Do you think it's going to be one of those stretch limos?" she asked. "Or a typical livery car?"

"As long as it's not a black Escalade, I really don't care," I said, regretting my words immediately. "Sorry, that was indelicate of me."

"Better that I'm prepared in case it is." Katya was all made up for the big event. She looked so spectacular that when she flashed me a smile my knees almost buckled. "And I'm not worried if you're here."

We made it to Door One at five minutes to six. The area was plenty busy. Not Monday morning or Friday evening busy, but enough that cars were double-parking to disgorge departing passengers. Several of them were even black Escalades, but none paid us any heed.

The road ramped up to the departures level around a curve just before Door One, so we only caught sight of approaching cars a few seconds before they arrived. The opposite was also true. Since there was no place for a driver to wait without drawing a squawk from a surveilling cop, ours either had a spotter, or he was circling, or he was counting on our being there as the clock struck six.

A cold wind took the air temperature down to forty-five degrees. Katya crossed her arms and began rubbing her hands over her triceps. I ignored the chill. Truth was, I hated the cold as much as anyone. I'd just learned to switch off that part of my brain when in the field. I wouldn't let it register until it began to compromise finger function. Then again, I never wore dresses.

A stretch limo appeared atop the ramp at precisely six o'clock, its windows dark as onyx. It wasn't one of the obscenely long vehicles that could house an entire football team, but it was good for a rock band, and it maneuvered to a stop right before us.

The door opened by itself. An anonymous invitation.

My phone started buzzing.

I had my iPhone forwarding to my burner, just in case. And I had Chris Pine's home phone forwarding to my iPhone, just in case. I pulled it to my ear and answered. "Hello."

It wasn't the driver, or someone looking for Chris. It was Max.

I held up my left forefinger to request a minute while I pressed the receiver to my ear. Between the whistling wind and buzzing traffic, it was hard to hear.

Katya looked me a question. *Should she get in? Or should she wait?*

I swapped my left forefinger for the halt sign.

She grabbed the door, but didn't get in.

The police car squawked.

Max said something about this being the only time he could get into the lab, and wanting to let me know right away. I did the calculation. In Moscow, it was four o'clock on Sunday morning. I stuck a pinkie in my left ear and closed my eyes, straining to hear his report.

The police car squawked again.

Katya called my name.

I opened my eyes to see the limo starting to roll away. An unspoken message. Now or never. I motioned to her to get in. I walked toward the door, slowly, buying time. Having trouble hearing while unable to believe my ears. "Are you absolutely sure?" I asked.

The police car started to roll. The limo inched forward again, this time with Katya inside.

I jumped in.

The limo pulled away.

The door swung closed.

The call dropped.

Chapter 79

Rule Three

MY MIND WAS ALIGHT with the fireworks of revelation, but the limo itself was black. Black seats, black carpet, and black windows. We couldn't see the driver. We couldn't see outside. We were in a rolling blindfold, but a comfortable one.

Soft light emanated from a LED strip that ran the perimeter of the ceiling, giving life to the droplets clinging to a frosty silver bucket of champagne. On the wall, two fragrant roses in a silver bud vase shared their blossom and their scent. Directly before us was the most enticing feature of all. Perched atop the backward-facing seats at the other end of the cabin, two black Prada duffel bags displayed numbers embroidered in white silk: *204* and *205*.

A soothing but authoritative voice, presumably the driver's, interrupted the analysis churning inside my head. "Make yourselves comfortable. We'll be driving for a couple of hours, give or take. Somewhere along the route you'll need to get changed. Everything you brought with you, and everything you're wearing, goes into your bag. Everything. Your bag will stay right there until we reverse the procedure on your return. Meanwhile, your chairs recline fully, in case you want to take a nap. I understand it's going to be a long night."

Music replaced the voice. Smoky instrumental jazz fit for dark clubs rife with romantic tension.

"A couple of hours of driving could take us north to Sacramento or Santa Rosa, or south to San Jose or Monterey," Katya said. She knew it had been Max on the phone, and I could see her real question in her eyes. She wanted to know what he'd said. I was dying to tell her.

We had agreed not to say or do anything suspicious in the car, assuming we'd be under audio and video surveillance. But Max's revelations were too momentous.

"Or we could circle San Francisco, the drive an illusion in support of Rule One," I replied. "In any case, we may as well get comfortable."

I put my arm around Katya's shoulders and pulled her close, turning my head and burying my nose in her hair as though I was kissing her ear. "Max says Brillyanc is entirely synthetic," I whispered. "Which means Vondreesen's endangered species story was complete bullshit."

Katya turned her face toward mine, as though she were about to kiss me. Despite the circumstances, I felt a thrill reminiscent of my teenage years.

I could have kissed her, ostensibly for the camera. But she would have known that I meant it. I'm no expert on women, but I know they tend to be extremely sensitive about those things. So I gave her my ear.

She whispered, "I'm sure that changes things, but I'm not sure how."

My thoughts exactly. I was going to need the two-hour drive to process these twists. Katya was no doubt eager to analyze the implications as well. God her hair smelled great.

I withdrew my arm from her shoulder. "We've got two hours. Let's see what's in the bags, and then follow the driver's advice and take a nap."

I passed Katya 205 and pulled 204 onto my lap. The leather-tabbed zipper opened to reveal a red silk lining and black silk garments. Pajama bottoms rested atop mine. Katya's held a slip-nightie. "That look like your size?"

Katya ran her hand over the fabric. "It looks tailor-made."

Next, we extracted full-length robes, accented with red liners and complete with hoods. The robes were followed by slippers and masks that tied in the back. "As advertised," I said.

"Rita also said we'd be getting the rules."

"There are three," the driver said. Apparently the powers that be wanted us to be aware of the surveillance. *Not unlike the CIA.* "Rule One," the driver continued, "Absolute secrecy. You are never to reference, hint at, imply, insinuate, or otherwise indicate the existence of Brillyanc to anyone, anywhere, ever." He paused to let that sink in, before continuing.

"Rule Two: Complete Anonymity. You are neither to give nor solicit information which could lead to the identification of yourself or another. This includes where you live today or have lived in the past. It includes where you've studied, worked, or grown up. It includes references to clubs or societies or political affiliations. And of course, it includes references to family members, lineage, and nationality.

"Finally, there's Rule Three: No Exit. Up until you leave the limo, you can back out. Rule One still applies, of course, but you can walk away and make like this was all a fanciful dream. The moment you step through the door at our destination, however, Rule Two becomes compromised. There's only so much that can be done to protect anonymity, even with sanitized costumes and masks. We're only working with the most elite, and that means that there's a certain amount of fame involved. So crossing the threshold raises the stakes. You'll be under no obligation to continue paying the fees and using the product, but thereafter, a certain amount of surveillance should be expected. Enough to ensure that you're not disregarding the first two rules. Think long and hard about that before stepping out the door. You'll get the question when we arrive."

"What's the penalty?" I asked. "For breaking a rule."

The music resumed. Apparently this was meant to be a one-way conversation. And silence was the polite-society answer.

Chapter 80

Masks On

I PICKED UP my Prada bag while Katya toyed with her seat controls. "I'm going to change."

I started with the top. Jacket, tie, button-down shirt, all refolded neatly and placed in my bag. Then the bathrobe went on and the rest followed. The material wasn't really silk, but some microfiber that was both stretchy and resilient. The robe probably cost a good two hundred bucks. Everything fit like a suit from Savile Row. "How do I look?"

Katya gave me an exaggerated once over and grew a mischievous grin. "Here in the limo you look like a guy who rents for a thousand dollars an hour. I mean that in the best possible way, of course. At the party, I suppose you'll look very comfortable, and very rich. What about the mask?"

"I'll hold off on that until we arrive."

I reclined my seat until I was looking at the ceiling, giving Katya privacy. Then I closed my eyes and started processing Max's startling news and its implications for the journey ahead.

I'd gone into plenty of operational situations without detailed knowledge of the lay of the land, but this was extreme. At a minimum, I'd always had a location and a target. A person to be neutralized or liberated. A document to be retrieved or destroyed. A charge to be placed. A photo taken. A trail erased. Tonight I needed to identify the person in charge, isolate him without drawing attention, and then force him to reveal the circumstances of my family's death. All beneath the watchful eyes of men in black suits.

"I think Rita must have worked in fashion before pharmaceuticals," Katya said. "She certainly sized me up."

I opened my eyes and sat up. "Gives a new twist to the little black dress."

"I'll say. It's not just little. It's incomplete."

"Incomplete?"

"A friend of mine in college had a euphemism for it. She called it going out 'alfresco.' She found it thrilling, but it will be a first for me."

We reclined and lapsed back into contemplative silence until the driver interrupted. "We're five minutes out. Time for your masks, and your decisions. Rule Three. If either or both of you want to go back, just remain in the car. Otherwise, welcome aboard. Get ready for the time of your lives."

Katya moved back next to me, and we donned our masks. The eyeholes and nose pieces were molded but the rest was free-flowing fabric that stretched and tied easily. Mine was integrated with a skullcap, producing more of a pirate look, whereas Katya's was just the strip, pure Zorro. "Reminds me of the movie, *The Princess Bride*. Ever see it?"

Katya shook her head. "Seems an odd piece of apparel for a bride."

"Her boyfriend Westley was a pirate. He wore a mask like this. Said it was terribly comfortable. I'm not sold yet, but we'll see."

On that note, the car slowed and the music crescendoed. The driver turned and the road began to rise. A different timbre emanated from the tires, and my stomach encountered butterflies.

Katya grabbed my hand and we looked at each other in anticipation. Would it be a nightclub, or a hospital? A five-star hotel, or cabins in the woods? Would there be ten other participants? A hundred? A thousand? We'd mused on these during the flight, but even with Brillyant minds, we'd come to no conclusion.

The car crunched to a halt, along with the music. We heard similar rhythms coming from outside, as though the entrance to a trendy Parisian club lay ahead. For a few seconds we sat in relative silence, stewing in anticipation. The car rolled forward only a few feet before stopping again, like our plane had on the Dulles runway, and limos did at the Academy Awards. The ambient music became a little louder with each promotion. One more roll and the speakers were right there, not just in front but also behind. Then the door opened with a click and a whoosh, and we found ourselves looking down a candlelit tunnel.

Chapter 81

Two Blows

GRIGORI IGNORED THE FLEAS buzzing around his head. They couldn't hurt him, and he was having too much fun with the girl. He'd bid on Green, an atypically early selection from the rainbow on auction, because he felt like fucking a lawyer. Well, a law student, to be precise. This one looked like a younger version of the plaintiff's lead council in a wrongful death case GasEx was trying to settle. Grigori suspected it might actually be her daughter. Wishful thinking.

She'd proven to be quite an athlete in the sack, but not the actual daughter. Sobyanin, his new security chief, had verified her identity with a little sleight of hand. But then somehow her law school classmates had all shown up in his bed, wearing plaid skirts like private school girls. He wasn't sure how that had happened, but he didn't fight it. Quite the opposite. Did fleas buzz? He thought that was flies. With a flash of insight that made the school girls vanish, he realized this was neither fleas nor flies. It was the damn phone, vibrating on his nightstand.

He'd been dreaming.

He opened his eyes.

The law student, his forty-one-hundred-dollar auction prize, was there, but without her friends. Grigori studied her while his brain came on line. Sleeping on her back with her blonde hair tousled, he noted that her breasts were still young enough to resemble the building they were in. Looking up, he saw that the glass panes at the pyramid's pinnacle were beginning to clear with the rising sun, placing the time shortly shy of five a.m. On a Sunday. Who would dare to be calling?

He hit answer, and brought the phone to his ear. "Yes?"

"Sir, it's Sobyanin. I've got important news."

Pyotr's replacement chose to go by his last name, which along with his first matched the mayor of Moscow. While they looked nothing alike, they sounded similar, and that could come in handy on the phone. Otherwise, the jury was still out on whether Sobyanin was a good hire or not. Among other things, he didn't have Pyotr's sense of discretion. "Go ahead."

"We've got Achilles and the mathematician. They're in our limo as we speak, heading to the California party."

Grigori propped himself up on a thick white bolster. "How is that possible?"

"I don't know all the details. I just know the facial recognition program nailed them. They're disguised to resemble legitimate guests, but our software is the best in the world, and they've been within a meter of a hidden camera for the better part of an hour, feeding it data. How would you like this handled?"

Grigori was about to say something about bullets and brains when a painful memory gave him pause. A memory that still shamed him, and made his nose twitch.

He and Vladimir were in Brussels, back in 1986. Fresh KGB academy grads, number one and number two in their class, with a coveted posting and the world at their feet. Their job was classic human intelligence gathering, and toward that end they had befriended the daughter of the personal secretary to one of NATO's division commanders.

Alice was homely and rebellious and thrilled to be receiving attention from the two Austrian brothers. Especially the younger, handsome one, named Vlad. He had enough charisma to become a movie star, or a president.

They smoked grass, complained about their parents, and mused about what they wanted to do after high school. Alice wanted to go to the Sorbonne and study literature. Greg and Vlad wanted to be diplomats, like their father. A routine soon developed, where Greg would play Super Mario on Alice's coveted Nintendo, while she and Vlad snuck off to kiss.

Once Vlad had Alice locked away in her bedroom, Grigori would shift the Nintendo into autoplay mode with the assistance of some special equipment from the KGB's Operations and Technology Directorate. Then he'd go about the Motherland's business while the lovers kissed and the game prattled away.

His catch was usually modest—unclassified interoffice memos or routine correspondence. But before the director's biweekly staff meetings, they often scored valuable handwritten notes on agenda drafts.

In addition to photographing papers, Grigori and Vladimir also bugged the bedroom phone, a pushbutton model on the nightstand between the queen-size bed and the secretarial desk where Alice's mother did her off-hours work.

Grigori was in the midst of swapping out tapes when Alice caught him red-handed. She'd gone to fetch baby oil from the bathroom but Vlad had stayed behind because his pants were around his ankles. Her face made it clear she understood everything in a snap. Homely correlated with lonely, but not stupid.

Grigori had panicked and hit her upside the head with her mother's glass paperweight. It was just a single, panicked blow to the temple, but enough to render her dead.

Alice dropped to the floor with staring eyes and a nasty round dent to the left of her brow. The glass-encased rose dropped right beside her. Vladimir heard the double thunk and came running.

He too read the situation in a split second.

He too lashed out—with a fist to a nose, rather than a paperweight to a temple. "Idiot!" he'd yelled. "I could have turned her. I could have recruited her to work for us."

Grigori heard the echo of those words as he looked back and

forth between the phone and the girl now in his bed. He asked Sobyanin, "Who knows about this?"

"Nobody, yet. Not even the driver. I'm the first to be notified when facial recognition gets a hit. In this case, I thought you'd want to be the second. I hope that was the right call?"

It was, but Grigori wasn't one for mollycoddling, so he left the question hanging. "I'll take it from here. You're to take no action. Tell nobody. Their cover remains intact. No one should suspect that anything is amiss."

Sobyanin agreed, and Grigori had no doubt that he would comply rigorously. The new security chief was well aware of his predecessor's fate, and appropriately acrophobic.

Chapter 82

Angels & Flames

THE CANDLELIT TUNNEL was really a tent, a canvas corridor, something the Secret Service would use to protect the president. The white candles that illuminated it were the size of paint cans. They flickered within glass fishbowls, bringing the corridor alive and beckoning guests down an enchanted path.

The limo's door closed automatically behind us as we stepped from the car onto cool flagstones, sealing our fate. Rule Three. I saw nothing but darkness behind and a big black door some thirty feet ahead. I expected the limo to pull away immediately, but it sat there blocking our retreat, waiting for us to move ahead while the music played, and the candles flickered, and our adrenaline surged.

Katya took my arm. "This feels like the modern reenactment of a fairy tale I read as a girl."

"I was thinking the same thing, except when my grandmother read it she skipped the part about Hansel and Gretel wearing skimpy black silk pajamas." Katya elbowed my kidney as we followed the path, descending below ground level toward a door set deep within a stone wall. It appeared to have neither handle nor knocker. I was about to say, "Open sesame," when it slid to the left.

We entered a dim vestibule sized about twelve feet square, with a second sliding door centered on the opposite wall. To the left and right, gold-framed dressing mirrors begged for our self-appraising gaze. Beside them, combs, sprays, and bubbling flutes of champagne rested atop Doric pedestals. As the door swished shut, a soprano voice greeted us from behind. "Welcome, two-oh-four, and two-oh-five."

We whipped around to see an angel emerging from an alcove beside the entry door. Our heavenly guide was an early-twenties model with long blonde locks and augmented breasts. She sauntered between us on strappy silver heels of dangerous height, an appraising index finger before her pouty lips.

The angel's outfit consisted of a white babydoll even shorter than Katya's slip, and nothing to mask her bright blue eyes. A long white cape of sheer material, crafted to resemble wings, trailed behind while she walked, as if blown by a breeze. "You'll use your numbers when checking in for your procedure, and when you're ready to depart. All in support of Rule Two, you understand. Just type your numbers into the pad." She gestured to a panel beside the door. "When they're ready for you, your number will appear on a screen over the door."

She began to circle us, slowly, with an appraising eye. "Meanwhile, feel free to ask an angel if there's anything at all that you need." After trailing a finger across my shoulders, she moved on to Katya. She pulled a pick comb and some spray from the nearest pedestal and began toying with Katya's hair, assuming the familiarity of a big sister, and demonstrating the skill employed in top salons. "There you go. Perfect."

She put her arms around Katya as though to embrace, but then pulled Katya's hood up into place. As I followed suit, the angel used a willowy arm to motion toward the pedestals and then the door. "Please help yourself to a flute of Cristal, and enjoy the party."

The door opened automatically to reveal a warm and fragrant space even dimmer than the vestibule, with no ceiling in sight. Smooth energetic rhythms issued from unseen speakers all around, enveloping us in a blanket of sound that gave me the urge to dance, relax, and release. Quite an accomplishment, all things considered.

Our eyes flew to a swirling tower of flame in the center of the room, and our feet followed. I knew I should be studying the room, but to do anything other than walk wide-eyed toward the flame would have appeared suspicious, so I went with it.

Surrounded by a cylinder of glass that rose majestically out of the stone floor, the centerpiece combined fans with revolving gas jets to bring personality to a duet of dancing flames. Katya took my hand and spoke into my ear. "Looks like a tango of sorts. I've never seen anything like it. It's practically alive."

It was the coolest sculpture that I had ever seen. But this wasn't the first time that I'd seen it.

Chapter 83

Unencumbered

I LOOKED UP to where the flames disappeared through the black ceiling far overhead. Given the contrast with the dark room, the glare blinded like the sun.

Katya reached out hesitantly to touch the glass. When she found it tolerable, I saw the same realization cross her face. I nodded back as her eyes went wide.

We couldn't risk discussing the revelation here. At least not until we had the lay of the land.

Turning our backs to the swirling flames, we found that the room was also alive. Our adjusting eyes picked up people all around. Most still wore their silky hooded robes, but a few were setting what was no doubt the coming trend, having shed their robes, or more. The fire gave a healthy glow to their exposed skin, and the shadows made their fit bodies appear even more toned and lithe. They were clustered in pairs and groups, some standing, some sitting, some in repose. They were talking and touching and drinking and watching—all confidently poised, but only about one in three striking me as entirely relaxed.

After thirty seconds of observation, I felt myself beginning to react. Made me suspect that they'd laced the perfume-scented air with pheromones. "Time to wander. It's only natural to explore."

Katya took my arm. "Judging by the body language, I'd say we're not the only ones here for the first time."

"I'd guess that within an hour everyone will feel loose as linguini. *Al dente* that is, warm but firm."

A labyrinth of interconnected rooms surrounded the central

chamber. Some were larger, others quite small. Some relatively bare, others filled with furniture or toys. All had beds or chaise lounges or thick fur rugs on the floor, and each was lit by nothing but candles. Most were occupied by attractive people engaged verbally or otherwise in various forms of congress, some all boys and others all girls, most mixes favoring one or the other.

Meandering, we discovered that the angels really were at our service. So far, I hadn't detected their male counterparts, although the guest list appeared to be evenly split between the genders. Perhaps that was for the best.

I mapped the floor plan out in my head as we walked, avoiding eye contact and pretending to sip champagne. We were looking for one man in particular, while trying to identify anyone who might be in management. Plenty of individuals were wandering around like us, but the hooded bathrobes made it difficult to discreetly judge their age in the dim light. Those without robes all appeared to be in their thirties or forties. All were suitable for fitness magazine covers. The only point of interest so far was a second large sliding door, located directly opposite the one through which we'd initially entered. "What do you think's on the other side?" Katya asked.

"A few hundred lounge chairs paired with IV bags. I suspect it will open when the time is right."

There wasn't a staircase, back room, kitchen, or exit to be found. However, there were plenty of bars and small buffets scattered throughout the rooms, all with top-shelf drinks and exquisite finger foods. French pastries, ripe fruits, petit fours, and an endless assortment of sumptuous hors d'oeuvres. All were serviced by silent angels who seemed to appear and disappear as needed. "Let's see if we can find out where they're coming from," I whispered in Katya's ear. "Maybe they'll lead us behind the curtain."

Katya jumped on that idea. "Let's wait here for one to follow. The black caviar on those blinis is calling my assumed name."

I handed her a small porcelain plate. While Katya covered it with caviar canapés, I forked a few oysters onto my own, and discreetly emptied my drink into the mountain of ice supporting the mollusks. Between bites, she said, "I wonder if they're watching surveillance cameras, looking for glasses that need refilling and plates that need carting away?"

"Good question. Let's find out." I cleaned my plate and set it down on the marble-topped pub table beside my empty glass.

Katya followed suit.

I took her hand and guided her to the darkest corner of the room, stopping directly beneath the position I'd choose to hide a camera. I turned to face Katya and grasped her hands. From this vantage point, I could see both of the room's archways, and the buffet. I also had a view of Katya's upturned face, her scintillating eyes, and plump red lips.

Katya met my gaze, and stepped a little closer.

I only had hours if not minutes to get a look behind the curtain, find the wizard, and somehow either wring out a confession or gather the evidence I'd need to bring him to justice. This was potentially the last chance I'd ever have to avenge the death of my family. But all I wanted to do was lock Katya in a long embrace. I'd never been affected by a woman this way before. I felt drawn to her at the molecular level, and proximity made the attraction stronger.

Mother Nature was compelling me to sweep her up in my arms, carry her across the room to a velvety red couch, and make a memory that could get me through the next fifty years without regret, if it came to that. Or maybe it was just the confluence of stress and circumstance. In any case, the battle between the Archangel Gabriel and Mephistopheles was raging inside my head.

The pheromones weren't helping.

Katya released my hands and reached up with both of hers to push back my hood. Once it fell, she slipped her hands inside my robe and slid them out to the ends of my shoulders. Her touch was warm and tender and seemed to send voltage across my skin.

As our eyes locked and my throat dried, my racing mind managed to ease off the gas. Months of tension evaporated beneath her fingertips. My muscles relaxed, my blood pressure dropped, and the puzzle pieces swirling around my mind finally fell into place.

Katya must have seen it in my eyes, as her own face crinkled. "What?"

Chapter 84

Last Piece

I LOOKED DOWN into Katya's beautiful amber eyes, simultaneously relieved and distraught by the break in sexual tension. "I figured it out."

"What did you figure out?" Katya switched from one form of excitement to another just as quickly as I had, but left her hands on my shoulders.

"All of it."

"Everything?" Her voice brimmed with the unbridled excitement of a little girl with a new doll.

"All the broad strokes. Vitalis's closure. The murder of my family. The assassination attempts. The sun bears. And this party."

Katya grew a contemplative look that I was beginning to consider her trademark. Pretty fitting for a mathematics professor. "I'm sure the sun bears are the key. But I can't figure out how to turn it, so to speak."

"That's right. Ask yourself what would make you invent that kind of grand deception?"

"Invent?"

"Yes, Invent. Remember that Max discovered Brillyanc is synthetic. Why fabricate a story that's not just esoteric, but potentially damaging to your business? What purpose does it serve?"

"I don't know. Marketing isn't my thing. Maybe to drive up the price by reducing supply? Or give it cachet by making it rare or elitist?"

I shook my head. "There are simpler means of accomplishing

those things. These are clever people. And completely unscrupulous."

"What purpose do the sun bears serve … " She was getting frustrated, but she was also getting close. I could feel it.

"You're almost there. Bring it home. How did this all start?"

"With Colin's murder."

"Before that. Why was he killed?"

I saw the light go on. "He discovered something."

"Exactly. Now connect the dots."

"He was killed to conceal his discovery." She was doing the thing with her nails again. One, two, three, four. One, two, three, four.

"How does the sun bear story fit in?"

"It serves the same purpose. Concealment. It's camouflage. Everything has been about concealing something."

"Exactly. This is all about a secret worth killing for."

"But what secret?"

Katya had hit on the billion-dollar question, but an angel had appeared over her shoulder as she spoke, quiet as a cloud. The angel gathered up our used plates and glasses.

Katya saw the white form reflected in my eyes and lowered her hands. "Should we follow?" she whispered.

I was torn. I wanted to get on with the physical investigation, but now that we were both on the same new page, I wanted to keep reading. It was helpful to talk things through with a mind as sharp, precise, and logical as Katya's. I'd never experienced a mental partnership quite so satisfying before, even with Granger.

I moved a couple empty plates from the buffet to the pub table where they'd look used. "Let's follow the next angel. I want to double-check my math with you."

Katya backed up a step. "What do you think the killer secret is?"

"It has to be product related. Brillyanc is the common denominator. My father and brother were working on it. Tarasova was working on it. All the activity surrounds it."

"But it works." Katya threw up her arms in an atypical display of emotion. "We experienced it. Max and Saba both swore by it. Colin was incredibly enthusiastic about it."

"Until he wasn't. You said he was confident one day and despondent the next."

"Right. He was."

"And shortly thereafter, Vitalis was shut down."

"Right. Vondreesen explained that with the whole sun bear, endangered species, gallbladder thing."

"But we know from Max that was a lie, because Brillyanc is entirely synthetic. So Colin must have discovered something else. Something *worse*. They made up the sun bear story to camouflage something more damning."

Katya was nodding along with me. "I like the concept, but what could that possibly be? As Vondreesen pointed out, the sun bear discovery was a triple blow. It decreased supply, and demand, and killed any chance of regulatory approval."

"It may have been a triple blow, but look around." I gestured back toward the main room. "They're still able to sell it for a thousand dollars a day."

"Oh my God, you're right. So Colin must have found something that would have prevented that."

"Exactly."

"But what?"

"It's a drug, right?" I prompted.

"Sure…" Her face lit up a second later. "Side effects."

Chapter 85

The Path

AS THE WORDS 'side effects' escaped Katya's lips, another angel walked through our room. Again Katya saw the white form reflected in my eyes. She spun around as the angel made her exit, and without a word we began to follow, our minds racing in one direction, our feet headed in another.

Within two seconds of the angel's disappearing through the archway to our right, we rounded the corner in silent pursuit—and bumped into a couple of the angels' male counterparts.

They wore black suits and black tees, and together formed the operational equivalent of a brick wall. The left suit spoke, his accent Russian. "Two-oh-four, and two-oh-five, come with us please."

I studied the faces of our adversaries, trying to get a reading on their disposition. The set of their jaws, the angle of their heads, and the tension in their necks told me they knew that I'd killed five of their friends.

Neither fight nor flight was an option. Not in that place. Not at that time. We'd have been running blind. Then and there, the smart move was to capitulate. "After you," I replied.

The left suit spun around and walked toward the back of the room, toward nothing that I could see. Katya and I followed, side by side, with the right suit trailing behind. It appeared that he was going to collide with the wall, but a panel slid silently aside just before he did. We followed him into a dark corridor lit only by blue LEDs embedded every few feet in the floor, like a luminescent highway divider.

He turned right, taking us back in the direction of what I'd speculated was the procedure room. We passed chest-high LEDs on the corridor wall every twenty feet or so, some red, some green. When I saw one slide aside just before an angel appeared, I understood that they marked the hidden doors. I couldn't tell how they were activated. They didn't slide open as we passed, so it wasn't a typical motion sensor. Still, the door into this hidden corridor had opened before the suit as though sensing his approach. Thinking about it with my Brillyant brain, I realized that was exactly what it did.

If a person had an RFID chip, a radio frequency identifier, then the system could be programmed to react specifically to him. This would explain how the angels came and went through doors that were invisible and inaccessible to anyone else. My next thought struck like a crashing wave, sweeping me up in a moment of darkness before delivering me into the light.

Katya and I had also been tagged.

RFID chips could be as small as a grain of rice. You could easily hide one on anybody, and they had created the perfect place: our masks. With that system, they could track every guest's every move on the equivalent of an air traffic control console.

But why?

I answered my question as quickly as I'd asked it. Security, of course. Rule One.

A minute into our tour, the lead suit stopped directly before a triangle of three green LEDs. A panel slid aside after two seconds, revealing a staircase going up. Rather than entering, he stepped aside. "They're waiting for you upstairs."

Chapter 86

Burning Man

KATYA AND I both turned to face the lead suit. His angular face looked evil in the dim glow of green LED lights. She spoke first. "Who's waiting for us?"

He scoffed for an answer. Looked like Rule Two applied within the organization as well.

We turned our backs on them and started climbing. There must have been forty steps, each lit by a twin pair of green lights. After the door slid shut behind us, Katya grabbed my arm and paused. "Do you think this is routine? Something they do for all first-time partygoers?"

"No. They know who we are." I spoke low and in Russian, assuming someone was listening in, and trying not to make it easy.

"But how?" Katya replied in kind.

"I was a fool. Again. They ID'd us in the car. Our disguises are good enough to deceive people who aren't personally acquainted with Chris and Alisa, but they won't fool a sophisticated computer. Not one that's looking for us. Not one that already has our real identities to match against."

Katya clutched my hand as we neared the top. "What do we do now?" She moved around me so that she was on the stair above mine, putting our heads on the same level.

"We fight back—when the time is right. We hit them with everything we have, and don't stop until we escape."

"But we're not armed. We're in pajamas."

"That means they won't be expecting much. And not all weapons are physical."

Katya pondered that for a second, then she leaned forward and kissed me on the lips—a quick kiss, but one that spoke volumes. Before I could react she turned around, and climbed the last stair.

I stood still for a moment.

Then another shock came.

As I stepped onto the landing beside Katya, the floor began moving beneath our feet. It rotated us clockwise around a six-foot section of wall into the adjoining room. A room we'd seen before. A room with twin staircases, eighteen-foot ceilings, and a wrought-iron chandelier.

The disk we were standing on didn't stop rotating after a half-turn. We had to hop off to avoid being taken back into the hidden corridor. I watched over my shoulder with childlike fascination as the wall returned to its original position behind us—displaying a large painting from the studio of Raphael.

Two men were waiting for us when we turned back to face front. They were dressed in robes and masks, rather than black suits. "Good evening, Vaughn. Hello, Casey."

"Well done," Vondreesen said, removing his hood along with Casey. "If not a few days overdue. Let's go up to the library. I'll tell you a story."

With Casey bringing up the rear, we followed Vondreesen up the winding staircase and back into the room we'd visited a few days before. The lights were dimmer now, and the back wall flickered and glowed like one of the entryway fishbowls, bringing the whole room to life. "Looks a bit different downstairs, doesn't it? I named it *Burning Man* after the annual desert festival that inspired the design. To my knowledge, there's nothing else like it."

"It's captivating, in a Faustian sort of way," Katya said, her tone reflecting a robust emotional state.

"Tell me, Vaughn, why's it circular downstairs, but semicircular here?"

"My bedroom and private study are on the other side. You don't see through to them because the lights are out." He led us back to the central of the three coffee tables as he spoke.

We sat in the same chairs as before, with Casey in the last seat. After we'd removed our hoods and masks, Vondreesen lifted an ornate crystal bottle from the coffee table. He poured generous portions of amber liquid into four brandy snifters. "Louis XIII Cognac. They say there's a century in every bottle. I thought that appropriate, given the perspective required for what we have to discuss."

It struck me that while the elder statesman in Vondreesen was on display in high resolution, Casey seemed much less at ease. It was almost as though he had a sense of shame. Nonetheless, he kept his right hand in his bathrobe pocket, where the silhouette of a silenced pistol cast a shadow over us. I recalled that he had been a Marine—and once a Marine, always a Marine. *Semper Fi.*

Vondreesen nudged a glass in each of our directions. An invitation in lieu of a tasteless toast.

With everyone leaning in to grab a glass, I thought about snatching the moon rock off the table and braining both my nemeses. In less than three seconds I could have my revenge. Casey would probably get a bullet off, but it would be the last thing he'd do. Pyrrhic victories didn't work for me, however. And besides, I was most curious to hear Vondreesen out.

"Can I get a cigar to go with it?" I asked, not because I wanted a smoke, but because I wanted to disarm Casey—and see if Vaughn would hand me a weapon more substantial than a snifter glass. Eyeballs and nerve centers reacted poorly to contact with tobacco burning at a thousand degrees.

Chapter 87

Gorilla Marketing

VONDREESEN SMILED at my request for a cigar. I couldn't tell if he thought I was caving, or if he'd read my mind. He rose and retrieved a box, torch, and cutter from a side table. Romeo & Julieta coronas, packed in the same tubes Rita used to camouflage her syringe. Hard to believe that was a coincidence.

Katya declined.

Alas, so did Casey.

Vondreesen clipped and torched our cigars. "I was in shock when your father brought me the news about the sun bears. I got the Russian on the phone then and there. He insisted on meeting in person to discuss it. So I flew to Moscow."

I knew this was a lie. The sun bear story was a fabrication. But I decided to play along and see where Vondreesen took it. Information was power, and knowing one of Vondreesen's secrets gave me some. "Did my father go with you?"

"No. I wasn't sure where that meeting was headed, so I didn't want to expose him. By then, there had been enough indications that the man I was dealing with could be dangerous. But he made me bring Casey. Called him my consigliere, no doubt having learned about Western business by watching *The Godfather*." Vondreesen paused, as if picturing the memory.

"We met in his Moscow office. Or rather *outside* his office. He took us out onto the ledge circling his penthouse. We were thirty stories up and walking a few feet from an open edge while he explained the facts of life to us. He treated it like a walk on the beach. I nearly peed my pants. Unbelievable.

"Meanwhile two of his goons trailed us at arm's length the whole way. Those security guys you keep, uh, dispatching—they aren't mine. None of them." Vondreesen gestured toward the door. "The large gentlemen you met downstairs, Boris and Ivan, they're his. Presumably provided for operational security, but most of the time they're watching me."

I was beginning to wonder if Vondreesen really had been duped with the sun bear story. Perhaps the Russian had fed Vaughn the same grand deception he was now dishing out. Or perhaps Vaughn was just that good a bullshitter. His accent made everything sound so prim and proper. "If you're looking for pity, you're speaking to the wrong person."

Vondreesen continued as though I hadn't spoken. "The Russian told me that he'd fundamentally changed our marketing strategy. We wouldn't be taking the traditional pharmaceutical path, with its regulatory approval and physician prescription and insurance reimbursement. We weren't going to be marketing to the masses either. And we wouldn't be selling Brillyanc for a lousy two or three grand a year."

He paused for a couple of cigar puffs. "You know where he went with it. You heard Rita's pitch. But did you do the math?"

Katya was all over that. "At $360,000 per year per user, your revenues will top a billion at just 2,800 patients."

"Exactly. And ten times that amount wouldn't be a stretch. The Russian mapped it all out for me, step by step. We'd start with operational centers in DC and the Bay Area. Hand select the ripest three hundred souls in each, the top 0.01 percent of our target demographic, and make each the offer you heard. An offer they'd be fools to refuse." Vondreesen's voice brimmed with excitement as he spoke.

"The plan is to expand to another major metropolitan area every six months or so. New York, Chicago, Dallas, and LA. Then London, Paris, Frankfurt, Zurich, and Milan. Followed by

Singapore, Tokyo, Beijing, Sydney, and Seoul. And let me tell you, it's happening exactly as he said it would. DC and San Francisco now have over two hundred Brillyanc users each. That's worth a hundred and fifty million dollars a year, most of it profit, and we've only been rolling Brillyanc out for half a year."

"So it's all about money?" I asked.

Vondreesen gave me a silly-boy look. "Is it ever about anything else?"

"But you have plenty of that. How much more do you need?"

Vondreesen took a long swallow from his snifter. "Let me finish. That was just the carrot. Attractive as it was to the businessman in me, of course it wasn't enough. The Russian knew it wouldn't be. So he had his goons show me the stick.

He had a big one.

You know those movies where the gangster dangles his mark over the edge of a building until he capitulates?"

"Sure."

"Well, he wasn't that kind to me. He said, 'I'll give you five seconds to think it over. That may not sound like much, but it will suffice—if you're in the right frame of mind.' Then his goons picked me up and hurled me over the edge."

Vondreesen mimicked a tossing gesture. "I was over three-hundred-feet up when they released me. That's where he got the five-second calculation, the amount of time required for a thirty-story free fall. It was dark out at the time, but the snowy ground below was illuminated by landscaping lights so I could see where I was headed. At least until I closed my eyes." Vondreesen shook his head and took another puff.

"I fell to within a few feet of an icy hedge, and then sprang back up. One of the goons had cuffed a bungee cord around my ankle while they were throwing me off. Had it hooked up to a device that looked like a fishing pole, keeping me away from the building when I bounced. The goons reeled me back up but left me hanging there by my ankle ten feet out from the edge. I was scared to death my shoe was going to come off and I'd slip loose. Haven't worn loafers since." He pointed down at his lace-ups.

"That's when he asked me if I'd decided to embrace the new marketing strategy.

"I agreed.

"Casey went along too, of course."

Chapter 88

Mission Accomplished

VONDREESEN LEANED FORWARD and poured more Louis XIII into all our glasses, although he had been the only one drinking. He took a slow sip with closed eyes before speaking. "Once I agreed to the new marketing strategy, we shut Vitalis down, just as we would have done otherwise. Your father and brother were none the wiser." He twirled the brandy around in his snifter, staring into it as he spoke.

"I had no idea the Russian was going to kill them. There was no reason for that, beyond paranoia. But as the rules have made you well aware, we're dealing with a paranoid personality. A megalomaniac with a cruel streak a mile wide." Pausing for a moment, he finally met my eyes.

I knew the big reveal was coming.

"He called me the morning after the accident, while you were still asleep. Told me what he'd done. Told me to put Casey on it. Told me that he'd impose the death penalty if you weren't convicted in court. No delays. No appeals."

I took a second to digest that twist. "You're trying to tell me that by getting me convicted for a triple homicide, Casey was really working in my best interests?"

"Yes, exactly. In that context, you can see that he did a great job. He effectively got the death penalty reduced to six years, for Chrissake. It was an incredible deal. But you turned it down." Vondreesen shrugged. "So Moscow ordered the hit."

I looked over at Casey, expecting to see him nodding along, vindicated.

He wasn't.

He just looked troubled. Preoccupied.

I turned back to Vondreesen. "You called Detective Frost after our last visit, didn't you? The minute we were out the door, you were on the phone."

"Actually, I called Frost the moment you arrived. Gave him an anonymous tip—for your benefit. Ever since your escape we've been trying to funnel you back to prison where at least your life expectancy would be measured in years rather than days. But that hasn't worked either. So here we are."

"Where, exactly, are we?"

Vondreesen set his snifter down. "I'm going to give you and Katya the same choice he gave Casey and me. But I'm going to give you a very different experience to help you make up your mind."

"What's the choice?"

"What do you do if you can't beat 'em?"

"Are you kidding me? You want us to join you? Team up with the people who killed my family? Are you out of your mind?"

"You'll be the one out of his mind, if you don't take me up on the offer. Literally. I snap my fingers and within three seconds Ivan or Boris will have put bullets in both your brains. So listen up!" Vondreesen let his words hang out there for a second. Then he patted the air in a calming gesture, sending cigar ash onto the carpet.

"First, let's get a bit of perspective. What we're talking about, in the worst-case scenario, is driving sun bears to extinction. Right? Setting spilled milk aside, that's the rub. Now, I've never seen a sun bear, and I don't expect that I ever will, but I'd still agree that their extinction is not a good thing. However, I'll ask you to ponder this: is it necessarily a bad thing? Does it really matter? Did you know that twenty-thousand species are near extinction, and that every single day dozens disappear forever? Granted, most of those are plants, and the sun bear is a mammal, but at the end of the day, doesn't it boil down to survival of the fittest?"

I wanted to end him right there. Show him who was fittest. But I held it in. The animal would emerge soon enough.

"Survivors do what it takes to survive. Are you willing to exert your positions as *prime*mates? Are you willing to do what it takes to survive? Join us and you can be a part of one of the greatest medical developments in the history of mankind, one that will help to catapult the human race forward. One that, for all we know, is just as ordained to be a part of our evolution as the printing press, light bulb, and automobile. Or you can cry over spilled milk, and join the sun bears." Vondreesen spread his hands, like a balance scale. Left, or right. The blue pill, or the red.

He seemed to genuinely believe the sun bear bullshit.

I studied the lit end of my cigar, blowing on it until the gray ash dispersed and the tip glowed red. The superficial radial nerve branches out from the base of the thumb just below the skin's surface. If I could get within striking distance of Casey's hand, I could take his trigger finger out of play in a single second. A few seconds more and I could brain them both with the moon rock. I took a puff and then met Vaughn's eye. "You killed my family. What makes you think I can ever get past that?"

"Two simple truths. First of all, Casey and I had no idea that was going to happen. It was a business decision made and executed by a paranoid mind. A changed mind. You've bested five of his men since then. Squashed them like high schoolers who walked onto an NFL field. He recognizes your talent. Appreciates it. Which is why he's sanctioned this offer."

I looked over at Katya to see how she was faring. Her expression showed that she was aghast. "What's the second simple truth?"

Vondreesen lit up before my eyes. His face regained color, and his voice resounded with verve. "Justice has already been served. The two guys you took out at Katya's apartment were the same men who set you up. They were the men who reconfigured the

Emerging Sea's exhaust system to kill your family. Your mission is accomplished."

Chapter 89

Prime-mates

VONDREESEN'S WORDS hit me with physical force. They were a blow to my operating paradigm. The men who had killed my family were already dead. I'd killed them without knowing it.

I didn't feel any better.

A quote by Martina Navratilova popped into my mind. *The moment of victory is much too short to live for that and nothing else.*

Katya reached over and put her hand on my knee.

Apparently satisfied with my reaction to his revelation, Vondreesen plowed on. "This brings me to the cherry on top of our proposal. Casey can present the evidence required to prove that those men did it. His investigators actually did find video. You'll be free and clear, wealthy and healthy, and part of the new ruling class."

I said nothing, but sighed inside. *Free and clear!* Now I just needed a healthy resolution to the dead-or-alive issue.

Vondreesen resumed his pitch. "Speaking of the ruling class, it's time for my final slide, so to speak. Ever read Plato's *Republic*?"

"I think I read a few excerpts in a poli-sci class."

"In book VI, Plato describes his version of utopia as a place ruled by the wisest among us. Philosopher-kings, he called them. Imagine it. You'll be helping us to create Plato's Utopia. It's an idea that's been 2,400 years in the making."

I wasn't sure how much more of this crap I could take. The cigar-ashtray combo move was looking pretty good, but a more elegant play had come to mind. "Don't tell me you're doing this because of some grand vision of social justice, Vaughn. This is all about greed, pure and simple."

"Granted, self-interest may be our prime mover, but that's Adam Smith's invisible hand at work. Capitalism at its finest. Do you begrudge Sergey Brin and Larry Page their billions? Or are you just happy to have Google?"

"You've really given this a lot of thought."

"I have. Believe me."

"Good. Then I have a question for you."

"I'm all ears."

"What do you think your guests would say if you told them about the sun bears? You haven't, have you? We heard the pitch. How would they react if they knew the cost of their brilliance?"

Vondreesen chuffed. "These aren't vegetarians, Achilles. They're meat eaters. *Prime*mates. Top of the food chain."

"Are you sure?"

"Absolutely. Most of them already know. We stopped including it in the pitch because it proved unnecessary. Nobody cared. You don't think about the newborn calf when you order veal piccata."

Actually, I do pass on veal for that reason. But I was pleased with Vondreesen's pitch. It would convince some people, and probably most of the power crowd. "Okay then. Prove it. If they're still aboard after learning the truth about Brillyanc, then Katya and I are aboard too."

Katya gasped.

Vondreesen's eyes narrowed. "I'm pleased to hear that. With your training, I knew that you'd be capable of putting reason over emotion, but I didn't know if you'd be willing. How do you propose that we prove it?"

"Let's go ask them."

Vondreesen leaned back in his chair, studying me with his cigar dangling over the left arm and his Cognac over the right. The fall of his robe sleeve made it possible for me to see that he had something strapped to his right forearm. A weapon, most likely. "You know I won't allow the presence of the goons to spoil the party atmosphere, so you think that will provide an opportunity to get away. It won't. First of all, even if you could escape the castle, where would you go? We know exactly where you'll be one week from Monday. Secondly, your attorney here is armed with more than a law license."

"Yes. A subcompact with a suppressor. I saw the silhouette. What is it, Casey? You get the Smith & Wesson, or a Glock?"

Casey withdrew the silenced sidearm from the pocket of his robe. It was a clean, controlled move. Unwavering. He was comfortable with the weapon. Clearly more Texas than California.

"A Springfield XD-S," I said. "The 4.0. You must have custom retrofit the barrel to get the suppressor on. Nice weapon."

Casey didn't comment. He remained uncharacteristically quiet. Perhaps guilt had gotten his tongue. How about that, an attorney with a conscience.

I turned back to Vondreesen. "I want to make sure everyone's still onboard once they have all the facts. You can appreciate that this isn't something that's naturally easy for me to get cozy with. Putting reason over emotion will take some effort. Hearing reinforcing opinions will help."

Vondreesen took a long puff and blew the smoke out slowly before answering. "This isn't a banquet. There is no master of ceremonies. There are no speeches. There's not even a podium. This is just a party that reinforces the elite status of the participants while reminding them of their vested interest in maintaining secrecy."

I began to speak, but Vondreesen held up his hand.

"Furthermore, I'm too familiar with your background to agree with any plan you may suggest without an appropriate measure of skepticism. Katya would have to stay here. Casey will see to her comfort while we're away."

Katya's grip tightened on my knee. I turned to meet her gaze. Tried to fill my eyes with confidence.

"That's okay with me," she said. "If that's what it takes."

Vondreesen tapped the burnt ash off the end of his cigar. "There's a group of nine here tonight. Elected officials. Members of the United States Congress, in fact."

"Your political connections," I said, half to myself.

"They've been with me from the beginning. They started using Brillyanc when your father was still running the company. Back before we knew about the sun bears. Before we got so strict about anonymity. Friends who I let into the fold."

"Why target politicians?" I asked. "Lawyers, businessmen, scientists, I get. But being a politician is all about charisma and connections. At least that's the impression I usually get when listening to some of those idiots blathering away on C-SPAN."

"Maybe that used to be the case. Maybe it still is in some districts for politicians who don't aspire to the national stage. But in an era when every word that ever comes out of your mouth can become a self-destructing missile, most politicians have to be on top of their game, all the time."

"Then there are debates and press conferences and interviews, during which the command of a tremendous array of facts can be crucial. And don't forget about all the legislation they're supposed to be reading. With Brillyanc in their bloodstream, these guys are actually reading the bills they debate."

I let my reply come out slowly, deflating tension. "Okay. I can see that. What are you thinking?"

"They get their infusions together so they can caucus. As a group, they're older than our average user by about fifteen years, and they've been to more parties than most, so they tend to be among the first to make their way back to the infusion room. They're probably already there, and at this hour we'll likely catch them before any IVs are hooked up. The solution contains a mild sedative, to make it easier to sleep with the IV in, so they won't have the angels attach them up until they're ready to sleep. We could go ask them to join us. They all know about the sun bears, and it will give you feedback direct from the representatives of over six million Americans. I'll even give you the nickel tour on the way so you can see our operation in action. Would that satisfy you?"

"Yes, Vaughn. A meeting with the congressmen would be perfect."

Chapter 90

The Tour

KATYA'S HAND was still resting on my knee. I put mine on top of hers and gave it a reassuring squeeze as Vaughn and I agreed to go fetch the nine members of congress. I could only imagine what was going through her mind.

She had said that she believed in me.

I was about to put that belief to the test.

We set our drinks and cigars aside, then donned our masks and hoods.

Vondreesen's willingness to take me without an armed escort confirmed my suspicion that he was packing something formidable up his sleeve. Turning to Casey, he said, "We'll be back in ten. Don't let her out of your sight."

Casey nodded.

Vondreesen gestured me forward. "We're going back the way we came." He wasn't going to let me get behind him. Smart move.

At the bottom of the circular stairs, the Raphael door opened before us as if by magic, revealing the hidden staircase.

"RFID, right?" I asked as we descended. "I bet you can track everyone in real time on that tablet of yours, using their numbers. That's why Boris and Ivan referred to Katya and me as 205 and 204, isn't it?"

"I take advantage of technology when I can."

Vondreesen guided me past a number of red LEDs and stopped us before one that had just turned green. The significance of the color dawned on me. Green meant the room was empty, or at least devoid of motion. The light emitting diodes made it possible to know if you could enter a room without being seen. Nice little parlor trick, quite literally in this case.

We passed through a series of sitting rooms, some in use, others not. About a third of the occupied rooms resembled cocktail hour at an exclusive members-only club. Distilled spirits, fat cigars, and lively debate on how best to master the universe. The rest were in use by groups who had shed everything but their masks. "People tend to start in twosomes, and move on to larger and larger groups as the night progresses," Vondreesen commented. "Like most of human nature, it's pretty predictable."

Eventually we entered the main room, where Burning Man was dancing. I looked up again, but even with the lights on in the library I still couldn't tell it was there. The big doorway at the back of the main room was open now, revealing a chamber lit by more than candle power. I headed toward it without prompting.

As we walked, Vondreesen began bragging. "We modeled the infusion room pods after the first-class accommodations on transoceanic jets. Each offers a broad leather chair that goes from fully flat, to seated, to any position in between. Along with a state-of-the-art entertainment system. We call it a *flight* instead of an infusion. Helps our jet-set clients put things in a familiar perspective."

"How many pods do you have?"

"Three hundred thirty-six. Enough that we could eventually handle a thousand clients by servicing one group a month, on a quarterly rotation. The way that averages out, it would make this location worth a million dollars a day."

Now there's a killer motive. "That's not bad, for a pension. Did you choose the winery for camouflage?"

"Exactly. With an estate like this, large parties with limousines coming and going are expected. That's something we think about when picking locations. I must admit, personal preference also played a role—picking Napa, I mean. Not a castle. At one time or

another, every Silicon Valley executive thinks about retiring to a
winery."

As we passed through the doorway, Vondreesen gestured
dramatically. "Welcome to the flight zone. You can see that
everyone flies first class." His voice resonated with pride. To give
credit where due, it was an impressive sight. The room did
resemble the first-class cabin on a Boeing 777, but was much larger,
since all the passengers were 'up front.'

We made our way toward a back corner, where the pods had
been rearranged into a circular configuration like tick marks on a
watch face. Vondreesen reached out and grabbed my arm. "Would
you recognize any member of Congress from a western state? I
believe you're still registered to vote in North Carolina, not that
most people would even recognize their own congressmen."

I pondered that for a sec. "I'd recognize Daniels. He was a
California senator before moving on to the vice presidency. Now
he presides over the senate. Not sure if that counts?"

"Well, I suppose it really doesn't matter. The point is that despite
the masks, you're likely to recognize some of the people you're
about to meet. I want to be sure you're completely aware of the
implications of learning their identities?"

I understood Vondreesen's question for what it was. He was
preemptively trying to assuage his guilt over killing me, should it
come to that. He was shifting the decision onto my shoulders. I
wasn't in the mood to lighten his load. "My understanding is that
you'll kill me if I don't join you, regardless."

Vondreesen frowned. "Very well then. I'm glad we have that
understanding."

Chapter 91

In the Balance

WE WALKED INTO the midst of the circular configuration. Nine pods were occupied, as advertised. One sat empty, like a dinner plate set in reverence for a loved one who had died. A lively discussion ground to a halt, and we found ourselves under the scrutiny of nine pairs of intelligent eyes.

"Pardon the intrusion," Vondreesen said, his British accent on full display. He was the gracious host again. He'd snapped back into that role like a turtle into a shell, and now he appeared bulletproof. "Allow me to introduce Kyle Achilles. He's brought us a bit of a special situation. One that would benefit greatly from your sage counsel. A question of ethics. Could I trouble you to join us upstairs in the library for a few minutes?"

A woman replied with a voice resembling the jazz singer I'd liked at Off the Record. She was probably in her early seventies but looked to be in her late forties. A vivacious face framed by chestnut hair so perfectly highlighted and coiffed that you'd swear she was headed for a national television appearance after paying some uber-stylist a thousand bucks. To my surprise, I recognized her. She was the one Kilpatrick said the DA consulted while covering her ass. The one who chaired a committee that oversaw CIA-related issues. Senator Colleen Collins. "We were having an ethical discussion of our own," Collins said. "It wasn't going particularly well. A side discussion might actually help to shake things loose."

To her right, a fit blonde man with a permanent tan flashed a twenty-tooth smile. "It's going to take a lot of shaking to loosen her up. But I'm game."

"Thank you," Vondreesen said.

As they rose, I got the impression that this was a group of friendly rivals—at least while the cameras weren't recording.

Vondreesen led us through one of his secret doors at the back of the room, avoiding a procession past other guests. He greeted each member individually as they entered the hidden corridor, and joked about burning off the banquet calories as we climbed the stairs, keeping the atmosphere light. The man really was a master of manipulation.

I was relieved to find Katya looking composed as we entered the library.

Casey's dour expression hadn't changed, but the room had. He'd rearranged the chairs to create a mini-amphitheater, and now sat in the corner with Katya.

Vondreesen led me to center stage while the Congressmen took their seats. With the flames behind me and the mob in front, it felt like the Salem Witch Trials.

This was it.

Time for the speech of my life.

My half-sample of Brillyanc was fading, but I hoped my jurors were still fully endowed. I needed them sharp and savvy. Modern murder trials lasted for months, but I'd only have minutes. Wild West rules, with the hangman present.

Vondreesen gestured my way, and I began. Since politicians were all professional bullshit artists, I went with the direct approach. No introduction. No small talk. "I understand you've been told that Brillyanc derives, in part, from the gallbladders of sun bears. An endangered species. Is that accurate?"

My opening hit them like an arctic breeze. Expressions turned sour, and the atmosphere morphed from convivial to grim.

I took that as a yes.

"I see you're all well aware of the implications. This makes Brillyanc a big secret. A secret my family was killed to protect." I paused in an attempt to meet each face for a second or two. Most eyes looked away, but a couple had gone wide at the mention of my family's death.

"The use of sun bear gallbladders explains why Brillyanc is not approved by the Food and Drug Administration. It also helps to justify an exorbitant price tag, while ensuring that you, its elite users, have a vested interest in keeping Brillyanc a secret." I began walking the semi-circle, addressing each audience member individually for a second or two like trial lawyers did when they were allowed to approach the jury box.

"It wouldn't do much for your reelection prospects if word of your habit got out. You'd get skewered from both sides. The tree huggers would condemn you for killing Winnie the Pooh. The bible thumpers would crucify you for using illegal drugs." All eyes were frigid now. The politicians' bonhomie replaced by steely stares.

Casey retained the serious demeanor befitting a sergeant-at-arms, but I was glad to see by the bulge in his robe that he'd shifted his aim from Katya to me.

Vaughn, suddenly looking no less nervous than Katya did beside him, extracted the tablet from the pocket of his robe and began swiping. If he was summoning the goon squad, I didn't have much time.

I returned to center stage and stood facing Senator Collins, holding her unflinching eyes. "It's all bullshit. Brillyanc is entirely synthetic. There are no animal products involved. To borrow Vaughn's phrase, you've all been duped."

I paused as a murmur broke out.

Casey tensed.

Vondreesen jumped into the gap. "Don't be silly. What would be the point of such a silly deception? There are plenty of other reasons to keep Brillyanc a secret. Everyone here benefits from our keeping it exclusive, and limiting its use to the elite alone. Am I right?"

A few congressional heads nodded. Others seemed less convinced. "Are you a chemist, Mr. Achilles? Or a physician?" The speaker had a rugged, weathered face. The Marlboro Man in his heyday, with a Texan twang.

"He's unemployed," Vondreesen said. "He used to be a spy. I thought he might be useful to us, but apparently I need to reconsider. I'm sorry to have wasted your time. Please forgive the interruption." Vondreesen turned to usher them back downstairs, but nobody moved.

I stood my ground.

Senator Collins said, "What was the point, Mr. Achilles? Why would Vaughn devise and propagate such an abstruse story?"

I needed to draw the other congressmen into the conversation, so I answered her question with a question. "When does a magician use his right hand to produce fire and smoke?"

That evoked thin smiles.

Collins said, "Were you up to something left-handed, Vaughn?"

Vondreesen said, "You've been benefitting from Brillyanc for over a year now. You know it works wonders. Your stars are all rising. As advertised. You of all people should know that talk is cheap and accusations are easy. It's actions that count, and you've all benefited from mine. Forgive me for this interruption with its spurious allegations. Let's get you back down to the flight zone."

As if on cue, Boris and Ivan entered through the doorway on the right. Seeing the crowd, they paused a few steps in.

While they looked inquisitively at Vondreesen, Casey spoke up for the first time that day. "I'd like to hear Achilles out."

"I too would like to know what he meant by *you've all been duped*," said a bald, bespectacled congressman, his voice a good fifty pounds heavier than his frail frame.

Boris and Ivan inched closer, rearing to be let off the leash.

This was the crucial moment. My life was in the balance. Would Vondreesen go with diplomacy, or war?

Chapter 92

Phone a Friend

VONDREESEN KNEW he was in a pickle. A sour one, judging by his face. His nature won the struggle. Ever the diplomat, he smiled and halted the black suits with the palm of his hand.

The room exhaled.

Boris and Ivan assumed an observation stance with their weapons still holstered.

All eyes turned to me.

With guns on both sides of me and the inferno behind, I returned my full attention to the congressmen before me. "The trick to telling a convincing lie is to stick close to the truth. I'm sure you've all heard that a time or two from political strategists."

A few nods, but only a few.

"It's true that Brillyanc will never gain regulatory approval. Vaughn was honest with you about that. But he lied when he told you it's because of the drug's provenance." I turned to look directly at Vondreesen. "The FDA would never approve Brillyanc because of its side effects."

Fear built on Vondreesen's face as I paused to let the revelation sink in and imaginations run wild.

Vaughn's reaction told me part of what I needed to know.

Up until that point, I hadn't been sure if he'd been among those duped by the sun bear story, or if he was one of the deceivers.

Now I knew.

Vondreesen was in on it.

That was bad news. If Vondreesen had been among the duped, then there was a chance I could have turned him into an ally—

enemy of my enemy, and all that. Instead, I was looking at a winner-take-all battle. Normally I wouldn't mind that proposition, but Vondreesen had the benefit of knowledge, whereas I had only speculation.

I returned my attention to the jurors. Their expressions had shifted from anger to a mixture of concern and fear.

"What side effects?" the bespectacled congressman with the heavy voice asked. All eyes shifted from me to him to me again.

Casey moved a step closer to me and said, "Congressman Neblett is a neurologist."

Having an authority other than Vondreesen in the room was a bit of good luck. Neblett would be the one to sway opinions on medical matters. If I could convince him, he would convince the rest.

I was comfortable in medical discussions after growing up as the son of a physician. I'd also gone through extensive medical consultation during my Olympic-training years. Unfortunately, physicians worked from data, and I had none. I had to bet all my chips on the next hand—before I saw the last card.

I turned back to Vondreesen. I needed to see his eyes for this. They'd give me the read on that final card. I'd be gauging his reactions using the same biofeedback clues favored by psychics and fortune-tellers. With raised voice, I said, "Vaughn can tell you that, doctor. He's been experiencing those side effects."

And there it was.

The telltale flash of panic.

Vondreesen's upper eyelids rose fractionally while the lower ones tensed, the edges of his mouth pulling back ever so slightly. With those micro-expressions as confirmation, I jumped in before Vondreesen composed his retort. "He's in the early stages of Alzheimer's."

"This is complete nonsense," Vondreesen blurted. "My mental faculties have never been better. Brillyanc has no side effects.

None."

Perma-tan jumped into the discussion. "Wouldn't our doctors have detected any side effects? I just had a thorough annual physical last month, and everything came out normal."

"Me too," emanated from around the semi-circle.

Neblett's head shake threw cold water on the crowd. "Neurological disorders like dementia and Alzheimer's are detected by comparative performance evaluations, rather than blood work. Those aren't routine yet."

"Could Brillyanc cause Alzheimer's?" Senator Collins asked. "Is that even possible?"

Again all eyes returned to the neurologist. "There's too much we don't know to say one way or another for certain. We do know that Brillyanc improves cognitive function. It's quite possible that it could be doing damage as well."

An idea struck me as murmuring broke out. I felt a fool for not thinking of it earlier. While the crowd digested Doctor Neblett's revelation, I walked to his side and whispered in his ear. Then I grabbed a phone off an end table, dialed, and handed it to Neblett with the speaker on.

Vondreesen dropped his diplomatic veil. "What the hell are you doing? You can't make a call. That's Rule One."

"Rules are made to be broken," I said, as the international double-ring commenced.

"Hang up! Hang up now!" Vondreesen walked our way, clearly intent on physically stopping Neblett, but Tex's hand reached out and stopped him instead.

The phone stopped ringing, and we heard, "Da, slooshayou," from the speaker.

"Max, it's Achilles. I've got you on speaker with a neurologist and some other Brillyanc users. Really quickly, tell us who you are and what you've learned about Brillyanc."

"Ah, hello. I'm a doctoral candidate in biochemistry at Moscow

State University. I've also been participating in the Brillyanc clinical trial for the past eighteen months," he paused there, his voice cracking.

"Are you okay, Max?"

"No, Achilles, I'm not. I've run more tests and calculations since we spoke. I discovered that Brillyanc exposes the brain to extreme levels of oxidative stress, which is the primary exogenous cause of dementia, Alzheimer's, Parkinson's, and other neurological disorders. While it's impossible to predict individual reactions, I'd estimate that an individual's odds of developing a serious neurological disorder quadruple with every infusion. I've had six, which increases my odds four-thousand fold. So no, I'm afraid I'm not alright."

The room sat still in stunned silence. We could even hear the whooshing flames through the glass. Max's tone had been as convincing as his words.

I looked at Neblett. His face was grim. "I'm afraid that oxidative stress makes sense. It's reasonable to conclude that as our minds burn brighter, so to speak, they'll generate more 'pollution.' Furthermore, there are no routine tests for oxidative stress, so it would go undetected."

"Thank you, Max," I said. "Hang in there. I'll call you back a little later, my friend."

Neblett hung up.

Vondreesen yelled, "This is crazy! One student's tests aside, you haven't seen a shred of evidence. Real doctors get things wrong all the time. Believe me. As a venture capitalist, I know. This one's talking about conditions that can't be predicted and a pathology that can't be tested. It's poppycock. Ask yourself, whom are you going to trust? Some student six thousand miles away, or your own bodies? You feel great, right? Your minds have never been sharper, right?"

Nine chins bobbed up and down. Vondreesen had personal

experience on his side, and theory rarely trumped that.

Chapter 93

Destiny

I LOOKED AROUND Vondreesen's study, meeting every gaze. Some were glowering, some closer to weeping. All verged on hysteria. The jury was still up in the air. Probably leaning against me. They all desperately wanted to believe Vondreesen. Their very lives depended on my being mistaken.

Vondreesen pressed his advantage. He spread his arms wide—a man with nothing to hide. "If what you say were true, then I'd be a victim as well. I've been taking Brillyanc longer than anyone. But it's not true."

A concurring murmur broke out.

I still had a card to play—or rather, a hunch. I took a deep breath, and did my best to speak with conviction. "Tell me, Vaughn, if it's not true, then why did you stop taking Brillyanc?"

Vondreesen's jaw slackened, but he recovered quickly and spoke confidently. "I haven't stopped taking it."

"Sure you have. It's in your eyes. They've lost their glow. At first I thought it was retirement, but looking at the gleaming eyes of all the users in this room, I know better."

"Now you're claiming to know what medicine I take? This is ridiculous."

"It's easy enough to test, Vaughn. You really want to take that path?"

Vondreesen didn't answer.

"Everybody, what's the value of Pi squared, out to ten significant figures? Raise your hand when you have it."

Neblett's hand went up after about forty seconds. Others began raising their hands ten seconds later. Within another minute all nine were up, as was Casey's.

"Time to speak up, Vaughn."

Vondreesen remained silent. He just stood there blinking.

"It's true." Collins' voice was now strained and weak. "We're all headed for the long goodbye. How could you, Vaughn?"

A room full of outraged eyes burned into the shrinking host like so many lasers.

"I ... but ... there was ... You have to understand, I–" Vondreesen turned to me. "It doesn't matter. So what if it's true? It wouldn't have changed anyone's mind. You of all people should appreciate that, Achilles." He stepped closer and poked me in the chest with his index and ring fingers, hard enough to hurt.

"Why me? Appreciate what?"

"Your namesake. Achilles. Besides his heel, what's he most famous for?"

"His choice," Collins said.

"That's right," Vondreesen said, whirling about. "Achilles chose to live a short life of glory, rather than a long life of obscurity. His personality is the archetype of everyone in this room. Nobody here would have chosen different if they'd known the truth. It's a lock. A glorious life versus an obscure chance of some disease. No contest. Hell, look at cigarettes. No glory in those, and the warning's crystal clear. Smoke these, get cancer. Yet people pay big taxes and slink off into corners to light up by the millions. I made you geniuses!"

Tex glared at his host. "You didn't give us the choice."

Vondreesen shook his head. "Don't you see? You never had a choice. Not really. It's in your nature. It's destiny." He spread his hands like a preacher.

Casey withdrew his hand from his pocket in a quick fluid move, exposing the silenced Springfield and surprising the guests. He pointed it at Vondreesen's heart.

Boris and Ivan reacted as one, leveling their sidearms on Casey.

Casey ignored them. "I want the truth. I want all of it. And I want it now."

I saw the calculation cross Vondreesen's face. Then I saw him begin to move. If he could take Casey out, Boris and Ivan would have the only other weapons in the room.

I had no great desire to save Casey. At the very least, he'd been complicit in my situation. But he was my attorney—and at the moment, one of just two people on the planet who both knew me to be innocent and had the ability to prove it. Bottom line, I needed him alive.

There's no secret to shooting accurately indoors. Outdoors, where distances are much greater and weather factors in, you need to make all kinds of adjustments for wind, and gravity, and drag. But indoors, it's simple trigonometry.

If a true barrel is pointed directly at a target, you'll hit it. How perfect the pointing needs to be, and how steady the barrel needs to remain during the firing sequence depends on the distance to the target. The shorter the distance, the more forgiving the requirements.

There were only a few feet separating Casey from Vondreesen. It would almost be harder to miss than to hit at that distance—even if Vaughn was shooting from a tiny weapon concealed up a sleeve.

Vondreesen was already raising his hands from the palms-up position he'd assumed while pleading his case. He was just a flick of the wrist and a squeeze of the finger away from hitting Casey with the last surprise of his life.

And I couldn't stop him. I couldn't get to Vaughn in time.

I yelled, "Semper Fi!" to shock the crowd and alert Casey while spinning in a counterclockwise move. My right arm snatched up the moon rock from the table as I began a full-body side-arm pitch. I put everything I had into the throw—legs, back, shoulders, and arm —building momentum and transferring power as if I needed the rock to reach orbit. I whipped around until I was facing the inferno, and then released it as the Russians drew their guns.

Chapter 94

Royal Flush

THE HEAVY HUNK of moon rock shot from my grip as if released from a giant sling. It hurtled through a few feet of open space and transferred all its momentum into the enormous pane of curved glass at the point closest to the Russians.

An ominous cracking crunch rang from the glass wall as the rock's high-velocity crystalline structure overpowered the glass's static amorphous one, sending shock waves and breaking bonds. Then the rock breached the distal plane, releasing the vacuum and putting a whole other set of forces into play.

The vacuum's implosion sent shards of glass shooting out of the new hole like a plume of water after a cannonball strike. Shock waves rippled across the wall's remaining surface, shattering it like the world's largest light bulb, with a pop loud enough to shake books off shelves.

I continued swinging around, propelled by the momentum I'd generated. I hit the deck in the fetal position, while a barrage of glass shrapnel blew past me and into the Russians. Not all of it. My back felt as if it had been lit on fire. But Boris and Ivan took the blast like straw scarecrows in a tornado. Their clothes were shredded. Their skin was scratched and sliced and punctured and scraped. I couldn't tell immediately if anything was lethal, and I never got the chance to find out. Casey's Springfield coughed twice and both Russians dropped.

But each got a round off first.

Both missed Casey. One flew past his right shoulder, the other his left ear. They pierced the inner glass wall instead. It shattered like a windshield, sending cracks out from the 9 mm bullet holes like giant spider webs, but the wall remained standing, thanks to the infrared film.

I rolled forward as the Russians dropped, grabbing one of their bloody Glocks in each hand. Ignoring the pain in my back, I leapt to my feet with both weapons aimed and ready. For a second I was thrilled by my reversal of fortune—then my heart turned to ice.

Vondreesen had a gun to Katya's head.

He'd popped it out of his sleeve and cudgeled Casey before bringing it home under her chin. As Casey dropped and Katya screamed and nine members of Congress looked on in abject fear, Vondreesen yelled, "Drop 'em, Achilles! Before this really gets out of hand."

Adrenaline had slowed time to a snail's pace, so half a heartbeat was all I needed to assess the situation. By aiming for the right corner of the fireplace, I'd limited the significant glass-blast damage to the part of the room where the Russians had stood. I saw a few flecks of red scattered among the congressmen, but no serious injuries.

Vondreesen had knocked Casey unconscious.

Katya was fine—other than having a gun pointed at her head.

I couldn't tell what the blast had done to my back, but I seemed to have full muscular control and wasn't feeling woozy from blood loss, yet.

Putting a bullet into Katya's head would get Vondreesen nowhere but killed.

I knew that.

He knew that.

I walked toward him without dropping my guns.

He changed tactics. He looped his left arm around Katya's neck and stooped to use her as a shield while pointing his weapon straight at my head.

I kept walking.

"I mean it. Not another step!"

I stopped with about six feet between us, judging that to be the limit beyond which fear might provoke an irrational reaction. I looked over the barrel of Vondreesen's gun to meet his eye. "What do I need to do to get you to release her?"

While Vondreesen tried to puzzle out an escape scenario, I shifted my gaze to meet Katya's wide-eyed stare, and added, "Do I have to drop and shout *rape*?"

As Katya's trigger word left my lips, I crouched to take my head below the immediate line of fire and sprang left.

Vondreesen fired once, high. Purely a reflex move, a startled response. His subcompact adding one more *crack* to the succession of explosions that had pummeled our ears since I'd released the moon rock and tipped the first domino. His next move would have been tracking my lunge to his right, where I was open and exposed and ripe for the plucking. Just a trigger squeeze away from no-more-problem. Would have been, were it not for Katya.

Before the echo of *rape* had died, Katya had bit down on Vondreesen's hand and swung her fist back between his legs with all the ferocity her fright could muster. Instead of swinging off to the right, Vondreesen's gun arm flew back toward center, coming home to cradle the jewels.

As Katya wriggled free, I brought my fist down on the top of Vondreesen's right hand, knocking the weapon from his grasp and breaking it free of the contraption that held it to his wrist.

He glared at me with fiery eyes. It wasn't Brillyanc burning there, but hatred unmasked.

Drawing strength from the emotion, he lashed out with surprising force, throwing a rapid series of left and right jabs reminiscent of engine pistons, pushing me back toward the fire. Not wanting to shoot him point-blank and risk a through-and-through that could injure someone else, I tossed the Glocks and delivered a haymaker to the underside of his chin.

He didn't drop.

He didn't scream.

He just kept coming like a possessed creature that had to let its demon out. Left-right-left-right. Punches with poor aim, but surprising force and relentless fury.

I absorbed the blows and timed my move to grab his recoiling left wrist with both hands. Planting my heels as his right fist glanced off my shoulder, I swung Vaughn around like an Olympic hammer, using his own momentum against him while throwing him off balance. Releasing my grip at the end of a forceful three-quarter turn, I sent him flying backwards into the inner glass wall at the point where the Russians' bullets had struck.

He slammed into it with his shoulders and kept right on going, the shattered glass caving in around him, the film and flame turning it into a hot crystalline hammock. For a long second Vaughn hung there like an enormous fly embedded in the windshield, startled by his situation and shocked at having survived the impact, but unable to extricate himself.

As the room looked on with rapt fascination, the added strain ripped the top of the wall free of the frame and gravity took over. Everyone gasped as the king of the castle plunged backward into the flames.

Chapter 95

Not Over

VONDREESEN'S SCREAMS CRESCENDOED, and then ceased like a phone that stopped ringing. The cessation exposed a cacophony of distressed mechanical noise. As my imagination filled in the picture, the flames changed color and smoke started billowing forth.

Everyone who had moved closer in a morbid trance now recoiled back from the smoke and the smell.

Then the Burning Man extinguished, the grotesque sounds stopped, and the heat subsided.

I looked over to see Casey beside a control panel on the wall. He'd flipped a switch.

He was standing with a dazed look on his face and the Springfield by his side. I had no idea what his next move would be, so I closed the gap with three quick strides and grabbed the weapon by its warm suppressor.

Casey didn't resist.

He let the Springfield slip into my hand.

I wasn't sure if that was a result of shock, or a tactical move. By some counts, he was next in line for a bullet.

I slapped his shoulder with my left hand as men sometimes do, and turned my attention to Katya. She was sitting in the same place she'd landed after sinking her teeth into Vaughn. I walked over and held out my free hand. She took it and I pulled her up into my arms. "You did it again, Katya. That combination move of yours is amazing."

"Promise me that will be the last time it's required."

"I can't promise until this is over. But I can hope."

"What do you mean, until it's over? It is over. Vondreesen is dead."

Before I could respond, Perma-tan shouted over the ruckus, authority in his voice. "Order! Order, everyone! Take your seats. There are decisions to make, and actions to take."

"Congressman Chip Tanner," Casey said, stepping over beside us. I turned to see lucid eyes. His moment of shock had passed. Semper Fi.

Tanner addressed his colleagues with a voice calm enough to quiet a child, but resolute enough to start a war. "What we've seen and heard tonight doesn't change the rules. We still need to maintain absolute secrecy and complete anonymity. Perhaps now more than ever. Are we agreed?"

A murmur of assent and a flourish of nods followed. Then a lone voice of dissent rose from the crowd. It came from an Asian woman who had not previously spoken. She was the group's youngest member, by my estimation. "I don't see how that's possible. We've witnessed three homicides. There's going to be an investigation. We'll have to give testimony."

"No point in any of that," Tex said. "Justice has been served. All we'd be doing is detracting from press coverage of issues that matter, and wasting taxpayer money."

"But we'll be abetting murder after the fact," she pressed. "We could be prosecuted."

Tanner wagged a finger. "With this many members of Congress involved, it's a national security issue. We're obligated to keep it quiet."

"If national security doesn't work for you, consider this," Neblett said. "If word does get out, the leadership will have no choice but to distance itself from us. We'll never see public office again, and we can forget about lobbying, consulting, and speaking engagements. We'll all become pariahs. And let's not forget the executive involvement. To quote the distinguished gentleman from Texas, what would be the point?"

Seven heads nodded back at the junior congresswoman as she looked around. She raised her chin. "I'll bow to your greater wisdom."

Senator Collins picked up the ball. "I propose that we plan to leave here in the morning, the same as always."

She turned to Casey. "Mr. McCallum, to use the appropriate euphemism, are you capable of cleaning up this mess? If we can count on you for that, it will give us a three-month window to deal with the big picture. Something I suspect Mr. Achilles will be keen to help us with."

For my benefit, Senator Collins confirmed what I already knew from Kilpatrick. "Santa Barbara is part of my constituency, and the DA is a personal friend. I'm aware of your predicament. And your history of national service."

Casey was raring to help. "First thing I'll need to do is confirm that nobody downstairs saw what happened. If anyone did, I'll remind them of the rules. Then I'll see to the cleanup."

"I'm with you, partner," Tex offered, walking over to join Casey.

Casey asked, "Any suggestions on disposal?"

I mulled that one for a few seconds, then leaned in to speak with a quiet voice. "I'm no horticulturist, but given that this is an active vineyard of considerable size, I'm guessing there's a fire pit for disposing of all the dead vines. Probably a woodchipper too."

Casey grimaced, but then swallowed it. Semper Fi.

"Look on the bright side," I said. "It's not snowing."

"What?

Tex got the movie reference, and put an arm around Casey's shoulder. "The woodchipper scene from *Fargo*."

Recognizing that my attempt to lighten the mood was probably ill-conceived, I moved to change the subject. Picking Vondreesen's tablet off the floor, I turned to Casey. "Can you unlock this?"

"Try 1999."

"A reminder of the good old days?"

Casey shook his head. "The year Vaughn's net worth went from seven figures to eight. He called it his 'no thanks' year, because with ten million in the bank, he would forever be free to do whatever he wanted."

I punched in 1999.

It worked.

As Casey and Tex set about cleaning up, I went to *settings* and switched the tablet's auto-lock feature to *never*.

I turned back to Katya. "I'm going to summon Melanie, the woman who served us coffee during our first visit. We've got to figure out if she's an asset, or a loose end."

"How could she be an asset?"

"For starters, she'll know if Boris and Ivan are the only enforcers, or if we've got more suits to dispatch. Also, we could use her help to clean up the mess. Both here and now, and then later with the bigger picture."

"But why? Why clean up at all? Isn't this perfect? Isn't this all the evidence you'll ever need to get out of jail? Especially with what you told me about Casey."

"You're right. I have what I came here for. But the picture has changed. It's grown much larger, much more devious and complex. To make things right, I've got to go back to Russia, back to where this all began."

Chapter 96

Angels

AN HOUR LATER, the congressmen were back in their pods, ostensibly playing along as though nothing had happened, but no doubt whispering up a storm.

Katya and I were on our way back to the library to regroup with Casey after a bit of first aid. I'd taken thirty-one pieces of glass shrapnel in the implosion. Fortunately, none of it had cut too deep. Katya had cleaned up my back with a pair of tweezers and a bottle of hydrogen peroxide. I'd be sleeping on my stomach for a few days, but it would heal without loss of functionality.

"We need to talk," Casey said by way of a greeting.

"You're damn right we do, but first things first. How's containment looking?"

"Six guests observed the barbecue downstairs. Tex and I have sworn them to silence. We put a little fear of the Almighty into them as well, in case they got second thoughts. You get the Russian situation figured out?"

"Melanie confirmed that Boris and Ivan were the only suits on the premises."

"That's good news. What's her personal perspective on recent developments?"

"Melanie appreciates both the legal precariousness of her position, and the danger she potentially faces at the hands of the Russians. She's eager to help in any way she can."

Casey smiled. "I bet she is."

"Now, if you don't mind, I need those details that Vaughn mentioned. The proof of my innocence."

"Don't worry about that. I mean, I've got you covered. Believe me. So long as you clean things up in Russia before the Russians start cleaning things up here, you've got nothing to worry about."

I studied Casey's face. He seemed earnest. Relaxed eyes, steady gaze, no tension around his mouth. Plus, he'd spoken pretty definitively when he pulled the trigger on Boris and Ivan.

"There's something else we need to talk about," Casey continued. "Something very important."

He motioned to the coffee table, where the five-thousand-dollar bottle of Louis XIII had miraculously remained intact, along with two of the four snifters. One still bore the lip marks of a dead man, the other remained untouched. "I'm ready for my drink now." He picked up the clean glass and took a long sip with closed eyes.

"I was so thrilled with Brillyanc," he began, his tone wistful. "I thought it was the best thing that ever happened to me. It was like my brain went from six cylinders to twelve. I reveled in the power of my own mind. I used to rev it all the time, metaphorically speaking, like it was a Lamborghini. Just like you did with the Pi multiplication bit. A brilliant move, by the way."

He took another sip and shook his head. "I should have known it was too good to be true."

He lifted his gaze and locked his eyes on mine. "And the truth is even worse than you think."

I saw Katya dry swallow at Casey's revelation.

He plowed on. "But let's get the Russian cleanup out of the way before we tackle that."

"Is Barsukov behind Brillyanc, or Antipin?" I asked, referencing GasEx's Chairman and its CEO. "I'd be inclined to say Barsukov, since he seems to have the right personality, but then Antipin is a Vondreesen clone. An elder statesman with charm to burn. Seems to me they're much more likely to be friends."

"It's Grigori Barsukov. He's been one of Russia's leading angel investors for the last ten years, which is about how long he's known

Vaughn. They live on different corners of the planet, but travel in the same small, elite circles. Grigori isn't charming like Vondreesen —far from it—but he's got his own sort of charisma. Kind of an evil magnetism. And he's very slick. He's also very well-protected."

Casey put his arm on my shoulder. "I don't know how you're going to get to him. But I'm sure he'll kill us all if you don't find a way."

Chapter 97

Priorities

CASEY LOOKED GENUINELY CONCERNED. Having seen Grigori's headquarters complex, I could understand why. The GasEx chairman worked in a fortress. "You said you met him at his office. Did he happen to invite you to his home as well, given that Vaughn is an old friend and you flew halfway around the world?"

Casey raised his brows. "We did, but not because Grigori is a gracious host. He lives in his office. Literally. Like the US President lives and works at the White House. I think he enjoys the analogy. He cultivates it. He refers to his office as the East Wing and his residence as the West Wing."

"Isn't it supposed to be the other way around? Doesn't the President work in the West Wing?"

"Remember where he comes from. Grigori is KGB. East versus West. The reversal is deliberate, I'm quite sure. And as long as we're on the topic and looking at parallels, I'm sure you know what Kremlin means in English?"

"Castle," Katya said.

"Right. And that's where Grigori lives and works. His so-called Rocket is a modern castle. A fortress. He's protected against assault by a wall, a gate, guards, and a lofty perch."

"We've seen it," I said. "At least from the gate. So I've got that picture in my head. Did you get a look at the security inside?"

"Not really. He brought us in by helicopter. When you're flying in and looking down, a fortress is what comes to mind. There's the main building with the pyramid on top, like the Washington Monument would look if topped with glass, but then each corner has its own square tower attached, making the footprint look like the classic X of a castle. Also there's this." Casey gestured to the room they were sitting in. "He chose literal castles for his American outposts."

"The Washington parties are also in a castle?" Katya asked.

"I haven't been there, but I've seen a picture. It's an old limestone manor atop a hill on a large piece of secluded real estate. Definitely something that would both make William the Conqueror smile, and impress modern Washington's elite. Which brings me to the main topic of our discussion."

My mind had been working that one in the background ever since Casey divulged that the truth was worse than we thought. "This is about the *executive involvement* Senator Collins mentioned, isn't it? It's about the empty tenth pod."

Casey gave me a grim look. "That's right. Before he became the Vice President, Daniels was the junior senator from California. And before he ran for his first election, he was a friend of Vaughn's. He was also one of the very first Brillyanc users."

"And he's still using?"

"He is. Vaughn visits him once a quarter. Brings Brillyanc with him. He spends the night at the vice president's home, at the Naval Observatory.

"So you see, this story can't get out. It really is a matter of national security. If the press got word, there would be a major global scandal. Members of both the executive and legislative branches of government using a mind-altering drug that causes dementia. The Brillyanc scandal would dwarf Watergate and Benghazi."

"And Barsukov knows that Daniels is using," Katya said. "Which means so does President Korovin. Which means the Kremlin has leverage over the White House. That's what all this is about. That's what the suits were sent here to protect. It's not about billions in drug sales. It's about the global balance of power."

"Precisely," Casey said, sounding very lawyerly. "I knew about the Russians, of course. But I had no clue about the dementia. Not until your revelation. But the second you mentioned it, everything fell into place. A benefit of Brillyanc itself, ironically."

Casey drained his glass and set it down with a bit of flair. "I always thought this was about money. It is potentially worth billions, and that's the way Silicon Valley guys think. But as Katya noted, this is really about power, power at the geopolitical level. We're talking influence worth trillions. The chance to change history, move armies, and relocate borders."

"That was the plan all along," I said, speaking to myself as much as the others as the big picture gained resolution in my head. "I wondered why they'd gone with Washington, rather than New York City. I had assumed they wanted to learn from a smaller market before going for the Big Apple, but now I know better." I felt my heart skip a beat as the next shoe dropped. "Wait a minute. If there are nine members of Congress coming to Vaughn's parties, how many more have been snared by the Washington office?"

"I don't know," Casey said. "But if you don't kill Grigori, I'm afraid the whole world is going to find out."

Chapter 98

Deadly Habit

CASEY AND MELANIE agreed to maintain the impression that the great Vaughn Vondreesen was still alive. I had no doubt that they'd work tirelessly and attentively. Both their lives were on the line.

With Vondreesen's iPad and her long familiarity with his style, Melanie would be an effective impersonator in the electronic world. Casey, as Vondreesen's lawyer and consigliere, would handle his phone.

They only had to sustain the illusion for a week.

My trial was set to start next Monday, and I planned to have Grigori Barsukov buried by then. How, I hadn't a clue.

To do our part to maintain the illusion, Katya and I spent the rest of the night in our assigned pods, draining our Brillyanc into the toilet rather than our veins.

I spent much of it on Vaughn's tablet, studying his email. I found one that had been trashed but not emptied during the automatic daily purge. It was from someone named *Archangel* at a popular Russian provider. It had arrived just hours before, and said simply, "Let me know how the recruitment goes." I replied for Vaughn with, "Achilles is aboard, but we lost Boris and Ivan." Hopefully, that would buy us time. Assuming *Archangel* was Grigori. If not, Archangel would assume Vaughn was confused.

There were no calls from Russian numbers in the log on Vondreesen's phone. That was disappointing, but given Grigori's ex-KGB status, I knew he'd likely use a masking relay, so I wasn't discouraged.

In the morning, we left the party as numbers 204 and 205, returning to SFO using the same limo in which we'd come. We retrieved our documents and cell phones from storage, and took a cab into the city.

Now we were holed up in a suite at a large hotel, planning my attack on Grigori Barsukov. It wasn't going as expected.

Try to focus as I might, I was preoccupied with thoughts of Katya.

She'd kissed me just before our final meeting with Vaughn, and despite being a man, I could tell there was something in it. Then we'd spent the night in pods, and slept for the whole limo ride. Tonight, however, was going to be very different. We were looking at a big fat fork in the road. Either we'd sleep together, or we'd drift apart.

I'd punted on the decision, to the extent that it was mine to make, by getting us a two-bedroom suite. We had momentum in that regard from our stay in Washington, so the choice had not been overly awkward. I hoped. I might have detected a flinch.

"There's quite a bit about him online, both traditional press coverage and blogs." Katya was studying the man, while I was learning what I could about his GasEx office. "So far, I've only found one reference to his habits. It's in an article about a trendy club called, get this, Angels on Fire. It's a strip club on the Garden Ring. They're writing about him because apparently he flies in for it every week by helicopter. Come look at this." Katya pointed to her screen.

I walked around to her side of the table. We'd picked up a couple of MacBooks to make our round-the-clock research easier, and we had them opened back-to-back, as if we were playing Battleship.

Casey had wired a quarter-million dollars into my account to give the hunting expedition virtually unlimited resources. He'd also chartered us a jet, more for the trip out of Russia than the trip in.

If I wasn't in the Santa Barbara County Courtroom at nine the following Monday morning, I'd be forfeiting my ten-million-dollar bail. With a mission as tight as this one was going to be, the hours saved by flying private might make all the difference.

The relaxed security that came with flying private would be a blessing too.

If it got to the point where I had to decide between completing the mission or making it to court, I wasn't sure which way I'd go. I was resolved not to let it come to that. Therefore Grigori had at most one week to live. His next trip to Angels on Fire was going to be his last.

Chapter 99

Gusts and Thermals

THE DRAMATIC PICTURE displayed on Katya's screen captured a wiry man in formal dress stepping from a helicopter beneath a red neon Angels on Fire sign. The caption beneath the photo read, "Pouring Gas on the Flames. GasEx Chairman Grigori Barsukov's secret indulgence."

Katya summarized the story. "Every Saturday, Angels on Fire has an auction in their Rainbow Room. Apparently it's become quite famous. A hot ticket. Seven women are selected to participate each week, and the club's owner swears none of them are professionals. Thus the excitement."

"Kind of an American Idol, but for strippers rather than singers," I said.

"There's more." Katya scrolled down. "Audience members bid while contestants dance. The winner gets a date for that evening, while the student—apparently that's what most dancers claim to be —gets the proceeds to help finance her education."

"We do that here too. At charity events. To my knowledge, the auctionees are high-society members rather than students, but what do I know?"

Katya clicked a link that brought up an arousing image. "Do high-society members perform the Dance of the Seven Veils? Because apparently that's what they're doing during the auction process. It says each contestant is assigned one of the colors of the rainbow, and is given a costume comprised of veils of that color with a matching G-string. Looks like the bidding goes on until only the G-string is left. I suppose the winner gets to remove that. If the date goes as planned."

I returned to my chair. "I'm pretty sure that here in the US, the participants don't do anything they don't want pictured on the society page."

"It says that no names are used, just colors, but the auctioneer reads a biography for each in order to flesh out the fantasy. Whoa, look at this! It costs the ruble equivalent of a thousand dollars for bidders to register. That's on top of the club's hundred-dollar entrance fee."

"Smart marketing. That's how they add cachet. They make it prestigious to hold a bidder's paddle. And you can bet the women who go to the club are all clued into that. Most won't see if you arrive in a Ferrari, but a paddle says the same thing, and it's on display all night. Tells you a lot about Grigori."

"Do you think it's a good place to get to him?"

I shrugged and drained my third cup of coffee. "First reaction? It might be. I'm not happy with the helicopter. That severely limits our options. I'm sure the club itself has security out the wazoo, on top of Grigori's personal bodyguard contingent, so taking him out inside the club would be risky for us and for bystanders. Special Operations Command would never green-light a mission with that profile. And we're not going to be equipped for an air assault. So that only leaves landing and takeoff. That might work if we could study it for a few weeks and identify a security gap. But we'll be doing this cold." The more I spoke, the less encouraged I became.

"On top of that, I've got to be in Santa Barbara Superior Court by nine Monday morning. Even with the ten-hour time change, a Saturday night operation would be cutting it close. So I'm thinking that Angels on Fire should be an option of last resort."

I was surprised to find myself feeling natural using *we* to discuss an assault operation with Katya.

She seemed to embrace it.

"Do you have an alternative? A first resort?" she asked.

"I'm thinking I'll need to treat it like a sniper mission."

"What's that mean? Are you going to shoot him from a mile away with a rifle?"

"Shoot him? Yes. With a rifle? Maybe. From a mile away? No. What I meant was that I'd lie in wait in a location that he frequents, and then take him out when he shows up."

"At Angels on Fire?"

"No. The architecture isn't suitable." I whirled my laptop around and pointed to a Google Earth image. "The distance between the helipad and door is less than ten meters, so I'd only get a few seconds, during which the helicopter's rotor wash would blow the bullet all over the place. And that's in addition to the gusts and thermals that are going to surround any building in the heart of a major city. Plus, there's no decent vantage point above the club, other than the Ministry of Foreign Affairs, and I can't hole up there with a sniper rifle."

"So where, then?"

"At his office."

Katya tilted her head and narrowed her gaze as though studying a calculus problem on a blackboard. She moved the mouse from Angels on Fire to the GasEx complex. "I'm confused. Maybe I don't get the whole sniper thing, but his building is the tallest for miles around. How do you make the trigonometry work? How can you shoot him up there? Are you just going to hope he comes out to walk around the edge, like he did with Casey and Vondreesen?"

"No, I couldn't count on that happening, and again the thermals would make it an impossible shot. I'm going to climb the building and wait for him up top."

Chapter 100

Disproportionate Response

KATYA GLANCED DOWN at me with incredulity in her eye and a question on her lips. "Even after everything I've witnessed, I still don't see how you could possibly hope to climb GasEx. I understand climbing a house with windowsills and drainpipes, but this is a skyscraper."

I was lying on a swatch of spandex like it was a bed sheet, while Katya traced my silhouette with a fabric marker. To avoid staining it with blood from my shrapnel wounds, I had thirty-one Band-Aids on my back, complete with thirty-one dabs of antiseptic. Bless her heart. The fabric resembled the blue glass of the GasEx building. We also had a swatch that matched the building's stonework, and a sewing machine.

The plan was to sew front and back sides together to create a formfitting jumpsuit. A bottom half that would fit like overalls, and a top half that would fit like a hoodie. Only my hands, feet, and face would be uncovered. The ghillie suit didn't need to be pretty. It just needed to fit without restriction through a wide range of motion. Since neither of us was an accomplished seamstress, we'd bought enough material to accommodate multiple attempts.

"Technically, the climb isn't going to be challenging," I replied. "There are corners running all the way to the top. Beyond basic skills, all that's required to conquer GasEx is physical endurance, and psychological control."

"What do you mean by psychological control?" Katya asked, as she started in with the scissors.

"Basically, that amounts to ignoring irrational emotions. In this case, the fear of falling."

"You think the fear of falling is irrational?"

"If you're not drunk or running on ice, falling is highly improbable. When's the last time you fell?"

"I don't remember."

"Exactly. But if we were walking near the edge of a cliff, you'd become very concerned about it. For millennia, only the wary lived long enough to reproduce, so now extreme caution is built into our DNA. This creates what military minds would call a disproportionate response. For example, say you were taking a bath and somehow a mouse fell in the tub. How would you react?"

Katya's face scrunched back and her lips thinned. "I'd scream and splash, then scramble from the tub and run from the room."

"Exactly. But there's no real threat posed, except to the mouse. Rodents and bugs rarely harm anyone in the civilized world, but we still react to them as if they're hand grenades."

Katya's expression told me I hadn't sold her.

"Working for the CIA, I frequently faced choices between tactics that *all* offered odds of survival much worse than rodent encounters. Over time, I conditioned myself to calibrate my psychological response to dangers based on their probability. I learned to evaluate before I react."

I'd anticipated the math bringing Katya around, but the downward tilt of her chin told me I needed to work harder. "Now I draw the line using a simple formula. If the odds of mortal harm are less than one percent, then a situation no longer triggers anxiety. And the odds that a critter will kill me, or a distant handgun can hit me, or that I'll randomly slip or trip while walking, or running, or climbing are all effectively zero."

Katya's expression told me I still wasn't there. I decided to move on.

"As for the physical endurance part, that's a combination of attitude and repetition. Can you ignore the pain? Can your muscles keep contracting? Climbing a hundred meters to the top of the GasEx building is going to be the rough equivalent of two hundred chin-ups. In prison, I was cranking out a thousand a day. So I know I won't fatigue. And I know from experience that I won't fall. Thus I can focus on the real threat, which is being seen."

Katya looked relieved, although her voice was still tentative. "Thus the camouflage suits. But they won't make you invisible."

"Right. They'll just help me blend in. So I'll still have to avoid attracting eyeballs. That means minimizing movement, sound, and length of exposure. I'm not too worried about movement or sound, since I'll be climbing at night. But speed is an issue. I'm sure there will be patrolling guards, and it could take a long time to free solo a hundred meters up a smooth corner, so I'm going to use a tool that should cut the ascent to under fifteen minutes."

Katya gestured for me to continue. Progress.

When the possibility of climbing the GasEx building first arose, I emailed an inventive climbing buddy. The latest tool he'd showcased on Facebook wouldn't arrive until morning, so I explained it to Katya along with the rest of my plan.

When I was done, Katya sat quietly for a moment, reflecting. "So your plan is to hide on the rooftop, wait for Grigori to appear, and then shoot him?"

"That's the way snipers work."

"But how will you get away?"

"That will depend on the circumstances. Probably either in the helicopter, or by climbing back down, or with a parachute."

"Will a parachute work from that height?" Katya asked with the skepticism of someone who could do terminal-velocity calculations in her head, even without Brillyanc.

"I'll pre-inflate it. There will likely be an updraft on the windward side of the building."

Katya pulled her first attempt at overalls off of the sewing machine.

I tried it on. "It's not pretty, but then, with luck nobody will ever see it."

"I hope you're not counting on luck. This hasn't been your lucky year."

Chapter 101

The Ghost

OVER THE NEXT couple of hours, we cranked out a matching pair of coveralls in the stone-colored spandex, and tops in both patterns. Then we sewed matching camouflage packs for my guns and gear. Between the two suits, I would be able to blend in anywhere on the GasEx building.

I checked the results in the hotel mirror. "I wonder if this is how Peter Parker felt after his first attempt at Spiderman?"

"More like Bruce Wayne," Katya replied. "Batman was the one with all the gear."

"How did you—" I didn't finish the question. I knew the answer. Colin was a big DC Comics fan. I'd invited a ghost into our hotel room.

Katya met my eyes.

She saw the ghost too.

"We both loved him," she said. "You, for your whole life. Me, with my whole heart. We'll never forget him. But we are forgetting something, perhaps the most important thing. Now that he's gone."

I took a step closer, catching my own reflection in the mirror. I looked like a creature from the movie Avatar, minus the big yellow eyes and prehensile tail. "What are we forgetting?"

"We're forgetting that Colin loved us too. He'd want us to be happy."

Katya's words reminded me of the first time Dix let loose on me during combat training. I never saw the blow coming. He hit me out of nowhere with a lightning combination that left me breathless and dizzy and disoriented and flat on my back. I felt like that now. Without thinking, I asked Katya, "Do you think I could make you happy?"

"You make me feel safe. And you make me feel loved. And I don't know what I'd do without you."

I found myself holding my breath. I exhaled, knowing from her tone that a *but* was coming.

"But I haven't put Colin behind me yet. And I can't move on until I have. I want to, but I can't. I need time. I've never gone through this before, so it's hard for me to estimate how long it will take."

I took a half step back.

Katya took a half step forward. "I tried looking up a ratio on grieving—some peer-reviewed study that would orient me. It's been six months since he died, and I knew him for sixteen months. I thought there'd be an algorithm, but I didn't find anything predictive. And of course I'd been hoping to spend my whole life with him, so that would have confounded the calculation even if I had found one. And now I'm prattling on. Because I'm nervous. Because I know that someday I will be ready to move on, and I'm afraid that you won't be there when I am."

I didn't know what to say to that.

I wasn't sure what I was feeling, and I knew better than to trust my feelings even if I did, given my current circumstances. As for the long-term, my thinking didn't go beyond the trial that started next Monday. What would be the point?

So I picked her up, cradled her in my arms, and carried her to the bed. I laid her down with my chest pressed to her back and my arm around her. Then I held her hand in mine, and we fell asleep, surprisingly content.

When I awoke I felt as fresh as a sunlit field after a short summer storm. Totally relaxed even without complete release. That was when it hit me, and I literally shook.

"What is it?" Katya asked, her voice soft and innocent, still half-cloaked in slumber's shroud.

"It's not going to work."

Katya rolled over, reacting to the timbre of my voice. "What won't work?" she asked, alarmed.

"The plan."

As Katya exhaled in relief, I realized the unfortunate ambiguity of my words.

"Why not?" she asked.

"Because I figured out what Grigori is really up to. We need to take him alive."

Chapter 102

Outmaneuvered

KATYA SAT UP so fast she looked like she'd popped from a toaster. "Why do we have to take Grigori alive? What do you mean, you figured out what he's really up to? I thought that was pretty clear."

"Remember our discussion with Casey? We concluded that the Brillyanc conspiracy was more about influence than direct profit. We concluded that the ability to blackmail the vice president was potentially worth trillions."

"Sure, I remember. Giving Korovin that kind of influence is a scary thought."

"Right. Except it doesn't."

Katya's face crinkled into a confused expression that was the cutest thing I'd seen in years.

"The vice president doesn't have that kind of power. Not really. The *president* is our government's executive. The vice president decides nothing."

"So it's a money thing after all?"

"No. It's still a power play. We just overlooked one critical move."

"What's that?"

"Do you know what the vice president's job is? He only has two constitutionally mandated roles." I held up two fingers. "He's a tiebreaker in the Senate. And he takes over—if the president dies."

I watched Katya's eyes turn to ping-pong balls as she put it all together. "Grigori intends to assassinate President Silver."

"Right."

"So that Daniels will become the president."

"Right."

"And since Korovin knows that Daniels secretly used a dangerous, unapproved, mind-altering drug, he can blackmail him."

"Right."

"And given Korovin's expansionist agenda, I'm sure he'll make good use of it."

"Exactly."

"But how could he possibly kill Silver? Assassinating the President of the United States has to be the toughest assignment in the world, even if you're Korovin."

"That's what I need to ask Grigori. That's why I need to take him alive. And quickly. Silver's going to Moscow next weekend."

As Katya sat up, I had a flashback to the morning this all began in a Santa Barbara hotel room. Sophie had been beautiful, but even clothed, Katya was more spectacular. A launch-the-ships and raise-the-drawbridge miracle, with very non-biblical proportions. My train of thought went off the rails, but Katya's question put it back on. "You think he'll risk killing Silver in Moscow?"

"No. KGB guys are too crafty for that. But he might tip the first domino."

"How do you think he'll do it?"

I shook my head to reboot my thinking. "In a word? Cleverly. Your countrymen are known within intelligence circles for devising innovative and ingenious methods of assassination. They took out one famous defector with a ricin pellet fired from the tip of an umbrella. They killed another by lacing his tea with Polonium-210. They assassinated a head of state by planting a bomb beneath a chair in a sports stadium during its construction, knowing that he'd be sitting there a year later for a national celebration. Who knows what they'll devise for a man with a briefcase that launches nukes. The only thing we can be sure of is that it will be innovative, and ingenious, and nearly impossible to defend against—unless you know it's coming."

"Can't you modify your plan to kill Grigori? Use a tranquilizer dart or something to capture him instead?"

"Kills and captures are totally different beasts. Shifting from lethal to debilitating force increases the risk tenfold, and that's just the beginning. Exfiltration becomes exponentially more complicated. I could account for all of that with proper planning, but I'll have neither the time nor the conditions. I won't know Grigori's procedures or habits, and ground zero is a hundred meters up, so I won't know exactly what I'm dealing with until I get there.

"Then there's the interrogation. It's going to be noisy and it's going to take time. That will be very risky without knowing the security arrangements in advance."

I'd tied my stomach into knots while pondering this problem. Now I rolled onto my back to loosen up and avoid distraction while I tried to work it.

Katya did the same.

She got there first.

"I'll enter the auction."

"What?"

"At *Angles on Fire*. I can't guarantee that I'll get in or he'll pick me, but maybe we could figure out a way to increase the odds."

I looked at her with a combination of astonishment, appreciation, and apprehension. I had to wonder where her courage came from.

"I know you're going to object," she continued. "You'll come up with all kinds of reasons why it's a bad idea. But I want you to do me a favor instead. I want you to pretend that I'm one of your fellow CIA operatives. What would you do then?"

What was it about this woman? How had God packed so much greatness into a single petite package?

Rather than questioning the divine, I did as she asked. I swapped her image for that of Jo Monfort, a French operative I'd worked with. The scenario flowed easily from there.

"You'll get selected. There's no doubt about that. There's a better chance of Grigori dropping dead of a heart attack between now and Saturday than there is of Angels on Fire rejecting you. The same goes for Grigori's interest at the auction, particularly if you play to him. Speaking as a hot-blooded male member of the human race, I can assure you that's an iron-clad guarantee. And I'll be there, helping steer things as a fellow bidder. The big question is what we do once you win—not that I'm agreeing to this approach."

"Let's order up breakfast and think about it," Katya suggested.

"Great idea." I put a rush on our order and it arrived just as we were ready for it. Pots of strong coffee and herbal tea. A carafe of freshly squeezed grapefruit juice. A lobster omelet with brie cheese and a side of fresh fruit for her. Eggs Benedict with a side of oatmeal and a berry plate for me. Plus, a couple of big bottles of water. We'd missed a few meals as of late.

"A medical emergency," I said, as the plan materialized inside my nourished head. "That's how we do it. Once you're alone you stick him with a tranq dart. Then you call me and Max and we'll show up a few seconds later at the gate in an ambulance."

"You sure they'll let you into the compound? Even in an ambulance?"

"After you call me, you'll need to find a guard. There will probably be one waiting nearby, ready to take you away once Grigori's had his fun. Tell him Grigori had a stroke or heart attack. The guard will likely have been at the club as well, which means he'll have heard your biography. If we present you as a medical student, then you'll be credible. You can even get specific to add urgency—say he had a heart attack. Those are common enough in older guys during sex. With heart attacks, time is muscle, which gives you an excuse to push the guard faster than he can think."

"Well alright then," Katya said. "Sounds to me like we've got a plan."

As much as the idea made me cringe, I had to admit that we did.

PART 4: POLITICS

Chapter 103

Blood on Fire

GRIGORI WASN'T SURE which he enjoyed more, stepping off his helicopter on his way into Angels on Fire, or hopping back on afterwards with the catch of the week. Going in, he got to enjoy the anticipation of wielding unrivaled power. He was Klitschko entering the boxing ring. Bono with a microphone. Tarzan in the jungle. Coming out was also about anticipation, but of a very different kind. That was all about the spoils of war. The pleasures of the flesh. The appreciation of beauty in its ultimate form. He decided that it was the combination that made Saturdays in the Rainbow Room the one appointment on his calendar that was chiseled in stone.

The owner, Leo, proffered a flute of Cristal while escorting him toward his reserved seat just in time for the show. Front and center. When it came to naked women, he wasn't a back-row guy.

Vondreesen had turned him onto drinking champagne. He preferred vodka, but drank champagne at the club for the effect it had on the women. Since his wasn't the friendliest countenance around, he used the bubbly to paint himself in a softer light. The pros didn't care about such subtleties, of course. But there was no sport in bagging a pro. That was why he liked the Rainbow Room. And of course, just winning an auction was no guarantee of ultimate success. The hunt didn't end when the bill was paid.

At the back of the room, behind a velvet rope buttressed by burly guards, hundreds of horny spectators gawked and cheered. Down in front, a rainbow-shaped stage was surrounded by three rows of wide, red, armless leather chairs, spaced to allow plenty of room for the girls to mingle and maneuver. Thirty-five chairs.

Seven girls. A spirited auction guaranteed, given the laws of supply and demand.

"How's this week's catch looking?" Grigori asked, accepting his drink and his chair with relish.

"Only five tens this week," Leo said with a double flash of his brow. "The other two are elevens."

Leo was a natural born salesman with a hungry wallet and a golden tongue, but Grigori knew the owner wouldn't BS him. Theirs was a long-term relationship. "Tell me about them."

"Indigo is a Mariinski ballerina whose career got cut short because her breasts grew too large. Her audition was one of a kind. I've never seen so much talent with the veils. And her energy, sheesh. Someone's up for the ride of his life."

Grigori wet his dry throat with a sip of Cristal. "And Violet? I know you save the best for last."

"I'm not sure if Violet is the best. She's definitely a contender, don't get me wrong. She's stunning, to be sure. Top to bottom, from facial symmetry to carnal chemistry, I don't think I've ever seen better. But she's different. A doctor. I know what my clients like, and I'm not sure she'll perform when it counts. I left her for last because she's a bit of a wildcard."

Grigori raised his glass to that.

The techno music shifted to a sultry rhythm reminiscent of the Strauss original, but more suitable for a modern Arabian night. Leo had a skinny DJ nicknamed Lic, which Grigori understood to be short for licorice stick. Lic was a master of mood whose massive mop of hair was forever swaying to a beat. He watched the auditions with a composer's eye, and customized mixes of the Dance of the Seven Veils for each performer based on her personality and moves.

The stage began to glow like sunrise. Leo had it backed by one of the massive screens used for the latest electronic billboards, and Lic's assistant used it to full advantage. Red made her entrance using a catwalk stride with a bit of extra wiggle, starting a chorus of wolf whistles and catcalls that Grigori knew would crescendo until all seven dancers were standing side by side in a rainbow of sexual desire.

Leo had been right, the first five all ranked as tens for someone, judging by the outbursts coming from around the room. Dark-skinned and light, slim and voluptuous, petite and modelesque. Leo had arranged to pick every patron's pocket.

When Indigo emerged, Grigori found himself on the edge of his seat. She had short, dark hair, coiffed to give her a catlike appearance that matched her moves, moves that Grigori would describe as evocatively animalistic. He made his selection then and there. He wanted a wild ride with that pretty kitty.

Finally, the doctor emerged in violet silk. Grigori inhaled sharply as she strutted his way, all luscious curves and firm jiggles. She was spectacular, but she was also different. Clearly less comfortable on stage than her fellow contenders. Not more awkward, but rather more innocent. Innocence was why these thirty-five men were here, rather than buying lap dances and massages in the club's other rooms.

The crowd seemed to sense Violet's disposition, and their moment of appraising silence erupted into an appreciative chorus that drew Grigori in. Perhaps he would have to take two home tonight. Then the good doctor winked at him as she strode past, and his blood caught fire.

Chapter 104

The FOB

MY HEART invaded my throat, as Grigori's helicopter rose toward the heavy clouds with Katya inside.

"Do you have a helicopter too?" my date cooed.

It wasn't a crazy question, given what I'd forked over for a single night of companionship. A new record according to Leo, the club owner and auctioneer. "No. When I want to fly, I use my jet." As soon as the words were out of my mouth, I knew I'd made a mistake. That was going to make my next move harder for Indigo to take.

I could see the beach at Cannes reflecting in her eyes as the ballerina digested my news. "I like jets."

My Mercedes limo pulled to the curb as we exited the club. We climbed into the back, where Indigo proceeded to lay her long, lithe legs across my lap. As I looked up, she placed a blood-red nail against her crimson lower lip.

The driver only took us a few blocks before pulling over behind an ambulance.

I gently laid my date's legs aside. "You're beautiful. But I'm going to have to take a rain check on tonight. While you were changing I got an urgent call. A close friend of President Korovin's had a heart attack. My driver will take you anywhere you want to go —anywhere but back to the club. I have my reputation to consider."

The image of Cannes faded from her eyes and her plump lower lip began to pout.

"I hope you'll leave me your number," I said, trying to avoid a scene.

Indigo pulled a lipstick from her tiny bag and scanned the limo's interior. "I don't have any paper." She gave me a grin that would jumpstart a Jeep, and wrote her number on the ceiling. "Now you can look me up whenever you want."

Indigo would land herself a jet. It was only a matter of time.

I escaped into the waiting ambulance. "Let's roll," I told an anxious Max. "Lights but no sirens."

He pulled onto the ring road, hitting the gas as the clouds let loose with a heavy spring shower.

Max was doing a lot better than when we'd spoken to him on the phone from Vondreesen's study. He was symptom free for the moment, and that news was apparently enough to let him revert back to his natural optimism. I admired him for that more than I could say.

"How'd it go?" he asked, his voice apprehensive, but tinged with excitement. We weren't in his comfort zone, but he appeared to be embracing the moment. A fellow backpacker, as Katya would put it.

"Katya's in the air, but will be touching down atop the Rocket any minute. Her call could come any time after that. Probably not less than five minutes but you never know, so use the siren if you need it."

"Any issues at the auction?"

"All the women were gorgeous. Grigori passed on the first five. They went for a low of eighteen hundred up to three and a half grand. But then he bid on the sixth. A buxom ballerina. Cost me ten thousand to win her from him."

Max whistled.

"Then only Katya was left. Grigori got into a bidding war over her with an Armenian. Neither of them wanted to go home alone. Given their egos, the auction had all kinds of hormones flying around. It threatened to get ugly."

"What did you do?"

"I covertly spritzed the Armenian with nausea-inducing spray to curb his enthusiasm, but our man still ended up paying twenty for Katya. The Armenian made a point of leaving with a whole harem on his hairy arms."

Max pulled to the side of the road precisely eighteen minutes after Katya set foot in the helicopter. We'd picked a spot roughly halfway between the presidential hospital on Michurinski Prospect, and the GasEx complex a few kilometers further south.

I had the Valdada scope from my CheyTac sniper rifle out before Max had the ambulance in park. I didn't expect to be using a long gun on this mission, but I'd come equipped for all kinds of contingencies. Better to have it and not need it, and all that.

"Keep the windshield wipers going," I said, scanning the dark sky before honing in on Grigori's rooftop lair. "The helicopter's there. Rotor's not turning."

"Any light coming from the pyramid?"

"Nothing bright enough to register."

"Is that a good sign?"

Max was subconsciously drumming his fingers on the steering wheel, relieving nervous tension. I'd seen similar tells emerge a hundred times at this stage in the mission. The team was fine as long as we were moving, but once we entered wait mode, anxiety kicked in. "It is. She'll tranq him as soon as they're alone. Lights off is a step in that direction."

That satisfied Max for about five minutes. As the windshield wipers sloshed a hypnotic rhythm, he hit me with his next nervous question. "What would be a bad sign?"

"Basically any activity other than our ringing phone."

"Should we move up to the FOB?" He asked, after another three hundred painful seconds had ticked by with his fingers drumming away. He was referencing the forward operating base we'd picked out, directly across the street from GasEx.

The FOB was a parking lot in an apartment complex. The front parking spaces gave us line of sight on both Barsukov's Rocket and the guard gate. They also left us exposed. Distant from the door was an odd and conspicuous place to park an ambulance. I hoped the heavy rain would fend off rubberneckers.

I considered asking Max to stick to the plan, and remain at our current location for another three minutes, but that would be pointlessly fastidious. Truth was, Max wasn't the only one growing nervous. "Let's do it."

Chapter 105

Alternative Scenarios

I POWERED ON the radio as we drove toward the FOB, hoping for something soothing. It came to life with a rapper venting frustrations about his mother. Odd choice for an ambulance driver. I turned it back off.

Max stopped the ambulance before the orange cones that reserved our parking spot. He looked over at me with an unstated request.

I looked out at the pouring rain, and prayed that an umbrella was the only thing I'd forgotten. "I don't want to get my makeup wet. Drive over the cones."

I'd made my face up to look like Scar's. Speaking of which … I craned my neck and spotted our stolen GasEx van. We'd parked it nearby in a less conspicuous spot. I wanted it handy, in case we needed Plan B.

Max rolled slowly forward, attempting to nudge the cones out of the way. It didn't work. Both tipped. We listened to them scraping the pavement beneath the ambulance. With a shrug, he shifted into park and glanced at his watch. "I'm sure she'll call any minute."

I indicated agreement.

She didn't call. Not within five minutes. Not within ten.

I gave the radio another try. Found some jazz.

"How long has she been in there?" Max asked, when the song ended.

"About thirty minutes. Tell me again about the tranquilizers you gave her." I knew all the details. I wouldn't have approved the mission otherwise. But it would relax Max to talk about biochemistry.

"The microinjectors in the haircombs you gave me have a very limited capacity, just a tenth of a milliliter. So we needed something that would work with a minute dose, and we needed something that would act immediately. I went with etorphine, also known as M99. It's a common veterinary tranquilizer that's lethal in humans because of our opioid sensitivity. A single drop will kill most people, a mere twentieth of a milliliter. She'll use that to knock Barsukov out. It'll drop the bastard like a bullet to the brain. Then she'll administer the antidote, naltrexone. I've got that stashed in the left cup of her bra. Before he regains his senses, she'll dose him with the chloroform stashed in the right cup, to keep him under." He nodded, reassuring himself.

"Overall the plan is more complicated than I'd like, but it's surefire, and it will leave him looking like something's definitely medically wrong. It will also wipe out his short-term memory. In that regard, M99 is like Rohypnol squared."

"Brilliant, Max. I don't know what we'd have done without you."

"Bastard killed Saba. You sure Katya's okay? What if there's more than one guy in the room. What if Barsukov wants his bodyguard to watch?"

"She's got four doses of M99. Two combs, two ends."

"Yeah, but wouldn't the presence of multiple bodies ruin the heart attack ruse?"

"Katya's very quick on her feet. She'll think of something. You should have seen her when we got attacked at the hotel. The guy who seized her was literally twice her size, and she latched onto his trigger finger like a pit bull on a bone. Saved both our lives. And then at Vondreesen's castle, she did it again."

I was speaking to myself as much as to Max. Truth was, I was kicking myself for agreeing to Katya's plan. I should have nixed it back in San Francisco, but we had the whole partner thing going. It was working for us and I didn't want to ruin it by vetoing her idea.

At the time, I'd expected to come up with a better proposal once we got here.

We had four days in Moscow to prep for the Angels on Fire plan. That seemed like a lot at first, especially with my trial less than a week away, but it proved barely adequate given all the practice, equipment, and contingency planning required.

I'd searched for alternative plans at every opportunity, but had come up empty. We didn't have sufficient data on Grigori's routines to uncover weaknesses—and none were apparent. He lived and worked in a fortress. But I could have gotten more aggressive. I could have broken into the complex and poked around. I had retrieved a blue key card from the stolen GasEx van, using safe-cracking equipment brought from the US.

"How long's it been now?" Max asked. He was working hard to keep calm, but his voice was cracking like an old telephone wire.

I looked at my watch. Two-thirty. Katya had been in there nearly an hour.

The hardest part of most missions was fending off demons while waiting in the proverbial dark, but this was the worst ever. This wasn't an A-Team gone quiet. This was Katya working alone. "She can't drug him until they're alone and getting intimate. Plenty of things could cause a delay. A late dinner to set the mood. A phone call requiring immediate attention. His waiting for the Viagra to kick in."

"How do we know when our worrying becomes legitimate?"

"It's not a question of worrying. It's a question of alternative action. The proper question is: when does it make sense to switch to Plan B? In this case, that will be when we decide Plan A is off track, because it's more likely that she's been identified or thwarted than delayed."

"And when will that be?"

I ran through alternative scenarios in my mind, weighing each against my probability meter, then racking and stacking the results.

"Right about now. I'm going in."

Chapter 106

Dangerous Heights

ONE GOOD THING about Plan B was that it didn't void Plan A. If Katya called, Max could still execute the ambulance scenario.

"If a guard asks why you're alone, tell him there's another emergency, an accident with members of the Duma involved," I said, referencing Russia's parliament. "Everyone understands the hoops that have to be jumped through when politicians are involved."

Since Plan B got me into GasEx using Scar's blue key card, I didn't expect to have any human interaction at all. But just in case, I'd made my face up and styled my hair to resemble Scar's ID. Our physiques and features were in similar ballparks. In my experience, that combination would be good enough for late-night guards. They'd be second-tier, tired, and focused on the deformity.

If not, I had the Glock.

I set about changing out of my EMT uniform, into a black suit and t-shirt. My other gear was waiting for me in the GasEx van, all pre-packed and ready to go.

Max watched me with his mouth half open. "I still can't believe you're going to climb that thing, in the rain no less. But I'm sure glad that you are. What are you going to do once you reach the top?"

"Depends on what I see. I'll have you on comm the whole time, so you'll know when I do. You just remain ready to roll down here. Hopefully Katya will call, but in any case, the ambulance will likely remain our best ticket out."

"You can count on me."

"I know I can, Max. Thank you."

We bumped fists, and I left to climb a castle wall.

The employee gate responded to the stolen key card without delay, and I rolled toward the Rocket like a lion stalking a gazelle.

I had identified the southeast corner of the tower as the best place for climbing. The wind was blowing from north to south, so the southern walls were the most protected from the rain, and the southeast was the least visually exposed. I'd be hidden from neighboring apartments, the guard building, and Max. Probably better for his blood pressure that way. I parked as near as I could get without being conspicuous, and went into the back to grab my gear.

I'd decided to climb wearing the black suit rather than one of my homemade camouflaging leotards since this was a covert assault rather than a lay-in-wait sniping mission. Nonetheless, those silly suits would come along in my bag for contingencies. I was also packing a large sport parachute, heavy-duty cable ties, and a lock-picking set in addition to my shoulder-holstered Glock. My specialty items were a sonic glass-shattering pick, and a pair of sophisticated suction cups.

"How's it looking?" I said into my headset mike.

"All quiet."

"Keep an eye on the pyramid and the guardhouse with the scope. Let me know if anything changes."

"Roger that."

I ran for the southeast corner and came to a stop with my back pressed into the southern wall. It was nearing 3:00 a.m. I paused there for my final pre-engagement reconnaissance, a black figure in the shadow of a stormy night. Quiet all around, except for the wind and the rain and my pounding pulse.

I was worried about Katya.

Turning back to the building, I raised the suction cups over my head. Fashioned from the shells of a popular push-up tool, my friend had designed them specifically for use on glass. Each had a suction cup the size of a salad plate. A thumb switch alternatively blew compressed air in, and then sucked it out, enabling swift and solid attachment and detachment. His clever invention would cut my ascent time by over fifty percent. I just had to be careful not to confuse my thumbs. That was one of those mistakes you only got to make once.

I pressed my left thumb, felt the cup suck in, and pulled myself up the length of my arm. Twenty-five inches from the top of my deltoid to the center of my clenched fist. My feet now dangling, I reached my right arm up as far as I could, and depressed my thumb. Feeling it engage, I pulled myself up another couple of feet. I hit my left thumb, felt the tension release, and began to repeat. *Katya, here I come.*

I wanted to test my ability to climb without the suction cups before I reached breakneck height, so after a few pulls, I tried wedging myself into the corner. Without a rope, this cornering grip was my only safety, my only alternative to falling if the suction cups failed. I'd lined the parachute pack with an extremely tacky rubber, similar to the soles of my shoes. The opposing sticky surfaces would normally make it possible for me to cling to the corner without the use of my hands, but the rain made the pollution-coated glass too slick. I tried every angle and every technique, but nothing gave me sufficient purchase to ascend.

I was about to break a cardinal rule of climbing.

I was about to risk my life on a piece of experimental equipment.

Rain poured down on me as I looked up to the sky. Somewhere thirty stories above, the most wonderful woman I'd ever known was battling the man who had brought nightmares into my life. The man who had ended my father's and brother's dreams. Those thoughts kicked my adrenaline into overdrive, and I resumed the climb with savage intent. Left. Right. Left. Right. Twenty meters. Forty. Sixty.

I was two-thirds of the way up, about twenty stories, when the lightning started. The first bolt came with a thunderous clap that made me glad I was conditioned to working around gunfire. I said, "I'm fine," for Max's benefit, then decided this was a good time to pause and replace the air canisters. My friend said each was good for well over a hundred cycles on the suction cups, but I didn't want to push it. Failure would be catastrophic, and Katya was counting on me.

Chapter 107

Lack of Transparency

A SIMPLE STRAP ran from my belt through each suction cup's handle and back down. This loop provided a measure of safety throughout the climb, and freed up my hands for the swapping operation.

The first time I'd used one of those simple tethers was in Airborne School at Fort Benning. During the final practice exercise, before they threw us out of an actual plane, the Black Hats hoisted us up a tower about the same height as the GasEx complex. During the ascent, our parachutes were held open above our heads by a giant ring. When we reached the top, the drill was to remove the safety tether running between our belt and the ring, and then give the thumbs-up to signal that we were ready for release.

I'll never forget watching one of my fellow paratroopers get confused and give the release signal without unclipping his tether. He ended up dangling by a thread still hooked to the ring, while his inflated parachute dropped below him, caught a breeze, and started pulling him toward the ground. I'd never seen someone so scared in all my life.

But the tether did its job.

We all walked away with a deeply engrained respect for our safety equipment.

"Anything happening?" I asked Max.

"All's quiet. I don't know if that's good or bad, but I'm glad you're on your way. I've been afraid to speak. I worry about breaking your concentration."

"Good instinct. I'll talk to you in a few from the top."

I rolled onto the roof fourteen minutes after my feet left the ground. My arms and deltoids were burning, but nothing like my heart.

Grigori's rooftop terrace ran about three-meters deep, from the edge I'd just clambered over to the base of the glass pyramid. The shiny black helicopter that had delivered Katya loomed behind me, off to the right. I rolled away from the edge so I wouldn't be silhouetted against the night sky and looked for a place to stash the suction cups. I didn't plan on using them to go down, but contingency planning was like breathing. It had often kept me breathing.

The roof didn't appear to have the usual assortment of exhaust pipes and HVAC units, so I made do with stashing my tools against the wall of the nearest corner tower, which rose about a foot higher than the main building. I stashed the parachute there as well, then turned up my jacket collar in an attempt to appear like a guard stuck on perimeter patrol in the pouring rain.

"I'm on the roof," I told Max. "You see any lights on your side?"

"All's dark. I still can't believe you climbed that thing."

I palmed the Glock and crawled to the wall to Grigori's East Wing office. Cupping my eyes, I put my face up to the glass. I couldn't see anything through it. Illumination from the next lightning strike confirmed my suspicion. The glass was electronically opaqued.

The last time I'd encountered this kind of glass was in the unisex restroom of a trendy Belgian nightclub. Customers had the choice of making the door to their stall clear or leaving it opaque. I remembered doubting that many patrons would take advantage of the exhibitionist opportunity, but being certain that all would talk about it. My practical take away from that experience was the knowledge that unlike most mirrored glass, the opacity worked both ways.

I stood and checked the triangular panes one by one. They were huge. Each was roughly two meters in height, and probably weighed a hundred pounds. Twelve rows of panes rose up into the darkness, beginning with twenty-three triangles in the first row on the bottom, and of course ending with just a single triangle in the last row at the top. The entire first and second rows appeared to be opaque.

I began making my way around the pyramid. Looking for doors and signs of life. I made the full three-sixty circuit and found neither. "There aren't any traditional doors on this thing," I told Max. "Just hinges on a few of the panes. I'm guessing they swing out like doors, but they don't have traditional handles I can lever or locks I can pick. Just touch pads."

"Can you get inside?"

"I figure the odds are fifty-fifty that the touch pads will respond to my palm. Either they are biometric, or they aren't."

"Why wouldn't they be?"

"Submarines and space shuttles don't have locks on their doors, and this is no less remote. But I hesitate to try without knowing if the coast is clear on the other side. I'm going to climb the pyramid. He's got the ground-level glass electronically opaqued, but maybe there will be clear panes higher up. I'll start on the southeast wall and will work my way around, so you'll be able to see me soon."

"Roger that. I'll keep watch."

Ten minutes later, I reported back to Max. "We're out of luck. Not a single pane on the pyramid is currently transparent." I sat on the apex and looked in Max's direction for his benefit.

"What now?" he asked. "She's been in there for two hours."

I scared myself with my own reply. "I don't know."

Chapter 108

Lost Luggage

PERCHED ATOP BARSUKOV'S ROCKET like Rodin's *Thinker*, I weighed my options. I considered picking a pane to shatter and dropping in with guns blazing, Hostage Rescue Team style. The core issue with that kind of breach was that I'd only get one shot at picking the right window, and it would literally be blind. If I guessed wrong, Katya and I would both be dead, and in all likelihood, so would President Silver.

"What are you thinking?" Max asked, breaking a long silence.

"I'm thinking it's time to try the doors."

The rain had stopped and the sky had cleared, but I was still wet as a washcloth as I worked my way back down the southeast wall to the hinged pane in the corner. An electric motor the size of an orange Home Depot pail drove the axle that hinged the triangular door. It resembled the engine of the Tesla I'd rented.

Electric motors tend to be quiet, but hinges often squeak. I readied the Glock in my right and pressed my left palm against the sensory pad. A tiny red LED illuminated. "Dammit!" I swapped hands but again struck red. Grigori had gone biometric.

"Try the other doors," Max suggested. "Maybe there's a servant's entrance."

I repeated the exercise three more times. Like a champion bull, I saw nothing but red. "Good idea, but no dice."

I pulled the sonic glass-shattering pick from my waist pack just to have something to fidget with while I thought things over. I loved tools. I could happily spend hours in a hardware store looking around. This one was a beauty. Shaped to resemble an ice pick, it delivered ultrasonic vibrations like a miniature jackhammer, and shattered glass the way its big brother did concrete. Unlike a jackhammer, however, it was quiet. Alas, the shattering glass was another, much louder story.

The triangular frames probably held two panes of quarter-inch glass, separated by argon gas and electronically-opaquing film. Going through would certainly draw the attention of everyone in an adjacent room, and probably anyone in the pyramid.

Testosterone was raging inside me like that bull who'd seen red as I imagined Katya suffering within, but thanks to years of training, I managed to retain control. Shakespeare's Falstaff had been right—at times discretion was the better part of valor.

"I can't risk going in blind. I've got to wait until I can see what's going on."

"That probably won't be until morning," Max said. "I mean, why would he open a window now?"

"You're right. He wouldn't. We're in for a long wait."

I weighed the options, and decided to wait at the apex, some seventy vertical feet above Grigori's floor. I'd be in for some fancy footwork if the pane I was resting on suddenly went clear, but I was up for that. Come daylight, however, I would also be visible from the outside. "I'm going to switch into the glass-blue spandex suit."

While I was changing, Max came through on the headset. "I've been thinking about your earlier comment. The one about submarines and space shuttles not needing locks. I'm wondering if that applies to helicopters."

I felt like the slow kid in class. Inspecting the perimeter was basic operational protocol, and I'd let it slip right by. "Thanks, Max. Even without Brillyanc, you're a genius."

Grigori's Ansat helicopter wasn't the sleekest design, but then neither was Marine One. The high-gloss black paint job went a long way toward making it a stylish toy, especially when viewed by moonlight.

I didn't plan to lie in wait inside, since I didn't know if Grigori would be flying anytime soon. But contingency planning made it a wise move to get the lay of the land, and clear it of any weapons. Perhaps I'd even get lucky and find a clicker that opened the pyramid. "The helicopter's doors have locks, but they're not engaged."

I slid into the pilot's seat and found a weapon the first place I looked, holstered to the front of the pilot's chair. "I found another Glock 43. Grigori must buy them by the case. Nothing else of value up front. Time to check the back."

The rear salon was typical private-aircraft luxury. Black leather armchairs with brushed aluminum accents. No weapons back there, but welcome bottles of water and bags of pistachios. I'd failed to pack either food or drink.

I moved to the back corner of the cabin to test viewing and firing angles. Now that I had two guns, I wanted to see if I could simultaneously cover all the doors.

Something dug into my backside. I twisted to inspect it and felt my heart skip a beat. "I found Katya's cell phone. It was wedged into her chair."

"On purpose, or by accident?" Max asked.

"No way to tell. Maybe she had some reason to hide it. Maybe it slipped out. Maybe she was told to leave it. In any case, it helps explain her silence."

"What now?"

"Good question."

"You should probably leave it there. In case it wasn't an accident."

"That's what I'm thinking. I'm going to head back up the pyramid now, before first light."

"Roger that."

I put the cell phone back where I'd found it and began to leave, but stopped when an idea struck me. I pulled the pilot's Glock from my pocket, ejected the magazine, and removed all six rounds. Then I racked the slide to pop the seventh from the chamber, and slapped the empty magazine back into place. Now nothing inside the Ansat would look amiss, unless Grigori was fastidious about his pistachio count.

A thought struck me as I abandoned the helicopter in favor of the pyramid. I couldn't even be certain that Katya was inside.

Chapter 109

Plan E

DRESSED ONLY in a lacy bra and panties, Katya looked down at Grigori's convulsing body, and wondered if she'd done something wrong. She thought she'd played it just right.

As soon as they made it to his bedroom, all hot with lust and tipsy from champagne, she'd taken charge using her 'Violet' alterego. She issued commands in a firm but sexy voice, while moving seductively and stripping down to lingerie.

Once she had Grigori where she wanted him, with his clothes on the floor and his guard dropped, Katya mimicked the moves of Vondreesen's angel. She circled him with an index finger alternatively on her lower lip and the top of his shoulders, purring intermittently while his breathing became audible. Then *whammo!* She drove the end of her hair comb into the back of his neck.

The hidden injector obviously delivered something. He dropped like a rock. But instead of slipping into sleep-like unconsciousness, he started flopping about like a landed fish.

What had she done wrong?

The answer struck her like a slap in the face. *The antidote!* She'd been so focused on knocking him out, that she'd forgotten part-two of Max's procedure.

But first the chloroform to keep him under.

Katya dropped to her knees and removed the chloroform and M99 antidote from her bra. She found herself shaking as much as her victim, so she closed her eyes and pictured a beach with rolling waves and swaying palms until her hands were sufficiently steady.

Now she needed something to absorb the chloroform. Her eyes

landed on one of Grigori's socks. Holding her breath, Katya poured half the contents of the tiny vial onto the black cotton, and placed it over Grigori's nose. She wanted him inhaling the anesthetic while she administered the antidote.

The naltrexone syringe had a long, thin needle. She pulled off the protective cap, took aim, and plunged it straight down into the thick muscle of Grigori's right thigh without second thought or ceremony.

His spasms ceased immediately.

In fact, everything seemed to stop. He looked dead.

Katya hadn't known what to expect. No doubt Max had told her, but the memory had slipped. God, she hoped she hadn't killed the pervert. The whole reason she'd gone through this humiliation was so that Achilles could learn how he planned to kill President Silver.

She put her ear to Grigori's hairy chest. His heartbeat seemed rapid for someone sleeping, more cha-cha than waltz, but it was steady.

Enough already! Time for the ambulance.

She threw her bra back on, but left the rest of her clothes on the floor, scattered amongst Grigori's. The setting would be crucial to duping his guards.

Where was her phone? It was supposed to be in the back pocket of her skinny jeans. She spent a frantic minute rummaging through discarded garments and around the bedroom, then another retracing every step they'd made since entering the door. There hadn't been much prelude to the striptease. Not at two o'clock in the morning.

Her phone simply wasn't there.

She couldn't remember seeing it while removing her clothes. Maybe it had been stolen at the club.

What did it matter? Achilles had made her memorize his number.

She plucked Grigori's cell from the front pocket of his pants—but couldn't unlock it. The query screen didn't want a fingerprint or a dot-connecting pattern. It just presented a keypad—and she didn't have the code.

Land line?

She found none.

She'd also have to use a guard's phone. That would be tricky, but since she was impersonating a doctor, she could swing it. She'd have to remain clothed only in her underwear. That would underline the sense of urgency while providing some distraction. One more indignity for the cause.

The elevator didn't respond.

She pressed and then pounded her palm against the reader, but got no response. No red light. No green light. No whirring motor. No chime. How could that be? Katya answered her own question. In the middle of the night, it was a sensible security precaution for a man waging geopolitical war.

So what then?

She could go out onto the terrace and try to catch Achilles' attention. Surely he and Max would be watching.

Neither of the doors responded either. Not the door to the terrace. Not the door to the office. Everything appeared to be locked down for the night. Grigori wasn't messing around.

Achilles had warned her that operations rarely went according to plan, but she hadn't expected so many frustrations. Time for what, Plan C? Plan D? She'd lost count. In any case, it was time to make some noise.

She retrieved a quart pot from the kitchen, and began hammering the steel base against the elevator's brushed aluminum door. The noise was jarring to nerves already on edge, but she persisted. And persisted. At least she wouldn't need to work at appearing hysterical over Grigori's 'heart attack'.

Nobody responded.

It seemed impossible that the guards didn't hear—until she thought about it. She was thirty stories up a building made of rock and steel, and it was pouring rain outside.

So what now? What was Plan E?

She couldn't do better than 'Wait.'

Wait for Achilles.

He was probably no less frantic than she. No that wasn't right. Achilles wasn't the frantic type. No less *concerned* than she. Actually, he'd be more concerned. She knew she was safe.

Waiting wouldn't be easy. This wasn't exactly a pass-the-time-watching-tv situation. As her new circumstances sank in, Katya realized that waiting was folly. She should be contingency planning. She should be setting the stage—in case Grigori awoke before Achilles arrived. Oh goodness, she didn't want to think about that possibility.

Chapter 110

Transformations

THE SUN PEEKED over the distant horizon at 4:31 a.m. Mid-May above the fifty-fifth parallel.

Birds began chirping as I did a quick and quiet perimeter walk to confirm that all the windows were still opaque. They were. That was bad news. I was becoming visible faster than Grigori's apartment.

Since my presence at the peak would change the pyramid's silhouette against the morning sky, I lay down with my head a foot below the crest. Max, can you see me?"

"Negative."

"Let me know if that changes."

"Roger that."

The transformation began at 4:57, when the sun's first rays touched the top of the pyramid like a golden crown. "I've got action. The triangles topping the northeast and southeast walls just turned clear. Ooh, there goes the next row, three more panes. They're responding to the sun."

I looked down into Grigori's lair, which had grown to mythical proportions in my mind. His enormous east wing office was decorated in what I'd call modern minimalist chic. Rich granite floors. Black leather seating. Dark wood tables polished to a diamond shine, and a glass kidney-shaped desk. There were rooms along the inside walls. A kitchenette and a bathroom.

No lights were on.

Nobody was present.

I unclipped the tether and slid down a row, just as the windows beneath me transformed. I could see all the way through the pyramid now. That meant the top triangle on the residential walls had also cleared. *Katya should be visible.*

I scampered around and lay with my head extending over a clear section. Cupping my hands to form a bridge between my forehead and the glass, I peered inside.

The tones were lighter and warmer in the living quarters. Golden travertine floors, and honey-colored wood. "The residential half just opened. It's split down the middle into two halves. I'm over the southwest section. It's a great room, combining a living room with a kitchen. The kitchen looks fit for a Michelin-starred chef, complete with a full suite of stainless steel appliances and crowned with an island that boasts a Viking grill fit to handle an entire pig. Again no lights, no bodies."

"Katya's got to be in the bedroom then," Max said, echoing the words in my head.

I circled around the empty office, and stretched my neck to peer through the corner of the bedroom's top pane.

"Well? What do you see?"

"Not enough. The angle's not right. All I see is the top of what I assume is either the bathroom or the closet. I'm going to scooch down and wait for the next level to clear."

"You're killing me."

Max only had to suffer for a few seconds before the sun did its thing. The glass transformed, and there she was—looking right at me.

She'd been waiting.

My heart filled with joy.

"Katya's there. She looks fine. She's lying in Grigori's big white bed. She sees me. She's smiling. She's okay. She's making the telephone sign with her hand and shaking her head. Now she's pointing to Grigori, and making the sleeping sign."

I mimicked jabbing him with a hair comb.

She nodded, then repeated the sleeping sign.

"She knocked Grigori out, but apparently couldn't call."

I looked a question at her.

She smiled, pointed toward Grigori's crotch, and shook her head.

"He didn't lay a hand on her."

I blew Katya a kiss.

The next set of window panes cleared, pouring more light into the room.

Grigori stirred, and opened his eyes.

Chapter 111

Disappearing Act

AS GRIGORI SAT UP IN BED, I ducked my head back, slowly.
Careful not to scrape anything that might make noise, I slid down
another level and peeked back in. "They're talking now. Katya is
smiling at Grigori. He's shaking his head. He looks like he's got the
century's worst hangover. He's getting up. Naked. Looks like he's
heading for the bathroom. Slow and wobbly."

Katya looked up and met my eye. She mimed a stabbing motion.

I shook my head. Used my thumb to give her the get-out sign.

She looked a question back at me. *Was I sure?*

I gestured with my thumb again.

Katya began pulling her clothes on.

Good move.

I brought Max up to speed.

~~Katya looked back up once she was dressed~~

I mimicked, "Your phone's in the helicopter," and then pointed
toward the bathroom.

She gave me a thumbs up. She understood. Sending Grigori to
get her phone was a good way to get his pants on.

I considered dashing to the helicopter to lie in wait for Grigori
to come to me, but tossed the idea. I wanted Katya safe before
moving on him—and I had a better plan. One that wouldn't put
Katya's safety on the line.

Grigori reappeared still walking with deliberate moves. He spent
some time on his tablet while talking with Katya, who played the
role of starstruck guest. Clearly he and Vondreesen had synced on
the technology thing, although I wasn't sure who had led and who

had followed. Another row of windows went clear, making it four of the ten.

"What's going on?" Max asked.

"I'm not sure, but Katya's dressed. Wait. She just left the room."

I made my way around the northern half of the pyramid, slow and flat so as not to capture the attention of anyone down on the street who happened to be looking up. "Katya's at a breakfast table. A woman in a maid's uniform is serving her tea. Another in a chef's outfit is busy in the kitchen."

Watching was getting dangerous. I was only about forty feet up now, and the kitchen had two hostile sets of eyes.

Then Grigori walked in, and there were three.

He was wearing black silk pajamas and fur-lined slippers. He had a coffee mug in one hand, and a phone in the other. He presented it to Katya, and they sat down to breakfast.

The next half hour was tense and painful. My cover slipped away as they ate and the sun rose, drawing me ever closer. Meanwhile Grigori was regaining his wits and getting more time to study Katya's face.

I didn't know if he'd seen the photos of her captured in the Santa Barbara courtroom, but the safe move was to assume that he had. Last night at Angels on Fire, wearing slutty makeup and silky lingerie, Katya had looked nothing like the meek mathematician who had presented herself to the Santa Barbara County Court. Even if she had, the context would have made it highly unlikely that an intoxicated, hormone-driven observer would manage to make the mental connection. But there, in the light of day, without sex on his mind and booze in his veins, the odds of Katya making it out the door were getting worse by the minute.

I studied Grigori live for the first time. He struck me as dark, energetic, and mischievous. His sunken eyes and sharp features made me think of a badger, which coincidentally was the translation of his last name. One thing I hadn't picked up on while studying pictures of him, was that his nose looked like it had been broken in a bar fight. I concluded that he hid it out of habit by turning his head for photographs.

Another layer of windows gave way to clear just as a black suit entered the room. I scrambled to slip out of sight. By the time I readjusted my position and peered back in, Katya was gone.

Chapter 112

Change of Plans

I GAVE GRIGORI'S great room a thorough visual inspection, reconfirming that Katya was gone. "Dammit!"

"What?" Max asked, alarm in his voice. I'd heard him nervously drumming away on the steering wheel, but now he was all ears.

"Katya's gone. I think she left with a man in a black suit."

"Did Grigori go with her?"

"I'm not sure. I don't think so. He was in pajamas. Hold on."

I made my way back around the pyramid, only to find that the pattern of clear panes over the office was no longer regular. Like the oculus of the Pantheon in Rome, it focused the sunshine on a single area. Peering in, I found it empty.

Only the bedroom was left. I sure hoped Grigori hadn't taken her back there. "Keep an eye on the front gate. See who's leaving. Be prepared to follow."

"Will do. But an ambulance isn't going to make for discreet surveillance."

Nothing we could do about that. "Katya's not in the bedroom either, but Grigori's there, getting dressed. Looks like he even wears a suit on Sundays."

Max's voice came back on, an octave higher. "There's a black Mercedes leaving through the front gate. The windows are tinted. I can't see inside. Should I follow?"

"Is that the only car leaving?"

"Yes."

"Go for it. Sunday morning, who else could it be?"

While Max followed the Mercedes, I had to figure out my next moves. I was running out of places to hide. With the sun rising, my silhouette would be visible to Grigori and his staff even when I was over the opaque portions of the pyramid.

I surveyed the roof in the morning light. The terrace surrounding the pyramid was featureless as a jogging track—and just as devoid of safety rails. The east and west towers were capped by skylights, smaller versions of the central pyramid. No hiding there. The north tower supported a traditional terrace, with an umbrellaed table, four chairs, and a pair of loungers. It looked like a nice place to enjoy your brandy and cigars while mastering the universe. The south tower had the helipad with the gleaming black Ansat I'd visited.

There was no decent point of concealment anywhere on the roof. If I tried hiding on a lawn chair, I'd look like a three-year-old kid who thought he was invisible while everyone chuckled. That discovery wouldn't end with tickles.

I had two options. I could either go into sniper mode by lying out of the way, still as a stone in my ghillie suit. Or I could return to the Ansat and kill anyone who came along. Not a tough choice, given the mood I was in. And I was ready for more pistachios.

I bid an Arnold Schwarzenegger farewell to Grigori as he was adjusting his tie, and slid slowly down the pyramid. From the base, I low-crawled toward the south tower and the gear I'd stashed, then made a dash for the copter.

Max broke radio silence as I shut the door, causing me to jump. "Katya just exited the limo in front of our MSU dormitory complex. She's alone. The limo is driving off. I'll pick her up, as soon as it's out of sight."

Relief flooded over me. As long as Katya was safe, everything would be okay. I could take care of myself. "That's great news! Please switch to speakerphone when you do."

I found myself nervously popping pistachios while waiting for news. This was the covert operative equivalent to giving birth. I heard the ambulance door open, and then Katya's voice. "I'm alright. I'm alright. Is Achilles on his way?"

"I'm not coming yet," I said. "I've still got to learn Grigori's plan. But tell us what happened, we're dying to know. Max, drive the ambulance someplace inconspicuous while Katya debriefs."

Katya's words came pouring out like an excited child's. "At first everything went as planned. He brought me home. I'd never flown in a helicopter before. Didn't know they were so loud on the inside. That was nice, because we didn't have to talk. I played the excited schoolgirl, and he seemed to like being the big daddy."

The tone of her voice gave me a warm feeling. I couldn't believe her level of enthusiasm. This was a math professor talking. Apparently, Max and I had been the only nervous ones.

"In his apartment, Grigori turned on classical music and poured us drinks. More Cristal. Then he led me back to the bedroom, where I took a page from that angel at Vondreesen's castle."

My phone beeped. Another call.

I interrupted Katya. "My attorney is calling. You guys keep talking. I'll be back on in a minute."

I clicked over, and Casey came on the line. "Before I go to bed, I want to be sure you're headed for the plane. The charter company says you haven't checked in yet."

"We still have time."

"Well, technically. But you're down to hours. Don't forget that in addition to flight time, which the pilot tells me will be a good twelve to thirteen hours depending on headwinds, you've got customs and clearances and bureaucracy. Then there's the traffic at both ends. You've gotta add four or five hours for that stuff, at a minimum. I don't need to remind you what's at stake, do I?"

"It's only money."

"It's ten million dollars, Achilles. Your birthright."

"Nine a.m. at the Santa Barbara Superior Court. Got it. That gives me until three a.m. Moscow time to reach the airport. How'd it go with Flurry?"

"She's happy with the evidence provided. She's been having fun with the two you left in the Escalade. Apparently they're wanted for other crimes."

"So I'm good?"

"You just get here. I'll take care of the rest. But do get here. I know this judge, and he's merciless on defendants who disobey court orders."

I clicked back over to Katya and Max. "Casey wanted to be sure I'd show up for court."

"You are tight on time," Katya said.

"It's going to get tighter. Unless Grigori flies somewhere today, I'm going to hit him tonight, when he goes to bed."

Chapter 113

Bad Reflection

IT WASN'T UNTIL AFTER MIDNIGHT that the lights went on in Grigori's bedroom —12:06 to be precise. The day of waiting had been no joyride, and I wouldn't eat another pistachio for the rest of my life, but now the departure deadline was whittling away at my nerves.

If I wasn't on my way to the airport in 174 minutes, I was going to be in contempt of court and out ten million bucks. My only ten million. Grigori's late arrival had left me precious little time for finesse during his interrogation. At the moment, that suited my mood just fine.

Judging by the extinguishing lights, Grigori finally slid between the sheets at 12:22. I gave him twenty minutes to start sawing logs, and then crept about twelve feet up until I was on the pane I knew to be directly over the center of his bed.

I'd waited so long for this moment.

Exactly 200 nights earlier, while my family and I were enjoying my father's sixtieth birthday celebration, Grigori Barsukov's men crept aboard the *Emerging Sea*. Using tools covered in my prints, they diverted the exhaust, bypassed the catalytic converter, disabled the carbon monoxide detectors, arranged the vents, and superglued shut every stateroom window but mine. Then, once everyone was sleeping soundly with full bellies and intoxicated brains, they started the motor that spewed the gas that claimed three precious lives.

Katya would be dead too, but for Colin's snoring.

I would be bearing those lost lives in mind throughout the next 138 minutes.

After readying the lock blade for action in my right hand, I buried my face in the crook of my elbow. With my eyes thus protected, I palmed the sonic pick in my left, pressed it into the glass, and hit the power.

The top pane shattered with a pop as the argon gas exploded outward. Then the second pane burst. I rode a carpet of broken glass down onto Grigori, landing on his chest with a whoosh and a crash and the melodic tinkle of crystal rain.

My nemesis screamed, but I didn't care. I already knew from Katya that nobody could hear. This scream would likely be the first of many.

I put the blade to his throat and clamped my hand over his mouth to control his movements and focus his attention before speaking. "Kyle Achilles. Pleased to meet you. Utter a word, one word, and I'll blind you."

We locked eyes.

After a second of intense staring, I moved the knife from the crease of his throat to the bridge of his crooked nose, then removed my hand, drew my Glock, and backed off the bed.

Grigori remained silent.

I grabbed hold of the puffy white duvet with my knife hand. Once my grip was solid, I backed up, pulling the duvet and about a hundred pounds of glass off my captive. "Roll over, then grab your ass with both hands."

I knew Grigori was dying to talk, longing to issue bribes and threats, but he managed to resist the urge while doing as I'd demanded. He was a man of discipline, if nothing else.

A door swooshed behind me. I spun to see two black suits entering the room, sidearms up but aimed at the moonlight coming through the missing window rather than my head.

Their eyes hadn't adjusted to the dark.

The lead suit spoke first. "You okay, Mister Barsukov? The roof alarm—"

I squeezed my Glock's trigger twice, once for each of them. The first suit dropped like a fishing sinker. The second staggered and tried to aim his gun with his right arm while his left pressed his stomach. I sent two more 9 mm parabellums on their way before he found his balance. The bedroom door slid shut as he collapsed, like the curtain on the final act.

"I might have mentioned the roof alarm. But I didn't want to end up blind." Grigori's voice rang out behind me, calm and cold. "Now drop it!"

Chapter 114

Hanging Out

WHERE HAD Grigori gotten a gun? The bastard must sleep with it under his pillow. I wondered if that was a recent development.

The gun was probably a slimline subcompact like mine. Probably from the same crate. Identical serial numbers but for the last couple of digits. Didn't really matter. What did matter was that he hadn't racked the slide. My ears pick up on that sound like a mother does her baby's cry, and I hadn't heard it.

Semiautomatics won't fire without a chambered round. Would Grigori, safe in his tower, sleep on a gun with a chambered round? Glock 43's didn't have a manual safety. I decided that a man who'd been losing bodyguards left and right just might.

I decided not to risk it.

Without turning, I slowly raised my gun arm out to my side. As it reached waist level, I said, "Did I forget to mention my friend?"

During Grigori's moment of apprehension, I flicked my left wrist with everything I had. The knife I'd pilfered from Gorilla back at the Korston Hotel was a lightweight ceramic model, so it soared a good twenty feet. As it clattered on Grigori's left, I dove to the right, spinning and bringing my Glock to bear. I had three rounds left and I used them all, aiming for Grigori's weapon. I couldn't afford a repeat of the Escalade situation, with no one left alive to interrogate.

Normally I'd have gone for the shoulder on an armed subject I needed alive, targeting the brachial plexus. Disrupting that bundle of nerves turns the arm into the functional equivalent of a bag of meat. But shooting on the move is never good for the aim, and I couldn't risk hitting his head or heart. Not with my president's life at stake.

The first two shots missed, but the third flew true. It amputated Grigori's trigger finger and sent the Glock flying from his hand. I rolled backwards and somersaulted onto my feet. Using my legs like springs to reverse my momentum, I dove and bowled Grigori back to the floor.

He howled like a dying dog.

Ignoring his screams, I rolled him over and pinned him with my knees. I trussed his wrists together behind his back, snugged them tight with cable ties, and then secured his ankles.

Still tuning out Grigori's voice so I could focus on ambient noise, I picked up his Glock and ran to the door, racking the slide as I went. Nothing ejected. There had been no chambered round. No round had loaded either. Strange.

I racked the slide again and confirmed it. The magazine was empty. That made no sense until I paired the thought with Katya spending the night in Grigori's bed. She must have emptied it just as I had the pilot's. What a woman.

Bending down over my fallen assailants, I used my left hand to confirm that neither suit's heart was pumping. Satisfied, I hit the lights and searched the corpses. No radios, just cell phones.

I dragged the nearest suit over to the corner and stopped before the panel marked as a door. Hoisting him up, I pressed his right palm against the reader.

The pane retracted.

Grigori moaned on in the background.

I released the corpse so that he flopped over the sill. There was something poetic about turning one's rival into a doorstop.

Returning to the man of the hour, I flipped him face up, grabbed the cable tie that bound his ankles, and dragged him outside onto the terrace like a caveman hauling a carcass from his cave. "Time to talk."

As we neared the building's edge, I readjusted my grip. I took him by both ankles, and swung him around until the top half of his body swept out over the building's edge. Satisfied with his precarious position, I crouched down and used my hands to anchor his ankles the way I'd do for a buddy during a sit-up test.

The little bastard had some strength in his abs. He remained rigid as a plank.

I stared into his dark, reptilian eyes and then tuned in his voice. "How's it feel to be on the other side of this equation?" I asked, remembering Vaughn's story.

Grigori said nothing. Showed nothing. His KGB roots had grown deep.

"You know me, and I know you," I continued. "So we'll dispense with the pleasantries, and get right to business. I just have one question for you. Are you ready for it?"

"I'm mildly curious," Grigori said, his voice now calm and steady. "But I won't make any promises."

What was with this guy? He had to know I'd happily kill him. I'd already gone through nine of his men. I had him dangling over a ledge. And yet we may as well have been talking about sports at the local pub. Somehow the threat had calmed him.

Normally I'd have softened him up before getting down to business, but I was very tight on time. I hit him with the trillion-dollar question. "What's the plan to kill President Silver?"

Surprise registered on his face. His scleras flared, his eyebrows rose, and his mouth opened ever so slightly. They were micro-movements, but they betrayed him. His surprise was nothing, however, compared to my own. My jaw fell when I heard his reply. "You can drop me now."

Chapter 115

Smoke Detector

I LOOKED PAST my captive toward the dark expanse beyond and the lights of Moscow far below. It was a beautiful night. Fresh air, clear skies, warm breeze. A good night for revenge.

To reach this lofty height, to mount one of the world's most powerful companies and the apex of a mighty nation, a CEO had to have superior negotiating skills. He had to be able to bluff with the best of them. But this was no ordinary negotiation. There'd be no *on-second-thought* moment. If I released Grigori's ankles, that was it. No replay. No do-over. It was all *call the priest, and make arrangements.*

You can drop me now. I let his words hang there for a moment, like a slow softball pitch. Then I did as he asked. I released my grip.

His rigid body pivoted over the rim like a seesaw.

I watched his face flash surprise once again, but the emotion that followed wasn't fear.

His words hadn't been a bluff.

I was the one who'd been bluffing.

I lunged and grabbed his ankles like an outfielder stretching for a ball. I pulled them back against the rim and slid forward on my elbows until my head was between his feet. Staring down past his crotch to his upturned head, a drop of sweat fell from my brow.

Grigori smirked as it landed on his crooked nose.

I ignored his jab and repeated my question. "What's the plan to kill President Silver?"

He didn't sniffle or stammer or spit a response. He did nothing.

Then I got it.

There were things worse than death.

For Grigori Barsukov, one of them was the repercussion that would follow from betraying his old friend, the president of Russia.

I was pretty sure I knew another.

But first I decided to shake things up, throw him off balance. "I know you've got McDonald's here in Moscow. Have you got Burger King?"

Grigori blinked. "What are you talking about?"

"I'm going to let you have it your way, Grigori." I worked my way into a crouch, then jerked up and back like I was doing an Olympic power clean. As soon as Grigori's head was clear of the edge, I took a couple of steps away from the rim and dropped him to the ground with a thud. As he groaned, I rolled him over and repeated the caveman drag. Facedown this time. Back past his fallen protectors, through the bedroom, and into the kitchen.

With another Olympic lifting move, I hoisted him up onto the island. While he watched wide-eyed, I selected a razor-sharp paring knife from the butcher's block. Setting it aside, I grabbed Grigori by the collar and hauled him atop the Viking range.

"What are you doing? I told you to drop me."

"I'm not here to do what you tell me, Grigori. I'm here to get an answer to a question."

Using cable ties, I fastened his neck to the Viking's heavy cast-iron grid. Then I secured his legs in a similar fashion. Sensing what was coming, he tried to flail, but there's not much you can do while strapped facedown by your neck and legs.

I sliced through the tie binding his wrists together behind his back. Power-handling his right arm over the edge of the island, I secured it to the handle of a drawer. His left wrist got the same treatment. The end result was no cross, but then he was no saint. The position, however, would most certainly suffice.

My watch read 1:15 a.m.

I was down to my last hundred minutes.

I walked around to the end of the island and crouched so I could meet Grigori's beady eyes. I was pleased to see him starting to sweat. "Does this place have smoke detectors?"

He closed his eyes, but didn't answer.

I hadn't really expected him to. I looked up and didn't see any, but then his was hardly the typical ceiling. I used the paring knife to slice off his black silk pajamas, just in case.

A switch on the wall caught my eye. I flipped it, and a big ventilation grid rumbled to life overhead.

Grigori began to tremble in anticipation, rattling the range's heavy grates.

I'd been tortured once, for days. That was more for sport than information. I didn't like receiving it, and I didn't like giving it. Despite what this man had done to my family, I wasn't eager to go medieval on him. But I was willing to do whatever it took to save my president. And the clock wouldn't accommodate anything but extreme measures.

Chapter 116

Nibbles

I LOOKED DOWN at the man who had killed my family, and felt my blood begin to boil. He was just a man. One man. But he'd wrought so much damage—and he was eager to inflict more.

Returning to the head of the island, I met his eye again. "I'll start with your left bicep, Grigori. I figure it'll take less than 5 minutes to cook all the way through. At that point I'll be able to snap your arm off like a chicken drumstick. Let me know if you find yourself ready to answer my question before then."

I stuffed a kitchen towel into his mouth. I figured this was the point where nine out of ten men would cave in. They'd spit out the towel and begin babbling. When Grigori didn't respond immediately, I gave him another nudge. "This Viking is my kind of art. Function meets beauty. What do you have, a dozen burners on this thing? All capable of going from a low simmer to high boil, I bet?"

Grigori's eyes remained panicked, but resolute. His jaw didn't move.

The gas burner lit right up, and I cranked it back to low. A beautiful blue flame, an inch below his flesh. He lasted longer than I'd expected. A good six seconds. Spitting out the towel, he groaned, "Okay," clearly straining to sound stoic.

"That's not an answer."

"Bugs. They're using bugs."

"What does that mean? Be clear, Grigori."

He was sucking air and rolling his eyes. "They're going to kill Silver using a custom bioweapon delivered by fleas."

1:18 a.m.

There had been talk of custom bioweapons at the CIA. Last I'd heard they were still theoretical, but just over the horizon. I'd been out of the game for over a year now, however, and with high-tech that was effectively forever.

Custom bioweapons were basically smart bombs engineered to attack a sequence of DNA. They could be designed specifically enough to only impact one person on the planet. In theory, if you could attach one to a vector that would propagate like the flu, it would go around the globe without harming anyone until it infected the intended recipient. But in practice, most biologics petered out in one or two leaps. If you wanted a real shot at success, you'd be well advised to launch it with just a single degree of separation.

"What do you mean, delivered by fleas?"

The smell was already getting to me. Much worse than what you got in the dentist chair.

"They figured out how to transfer the pathogen through flea bites. One will suffice. Now get me off this thing!"

"One more question first. Who's making the delivery?"

"Who do you think? Turn it off!"

It couldn't be, could it? "Say the name!"

"Korovin. Korovin's going to release the fleas personally."

I turned off the burner beneath his bicep, but lit the one beside his head. This one didn't expose him directly to the flame, but it was close enough to singe hair, and he'd still roast, given time. I wanted to keep him feeling the heat.

The Directorate of Operations at the CIA is essentially the military arm of the State Department. During my five years within their Special Operations Group, I'd learned to look at military matters through a diplomatic lens. I applied it now. Diplomatically, this situation was analogous to a tightrope-walking porcupine in a balloon factory. The Secret Service couldn't strip search a foreign head of state. They couldn't even pat him down. Nor could they confront him verbally. Even if they could find a pretext, that was no solution.

You can't catch the head of a nuclear state red-handed in the ultimate act of war, and expect to avoid a major geopolitical crisis. You couldn't even hint at your suspicion. The more I thought about it, the sicker I felt. If the press caught wind of this, the talking heads of 24-hour news would have the citizens of the planet's two most heavily armed nations clamoring for military action.

I couldn't allow that to happen under any circumstances.

Preventing it would be a challenge. With gossip this juicy, there would be no keeping it from the press. Saint Peter himself would be tempted to talk. I was going to have to work to contain the story with the same fervor I'd employ to stop the act itself.

Assuming everything Grigori had told me was true.

Time for verification.

I put my hand on the burner control inches from Grigori's nose. "How'd you get Silver's DNA?"

I knew a DNA sample was necessary to create a personalized bioweapon, and I knew the Secret Service actively guarded Silver's, sweeping up behind him wherever he went like the hypervigilant mother of a newborn

"They got it early. Before he even announced his candidacy."

That made sense. I suspected my former colleagues did the same with most global VIPs, as a precautionary measure. "Who created the weapon?" I asked.

"Bioresearchers in Kazan. Led by Dr. Mikhail Galkin."

"Where do I find Galkin?"

"He was at the medical school, but I think he's gone now. His contact info is on my tablet."

I ran back to the bedroom and retrieved the iPad from Grigori's nightstand. I held it up to his right index finger until it unlocked.

The first thing I did was disable the password protection. The next thing I did was find Galkin under the contacts. Kazan State Medical University. One of the best in Eastern Europe. He appeared legit.

"When's Korovin planning to expose Silver to the fleas?"

"On a hunting trip."

"Be more specific."

Grigori managed to smile through his tears. "Sunrise this morning."

Chapter 117

Russian Brillyanc

SUNRISE THIS MORNING! If that really was Korovin's plan, it might already be too late to save the president. I didn't have Silver on speed dial. I couldn't warn him.

What were my options?

Calling the Secret Service tip line wouldn't be fast enough. They were fielding over three thousand threats a day. 'Weaponized fleas' probably wouldn't sound like the most credible among them. By the time I got anyone to believe me, the president would be infected. Even if speed weren't a concern, I couldn't risk dumping information as sensitive and juicy as this into such a big bureaucracy. It would inevitably leak.

My own thoughts echoed in my head. *If that was true.* How did I know? "What will the flea bite do to Silver?"

I saw indecision cross Grigori's face, so I twisted the burner control.

"It's going to make him blind. He's genetically susceptible. It won't appear suspicious."

I believed him.

I had what I needed. I had what I'd come to Russia and risked my freedom and Katya's life for. Now I just had to deliver the news, quickly, and without instigating a nuclear war.

"Would you like me to leave?"

Grigori turned his head to study my face.

I supposed it was a loaded question.

"Yes."

"Call your pilot."

"My hands are tied."

"Walk me through it."

I turned off the burner, and he did. We called right there from his tablet. ETA twenty minutes. It would be 1:40 in the morning. Adding five minutes for the Ansat to be flight ready took the clock to 1:45.

Grigori told the pilot to go straight to the helicopter. Said he'd come out once the rotor was spinning.

I dialed Katya and Max, although there was no way I could reveal what I'd learned over the phone. Every major intelligence service in the world was dialed into Moscow's cellular networks. And with President Silver in town, they'd all be tuned in. My update could snowball into Armageddon. "The good news is that the mission is accomplished. The bad news is that we have another emergency. I need you to red-light and siren the ambulance over to the American Embassy. Let the Marine guard know that former CIA operative Kyle Achilles is about to arrive by helicopter with 'information critical and urgent to US national defense.' Use that exact language. Make it clear that the helicopter is a civilian Ansat, with no explosives or armaments aboard."

"What's going on? Are you okay?" Katya asked.

"What if they don't believe us?" Max asked.

"I'm fine. If there's an issue, have them contact CIA Director Wiley in Langley. He doesn't like me, but he'll definitely remember me." I gave them my agency identification number, then I hung up. My brevity was cruel, but there would be time for kindness later.

Running to the bedroom, I killed the lights and pulled the corpse out of the doorway and out of sight. I used the butcher block to prop open the door so I'd hear the helicopter turbine come to life.

Grigori's moans and groans were gaining volume. His self-control had been depleted.

I hit the bathroom next and inspected myself in the mirror. I was a mess. I'd worn the black suit over the blue spandex for extra protection from the breaking glass, but had suffered dozens of tiny glass cuts nonetheless. They covered my front side, including the parts of my face not shielded by my elbow. A Marine security guard wouldn't get much flack if he shot me first and asked questions later.

Grigori's suits weren't a viable alternative. Much too small. I'd have to go with something less fresh.

I swapped clothes with the first guard I'd shot. His only had a single bullet hole, and the black fabric hid the blood. In the back of my mind I wondered if that was the reason for the color selection.

I used the kitchen's main sink to quickly scrub my face, hair, and hands. Not perfect, but hopefully sufficient to avoid a bullet between the eyes.

The sound of a rotor revving-up reached my ears.

Time to bid farewell to Grigori.

I returned to the crouch that allowed me to meet his eyes. I studied the man who had ruined hundreds of lives, and was attempting to impact millions more. "One last question. Why did you keep the clinical trial going after Vitalis folded?"

Grigori's eyes lit up, and he managed a twisted smile. "Americans." He spit the word out. "You may have power, but you certainly lack cunning. The trial was for the next phase of the plan, of course."

"The next phase?" I couldn't help but ask, as worry seized my heart.

His smile grew. "The Russian phase. Brillyanc without side effects."

I thought about that for a moment. What he said made sense. Perfect sense. Yet he'd ultimately cancelled the trial. "But you failed. Seems to me, you're lacking American ingenuity."

His smile faded.

"You killed Martha Achilles, and John Achilles, and Colin

Achilles. You killed Saba Mamaladze, and Tanya Tarasova, and her husband. No doubt you've killed many others. I'm going to light a candle now, one in each of their memories."

While I ignited the first of the Viking's six burners, Grigori began bellowing like no man ever had before. He roared and he moaned, he wailed and he screamed. By the time I'd set the sixth burner aflame, I was wondering if his cries would shatter the pyramid.

I made it halfway to the door.

As much as I hated this man, as much as Grigori deserved to roast in the flames of hell, I wasn't that guy. I spun around and shot a bullet through the flaming tip of his crooked nose.

Chapter 118

Tough Old Bird

DRESSED AS I WAS in a GasEx guard's uniform, I didn't raise the pilot's defenses until I was in the copilot's chair with my weapon trained on his heart.

My conscript was probably around sixty in calendar years, but a hundred experientially. He was what most would call a tough old bird, with thick gray hair kept close-cropped, a weather-beaten face, and eyes that told you they'd seen it all. The no-nonsense type.

I got right to it. "The US Embassy. Land inside the fence."

He looked from my gun to my face. "I can't do that. The American Embassy is just a block from the prime minister's office. It's restricted air space. We'll be shot down."

"What's your name?"

"Erik."

"You fly Hinds in Afghanistan, Erik?" I asked, referring to the iconic beefy Soviet attack helicopter.

"I did."

"Then figure it out. Fast and low."

"That may get us to the compound, but we'll be shredded by ground fire if we try to land inside. Marines don't mess around."

"I've arranged for clearance."

Erik didn't appear convinced. I couldn't blame him. Unlike Hinds, I was pretty sure the undersides of Ansats weren't armor-plated. "And if I say no?"

"I'll shoot you, and steal a car."

His eyes drifted toward the base of his chair.

"I emptied the magazine. Nonetheless, I'd appreciate your keeping your hands on the controls."

Something flashed across Erik's eyes. Might have been admiration. Might have been hope. "What about Grigori?"

"He's tied up in the kitchen. Won't be joining us."

Erik turned to the windshield. "Flight time is about four minutes." He lifted the collective and pushed the cyclic toward the moonlit silver snake that was the Moscow River.

"I've got no beef with you, Erik. Take care of me, and you'll be fine. Cross me, and I'll add you to the list."

He didn't ask what list. Afghan vets had instincts.

I pointed my Glock at his crotch, and called Katya. "Are you there yet?"

I had to struggle to hear her reply over the rotor noise, even with my earbuds placed under the helicopter's headphones. "We're at the front gate."

"They still haven't let you in?"

"We're still talking over the intercom."

"Dammit! Do you know who's on the other side?"

"I think it's still the duty sergeant. It is two o'clock in the morning."

"Tell him the helicopter is three minutes out. Tell him to get the ambassador out of bed. Repeat the words, 'information critical and urgent to US national defense.'"

"I told him all that, Achilles. I don't think he believes me. I may have authority in the classroom, but I'm just a Russian girl to this Marine."

"He'll believe you when he hears the rotors. Tell him to open the window."

"Okay. Also, Casey called to remind you that we need to get to the airport."

"I'll see you soon."

Erik flew us north over the Sparrow Hills, then down to the

middle of the Moscow river, low and fast. Low enough that I could have yanked fish from the water with a hand net. Fast enough that the net would have snapped like a twig in a hurricane.

We flew under the third-ring road, wetting the skids. Then we splashed them again beneath the Borodinskiy Bridge. Just before the metro bridge, we cut inland and skimmed over side streets like an experienced cab driver.

This vet knew his stuff.

The US Embassy compound occupies an entire city block at the nine o'clock position on Moscow's Garden Ring Road. The public face is a famous white and yellow building of the same grand old architectural style used on most of Moscow's classic buildings. This was where the ambassador had his formal office, and where Russian visa applicants and Americans requiring consular assistance were serviced. But this building wasn't where matters of critical import were discussed. To see sexy foreign-policy action, you had to go deeper into the compound, to a cube-shaped edifice of sandstone and reflective glass.

Approaching at a height lower than many of the surrounding buildings, I was pleased to see floodlights covering the parking lot before the cube. As we swooped in, I also saw a familiar ambulance parked outside the gate.

Lights began to swarm around us from every direction, like TIE fighters defending the Death Star. Even more directed were the red dots of laser sights shining from dozens of M4 carbines.

Erik set us down center circle, killed the rotor, and raised his hands.

Chapter 119

All the Fuss

I LOOKED OVER at the pilot as the Marine embassy guards surrounded our helicopter. "Thank you, Erik. You're dismissed."

He didn't reply.

I exited the Ansat with my hands behind my head, and walked slowly toward the building's entrance. Marines in full battle gear materialized on my left and right. They grabbed my wrists and shoulders and marched me clear of the decelerating rotors.

We stopped before a third Marine who searched me while two more stood ready with M9 Berettas directed rock-steady at my head. Within seconds, my Glock and lock blade were gone, as was my cell phone and Grigori's tablet. A metal detector followed, and an explosive-sniffing German Shepherd did its thing. Finally, the Berettas backed off and a familiar freckled face appeared. "Hello, Achilles."

Michael McArthur and I had gone through the advanced field-operative course in the same six-man cohort. The experience hadn't been entirely pleasant. Granger had put me through an individual training program in lieu of the CIA's basic course—on account of my atypical background. Therefore, at the advanced-course, I was the new guy.

Initially, they all resented my special status, considering the Olympics a cake walk compared to what the five of them had been through. But between my marksmanship and stamina, I eventually earned their respect, and there was no bad blood at graduation.

Five years had passed since then.

I hadn't seen or heard of Mac since.

If inclined, he could slash through all the red tape surrounding my unusual arrival and brazen request. The identity verification. The credibility assessment. The escalation to a primary decision maker. If inclined.

Knowing he'd have an appreciation for human intelligence hot from the field, I opened with, "I've got ears-only intel for Ambassador Jamison. Information of a hyper-critical nature."

Mac studied me in silence for a good three seconds. "What about my boss, the Moscow Station Chief?"

I'd thought about that while Erik was dodging telephone wires on our flight in. "My information is diplomatically inflammatory and extremely sensitive. I think that should be Jamison's call."

Mac waved off the Marines. "Come with me."

I followed him through an anonymous federal corridor to a room with a thick door, no windows, and a round table suitable for six. He motioned for me to take a seat, but remained standing by the door. This wasn't the occasion to catch up or relive old times, so he remained silent.

I spun a chair around so I could sit while facing him. "The other two, the Russian man and woman who arrived by ambulance. They're on our side."

Mac acknowledged with a single nod. "They're comfortable in another room. What about the pilot?"

"I can't say. He flew me here at the point of my gun. His boss was evil incarnate, but as far as I know Erik was just hired help."

"Good to know."

Ambassador Jamison entered, dressed in jeans and a Naval Academy sweatshirt. The job of US Ambassador to the Russian Federation was the pinnacle post in the diplomatic corps. It didn't go to top contributors or friends of the president, like some island nations and minor European states. It was assigned based solely on merit. Jamison was nearing seventy, but word was that his mind was sharp as ever, and he looked amazingly fit.

As Mac closed the door behind him, Jamison took a seat. He studied my frazzled face for a silent second before speaking. "Tell me, Mr. Achilles. What's all the fuss about?"

Chapter 120

Two Vials

JAMISON AND I rocketed across the Russian countryside in his ambassadorial limo, blue lights flashing on the roof, American flag flapping on the hood, sirens silent. They would have been superfluous. The ambassador had requested a police escort, and the mayor of Moscow had accommodated. With the US President in town, this was no time for petty power plays.

We were sixty-five kilometers from the Kremlin when the limo roared through gates that armed guards closed behind us in haste. Sixty-six kilometers by the time we pulled up to the main entrance of President Korovin's hunting dacha.

I looked over at the ambassador. He appeared nervous. We'd spent one hour at the embassy debating tactics, and another perfecting the plan during the drive. Two hours wasn't a lot, given the diplomatic minefield we'd be navigating. Maximizing the odds of President Silver surviving while minimizing the odds of instigating a war required a tightrope balancing act.

I voiced a final word of encouragement. "Ninety-nine-point-eight percent is pretty good. Nothing's ever a hundred."

He nodded, but his expression didn't change. "Beyond that door, two rivals are having breakfast. Both have nuclear briefcases. I pray we're right."

Stepping from the limo to the snap of an enormous presidential security service officer's salute, I experienced a first. I cringed at the sight of an American flag.

"Ambassador Jamison, Mister Achilles, if you'll follow me please." Without another word, the officer did an about-face and led us through double doors held open by silent soldiers. Our guides' shoulders were so broad, I wondered if he'd have to twist to pass cleanly through a normal door. I wasn't sure how nimble that made him, but his physique certainly was intimidating. To Korovin's further credit, I'd never seen a better body shield.

We paused in the vestibule, ostensibly for our guide to receive instructions through his earpiece, but almost certainly for us to be scanned. You couldn't pat down diplomats without raising eyebrows, but you could secretly subject them to millimeter wave scans that produced detailed 3D images.

The pause gave us a moment to look around.

I'd never been to Naval Support Facility Thurmont, better known as Camp David, but I understood that the US President's weekend retreat was essentially a compound of high-end log cabins and lodges. By contrast, the Russian President's was more like the home of a German king. Marble floors, arched plaster ceilings ornamented with gold filigree, and large oil paintings of men with muskets and dead animals.

Satisfied, for one reason or another, Shoulders resumed walking. We wound our way to a dining room large enough to house an orchestra, and ornate enough to host a black-tie dinner. A left turn through an archway in the corner took us to a private dining room with a bay window that hinted at first light. Seated before it, dressed not in tuxedos but rather in hunting garb, were two of the world's most famous faces.

We stopped and waited to be acknowledged.

President Silver put down his coffee cup and turned our way. "Good morning, Ambassador."

"Good morning, Mister President. President Korovin. Pardon the intrusion at this early hour. We understood that your plan was to be in the hunting blind at dawn, and we needed to catch you first."

"Well then, you're just in time," Silver said.

"Mister Achilles needs a word in private, if you don't mind, Mister President. This will only take a minute."

Silver turned back to Korovin. "If you'll pardon me, Vladimir, apparently I need a minute."

Korovin inclined his head with no change of expression. "But of course."

Silver stood and Shoulders led us toward the back of the room while Ambassador Jamison remained with President Korovin. The guard paused beside a doorway and motioned for us to enter the sitting room beyond.

We did.

Shoulders shut the door behind us.

Two hundred days had passed since my family had been murdered. Fifteen days since a dedicated master sergeant had broken me out of jail. Nine days since Katya and I had gone undercover at a dead man's party. And four hours since I'd killed the man who was ultimately behind it all. Now I was twenty meters from the most powerful man in the world, and alone with his intended victim, the President of the United States.

President Silver looked older than on TV, but somehow more charismatic and intelligent. His thick head of hair befit his surname, and his deep blue eyes had a magnetism I knew I'd never forget. "Please allow me to see if that's a bathroom," I said, heading for a door a few steps from the one we'd entered.

It was.

I flipped on the light.

"If you'd come this way, Mister President."

While Silver complied, I turned on both faucets and motioned for him to close the door. To his credit, Silver went along without question. I supposed that handlers and security practices were among the many things to which presidents are forced to become accustomed.

"I'm sure you've got one hell of a story for me, Mister Achilles?"

I removed two vials of insect repellant from my breast pocket. "I do. While I relay it, would you kindly remove your clothes."

Chapter 121

Epic Choices

I STEPPED OFF the chartered jet into the balmy Santa Barbara air at eight o'clock, Tuesday morning.

I was a full day late.

My bail was forfeit.

I couldn't explain my tardiness. Not to Casey. Not to ADA Kilpatrick. Not to Judge Hallows. Long ago I'd sworn to keep my nation's secrets—regardless of how inconvenient. I suppose I could have asked President Silver for a favor. But that would have felt like putting a price on what I'd done. Besides, I didn't need the money —not now that I was done with legal fees.

As I walked out of the courtroom later that morning, a free man on the broad marble steps with a beautiful woman by his side, I heard a familiar voice. "I owe you an apology."

Katya and I turned to see a petite, ship-shape form approaching from a few paces behind. "Detective Flurry. How nice to see you where the sun is shining."

"I swallowed their bait," she said. "Hook, line, and sinker. I'd hoped I was better than that."

"Neither of us had a clue what we were up against."

"But *you* figured it out."

"Not for six months. And even then, I had to go to extremes."

Flurry half smiled, then got down to business. "I know how they did it. But I don't know why. Care to clue me in?"

"Professional curiosity?"

"You could call it that."

"They had a big secret to keep." I turned back around, put my arm around Katya's waist, and resumed walking down those broad marble steps.

"What about Rita?" Katya asked. "Will she be going to jail?"

"No. That would require a trial, and we can't have that. She's a victim of Brillyanc herself. She'll live in fear for the rest of her life. That's punishment enough for someone who didn't know what she was really doing."

"You're just being nice because she's pretty."

Perhaps I was. Perhaps I was just sick of negativity.

"Where to?" Katya asked, as we closed the doors of her Ford. Just two words, but a gigantic question. She knew it. I knew it. It had been hanging out there since that day she walked into the visitation room at the Santa Barbara County Jail. Now that those bars were forever behind me, a decision was finally due.

"When I left government service a year and a month ago, it was because I was disillusioned with the bureaucratic process that's baked in. I wanted to have right and wrong guide my life, not politicians. The question I couldn't answer was what to do next. Politics is the way of the world, after all. Whether it's the government or the private sector, if you have a boss, he's going to be looking for personal gain." I shook my head at the memory of my last boss and our final confrontation in his corner office at Langley.

"I spent a year throwing myself against rock faces and wandering about the corners of Europe, trying to find an answer. Then I spent six months in jail, learning to count my blessings."

I turned to face Katya, whose attention was locked on me so intently that I felt I should remind her to breathe. "The last two weeks were the toughest of my life. They were also the most productive. We altered history, Katya. Together we saved hundreds if not thousands of lives. We rid the world of a scourge. Wielded justice where it was overdue. No bosses. No rules. Just you and me and boundless determination. That's what I want to do. For the rest of my life."

Katya crossed her arms. "Like your namesake, the original Achilles. You've made the epic choice."

I said nothing.

"But how? How do you—I don't even know how to phrase it—identify the dirty work that needs doing? The Barsukovs and Vondreesens are hidden beneath cloaks and shadows. They're few … and far between."

I took her hands. "I'm not so sure about *few*. But I fear you're right regarding *far-between*."

Katya's eyes darted back and forth between my face and our hands. "But I work at a University. I'm not free to wander about in search of adventure."

"I know. And it's eating me up."

Chapter 122

From Time to Time

THE SAN FRANCISCO OFFICE of Senator Colleen Collins was elegant, but not grand. It befit a woman who was both distinguished and of-the people. The sky-blue carpet she'd selected was appropriately uplifting, and it had the added benefit of bringing out her eyes, eyes that were smiling at me.

She motioned me to a cream-colored armchair that looked great but was probably a bear to maintain. With that voice that should be singing jazz, she said, "Thank you for coming."

"It's a pleasure, if an unexpected one. I didn't think I'd see you again."

"Really? It was inevitable."

"How's that?"

"Allow me to enlighten you, Mister Achilles. Secrets are like walls. They have people on both sides. They try to keep you out, but once you're in, you're in. You've scaled a couple of tall walls of late. That puts you in rarefied air, with some pretty lofty company."

"A couple of walls?"

"I chair the Senate Subcommittee on Emerging Threats and Technologies, and in that role, I have regular contact with the National Security Committee. President Silver told me what you did."

I hadn't told the president the full story there in the bathroom. Ambassador Jamison and I had agreed that it could be diplomatically dangerous to give Silver news of such a vile, personal attack right before he spent the morning with the man who had plotted his genetically engineered demise. Not while they were both just an arm's reach from nuclear triggers. So I'd told him part of the truth. Enough to make him sufficiently worried about the dangers of insect bites to be extremely thorough in his bug spray application. "How is the president?"

"He's still pretty shaken. Theory is one thing, but having someone actually create a personalized smart bomb with your name on it is quite another."

"I can only imagine."

"It goes without saying that he's deeply grateful for what you did. He told me he's comforted to know that you're out there." She paused, her face fraught with emotion. "That wasn't just a political bromide. He really meant it. He went on to explain that despite having a dozen forces out there working to protect him and our nation, from the Secret Service to the FBI to the United States Marines, there are still gaps. Gaps that no federal force could ever fill, because they're too small, and we're too big and bureaucratic."

She shrugged. "Of course he could never admit any of this publicly. Never even hint at it. But I could, I can, with you. Because you're already on our side of the wall."

Climbing has its privileges.

"Silver suggested that on occasion he might need a force of one. And that on such occasion, he might want to call on you, through me, to help out. He wanted to know if you'd be willing? As would I."

At that moment, I wished I had a shot of Brillyanc to help process the load Senator Collins had thrown at me. Not really, but that got me thinking. "How's the cleanup going? The elimination of Brillyanc?"

"Grigori Barsukov's penchant for secrecy made that a relatively simple task. Very few people knew the formula, and we were able to identify and neutralize all of them—one way or another. Federal forces are excellent for that. We've also put flags in place that will alert the FDA if someone is purchasing the raw materials in suspicious proportions."

"What about the users?"

"They've all been discreetly informed of their situation." Collins paused, and I noted that she was playing nervously with the hem of her jacket. "I see by your eyes that you're thinking about my situation. In short, I got lucky. Good genes and a California diet overflowing with antioxidants. Looks like I dodged a bullet. But of course I'll be monitoring my mental health as regularly as my blood pressure. That will be a monthly reminder of how close we came to a dangerous fork in history's path, not that I'll need one. Every time I forget something for the rest of my life I'll probably be holding my breath."

"And Daniels?"

"The jury is still out on the VP. And by jury, I mean his medical advisers. He'll be taking monthly tests as well. Meanwhile, he's started playing one of those computer games specially designed to keep an aging brain sharp, and he's dining on fruit and vegetable smoothies three times a day."

I wondered if there had been a heated debate in the White House Situation Room involving everyone from political strategists to constitutional scholars to medical and security advisers, or if the discussion had been limited to a quiet three-way between Silver, Daniels, and Collins in the president's study.

I was enjoying this backstage pass to history in the making, and longed to know more, but didn't press. That feeling gave me the only answer that really mattered.

I wanted to spend more time behind the curtain.

"So what do you think, Achilles? Can I call on you, from time to time, at the behest of a grateful president?"

NOTES ON PUSHING BRILLIANCE

In the last words of this novel, Achilles faces the toughest decision of his life. Does he follow his passion, or follow his heart? It's eating him up. I didn't answer it here because to do so would not have been genuine. Neither Achilles nor I can answer it until the dust settles and he sees what comes next.

[Update: Achilles and Katya are both back in THE LIES OF SPIES, on sale now.]

If you're skeptical about Achilles' climbing feats, search "free solo climbing" on YouTube. What you'll see is mind-blowing.

For more information on the threat faced by bioengineered weapons, read "Hacking the President's DNA," published in the November 2012 issue of The Atlantic.

Brillyanc is a fictitious product, but the link between oxidative stress and cognitive function is well established. Google Scholar is the place to search if you're in the mood for heavy reading.

All of the above and more can also be found on the Pinterest Board for PUSHING BRILLIANCE.

ALSO BY TIM TIGNER

Kyle Achilles Series
THE LIES OF SPIES, CHASING IVAN, FALLING STARS,
TWIST AND TURN, and more to come…

Standalone Novels
COERCION, BETRAYAL, FLASH, THE PRICE OF TIME,
LEONARDO AND GABRIEL

TURN THE PAGE
for a preview of book #2 in the Kyle Achilles series.

The Lies Of Spies

PART 1: ASSIGNMENTS

Chapter 1
Damned Spot

Washington D.C.

"CAN YOU GET THE BLOOD OUT?" Reggie asked, unbuttoning the pinpoint oxford and handing it to his landlady.

Mrs. Pettygrove accepted the soiled shirt with a liver-spotted hand and an inquisitive glance. "Solid white is easy, dear. Lots of options. Don't you worry, I'll get it out. Leave your shoes too. They'll be waiting for you in the morning."

Reggie looked down to study his black wingtips in the dim glow of the Georgetown brownstone's entryway light. "My shoes are fine. You shined them just two days ago."

"*Fine* isn't good enough." Her singsong voice was tinged with excitement. "Not for you, and certainly not for the White House. I want them to be beautiful."

Reggie slipped off his shoes — more to see the twinkle in those wizened blue eyes than for the service itself. "You're too good to me."

"Better than some people, apparently. Would you care to tell me whose blood you're wearing?"

Reggie showed her some teeth. "Let's just say it's a lawyer's."

"Everyone in Washington's a lawyer, dear."

He winked and turned toward the stairs that led up to his room, knowing that no offense would be taken. She understood that discretion was his first duty. "Good night, Mrs. Pettygrove. Thanks again."

Reggie served as President William Silver's personal aide, or *body man* as most referred to him. It was a unique role. On the one hand, he was a servant, a valet. On the other, Reggie enjoyed virtually unparalleled intimacy with both the great man and the highest office. Only Brock Sparkman, the president's new chief of staff, was as tapped into the psyche of the commander-in-chief.

Reggie went everywhere the president went, mentally two steps ahead while physically three steps behind. His job was to anticipate Silver's personal needs and attend to them. With Reggie relieving him of petty problems and everyday worries, America's chief executive was free to dedicate his big brain to the nation's business.

Officially, Reggie knew little of import. Although he held a Top-Secret clearance, as everyone close to the president did, he didn't have SCI clearance. He didn't have access to the Sensitive Compartmented Information, the sexy stuff. Nevertheless, very little happened in the Oval Office or on Air Force One of which Reggie wasn't aware.

He pieced together a few words here, and a few words there, when a door was left open or he was leaving a room. The subsequent amalgamation was unavoidable when one had a keen intellect and a curious mind. Sometimes it didn't even take that much. Today in Cadillac One, for example, in between the president's routine update with his chief of staff and a call with the governor of Wisconsin, the secretary of defense had phoned regarding an administrative matter but had ended up briefing the president on a space-based defense platform that was right out of the movies — except that apparently it wasn't.

Of course, Reggie would never even hint at the knowledge he'd acquired, much less speak of it. His loyalty to his president was absolute. His patriotism emphatic and sincere. Still, late at night, when the president was finally tucked in and Reggie got to enjoy a few quiet moments before passing out on his pillow, he found pride in knowing as much about Silver's social relationships as the first lady, as much about Silver's congressional relationships as the minority whip, and as much about Silver's foreign relationships as the director of the CIA. Not bad for a young man whose upbringing had been anything but privileged.

Pulling back the covers, Reggie found himself shaking his head as he reflected on his conversation with Mrs. Pettygrove. *Can you get the blood out?* In this town, that was a loaded question. Reggie's conscience was clean, but he knew that many on Capitol Hill had souls resembling Lady Macbeth's. How fortunate he was, to be working for the good guys.

As he drifted off, Reggie had no inkling of the remarkable revelation he'd overhear the next morning while in the presence of those good guys — or the colossal confrontation that would result.

Chapter 2
Big Decision

Air Force One

PRESIDENT WILLIAM SILVER looked out the window to the left of his desk as Air Force One broke through the morning clouds. Funny how it was always sunny if you just climbed high enough. He tried to use that analogy as a guiding principle for his presidency — but Washington didn't make it easy.

Today, however, he wouldn't be rising above. Today, he would be diving down. He'd be sinking to the bottom of the barrel, taking the fight to the enemy.

Silver wasn't entirely comfortable with that.

Without turning from the window, he said, "Reggie, I'm ready for Collins and Sparkman now."

"Right away, Mr. President."

Used to be you had to press an intercom button, Silver mused. Nowadays, all he had to do was begin speaking with a name and the walls somehow knew who to connect. It was convenient, and the Secret Service loved it, but Silver found it a bit creepy — if he thought about it. So he tried not to.

Collins and Sparkman arrived simultaneously, but not together. Senator Colleen Collins was still getting to know his new chief of staff. She was a Californian with 36 years of Capitol Hill experience — and the new chair of the Senate Select Committee on Intelligence. A *grande dame* as it were, with power, class, and a scintillating intellect. At seventy-something, she appeared early-fifties, with perfectly coiffed chestnut hair, glowing skin, and a perky disposition.

Brock Sparkman, on the other hand, was a behind-the-scenes bulldog of a guy. The Washington Beltway equivalent of a 4-star general. Lots of bark, lots of bite, and a reputation for sacrificing political correctness in favor of expediency. Having Sparkman prep the battlefields allowed Silver to drive hard bargains without sacrificing affability.

Both Collins and Sparkman were extremely effective, albeit in very different ways.

Standing before his desk, both were giving him a funny look, as though a big bug was nesting on his nose.

"What?"

"Are you feeling well, Mr. President?" Collins asked.

She knew him too well. "I've been struggling with a special circumstance for some time now, and the accompanying decision. I finally made it, and it's *execution* time, which is why you're here."

"Execution time?" Sparkman repeated, while he and Collins took seats in response to Silver's gesture. "I haven't heard you use that phrase before."

Silver concurred with a nod, pleased with his chief of staff's astute grasp of nuance. "How long do we go back, Brock?"

"All the way to freshman orientation, Mr. President."

"Right. And in the forty years that have flown by since, have you ever known me to be vengeful?"

"No sir."

"Impulsive?"

"No sir."

"Irrational?"

"No sir. You battled your way to the pinnacle of political power by never allowing rogue emotions to get the better of your fine mind." Sparkman's tone was analytical rather than obsequious.

Silver nodded in acknowledgment, and turned his attention to Senator Collins. "And you, Colleen. Have you ever known me to put the personal above the professional?"

"No, Mr. President, I have not."

"Have you ever known me to be reckless with affairs of state?"

"No, sir."

"And as the ranking elected official focused on intelligence affairs, have you ever known me to be daft, rash, or unreasonable?"

"No, sir. I've always been proud to have you as my president."

Satisfied with the results of his verbal priming, Silver found the courage to proceed as planned. "I've asked you here to discuss a personal issue involving the Russian president. One which, as far as I know, has no precedent."

Collins and Sparkman leaned closer, but kept quiet. Their eyes were locked on his, their expressions anxious.

President Silver mimicked their pose and lowered his voice. "The bottom line is this: I've decided to order President Korovin's assassination."

ABOUT THE AUTHOR

Tim began his career in Soviet Counterintelligence with the US Army Special Forces, the Green Berets. With the fall of the Berlin Wall, Tim switched from espionage to arbitrage and moved to Moscow in the midst of Perestroika. In Russia, he led prominent multinational medical companies, worked with cosmonauts on the MIR Space Station (from Earth, alas), and chaired the Association of International Pharmaceutical Manufacturers.

Moving to Brussels during the formation of the EU, Tim ran Europe, Middle East, and Africa for a Johnson & Johnson company and traveled like a character in a Robert Ludlum novel. He eventually landed in Silicon Valley, where he launched new medical technologies as a startup CEO.

Tim began writing thrillers in 1996 from an apartment overlooking Moscow's Gorky Park. Decades later, he's still writing. His home office now overlooks a vineyard in Northern California, where he lives with his wife Elena and their two daughters.

Tim grew up in the Midwest. He earned a BA in Philosophy and Mathematics from Hanover College, and then an MBA in Finance and a MA in International Studies from the University of Pennsylvania's Wharton School and Lauder Institute.